KU-615-963

Chasing Lucky

Jenn Bennett

SIMON & SCHUSTER

First published in Great Britain in 2020 by Simon & Schuster UK Ltd

First published in the USA in 2020 by Simon Pulse, an imprint of
Simon & Schuster Children's Publishing Division

Copyright © 2020 Jenn Bennett

This book is copyright under the Berne Convention.
No reproduction without permission.
All rights reserved.

The right of Jenn Bennett to be identified as the author of this work
has been asserted by her in accordance with sections 77 and
78 of the Copyright, Design and Patents Act, 1988.

1 3 5 7 9 10 8 6 4 2

Simon & Schuster UK Ltd
1st Floor, 222 Gray's Inn Road
London WC1X 8HB

www.simonandschuster.co.uk
www.simonandschuster.com.au
www.simonandschuster.co.in

Simon & Schuster Australia, Sydney
Simon & Schuster India, New Delhi

A CIP catalogue record for this book is available from the British Library.

PB ISBN 978-1-4711-8074-3
eBook ISBN 978-1-4711-8075-0

This book is a work of fiction. Names, characters, places and incidents are either
the product of the author's imagination or are used fictitiously. Any resemblance to
actual people living or dead, events or locales is entirely coincidental.

Printed and bound by CPI Group (UK) Ltd, Croydon, CR0 4YY

MIX
Paper from
responsible sources
FSC® C020471

To all the booksellers I've loved before

STOCKPORT
METROPOLITAN BOROUGH COUNCIL

Libraries,
Advice and
Information

Mar 12/20

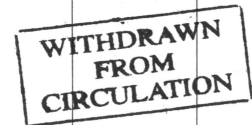

WITHDRAWN
FROM
CIRCULATION

Please return/renew this item by the last date
shown.
Books may also be renewed by phone or the
Internet

TEL: 0161 217 6009
www.stockport.gov.uk/libraries

WITHDRAWN
FROM
CIRCULATION

WELCOME TO BEAUTY: This faux-colonial sign greets travelers entering the small seaside town of Beauty, Rhode Island. A popular summer resort, the historic harbor area connected to Narragansett Bay attracts well-to-do New England vacationers. *(Personal photo/Josephine Saint-Martin)*

1

February

There's a long-held belief in my family that all the Saint-Martin women are romantically cursed. Unlucky in love, doomed to end up miserable and alone. Supposedly, one of my early New England ancestors angered a neighbor—big surprise—who then paid the wise woman in the village to curse us. *All* of us. Generations upon generations. Like, *None of you will ever get your happily ever after, so mote it be, enjoy the heartbreak.*

I'm seventeen and have never had a boyfriend. Only had one true friend of any kind at all, really, and that was a long time ago. So I haven't had a chance to personally test the curse in action. But even though my family is ridiculously superstitious, I know that everything bad that's happened to us amounts to a bizarre series of unfortunate coincidences. Moving back here to the curse's place of origin isn't the end of the world, no matter what Mom may say.

As I stand in front of Beauty's city limit sign, taking the photo I always snap when we relocate to a new place, I ignore my mother's irrational *woe betides!* about love and instead focus my lens on what this sign represents to me—my future.

See, Mom and I move around a lot. And by "a lot," I mean seven moves in the last five years . . . seven different cities up and down the East Coast. We're pros. We can skip town faster than a mobster who got tipped off that the cops were on their way.

One place is like another, and after a while, they all start to feel the same.

Except Beauty.

It's the place where the all the important things have happened in my life. It's where I was born—the birthplace of every Saint-Martin woman, all the way back to that silly love curse. It's where Mom and I lived until I was twelve years old, and where I'll finish high school next year, fingers crossed.

But most importantly, if things go as I hope they will, it's also where my life is going to change. Monumentally. I have epic plans for the future, and they all start with this sign, right here. Everyone else may just see "Welcome to Beauty," but not me. I see:

Hello, Josie Saint-Martin. Welcome to the Beginning of Your Life.

"It's freezing out here, shutterbug," Mom calls from the small moving truck parked behind me on the side of the highway. Our car, aka the Pink Panther, a 1980s cotton candy colored VW Beetle with too-many-thousand miles on the odometer, is hitched to the back. "Haven't you taken this one before? Forget tradition. It's not going anywhere. Shoot it later."

"Don't rush me, woman," I call back, capping the lens of my vintage Nikon F3 camera before I settle it into the brown leather case that hangs around my neck. The City Limits photo is tradition, sure, but taking photos of signs is my artistic vision as a photographer. Some people like photographing landscapes or people or animals, but not me. I like billboards, snarky church signs, obnoxious neon diner signs, street signs riddled with bullet holes. They all tell a story. They communicate so much with so few words.

And Mom is right about one thing. Unlike people, signs are always there, twenty-four seven, waiting for you to take their picture. You don't have to text them to ask if they're coming home for dinner. You don't have to be mad at yourself for being disappointed when they text back: go ahead, order takeout and eat without me. Signs are dependable.

I climb back into the moving truck, and as I pull on my seat belt, some rare emotion flickers behind Mom's eyes. Whatever the opposite of excited is, that's what she looks right now. Her anxiety over our move to Beauty started with Mildly Stressed, and on the drive here it escalated to High Anxiety, but now I do believe we're up to Scared Shitless.

And Winona Saint-Martin isn't scared of anything, so that leads me to believe that something big is waiting for us here— something Mom has failed to tell me about. Again.

Whatever it is, it must be *bad*. Worse than an old family story about doomed love.

"Seriously, you're starting to freak me out," I tell her. "Why are you so nervous about moving back here?" The reason we left when I was twelve is temporarily gone: the matriarch of the Saint-Martin family, Grandma Diedre. My mom's mother. They had a major falling out. Shouting. Tears. Police were called. Huge drama, and some of it was about me. They've since made up . . . sort of? But whenever we come back to visit, it's never for more than a day or two, and things are always strained.

Our family is kind of messy.

Mom's distracted and not listening to me, as usual. "Crap. Think that was one of your grandmother's friends who just passed us," she tells me, eyes on the rearview mirror. "She's probably on her phone right now, calling up half the town to alert them that Diedre's harlot of a daughter is crossing the border."

"You're being paranoid. Grandma would never call you that." Probably. Fifty-fifty chance.

Mom snorts. "Oh, to be young. Be glad I shielded you from that old bat the past few years. Thank God for Mongolia."

"*Nepal.* You know Grandma's in Nepal."

My grandmother and my mom's older sister, Franny, joined the Peace Corps and left to teach English in Nepal last week. Just like that, Grandma temporarily gave up the independent book-shop that had been in our family for generations and handed over the keys to my mom—someone she doesn't trust to post a

4

letter in the mail, much less run an entire business. And between you and me and this bargain-priced moving truck, my mom isn't exactly the most reliable person in the world.

Which was why Grandma and Aunt Franny running off to Nepal and leaving us as stewards of the family bookshop was a shock to all. Aunt Franny's daughter, my nineteen-year-old cousin Evie, is currently minding the store and will be helping my mom run it while attending college and shacking up with us in my grandma's above-shop apartment.

"There's no reason for you to be nervous. Grandma's gone. Aunt Franny's gone. You can make a fresh start here in Beauty—"

"Dream on, baby." Mom rummages through her purse for a tube of lipstick labeled Ruby Kick. Bright lipstick and pointed cat-eye glasses are the two things my mother wouldn't be caught dead in public without. "You have no idea what we're about to walk into. You were twelve years old when we left this wretched village of the damned. You don't remember what it's like. Beauty is a viper pit for people like us, Josie."

"Then don't give them a reason to gossip."

"What's *that* supposed to mean?"

I clutch my camera case tightly. "You know what it means." Blame the stupid Saint-Martin love curse if you want, but my young-and-single mom never has long-term boyfriends. Never brings men home. But she swipes right and sneaks out to meet guys . . . a lot. I used to keep track of the numbers, but it got depressing. I mean, hey. We aren't living in eleventh century feudal France: I know women can and should have whatever sex life they want. But it's my mom, and I know she's not happy. Also, the lying. If it's no big deal, why lie about it?

If I end up with trust issues, this is why.

Anyway, Mom did imply that she'd cool it with all the online hookups if we moved here. It's not something we *directly* discussed, because we don't talk about anything uncomfortable, so it wasn't a firm promise. But she gave me a silent nod that said: *I will not sleep with everyone in our small hometown, where people know us and our family, and gossip is currency.* And I gave her a return nod that implied: *Okay, cool, but mostly because I'm tired of you lying to me.*

I can tell by the way she's biting a hangnail that I've hurt her feelings by bringing this up right now—the forbidden subject of the dates she doesn't really have. And because I'm always forced to be the adult in the room, I opt to cool things down and switch subjects before we end up in a fight before we even get into town.

"Now you've got me all freaked out about vipers and pits and black holes," I say, trying for lighthearted. "Is it really going to be that bad here?"

"Worse, shutterbug. So much worse. It's not too late. We can turn back around and go right back to Thrifty Books in Pennsylvania."

Mom has managed every chain bookstore on the East Coast, along with some amazing indies . . . and a couple of complete hellholes. The one she just quit in Pennsylvania was in the hell-hole category.

"You emailed your district manager that 'Take This Job and Shove It' song and walked out on your staff in the middle of your shift," I remind her.

The corner of her mouth tilts up. "Okay, sure. Pennsylvania may technically be what people call a burned bridge. So we'll drive straight through town and head down the coast to Connecticut instead. You liked Hartford, remember?"

"Too many murders, too expensive. We lasted five months and got evicted."

"We could go farther south. Maryland?"

"Or we could just stay here in Rhode Island and do what we planned. Live in Grandma's apartment rent-free for a year and save up money for Florida. It's your dream, remember? Palm trees and white, sandy beaches? No digging cars out of snow?"

"Palm trees and white, sandy beaches . . . ," she murmurs.

"And you promised I could finish high school here. Henry said—"

"Oh my God, Josie. Seriously? Don't bring up your father when I'm in the middle of a panic attack."

"Fine," I say, protectively crossing my arms over the soft leather of my camera case. One of the few gifts he's ever given me, the Nikon is my most prized possession . . . and a point of contention between Mom and me. My parents hooked up in college, when she was enrolled at a prestigious state art school for a couple of semesters. He was a thirty-something photography professor, and she was a rebellious nineteen-year-old student who did some nude modeling for him that turned into a one-thing-led-to-another situation.

I'm not sure how I feel about that, but I try not to think about it too much.

Regardless, they never lived together, much less married. And now Henry Zabka is a famous fashion photographer in Los Angeles. I see him every year or so. I think Mom wishes I would forget he even exists. "Look," I tell her diplomatically. "There's no need for panic. This is easy. It's not a viper's pit. Besides, even if it is, Evie is counting on us. She's alone. Support Evie. Save money. Let me finish high school. Then you can head down to Florida, just like you've been dreaming."

"I'm not going alone."

I let out a nervous laugh and hope she doesn't notice. "Both of us . . . Florida . . . yep. That was implied." Wow, that was close. Gotta be more careful.

"Okay, you're right. We can do this," she says, calming down as gabled buildings and picket fences appear up ahead. "And Beauty is just a town, right?"

"Like any other."

Only it isn't. Not even close.

Beauty is a strange place with a long, dramatic history that stretches back to colonial America. It was founded in the late 1600s by a man named Zebadiah Summers, who helped King

Charles III of England "purchase" the "goodly" waterfront land here from two warring New England tribes, the Narragansetts and Pequots. A large quarry of high-grade marble at the edge of town made the English settlers stinking rich. And the postcard-blue harbor—which stretches beyond our U-Haul windshield as Mom drives the curving main road around the coast—later attracted other members of New England high society, who built their summer homes here in the 1800s and helped make this one of the most affluent communities in Rhode Island.

Being a harbor town, Beauty has a lot of boating action. A private yacht club. Racing cups. Boating festivals . . . A public pedestrian path called the Harborwalk circles the water for several miles, and if you like sandy beaches and saltwater taffy, you'll find that here too.

But it's the kooky parts of Beauty that I like. Things like that the town nickname since the 1920s has been—no lie—"Clam Town," because it has more fried clam shacks per capita than any other New England town. (Suck it, Providence!) Or that a slightly famous gothic nineteenth century American poet lived here and is now buried in Eternal Beauty Burial Grounds, a historical cemetery—and here's the weird part—inside the grave of one of the original female colonists who was found to *not* be a witch when she drowned in one of those "if she floats, she's a witch" tests given by Beauty's early paranoid townspeople.

Graveyards and clam shacks aside, the beating heart of Beauty is its historic harbor district. Hazy childhood memories surface in the setting sun as Mom drives us past a horse-drawn carriage trotting alongside gas streetlamps. I crack my window and breathe in the familiar briny air. Along Goodly Pier, sailboats bob in their winter moors, and tourist shops along the waterfront begin closing up. Glassblowers and candlemakers sit across from a row of gated historical mansions, some of which are occupied by families whose kids go to Ivy League schools.

It's another world here. A strange mix of money and weird.

We make our way to the southern side of the harbor, down a one-way street still paved with eighteenth-century granite setts. The South Harbor is the working- to middle-class side of town. It's pretty here. Quiet. A few shops. Waterfront warehouses. But Mom parks the U-Haul in front of the best thing in the South Harbor.

The Saint-Martin family business.

SIREN'S BOOK NOOK

OLDEST INDEPENDENT BOOKSTORE IN THE SMALLEST STATE.

Our street-facing family shop, known to locals as "the Nook," occupies the ground floor of a white bay-windowed house that's on the National Register of Historic Places because of its Revolutionary War connection. A private living space is on the second floor—an apartment that's accessible around back via an exterior flight of rickety wooden stairs above a three-hundred-year-old cobblestone alley. Mom and I lived here with Grandma until I was in sixth grade, but since Grandma Diedre and Mom do a lot of bickering every time they spend quality time together, we stay with Aunt Franny when we come to town, which isn't often.

Still. The quaint shop looks the same.

Generations of Saint-Martins all lived in this one building.

A large, paned window holds a display of books about ships, and over the recessed doorway, a wrought iron mermaid holding an open book juts horizontally from a pole over the sidewalk.

"Salty Sally," Mom says cheerfully to the mermaid, earlier anxiety left behind. "Mermaid boobs looking perky, as always. Guess we're stuck here together again. At least for the time being."

Pushing open the shop door, I'm engulfed by scents of old and new paper. Musty foxing on parchment. Ink. Worn leather. Orange wood polish. It smells inviting, and the New England folk music playing over the speakers is familiar and haunting; my Grandma Diedre collects recordings of traditional sea shanties and local broadside ballads.

Back during the Revolutionary War, this building housed both the Beauty post office and a printshop—I come from a long line of people who worship the printed word—which not only published the local newspaper but also seditious leaflets urging the rebels that lived in our Crown-supporting Loyalist town to "rise up against our redcoat overlords." Several of those leaflets are framed on the walls, and the original eighteenth century printing press crouches in the middle of the shop, now used as a prop to display books about Rhode Island history.

The shop appears empty of customers as Mom and I circle

around the old press and head toward the shop counter. Behind the register, lounging on a stool that squeaks loudly when she moves, is a nineteen-year-old community college student with her mother's long legs and her late African American father's warm brown skin. Her nose—which is dusted with the same pattern of splotchy freckles that all the Saint-Martin women have inherited—is buried in a historical romance paperback with a pirate on the cover.

Evie Saint-Martin.

"Credit card only. No cash. We close in two minutes," Evie says in a bored voice from behind her book in the same way a spooky butler would sound answering the door in an old-dark-house horror film. A ceramic cup of tea steams at her elbow, her own private fog machine.

"I need to pay half in a sock full of pennies, half in a check that looks like it's been dug out of a trash can," I say.

She lowers her paperback until big eyes outlined dramatically with Cleopatra-style makeup peer at me from beneath thick bangs that have been chemically straightened and smoothed with a flat iron.

"Cousin," she says brightly, her grin broad and slow as she pulls me into a hug over the counter. We nearly knock over a display of mermaid-topped writing pens near the register. She grasps my shoulders and pulls back to look me over. "See? This is why you should post more selfies. I had no idea your hair is longer than mine now. You should let me snip-snip it into something strange and beautiful," she says, eyes twinkling like a mad scientist.

Evie cuts her own hair. She's strange in a very good way and a million times cooler than me. And though her parents moved back and forth between Beauty and a couple hours away in Boston, causing us to miss some time growing up together, we've developed a long-distance friendship over the last few years.

She shoves me softly. "Can't believe you're here. Thought you'd be arriving after dark?"

"We downloaded an app to avoid police radar," Mom explains, sliding around the counter to wind long arms around Evie. "You've never lived until you've been in a U-Haul going eighty in a fifty-five zone."

"It was terrifying," I inform my cousin. "Seriously thought the Pink Panther was going to disconnect and fly off."

"How you and my mama are sisters is a complete mystery, Aunt Winona," Evie says as she leans around Mom's shoulder to peer out the front window. "Um, you know you'll get ticketed if you park there without a permit. Massive fine."

Mom groans. "Ugh. Beauty. Nothing changes—even the Nook's counter stool still squeaks. What the hell am I doing back here again?"

"Saving up for palm trees and white, sandy beaches," I remind her.

"And saving me," Evie says. "Grandma Diedre left too many instructions—the store window has to be changed out to her exact list of boring books every month, because God forbid anything changes around here. And even though I've counted everything a hundred times, the safe has somehow been $6.66 short for two days, because the vengeful spirit of the town is smiting us for selling fiction with dirty words in a town settled by puritans and yachting fanatics."

"Ah ha! Knew it!" Mom says. "I was *just* reminding Josie that this place is built over an actual portal to hell, and everyone who lives here is a minion of the dark lord."

A creaking floorboard near the old printing press makes us all turn our heads at once. A boy about my age stares back at us—at *me*.

Big, black Doc Martens. Black leather jacket. Dark waves of hair eddy and swirl around his face like fog circling a lamppost, overlapping a network of scars that mark one side of his face and forehead. Part of his eyebrow is missing. A tiny black cat is tattooed on his hand between his thumb and forefinger.

Carrying a book, he grips the strap of a brain-bucket style motorcycle helmet with the words LUCKY 13 curving around the back in a wicked font. He squints at me through a fan of black lashes—first at the camera case hanging around my neck, then at my face.

He stares at me like I'm the ghost of his dead dog. Like he's surprised to see me.

Like we're old friends . . . or enemies.

I feel as if I've just been asked a question in a foreign language, and I'm struggling to pick through a tangle of words, syllable by syllable, searching for meaning. *Who* are *you, and what do you want from me?*

A funny feeling sprouts in the pit of my stomach. Suddenly there's a word puzzle in my head, and the blanks are slowly filling in, and it's dawning-dawning-dawning on me what the answer to the puzzle could be. Because as much time as I've spent away from Beauty, the last five years, I did spend my childhood here. And during that childhood, I had a best friend. But I haven't seen him since I was twelve, and he was twelve, and . . .

Oh. My. God.

Lucky Karras.

He grew up. Good. And I do mean *good.* How did he get so big? He looks intimidating . . . and sort of angry. Don't think *Hey, old pal o' mine! How about a hug?* is the appropriate response.

He was pretty mad at me when I left town. That was five years ago. And not my fault. Surely, he's not holding a grudge. I wish I would have had time to brush my hair. I didn't know I was going to be getting out of a moving truck and seeing . . . Lucky 2.0.

Mom the Obvious, however, doesn't notice the electric stare-down that's happening right in front of her very face. She also doesn't recognize him and is all jokes and fake chagrin. "Oh, sorry. Not *you,* though," she calls out to him lightheartedly. "I'm sure you aren't a demonic minion."

"Clearly you don't know me," he says in husky voice that sounds like smoke and gravel—one that's changed along with his body.

"But I'd like to. Winona Saint-Martin." She sticks out her hand, but he doesn't take it.

"Know who you are," he says, switching his cool gaze to her briefly.

And as he walks past me, he slows long enough to murmur, "Hello, Josie. Welcome back to the portal to hell."

Then he tosses the book onto the printing press and strides out the shop's front door.

I exhale a long, shaky breath.

"Yikes," Mom says. "Already driving away customers. My mother will be so proud."

Evie waves a dismissive hand. "That's just Phantom."

"Who?" Mom says.

"Lucky Karras. Remember the Karrases? His parents used to own the tiny boat-repair business a block away? They bought the big boatyard across the street. Father's a boat mechanic. Mother runs the business."

"*That's* Nick and Kat Karras's kid?" Mom says. "Josie's Lucky?"

A warmth zips up my chest. "He wasn't *mine*. We were just friends." Good friends.

"Did you recognize him?" Mom asks without giving me a chance to respond. "I don't think he recognized you."

"He did," I say, a little dazed.

"He's been camped out here, watching the window for your U-Haul," Evie murmurs, giving me a suggestive smile behind my mom's back.

"Really would have liked to be warned about this before we showed up," I say through pinched lips.

"Last time I saw him," Mom muses, oblivious to Evie's comment, "he was a snotty-nosed little punk with a head full of black curls. When did he grow up into a dark and disenchanted Holden Caufield?"

Evie snorts a short laugh. "A couple years after you guys left town? I call him Phantom of the Bookshop, because he's in here all the time, brooding in the back."

"I thought the Karrases moved?" I say, still stunned.

"They did," Evie says. "Like I said, their business moved across the street."

That's not what I meant. I thought they moved out of town—gone. I had no idea he still lived here. All the times we've been in and out of Beauty for the occasional weekend over the past few years, I've never once seen him or heard about the Karrases.

"He was in that fire before we left town," Mom says. "At the lake house."

"His scars . . . ," I murmur. The last time I saw him, it was about a week after the fire, and he was bandaged up, in the hospital, awaiting news about surgery. I remember his parents being worried, whispering with doctors when I'd come see him every afternoon at Beauty Memorial during visiting hours, but they said he'd be fine.

Mom and I left town in such a hurry, I never got to say goodbye.

"He had a lot of skin grafts," Evie says. "I don't know . . . I think it changed him, because he sort of withdrew after that. He's been in and out of a little trouble ever since, but—"

"Whoa. What kind of trouble?" Mom interrupts.

"This and that. You know Beauty," Evie says with a shrug. "Hard to know what's gossip and what's fact."

"This town eats you alive, one way or another," Mom says. "Hope he keeps his trouble out of this shop."

"Don't worry," Evie assures her. "He just reads and sulks."

I stare out the bookshop window, watching Lucky straddle an old red motorcycle parked across the street in front of a building with a sign that says: NICK'S BOATYARD. REPAIR AND MAINTENANCE. Matching his tattoo, an actual black cat sits in a patch of sunlight inside the boatyard's office window.

How could that be the same boy I knew? Impossible.

As he straps on his Lucky 13 helmet, Mom clears her throat, catching my attention.

"Nope. Don't even think about it," she warns me.

"I was just looking out the window, jeez." Is my neck warm? Grandma Diedre needs to invest in some modern AC in this stuffy, old shop.

"The Saint-Martin love curse is stronger here," Mom insists. "Look at our record in Beauty. My grandfather kept three mistresses in a hotel across town. My dad left my mom for a business deal in California. My sister Franny . . . well"—she turns to Evie—"you know what happened to your own mother."

"*Mom,*" I say sharply. Ugh. Talk about foot-in-mouth disease, my mom has it.

"It's fine," Evie says.

But is it? Evie's father died of a stroke last year. He spent a couple of days in the hospital but didn't make it. The funeral was awful; that was the last time we were in town, in fact, just for a short time. Evie coped, but her mom kind of had a nervous breakdown and never really got over his death—and Mom thinks that's why Grandma encouraged her to rent out their house and run off to Nepal, leaving Evie to move in with us in the above-shop apartment. Mom says Evie's mom was always Grandma's favorite. You would think two adult sisters with kids of their own would be long past the Petty Jealousy phase, but I guess it's something you never grow out of.

"Regardless," Mom says, a little embarrassed, "everyone in Beauty knows I got hit by the Saint-Martin curse too. Tried to leave town to outrun it and ended up a single thirty-six-year-old mom of a seventeen-year-old. Now just imagine what the curse will do to you here, Josie. Heartbreak city, that's what."

Before I can protest, Evie picks up her paperback pirate romance and waves it, several slender silver rings clinking together on her thumb and index finger. She exclusively reads historical romance books. Earls and governesses. Princes and governesses. Governesses and governesses. If it involves the moors and a gothic castle, even better. She recently made the decision to give up real-life love in exchange for vicarious romance on the page. "Relationship-free and zero regrets." Or so she claims . . .

"Not here for relationships of any kind," I inform both of them.

Never had one, never want one.

Honestly, all I care about right now is building up my portfolio so that my father will agree to take me on as a photography apprentice in LA next year, after I finish high school. But I don't say that out loud. It's my own private secret. If there's one thing that will break my mom's heart, it's not romance—it's the thought of me leaving her. The ultimate betrayal.

I know it makes me a monster. *I know.* But the thing is, even though I may be cursed on this side of the family pie, there's a whole other half of the pie that I don't even know. Grandparents I've never met. Aunts. Uncles. Cousins. My dad even has a new wife, a painter. And once I'm eighteen, Mom can't stop me from traveling to see my dad. I only talked to him about it in a general sort of way, but I think I can convince him to let me apprentice for him. And that would be such a dream—to learn photography from a real master.

To learn how to be a real daughter in a real family.

Maybe one that communicates better than this one does.

That's my exit strategy. Beauty is my last layover town, then I'm going as far west as I can, seeking meaningful connections. People who eat dinner together and talk about their problems. People who do normal family things—backyard barbecues and trips to the zoo. Parents teaching kids how to swim and ride bikes. I want all that.

And I have a solid three-step plan to make it happen:

Step One: Prove to my father that I'm motivated and talented.

Step Two: Save up enough cash to get to LA.

Step Three: Graduate from high school before my grandma returns from Nepal.

That last one . . . that's tough. Next summer, Grandma Diedre's overseas tour in Nepal is up, and that's when Beauty will go from Layover Town to Family Fight Zone. My mom knows this; we're on borrowed time here.

Beauty's a ticking time bomb. I'm just clearing a path forward before it blows.

"Not here for relationships," I repeat to Mom and Evie. So I don't care how good he grew up, Lucky Karras can go sulk in someone else's bookshop. "I just want to tough it out long enough to finish high school in one piece."

But when I see the pitiful way Evie's sad eyes look down at me, as if both my three-step plan and the future are spread out before her like a bad tarot card reading, I begin to wonder if I'll even survive this town until summer.

BEAUTY HIGH, GO BREAKERS!: This quintessential 1980s plastic school sign molded into the shape of an ocean wave flanks the front sidewalk of the public high school. Last renovated in 1985, the building sits downhill from the well-funded Ivy League preparatory private school, Golden Academy. *(Personal photo/Josephine Saint-Martin)*

2

June

First impressions can be deceiving. Maybe I shouldn't have kindled any excitement whatsoever about returning to Beauty, because it only took four months for my initial hope to drain, and now I'm basically functioning on low-power mode and praying my battery doesn't die completely.

Between third and fourth period on the last day of school before summer break, I summon what's left of my energy, make myself as small as possible, and head down the western corridor of Beauty High, music thrumming through earbuds that block out the discord of the hallways—all the lockers slamming and all the football players shouting out to their bros. The laughter and buzzy excitement about graduation parties. The freshman kid crying in the restroom. Summer plans being solidified. Drug deals being made.

I keep as far away from these people as possible. Some of them I used to know when we were kids, and some of them might be okay now, but I'm in a full-on survival mentality, and I can't take any chances. Whenever Mom and I move somewhere new, I usually keep to myself and don't make many friends. People aren't disposable. It hurts when you get attached and have to leave them a few months later—something Mom doesn't seem to understand.

But unlike in other places we've lived, the students at Beauty won't leave me alone. They've poked and prodded me as if I'm a prize poodle who's unwittingly stumbled into some kind of kennel club competition for Worst in Show. Since the day I registered for school here, it's been one long series of invasive questions. *Did you really live in a cheap motel for two months? Were you on food stamps? Is your mother a sex addict? Does your father really know Prince Harry? Why did your grandmother really go to Nepal to live with Sherpas? Is she involved in some kind of cult?*

Leering eyes, the constant texted rumors zipping around school . . . sometimes just walking from one class to the next feels like I'm walking through a war zone. I might step on a land mine and lose a foot—or gain an illegitimate baby, you never know. I'm taking both my life and my flimsy reputation into my own hands every time the bell rings.

Everywhere else Mom and I lived, no one knew us. But here, people know *just* enough. Intimate details of our life are tossed around for entertainment. Not everything they say is true, but some of it is. And some of it hurts.

I'm starting to think that saving up for my exit strategy to LA to live with my dad might not be worth the torture of staying here for an entire year. But at least I have the summer to recharge. To retreat into the bookshop and my photography.

"Josephine?"

And I may have something else—this is the other thing, right here.

Please let me have this.

Pulling out my earbuds, I jog across the corridor to the journalism classroom to meet a bespectacled middle-aged teacher with a shiny bald crown, Mr. Phillips. He's in charge of the Beauty High yearbook and the school paper. More importantly, his wife works at a regional magazine that's published right here in Beauty—*Coast Life*. New England travel, food, lifestyle . . . that sort of thing. And it's his wife's job that interested me most, because where there's a magazine, there's photography. And where's there's photography, there are internships.

The summer internship at *Coast Life* is a good one.

"Miss Saint-Martin. See you made it through junior year." Mr. Phillips smiles as he adjusts round, gold-rimmed eyeglasses that are, style wise, somewhere between John Lennon and Harry Potter. "Got any big plans this summer?"

I *always* have plans.

"Working at the Nook part-time," I tell him, anxious for him to give me the news.

"Sounds fun. And what about your photography? Will you be

taking more pictures of signs around Beauty for your portfolio?"

"Always on the lookout for a good sign. They're humanity's communications, and I'm just the messenger with the camera."

"Love that," he says.

Is he making small talk to let me down easy, or to withhold the good news longer? I can't tell, but it's making me nervous. Mr. Phillips is nice and one of the few teachers I actually don't mind here. But the truth is, I need his help if I'm ever going to make it to Los Angeles next year.

The problem is that my famous father is famous for a reason, and he's notoriously tough. I need to prove to him that I have what it takes. See, *I* know I can take pictures. I'm mostly self-taught—my dad's given me pointers—but I've got a good eye, and I've taken thousands and thousands of photos over the years. I develop my own film, old-school style, in a darkroom. I've even got an online funding account—Photo Funder—a photography donation fan site on which I post exclusive photos for paid anonymous subscribers. Most months, it only brings in around a hundred bucks, and I'm pretty sure the majority of my subscribers are Mom's friends and my grandmother. Not enough to prove to my father that I'm worthy.

For that, I need something more. Like a photography internship under my belt. I need to show him that *other* people think I'm talented enough to take me under their wing. And at the end of the summer, *Coast Life* takes on a Bright Young Thing to help them do fashion shoots for Regatta Week. Rich people partying on boats. To be honest, it sounds like a total nightmare—absolutely the opposite of my artistic interests. But it probably looks fantastic on a résumé, and the person shooting it is a semi-big-name fashion photographer. Someone my father respects.

"What's the final word?" I blurt out to Mr. Phillips, unable to keep up the small talk any longer as my chest tightens.

He hesitates. "I'm sorry, Josie."

My stomach sinks.

And sinks . . .

"It has nothing to do with your photo submission," he assures me, "which they loved. The internship just normally goes to someone in college, and they just think you're too young."

"But I'm almost eighteen," I argue. "And they know who my father is, right?"

I hate to throw around his name, but this is an emergency situation.

"Of course your father's name doesn't hurt. But . . ."

But.

"I shouldn't be telling you this," he says in a low voice, "but if you want to know the truth, they were going to give it to you. However, the big boss who owns the magazine came into the board meeting. Mr. Summers is a stickler for rules, see, and you're underage."

"Mr. Summers?"

"Levi Summers. Big boss," he explains.

Oh. Right. Summers. His name is on every building in town.

Descendant of the founder of Beauty. Talk about privilege. I had no idea he owned the magazine. Rookie mistake.

Mr. Phillips holds out his hands. "That's why Levi Summers yanked your application, so I'm afraid you won't be getting the internship this summer. I'm sorry."

Yanked. Just like that. *Poof!* One more thing that's gone wrong in Beauty over the last few months.

Mr. Phillips is telling me some other things I barely hear, about how the internship itself is four days in August, before school starts back, and the work is rigorous, from early morning until midnight, so there would be problems anyway because of age restrictions and labor laws.

"Besides, maybe it's for the best, because you'd miss the Victory Day flotilla."

"Huh?"

"At the end of Regatta Week—the big Victory Day celebration. Surely you went to the nighttime flotilla when you were a kid?"

Oh, I went, all right. Rhode Island is the only state in the U.S. that still observes a legal holiday to mark the end of World War II. And for Beauty, that means an outlandish patriotic flotilla. At twilight, every boat is covered in strings of white lights, and they light the big braziers in the harbor. It's as if the towns-folk of Beauty sat around and said: *How can we outdo Fourth of July and stick it to those assholes in Boston by stealing all the end-of-summer tourists?*

"If you were interning, you wouldn't be able to enjoy the flotilla," Mr. Phillips says solemnly, as if it's my one dream in life.

Yeah, okay. I don't really care about yachts covered in fairy lights. The internship was going to help me get to Los Angeles, and now I'm feeling like my ship is sinking in the harbor along with my dreams. I can't explain to Mr. Phillips about the ticking time bomb that is my grandma returning from Nepal and the mess that is Mom's relationship with Grandma, but now it's summer, and I'm no closer to getting to LA than I was a few months ago.

A group of senior boys rolls past us down the hall, radiating arrogance and a toxic kind of laughter, and though I try to turn my head away, the leader spies me—an asshole varsity football player everyone calls Big Dave.

"Josie Saint-Martin." My name is thick in his mouth, too familiar. He doesn't even know me, not from childhood or now. "Coming to my party tonight? I'll let you take my picture," he says, kissing the air. "Private photo session."

His boys laugh.

"Hard pass," I tell him, hoping I sound tougher than I feel.

"All right, Mr. Danvers. Keep walking," Mr. Phillips says, pointing down the hallway.

They shuffle away, Big Dave miming snapping photos while one of his buddies makes suggestive gestures behind Mr. Phillips's back. I hate all of them. I hate Mr. Phillips for quietly apologizing for their obnoxious behavior, like he just saved me, but you know, boys will be boys. I hate that he doesn't have a clue that I've had to endure this garbage day in, day out for months when teachers aren't paying attention. I hate being angry all the time.

But most of all, I hate that after Big Dave and his gang of lunkheads have passed, I spy a lean figure in a black leather jacket across the hall, shutting his locker.

Lucky Karras.

Everywhere I go, there he is. The bookshop. The curb outside, where he parks his vintage red motorcycle. Silhouetted in the window of the boatyard's offices across the street, petting their black cat. Standing in line in the doughnut shop down the block. And here at school.

We never talk. Not really. He's never said, *So, let's catch up!* Or, *How's life been treating you?* Nothing normal like that. We don't acknowledge that we were once best friends and spent every day after school together. That I spent every Sunday eating dinner at his house. That we used to secretly meet up after school at an abandoned cedar boatshed at the end of the Harborwalk—*secret code: "meet me at the North Star"*—to listen to music and run terrible Harry Potter D&D campaigns.

No. He's just . . . around. Like now. Dark eyes staring at me from across the corridor.

Did he hear Big Dave just now? Lucky is always witnessing my little humiliations at school, and I can't decide if I'm angry or grateful that he never tries to intervene. All I know is that I'm weary of thinking about him all the time. Weary of wondering why he won't talk to me. And weary of enduring his haunting stares.

I'm *so* glad my junior year is over.

When the last bell rings, everyone pours out of the hundred-year-old brick school building like ants deserting an anthill. Sad sack that I am, I hike the five blocks back to the South Harbor district, trying not to the let the internship rejection get to me. After all, I've weathered bigger storms than this. I just need another angle. Talk to someone else. Show the right person my work—someone who'll be willing to go to bat for me and stand up against Levi Summers and his stupid age rules. Something. I'll figure it out.

Tenacious. Wily as a fox. Schemer. Plotter. That's me.

Once I get to the Nook and pass under Salty Sally the mermaid, I glance through the front door and spy Mom talking to a customer. Then I make my way around back where I march up rickety steps that are eternally covered in seagull shit. Up here is my grandmother's old apartment—where I lived when I was a kid. It's got a fussy old lock and a new security system, into which I tap a code before kicking the door closed behind me.

The front end of the apartment is basically one big living room with a fireplace and a tiny, open kitchen. It's decorated in a mix of my grandmother's left-behind furniture—New England antiques, worn rugs on hardwood floors, and her mermaid collection—and the few things that we've U-Hauled from state to state. A 1950s pinup-girl lamp I discovered in a junk store, which looks uncannily similar to my mom. Framed photos I've taken of all the cities we've lived in over the last few years. Mr. Ugly, a blanket Mom crocheted during one of her crafty phases. No matter where we go, those things follow us. Those things signal that we're home.

At least, they're *supposed* to. Right now, they're sort of duking it out with Grandma's things, and I'm constantly reminded that we are living in someone else's space on borrowed time.

I shuffle down a narrow hall past Evie's room—weird and spooky taxidermy, racks of altered retro clothes, stacks of worn historical romance paperbacks—and retreat into mine, which contains one hundred percent fewer taxidermized squirrel-cobra mashups.

In fact, my old childhood bedroom might as well be a hotel room because it contains little to nothing but clothes and photography stuff. I have a single bookcase filled with essential photography books, including my father's coffee table book of fashion photos, and all my vintage cameras. My oldest is a No. 2 Brownie from 1924 (doesn't work), and the rarest one is a Rolleiflex Automat from 1951 (it does), and of course, there's my Nikon F3, my most used camera. My digital pictures are stored online like everyone else's, and most of the film I develop is organized in containers that are stacked in the corner. However, the space above my pushed-against-the-wall bed is lined with curated photos I chose to display, hung on strings with wooden clothespins. I can take them down and pack them in under a minute. I've timed it.

All the bedrooms up here are super tiny, but mine has a bay window that looks out over gabled rooftops and steeples toward the town common. I stumble out of my shoes and head there now, to the window seat and its cushioned nest of pillows—a nook where I've spent a good chunk of the last few months reading and watching seagulls.

Might as well feel sorry for myself here, too.

But though I'm fully prepared to stay in all night and sulk, Evie shows up an hour later with other plans for both of us, pulling me out of my room to eat cold leftover takeout noodles while Mom is buried in some accounting mess downstairs in the bookshop.

Evie closes her eyes and holds up a finger to one temple. "Madame Evie the Great is getting a vision from the beyond. The spirits are showing me . . . wait. I'm seeing you and me on First Night."

"Is this a biblical vision of the end times?"

"It's tradition here for everyone to throw First Night house parties—as in first night of summer. School's out, students are home from college, and the tourist season is about to begin."

"And all of that equals an excuse to cut loose and throw wild ragers?"

"Pretty much," she agrees.

And after months of watching me suffer through gossip at Beauty High and misunderstanding my depressed state over not getting the magazine internship, Evie thinks a First Night party—the right party—will help my social situation. Which is nonexistent by choice, but she thinks if I tried to reach out to people, they wouldn't gossip as much.

Okay, fine, but I definitely can't explain why I'm not sticking around Beauty long enough to make friends due to my entire exit strategy to Los Angeles. And I love Evie, but like everyone else, she would just tell me I'm too young, and how much it would hurt my mom. She doesn't understand what it's like to live with Winona Saint-Martin. She only sees Fun Winona. Or Dedicated-Manager Winona, who is smart and determined to run the bookstore and trying really hard not think about hooking up with nameless guys in bars across town *right this minute*.

Evie doesn't know the Never-There Winona.

Or my favorite, the We-Don't-Talk-about-*That* Winona.

"Look, cuz, I've got a ticket to a great party. Not a Beauty High party. We'll go together. You'll meet some new blood. Maybe I will too. Not everyone is horrible here, believe it or not."

Evie just briefly dated and broke up with some Harvard guy named Adrian who's been low-key stalking her and being a total dick. Evie hasn't talked about it much, but I think it's starting to upset her.

"I thought book relationships were better than real-life ones?" I remind her.

"They're teaching me to have better real-life relationships," she says.

"Because you run into so many dark dukes and gothic widows in Beauty?"

"The world is a haunted castle on a moor," she says. "Your duke can be anywhere. Maybe at a First Night party tonight, even. Just have to be receptive to letting him into your life."

"Until the Saint-Martin curse hits, and my duke is drowned in a lake or cheats on me with three mistresses."

"I'm not entirely sure how I feel about the Saint-Martin curse anymore."

"You aren't a believer?"

She shrugs. "Yes and no? I believe all the women in our family are a little weird, but that's another matter," she says with a grin. "Now, come on. Let's get out of this apartment. Fresh air and new faces will do us both good. Let's just relax and have a chill night out, okay?"

Fine.

The house party we're heading to isn't that far, fifteen or twenty minutes, and we dare to walk down Lamplighter Lane to get there—a tiny street between our neighborhood and the Historic District that's full of old shops and a wax museum, and, according to my superstitious mother, the actual, precise location of Beauty's portal to hell.

"Not sure if she's mentioned this to you," I say to Evie, "but Mom claims if you stop on this corner at midnight, you'll meet the devil and he'll make you an offer for your soul."

"Do you have to enter a fiddling contest for it?" my cousin asks, amused, stepping sideways to avoid a crack in the sidewalk.

"Probably," I say. "You know she literally drives two blocks out of her way on the bank run to avoid this street, right? Always has, ever since I was little."

"They do ghost tours down here around Halloween. Maybe she got scared when she was a kid. I'll ask my mom on our next Skype call. In the meantime, if you see any devilish looking figures with fiddles, warn me. Come on—this way."

The party is in the sprawling backyard of one of the historic mansions near the center of town. I don't even know whose house this is, one of Beauty's Old Money families with a multimillion-dollar manor. Evie hands over a party invitation at a gated driveway filled with luxury cars, and we're allowed to come inside. We're directed to follow a path that leads to a pool and pool house—one that looks bigger than our apartment above the bookshop.

"Uh, Evie? Who are these people?" I ask as we make our way toward the pool's blue water, around which dozens of teens are laughing and drinking and dancing to loud music.

"Mostly Goldens," she says. Golden Academy, the private school in Beauty. Elite. Ivy League prep. Out of reach. "A lot of college students, home for the summer. Harvard's only a couple hours away. Wish I could afford it."

My goth cousin at an Ivy League? I wonder if this is because she briefly dated the Harvard guy. She's taking some basic biology courses at the local community college for a couple of years, but she wants to be a forensic anthropologist. Or a historian. Or a writer. In typical Saint-Martin fashion, she's always changing her mind. Even her mother, Franny—the straitlaced sister, compared to my mom—changed careers a dozen times before she rented out their house and ran off to Nepal with Grandma.

I get a little nervous the closer we get to the pool, where everyone's congregating. These kids don't just look rich, they look older. Prettier. Bigger. Faster . . . Better. I see them swaggering around town, but it's weird to be invading their personal property. I feel like an interloper. "Um, Evie? How do you know this crowd again? Because you dated that guy?"

"Adrian. Yeah, sort of."

"If you broke up with him, why are we here?"

"He's one person. Plenty of other fish in the sea. Besides, I was assured he wasn't invited, so we won't be running into him. One hour, okay? Then if you want to jet, we're out."

One hour? Dream on. Twenty minutes of weaving through the bikini tops and top-siders, hearing snatches of conversations about Harvard's rowing team and summering at the beaches north of the harbor and trips to Europe . . . and it's all. *Too. Much.*

Evie finds her people, though. One is a friendly brown-eyed girl from Barcelona named Vanessa who goes to college with Evie and knows enough about me to catch me off guard. "Feel like I already know you," she says in a pretty Castilian accent.

Which is odd, because Evie's never mentioned this Vanessa person before. Guess they're close friends, because they link elbows and Evie visibly relaxes around her. There's another girl with them who's headed to Princeton next year, but I don't catch her name. They pretend to try and include me in their conversation in an obligatory kind of way, but they're older than me, and it's pretty clear that I'm deadwood by the way they turn their shoulders to exclude me.

While Evie gets caught up in a deep conversation with Vanessa about environmental activism and the rising temperatures in the harbor, I wander around the pool, pretending that I know where I'm going, feet matching the rhythm of the thumping music that blares through unseen speakers. And after making the mistake of wandering into the pool house—drinks and a bathroom, sure, but too many strange eyes staring at me—I head through French doors to a secluded patio around back.

It's shadowy out here, lit only by a few globe lights, and there's a shrub maze that shields the back patio from the pool; it's segmented into a couple of seating areas. Plastic cups and cigarette butts litter a glass-topped side table next to a patio chair—unofficial smoking area, I suppose. I plop down in the chair and sigh heavily. This is a good moping spot for me to lick my wounds about the magazine internship. Maybe come up with a plan B. Maybe even a plan B through D.

Almost immediately, I feel a prickle on the back of my neck and suddenly realize my secluded oasis isn't as private as I'd originally thought.

I'm not alone.

SUMMERS & CO: An early twentieth-century sign curves around the Art Deco entrance of one of the last thriving independent American department stores. Open since the 1920s, the multifloor store is known for its custom tailoring and elaborate holiday window displays. *(Personal photo/Josephine Saint-Martin)*

3

"Well, well, well," a gravelly voice says.

I jump, startled, and peer into the darkness. Someone's sitting, legs kicked out casually, on a loveseat-style piece of patio furniture tucked behind a tall, trellised shrub. When he leans forward to rest his forearms on his knees, the angular planes of his scarred face shift from shadow into light.

Lucky Karras.

Why is he everywhere I go in this godforsaken town?

"Josie Saint-Martin, as I live and breathe," he says.

"I didn't see you there," I quickly say. "I wasn't . . ." Following you? Stalking you? Always managing to bump into you whenever I step outside my door? "I didn't realize you were out here. Or here. At this party. Here at all." Good God, I sound like a moron.

"Oh, I'm here, all right," he announces sarcastically, lightly lifting both hands and then dropping them. His gaze trails over the long, single braid of my hair that falls over one shoulder.

"Question is, why are *you* here? Didn't peg you for a partyer. Especially surprised to see you popping up at a Golden event."

"Evie brought me along," I say, gesturing toward the lights and sounds of the pool that seep between the dense branches of the shrubbery behind me. I try to remember the names of her friends. "Vanessa? From Barcelona? I think she's taking a class at community college with Evie? I guess they're friends or classmates or whatever."

Lucky chuckles. Black lashes cast shadows over high cheekbones as he looks down.

"What?" I say, feeling defensive.

He shakes his head. "Nothing."

"Look," I tell him matter-of-factly. "I'm just waiting on my cousin, okay?" I intend for this to be a signal. Like, *hey, move along and join the party; give me some privacy*. Why is he sitting in the dark, away from everyone else? He's usurping my loner throne, and I don't like it.

Lucky and I had one class together this semester at Beauty High: AP English. Because our teacher would do anything to avoid teaching, we watched a lot of old movies in that class— adaptations of the books we studied—and Lucky slept on his desk when the lights went out. I let him borrow my notes once; he returned them to me at the bookshop with a couple of smart-ass corrections in red pen. That was most intimate interaction we've had in the few months I've been in town. Unless you count all the silent staring. Staring from Across the Street. Staring from

Across the Bookshop. Staring from Across the School Cafeteria.

If you count staring, then we interact on a regular freaking basis.

Like now, for instance. His gaze sweeps over me as if he's playing a memory game and cataloging every detail of my outfit for points: loose, brown hair braid down my shoulder; striped top; tight jeans with a tiny hole in the left knee; red low-top sneakers.

No one looks at me like Lucky does.

It's disarming. Way too intimate. And it makes my pulse speed like I'm running a marathon. Especially since this is the first time we've been alone together since I've been back.

I don't want to be here, alone with him. I want to be at home, trying to figure out how I can talk my way into that magazine internship. Looking for local galleries that might let me exhibit my work. Developing a roll of film. Doing anything but enduring the never-ending thump of electronic dance music and Lucky's honey-slow gaze.

It's been a bad day. A bad four months. Something inside me just . . . snaps.

"Do you have something to say to me?" I blurt, exasperated.

"Excuse me?"

"You glare at me all day long, and you've barely said two words to me since I've gotten back into town."

"Don't have anything to say to you, I guess. Don't really know you anymore, do I?"

"We used to be best friends." *You used to be my boy.*

"When we were twelve," he says, eyes narrowing. "I was on math team and building robots on the weekend. I hadn't figured out how to disable the parental controls on my phone so I could access free porn on the internet. It was a different time." He shrugs with one shoulder.

Wow. Okay . . .

"If you're trying to shock me, you'll have to do better than that," I say, a little miffed.

"Thought we were besties who could say anything to each other. Can't have it both ways, Saint-Martin."

"My former best friend wasn't a dick."

"Your former best friend has been through some dark shit," he says, face tightening into sharp planes that make the ragged scars on his forehead stand out, white against olive. "So you may want to slow down before you get all high and mighty, pointing the finger of judgment in my direction."

I know what he's talking about. Of course I know. I glance at the black cat tattooed on his hand. "I'm sorry about the fire and everything you went through. I know when I left town, we didn't, uh, end things on the best of notes. . . ." I feel ill at ease, talking about this now. Sweat blossoms across my brow, and I have a fierce yearning to bolt out of my chair and flee this party, to never look back.

He blinks for several moments and looks at his hands. "Yeah, well, I was a stupid kid, and I was already hurting, physically and mentally. It was easier to shut you out. I guess I thought I was punishing you, but I didn't realize that it would punish me, too. Because when you left, I didn't have anyone."

I'm caught off guard by his confession. Some part of me wishes I had my Nikon with me to hide behind, because it would be easier . . . safer. I'm not used to anyone confessing anything to me. Ever. I think I've forgotten what it's like to speak to someone openly.

I've forgotten what it's like to communicate with a human being.

We stare at each other for a moment, then I say, "Thought maybe you hated me."

"Don't hate you," he says, the tiniest of smiles lifting one corner of his mouth. "Anymore. Much. Unless *you* hate *me*, then I'd like to change my answer. Because you *did* avoid my mom when she came to the Nook to bring food when you guys came back to town."

Oh, right. I totally did. She showed up with a ton of Greek food, and I hid upstairs. I used to eat Sunday dinner at her house every week for years. She was my second mother. Then she was gone. "Classic coward move," I admit. "A lot of old feelings. I wasn't sure what to say to her, and it was weird."

"Guess we're both fools."

"Maybe," I say, "but that was your mom, and this is us. You could have said, 'Hey, Josie, let's settle this mano a mano.' And we could have had a fistfight back when I first came into town, or maybe a Mario Kart race, or a few hours of D&D at the North Star—"

He snorts a little laugh.

"—and then the air could've been cleared. But instead, I've been freaking out, because you barely talk to me, and I've been trying to figure out why, because you're always staring—"

"Staring?"

"Look, I know it's hard to resist the Saint-Martin beauty, and all. . . ." I'm joking, of course, but it's weird how good it feels to joke with him again. *Really* good. Something icy in my chest is melting.

"You're the one who's been staring at me."

My jaw drops. "Pardon me? I think you have that backwards. You're the star*er*. I only look back at you because you instigate the staring. I'm the star*ee*."

He makes an amused noise in the back of his throat. "Hey, I stare at lots of things. Restored vintage motorcycles, sunsets on the beach . . . and trouble."

"Oh, *I'm* trouble?" I say, pointing to myself. "Me?"

"Got 'Siren' right over your door, don't you? Might as well add a red flashing light."

"Oh, *r-i-i-i-ight*. Saint-Martins are temptresses. Never heard that one before."

"Hey, you asked why I stare. I'm being honest. Just recognize temptation when I see it. Talented. Pretty face. Mysteriously keeps to herself. All my weaknesses." Lucky holds out both hands loosely, palms up. "Know thine enemy."

"Wait. Now we're enemies instead of friends . . . because I have a pretty face? *Pretty* sure I should be insulted."

"Why? It was a compliment."

"Didn't sound like a compliment."

"Hey, I tried," he says. "You're probably just better at flirting than I am."

I snort. "Oh, is *that* what we're doing?"

"You tell me. . . ."

I don't know. A sticky feeling forms in the middle of my breastbone. We've never flirted before. Ever. *Ever-ever-ever.* We played video games and read books. We painted backdrops for plays at school. When people kissed in movies, we both rolled our eyes.

Maybe I should think about . . . uh, whatever this is before I say or do anything I regret. It's Lucky, after all. That's first. And second, I'm not good at this. And third . . . the Saint-Martin love curse. And fourth, the utter pit-pattering-panic I'm feeling in my chest—something between excitement and fear.

I quietly clear my throat. "Um, I just remembered that I'm almost positive you're not single, so I should probably . . . um, maybe . . . ," I say in the most awkward way possible, trying to remember what I've heard about Lucky at school. "You have a girlfriend, I think, maybe?"

"I don't have a girlfriend."

"Boyfriend?"

"Nope."

"Huh." I waver at the edge of my seat. "Okay. Guess I got my gossip mixed up."

"Come on, Saint-Martin. I'd think you'd know better than most folks that you shouldn't listen to gossip," he says. "But if there's anything I can clear up for you, ask away."

He's right, of course. I *shouldn't* listen to gossip. But most of what I've learned about Lucky 2.0 has been gleaned from hallway whispers at Beauty High, which shockingly isn't the most reliable source of information. There are rumors he spent time in juvie. And that he once had his stomach pumped after OD'ing on drugs.

That he got Bunny Perera pregnant earlier this year.

Is any of that true? I don't know. But Beauty is an insanely finger-wagging, gossipy town that has made an art of shunning outcasts since it was a colonial village, and people are publicly judged, facts or no facts. More dirty laundry is aired here before nine a.m. than most towns manage all day.

I *do* know that more than half the things people whisper about me and my mom aren't remotely true, so I'd imagine this general percentage of *truthiness* could apply to Lucky as well. I just don't know which parts of his gossiped history are made up and which parts might be based in fact.

Here's what I *do* know about Lucky Karras: (1) His family has owned a boat-repair business in various locations around town for a few generations. (2) They live in a house west of the harbor in a small residential area called Greektown. (3) Lucky works part-time as a mechanic after school in the boatyard. (4) He reads a lot in the Nook, but he almost never buys anything. (5) He's a loner, like me. (6) He likes the same grape gum that he used to chew when we were kids, which I only know because he folds up the waxy wrappers into tiny, neat shapes that he leaves on his desk at school, like gum-wrapper origami.

Splashing and laughter float from the pool behind us during a break in the dance music. No way am I brave enough to ask Lucky to confirm or deny the nasty rumors about him. I try for a safer subject and ask, "What are you doing out here alone in the bushes, anyway?"

"Meditating on the meaning of life and how to live it."

"What is that? Some kind of code for smoking up?"

"You offering?"

"I have a peppermint candy in my pocket."

He whistles softly. "*Now* it's a party."

I smile. Just a little.

He smiles. Just a little . . .

"Seriously," I say. "What are you doing back here?"

"Antony invited me." When I make a face he elaborates, "Adrian's cousin."

Huh. Hopefully that's not the same guy Evie is trying to avoid. "Which Adrian?"

He looks at me as if I'm a big-eyed space alien who just walked out of a flying saucer. "Adrian Summers? As in descended from the founder of Beauty? Father is Levi Summers? This is his cousin's house."

I stare at Lucky, blinking.

"You know Evie just broke up with Adrian Summers, right?"

Lucky says. "I thought you and Evie were close, or whatever. You live in the same house and work together."

Oh.

Now I feel completely blindsided. Why didn't Evie tell me this? I pretend like my cheeks aren't suddenly ten degrees warmer and try to cover it up with more sarcasm—a tried-and-true Saint-Martin technique for avoiding humiliation. "And you got a personal invite to a Golden party, huh? Didn't realize you were part of the crème de la crème of Beauty."

"Yeah, no. My pops made me come," Lucky admits. "We take care of all the Summers family's boats. Gotta flaunt my handsome mug around all these future yacht owners, so one day, when he *thinks* I'm taking over the family business, which I'm not"—he holds up a finger to his lips—"I can charge them ridiculous prices for oil changes and repairs." He shrugs.

"Circle of life, and all that?"

"All that," he agrees. "And what about you, shutterbug?"

I frown at him. "Don't call me that."

"Your mom still does."

Sure. It's been my nickname since I was old enough to steal her phone and take pictures of my own feet. He knows that. What surprises me is that *he's* heard my mom calling me this recently.

"Just how much do you hear, brooding in the back of our shop?"

He threads his fingers together. "I hear some things, figure others out. I have some theories about you."

47

"Is that so?" I say. "Enlighten me, then. What are your theories?"

"I think you know that Beauty isn't your mom's forever home. So when your grandmother comes back and your mom inevitably hits the road, I think you plan on going out West to crash with your father."

Every muscle in my body tenses.

His smile is slow and smug. "Knew it."

"What the hell?" Has he learned some new hacking skills over the past few years? Paranoia skitters down my spine.

"Travel books about Los Angeles," he explains. "Seen you flipping through them at the Nook when you think no one's watching and hiding the notes you make from your mom. Your dad's an LA fashion photographer who has a multimillion-dollar beachfront mansion in Malibu, and you always wanted to go out there. One plus one plus one equals you're planning a secret trip to California. . . ."

My stomach twists. "You're spying on me in the bookshop?"

"I've got two eyes, Josie. That's not spying."

"It's *exactly* spying!"

"If you don't want people to see, stop doing it in public. You've always been terrible at hiding things, so that hasn't changed, just for the record. You left a printout of Los Angeles airfare comparisons next to the register two weeks ago. I swiped it and dumped it in the trash before your mom found it. You're welcome."

I'm stunned—*stunned*. And furious. "I didn't ask for your help."

"Sorry?"

I lower my voice and point at him. "You cannot say anything, okay? This isn't a joke. This is . . . I'm just looking at airfare. It's not a crime to look!"

"Whoa," he says, dark brows knitting together. "Not accusing you of murder. Jesus."

"I don't have firm plans or anything," I insist. "But you know my parents aren't friends, right?"

"I remember."

"Well, my mom would be really upset if she knew I was even thinking about it. Please."

He straightens his posture and holds up both hands in surrender. "Hey. No judgment. And I won't say anything. It's just something I noticed, is all. I wasn't snooping. I just happened to see it. Okay?"

I nod and scratch my arm, feeling exposed and uncomfortable.

We don't say anything. Behind the shrubbery, the dance music thumps on.

"Have you gotten to know him better?" Lucky finally asks.

"What? Who?"

Lucky lifts his chin. "Henry Zabka—your dad. He's gotten a shit-ton of big projects over the last few years. His work is gorgeous."

"Uh, yeah. He's amazing. He's still . . . tough."

"Tough," Lucky repeats.

I'm not sure how else to describe a man I barely know. He's candid in both his photos and his manner. Interviewers call him rude. "I still don't get to see him much. Every year or so he visits or we'll meet up somewhere for the weekend. He took me to see a bunch of photography galleries in New York the year after I left Beauty. I was thirteen. I shook Annie Leibovitz's hand."

"Yeah?" He seems impressed.

"It was pretty great," I say. Truth be told, I was so nervous that it's hard to remember anything about it other than I felt overwhelmed, and that her hand was cold.

Lucky studies me. It's hard to read his expression.

I sniffle and scratch my nose. "But, anyway . . . yeah. Henry—my dad. He's, still, um . . . very much a tough-love kind of guy. Nothing for free. He takes on apprentices every year, but you have to earn it. Aspiring photographers fight for those slots."

"At his home in Malibu?"

"Yeah."

"And that's where you plan on going after your grandmother comes back?"

"You do remember what happened the last time my mom and grandma spent more than a few hours together, right?" Ticking time bomb.

Something clicks behind his eyes. "So, that's why you're bailing and going to Malibu?"

"I'm not *bailing*. It's not a sure thing, but yeah. After I graduate, maybe. I don't know."

"You plan to move in with your dad."

God, he's nosy. "Maybe. If he'll have me as his apprentice."

Lucky makes a funny face. "*If?* Jesus, Josie. You're his daughter."

"So? Just because we share blood doesn't mean I should get special treatment."

"Suppose not," Lucky says, but he doesn't look convinced.

"I don't want a handout," I say, feeling like I have to explain myself. "I want to earn it and prove to him that I'm worth taking on after I finish high school next summer."

"Like, how?"

"Like, by building up my portfolio. And . . . I was . . . hoping to get a photography internship at a magazine."

"Magazine?" His brow lowers. "You mean . . . *Coast Life?*"

"You know it?"

"Only magazine in town. Started up a few years ago."

Oh.

"Had no idea they offered an internship," he says.

"Shadowing the photographer who's shooting Regatta Week at the end of summer," I confirm. "I think it's the only photography internship in the area, so getting it would be a huge deal for me. My dad would really respect it," I tell him, feeling a little despondent but unable to admit that I lost the internship already. *Because I'm too young.*

"Hey, Regatta Week is a big deal for everyone with status in Beauty. More money is blown in one pointless weekend than on entire wars, and nearly no one gets killed, so hey. Good luck with snagging that, if that's the kind of thing your dad will respect."

I think he's looking down on the internship. Pretty sure. *Al-l-lmost* positive.

"And I guess it confirms what I suspected," he adds.

"What's that?" I say.

"It's just how it was before," he says, eyes darkening. "Don't get too attached to Josie Saint-Martin because she's just passing through."

Okay, fair . . .

But it also feels a little bit like a punch to the gut.

A shout snaps our attention to the French doors of the pool house. Someone's fighting. Not the kind with fists and punching. The kind with name-calling and crying. Normally, that would be exactly the sort of drama I would try to avoid, but I recognize the tenor of one of the muffled voices beyond the paned doors, and my pulse goes wild.

"Oh no," I whisper.

I push out of my seat, rush to the pool house, and swing open the doors. A crowd of gawkers cranes their necks away from a big-screen TV to see what's transpiring across the open room. A couple is arguing near the kitchenette area. Half of that couple is my cousin.

"Just leave me alone!" Evie's shouting across a granite kitchen counter littered with plastic party cups and half-eaten plates of catered food. Tear tracks stain her cheeks. She's not crying now, but she has been recently. Now she's just angry.

And the object of her anger is a very tall, very muscular guy with cropped blond hair and intense eyes. His crimson Harvard Crew T-shirt stretches over shoulders broad enough to hold up the world. "You're the one who showed up at my cousin's house after breaking up with me," he shouts back, aggressively pointing at her over the counter. "You're sending me a lot of mixed signals, Evie."

Jesus. *This* is Adrian Summers?

"Here's a signal for you," she says, holding up her middle finger. "Leave me alone."

As she stomps around the counter, he drunkenly calls to her, "So typical. You Saint-Martins are a three-ring circus, you know that? Diedre's the world's greatest hypocrite. Your mom's a sociopath. You're an emotional seesaw. And now Wild Winona, the Whore of Babylon, is back in town, along with her little mistake, the amateur photographer."

I make a noise, and his attention slides from Evie to me.

"There she is. And who doesn't love a good amateur, am I right? Word on the street is that all your best pics are behind a paid subscription wall online. Twenty bucks and you get access to all your nudes."

"What?" I say, but it comes out as a whisper.

"Isn't that how your mom met your famous photographer dad, posing in the buff for him? Like mother, like daughter, huh?" Adrian whips out his phone. "We were just enjoying one tonight, weren't we boys? Where was that? Oh, here we go."

He turns his phone around to show me the screen. It's a nude, all right. One I've seen before by accident, when I was younger. It's my mother, photographed by my father when she was nineteen. It's in black and white, and the top of her head is cropped off, so it's hard to identify that it's her. In fact, it would be easy to mistake the girl in the picture for me.

Except that I know for a fact it's not. But that doesn't matter to anyone here.

Adrian puckers his lips and makes a kissy face at me.

Dark laughter swirls around the pool house.

An earthquake starts in my belly and spreads up into my chest. I feel sick. Humiliated. And completely unable to do a damn thing about it. So I just stand there, staring at a naked picture of my mother. Hating her a little for ruining my life once again. Hating all of these people for objectifying her. Wanting to rip the phone away from Adrian and beat his smug face with it.

Adrian just clicks off the screen, turns away from me, and finishes his grand speech to Evie, saying, "Your family's cursed, all right. You're all a blight on Beauty!"

"And you're an asshole," a smoky voice says over my shoulder.

I glance behind me to see Lucky glaring at Adrian.

"Stay out of this, grease monkey," Adrian says. "This is above your pay grade."

One of Adrian's friends pulls on his shoulder. "Come on, man. You're wasted. You'll regret this tomorrow."

Adrian shoves his buddy away. "The only thing I regret

is coming back home this summer. I should have stayed in Cambridge. All of you are losers. All of you!" And with that, he stumbles around the counter and out the door, heading toward the lights and music of the pool outside, where the main party is oblivious to what's happened in here.

Evie pushes through the crowd and grabs my arm. "I'm so sorry," she says near my ear. "Are you okay?"

No. I'm not. How did Adrian, some rich fool I've never even met, get a nude photograph of my mom? And how did he know about my Photo Funder subscription service and get the two things mixed up together? That's a complete and utter lie. I've never taken a nude selfie in my life. I don't even take clothed selfies. It's rare that I even take photos of people at all.

I suddenly remember Big Dave at school, asking about private photo sessions . . . blowing me a kiss in the hallway like Adrian just did. Now I realize that's truly what people think I do. Not just the dimwits in my school like Big Dave, but the Goldens. I wonder how far this photo has spread. Does everyone in town believe they've seen me in the buff?

I don't know whether I want to punch something or cry.

"I'm fine," I tell Evie, even though I'm not. "Are *you*?"

"Just typical drama." She glances around at everyone staring at us and calls out to the pool house: "Nothing to see here. That photo is a fake. Adrian's just drunk and spouting off because his feelings are hurt. What else is new? Enjoy your evening, folks."

Um, this is *not* typical for me, *thankyouverymuch*. I want to ask her more. I want to tell her that I'm ready to leave and get away from these people. She can tell me everything on the walk home and, and—

"I'm so sorry I dragged you into this shit. Don't listen to what he said or worry about the photo."

"Evie," I whisper. "You know that wasn't me, right?"

"Hush. I know. I'm going to see if I can find out where he got it." She looks toward her friends who are saying something to her. "Can you hang on for a while? It's just, I need to . . . I'll be right back, I promise."

Before I can protest, she's striding away, being comforted by Vanessa from Barcelona.

And now I'm alone. Stunned. Confused. Enduring stares and whispers.

And very angry.

I see Lucky though the crowd, but I can't handle him right now. I can't handle any of this. I'm completely overwhelmed, and I can't "hang on." I just need to get out of here. Away from all of it. I could call Mom to come pick me up, but honestly, she's the last person I want to see right now. So I don't call her. I just stride out of the pool house, around the pool, and across the perfectly manicured lawn, listening to the sounds of the party fade as I trudge around a curving gravel driveway filled with parked cars. In a few minutes, I'm out of the gate and walking down the dark sidewalk into town.

It's not midnight yet, and Beauty prides itself on being safe, so

I'm not all that worried about walking home alone—it's not far. Still, I try to stay aware and stick to the gas streetlamps, following the main road through the historic district.

Adrian Summers. Who the hell does he think he is? God only knows who heard him say all that stuff tonight and saw that photo. Probably a bunch of sons and daughters of other rich families around town . . . people who will gossip about this tomorrow over brunch at the Lighthouse Café and cocktails at the Yacht Club. I suppose this means I can now look forward to customers coming into the shop and snickering behind the bookshelves.

The more I think about it, the madder I get. The madder I get, the faster I walk. Moonlight shines on Georgian-style roofs as I stride down the block, past a marble statue of one of the town elders—probably someone who drowned the so-called witch buried in our graveyard. Every white fence is perfectly painted. Every shop window gleams. But when I turn the corner and head toward the grassy quad in our historic town common, I slow my pace in front of a multistory brick building.

Summers & Co Department Store.

Angry aftershocks rumble through me. I ball up my hands into fists to keep them from shaking as I stare up at the art deco letters that curve around the side of the old building. I mean, why does this even exist? It looks like a movie set through which Cary Grant might stroll. A dinosaur that should have died out decades ago. But no. Here in Beauty, it's still going strong. Enormous pane glass window displays from the 1920s, mannequins wearing pastel boating shorts and bright yellow sundresses. And all of it lining the Summers family's pockets.

For a moment, the rumble in my chest seems to have a real-life echo somewhere around me that I can't find. Then I see a single headlight and hear the insect-like buzz of a vintage motorcycle engine. A red Superhawk glides up to the curb.

"Are you following me?" I shout at Lucky over the vibration of his bike.

He shuts off the engine. "It's late, and we're going in the same direction. You shouldn't be walking alone. I can drop you off on my way home."

"No, thank you."

"I'm not a creeper. Seriously. Someone was mugged out here last week."

"I appreciate your concern," I say. "But I can take care of myself. You know, seeing how I'm an entrepreneur who makes my own porn to sell online, apparently. Even though it wasn't—goddammit!" Great. Now I'm crying.

"Hey—" He pops his kickstand, stands up from his bike.

I brush away angry tears—Temper Tears, Mom calls them, and they are the absolute worst—and turn away from him, walking in a circle.

"That wasn't my picture," I say. To him. To myself. To the empty, dark town common.

"It doesn't matter if it was. He's an asshole, and if you had a lawyer, you could sue him."

"But it wasn't! Lucky. Don't you get it? It was my mom's photos from college."

He stills. "Oh shit."

"Yes, shit!" I say, watching realization dawn over his face. He knows all about my origin story. At least he used to. I guess he remembers, or he's heard gossip, because he looks *mighty* uncomfortable right now. "As far as the other thing Adrian said, I mean, I do have an online non-nude—I can't stress that enough—subscription service. But I don't even know how anyone here would know about it. We haven't lived anywhere close to here in years. I know it's not Evie spreading gossip about me."

"It's not Evie," he confirms, taking off his helmet—the one with the Lucky 13 design.

"Can't be Evie's mom. Aunt Franny is kind of uptight, but she's not mean. She's more of a mind-my-own-business kind of person."

"She makes good carrot cake," he says.

She does. "Maybe my grandmother told people about my subscription service and it got distorted through gossip . . . ?" I make a frustrated sound at the night sky.

I'm so tired. I'm tired of gossip. And Beauty. And my mom. And defending my mom. And our terrible, broken communication. I'm tired of moving around. I'm tired of trying to prove myself to my father. I'm tired of feeling both too young to start my life and too old to cling to the way things were, and I'm tired of feeling so damn unstable and unsure about the future.

I'm tired of losing everything that's important to me.

But most of all, right at this moment, I'm tired of looking at those polished steel letters of the Summers & Co sign, because why does this family get to be on top of the food chain?

His father cost me my internship.

And now Adrian's blond, stupid I-row-at-Harvard head gets to humiliate me and hurt my cousin while I have to scurry into the shadows and hide.

The Summers family. I hate all of them.

And I hate Beauty.

Furious, I pick up a rock near my feet. It fills my palm with a delicious weight.

"Uh, Josie?"

I pull back my arm, use all my strength, and lob the rock at the shiny steel letters of the Summers & Co sign.

"Wait, wait, wait!" Lucky says, holding out his hands to stop me. But it's too late.

Funny thing about rage. It makes you think you have more power than you do. My pipsqueak-size arm sends the rock sailing through the night air, sure enough, but it fails to reach the art deco sign. Instead, it lands smack in the middle of the giant display window.

It shatters violently. Glass tumbles like a waterfall. Everywhere, a horrendous sound that echoes around the town common. Mannequins fall. Stubborn shards stuck to the top of the casing fall a few seconds later like an afterthought, as if they're melting icicles of death.

"Ho-ly *shit* . . . ," Lucky mumbles.

What.

Have.

I.

Done?

My chest hardens like cooling lava as shock floods my limbs. This isn't just any old window. It's a local legend. People come from miles to see the live models who pose in it every fall and the lavish orchid displays at Easter. Every December for almost a hundred years, people have gathered around this sidewalk to see the unveiling of the annual holiday display.

OH MY GOD. I RUINED CHRISTMAS.

I don't have time to wallow in this realization, because when the last big shard of glass falls, shattering on the concrete with a terrible crash, an even worse sound follows on its heels:

The store's security alarm.

It roars to life, a sleeping bear that's been poked, emitting a harpy-like screech that sounds as if it's a civil defense siren warning the entire town that an atom bomb is incoming.

Panic roots me to the sidewalk. *RUN!* I tell my legs. *FOR THE LOVE OF ALL THINGS HOLY, RUN.* But all I can do is stare in a stupor at the broken window.

"Josie!" Lucky shouts, pulling my arm. "Get out of here. Come on. On my bike."

But it's too late. A security guard appears from nowhere, beaming a flashlight over the broken glass . . . and then into our faces.

I'm toast.

BEAUTY POLICE, ALWAYS ALERT: A no-frills carved wooden sign with a giant open eye guards the lone law enforcement station. Six double jail cells can accommodate up to twelve prisoners comfortably—but rarely is more than one cell in use on any night. *(Personal photo/Josephine Saint-Martin)*

4

The Beauty Police Department is a model of small-town efficiency. An hour after my shortsighted moment of rage went sideways and fell on its ass, I've already been scared straight, given a Breathalyzer test, and hauled off in the back of a cruiser to await my fate here. Any moment, I'm sure I'll be mugshot-ed like a badly behaving popstar after a drunken weekend of strippers and fast cars in Miami.

But I'm not alone. They hauled both of us into the station.

Me *and* Lucky.

Now that we're here, we've been shepherded into a holding room together. I don't think the door's locked; guess they believe we're no flight risk. But hey, joke's on them, because that's *exactly* what I'm thinking about right now—running right the hell out of here the moment I get a chance. Run and never look back. Forget high school, the Nook, and my family. It's too late to salvage any of that now. I'll have to change identities and sneak aboard a ship bound for Iceland. Josie Saint-Martin is dead; long live Jamie San-Miguel.

Even the fluffy-haired woman running the front desk, Miss Bing, looked me over when the officer brought us in and shook her head slowly, as if to say: *Oh . . . It's the Saint-Martin girl. Can't say I didn't expect this.* And you know, with my family's track record and all the rumors swirling around town, in a way, can't say I didn't either.

I just didn't think it would be *me* doing the screwing-up.

Being both seventeen and very much minors, Lucky and I aren't being straight-up arrested and charged with a crime—at least, not yet. It's all very confusing. The security guard back at the department store couldn't get in touch with anyone higher up in management, what with it being a weekend and so late, so we'll have to wait to find out what's going to happen . . . I think? It's been a blur, and they aren't exactly keeping us in the loop.

All I know is that for the moment, we have to sit tight until our parents arrive. Lucky was able to reach his folks on the first try. Of *course* my mom didn't answer. Where is Winona Saint-Martin at midnight? Good question, and despite all her promises to cool it with the online dating, I'm pretty sure that's what she's doing right now. But, hey. It's hard for me to be righteous in the middle of a police station.

And wherever she is, I finally got Evie to answer, and she tracked Mom down, so I guess I won't be locked up in the slammer all night. Small miracles.

Right now, I'm sitting next to Lucky in an uncomfortably hard blue plastic chair at a table that smells nauseatingly of stale cigarette smoke. We haven't said much to each other. Haven't had the chance. Now that we're alone, I feel sick to my stomach that he's even here.

After all, Lucky didn't throw the rock.

"I tried to tell the security guard it was me . . . ," I say quietly. My voice is hoarse.

"I know," he says. "It looked bad for both of us."

"Oh God," I moan. "I'm so sorry. Can you explain to your parents that you weren't involved? Surely they can talk to the cops, and they'll just let you go."

"Me?" He makes a derisive noise in the back of his throat. "Have you gotten a whiff of my reputation lately? It stinks like the dumpster behind Clam Shack number thirteen before garbage pickup day."

I groan. "I didn't mean for any of this to happen. I don't even know why I did it. I'm not a criminal! I've never even gotten detention at school."

He snorts a little laugh. "Goodie for you. I haven't had it this month. Look, this isn't new territory for me. I've been in this room before. It all worked itself out. Had to do some community service. That's it."

"I doubt they're going to make me mow a lawn." I say.

He shakes his head. "Probably not."

I cover my face. "What was I thinking? My mom is going to

murder me. Am I going to be shipped off to juvie? Will I have a record? I'll never be able to convince them to give me another shot at that magazine internship."

Lucky scratches his chin. "I thought you said you were trying out for it?"

"They turned me down. Levi Summers came into the meeting, and he's a stickler about rules. He pulled my submission because I'm too young."

He exhales, long and low. "That's why you got so mad?"

"I needed another reason?" I say, angry tears threatening again as Adrian's drunken face pops back up in my mind.

"No," he agrees. "Definitely not. Sorry."

"Oh God. I'm screwed," I murmur. "All of my big plans . . . My father won't let me move up there now. Not with a police record. I'm stuck here. I'll probably never go to college, and I'll end up like my mom, completely resentful about her life choices and unable to hold down a job."

"Whoa," Lucky says. "Back it up. Let's not get ahead of ourselves."

"Maybe the Saint-Martin women don't have a love curse. My mom's right—this whole town is cursed."

He squints at me. "That stupid love curse? Don't tell me you're buying into that now."

"Hey, it's just like you said—we've got the word 'Siren' plastered right above our door. Temptation, right? We're cursed! Wanna know a secret? I'm a virgin. How's that for irony, huh?

Wild Winona's daughter—who's allegedly running a sordid nude subscription service online, proof provided by Adrian—is a virgin. There's your curse, right there. Happy?"

"Jesus, Josie," he says, looking embarrassed as he scans the corners of the room. Like maybe we're being watched or recorded. "I didn't—"

Well? We used to tell each other everything. Besides, he's the one who brought up porn outside the pool house. I don't even know what I'm saying anymore. "Know what's funny? Between me and my mom, I'm the adult," I tell him. "The responsible one who sits at home alone and does my homework and has to remind Mom to pay the electricity bill on time so I don't have to sit in the dark or walk to Starbucks for Wi-Fi until she can get it turned back on again."

"Josie," he says. Feeling sorry for me, pleading for me to shut up . . . it's hard to tell.

But it's too late for that. I have held myself under tight, careful control for too long, not communicating with my mom, not communicating with anyone, and now the levee's broken.

I'm awash in emotion.

"This isn't me. I'm a good girl," I insist, feeling tears prick the backs of my eyelids. "All I wanted was to get out of here before the time bomb exploded between Grandma and Mom when the Nepal trip ended—and for a chance for a real family with my father in LA. Now I won't be surprised if my mom shoves me back into the Pink Panther and drags me off to some other town once she hears what I've done here in the portal to hell."

"She'd really do that?" he asks, sounding shocked. "Make you leave Beauty again?"

"Maybe? I don't know. I . . . I was trying to keep my head down and mind my own business. Now everyone is going to be getting their jollies looking at a photo of my mom, thinking it's me? What is wrong with this town?"

"It was so small on Adrian's phone screen, probably half the people in the pool house didn't see it."

"You looked?"

Face long, he lays his head on the table, and that only makes me more miserable.

The door to the holding room opens. An officer tells Lucky his parents are here to pick him up, and he can leave the station with them. A little panic rises in me when Lucky stands to leave. Suddenly I don't want him to go. It's as if the past few years have disappeared, and we're twelve again—two geeky shy kids who bonded over books and video games and bad D&D campaigns at our secret North Star boatshed hideaway at the end of the Harborwalk. This night has turned me upside down.

"Hey," he says to me in a low voice. "Don't sweat. It's going to be fine. One of the good things about Beauty is that if people here expect you to be something, it's easy for them to continue believing it."

"What?" I say, confused.

But he doesn't answer. He just walks out of the room, briefly stopping to add, "By the way, there's no such thing as curses."

"Says you, the person with a black cat tattoo and a number thirteen on your helmet."

"Keep your head up, okay?"

Instead of a goodbye, he gives me a little lift of his chin, and when the officer fails to shut the door, I enviously watch Lucky as he's greeted by his parents, a wave of nostalgia hitting me right in the solar plexus when I see them. His dad, Nick Karras, friendliest man in town. His graying overlong curls hit his shoulders and gleam in the station's harsh lights. And his mom, Kat, with her short black hair and Lucky's chiseled cheekbones. Both of them are clearly concerned about his well-being. He doesn't resist when his mother hugs him and floods his forehead with kisses, or when she slings her arm around his shoulder protectively, like he's some frail and precious thing.

They both used to hug me like that. And when Kat looks up and sees me, lifting a hand to wave, I almost start crying all over again.

Then they're all out of sight.

There's some commotion with the officer who brought us, but I can't hear what's being said or see anything. Something dramatic is happening. What that is, I'm not sure.

Ten minutes later, though, I see Lucky and his parents leave.

While I'm having a minor panic attack, trying to puzzle out what's going on, I finally spy cat-eye glasses and red lipstick coming into the station lobby and wilt in relief. When I look into Mom's eyes, I see everything she's feeling at once: relief that I'm in one piece, shock over my mascara-smeared face. Disappointment that I've disgraced myself and our tiny, proud family.

"Are you hurt?" my mother asks, concerned.

I shake my head. "Not physically." Mentally, I'm pretty much a ten-car pileup.

Mom nods curtly. "Can she leave?" she asks the officer standing behind her.

"Just need to sign for her release. Did you bring an attorney?"

"Surely it's not that serious." Mom looks down her nose at him, both literally and spiritually. "It's only a misdemeanor. A prank."

The somber man with the somber mustache says in a low voice, "Like I told the Karrases, Summers & Co is owned by Levi Summers, ma'am. It's a historical landmark, and that window likely will cost a pretty penny to replace. I'd strongly advise you to find a good criminal defense attorney before the arraignment."

There's an arraignment?

"Levi Summers is not God," she says coolly.

"Here in Beauty? He's close enough," he says, hooking a thumb in his belt loop.

Mom points a finger in his face. "When my mother left me in charge of Siren's Book Nook, I moved my daughter back here with the assumption that this was a kinder, better Beauty. I was told by the board of selectmen that I was going to be accepted back into the fold as a respected member of this community—"

"Ma'am," he says impatiently.

"Don't you 'ma'am' me. I'm thirty-six years old, not a decrepit spinster on her deathbed."

"I didn't—"

"And furthermore," she says a little louder, speaking over him. "I'm not going to allow Levi Summers to hump my leg in a show of dominance. So you can do yourself a favor and scamper off to your master."

"Mom," I caution, but she's too caught up in being my hero. This right here? This is our problem. Quick to anger, *way* too defensive of each other. Oh, she'll bite my head off in private later, but she'll never in a million years admit to another person that I did anything wrong.

"Hold up," another officer says, striding up to the room. "She's free to go. Karras admitted to breaking the window."

"What?" Mom and I say in chorus.

"The Karrases said they'd get a lawyer and agreed to appear at the arraignment. It's all settled. Your daughter is free to go with you, Ms. Saint-Martin," he says to my mother. "Word of advice? Keep her away from Lucky. Have a good night."

What the ever-loving hell is happening?

If people here expect you to be something, it's easy for them to continue believing it.

People here think that Lucky 2.0 is trouble.

He told the police he threw the rock.

He saved me?

A funny kind of panic swirls around my stomach and grips my chest. I don't understand this. No one is ever nice to me for no good reason, and Lucky doesn't seem like the kind of guy who just goes around doing good deeds. One minute I was in the middle of a sob fest—telling him stuff I shouldn't have told him—and the next . . .

He was taking the fall for me.

For me.

For *me*?

"Oh, thank God, thank God, thank *God*!" Mom says, shoulders sagging. "Of course you didn't do this, right?"

"Uh . . ."

"Jesus. You scared the life out of me. Come on. Let's go home before someone sees my car parked here," she says with an anxious little laugh.

In a daze, I push through the front door and inhale a lungful of early summer air. Freedom, sure, only it doesn't feel all that sweet. I glance around the parking lot, looking for Lucky and his parents, but they're long gone.

Wired and paranoid, I climb into the creaky passenger seat of the Pink Panther and slam the heavy door shut, unsure what to say when Mom gets behind the wheel. She exhales a long breath and sits in silence, staring out the windshield.

"Where's Evie?" I ask.

"At home. She's freaked out that you left the party without

her and wanted to come along, but I made her stay. Shutterbug?"

"Yeah?"

"Why did you send me those texts if you didn't smash the window?"

Right. The bajillion panicked texts I sent when I was stuck at the police station. Texts like: I did a stupid thing. And: You're going to kill me.

How do I explain those?

"I'm just confused," Mom says. "Evie told me she had a bad fight with her ex at that party, and that he said some things that may have upset you?"

I rub my knuckles with my thumb. "He's such a jerk, Mom. He was drunk and . . ." God. I don't want to tell her about the nude photo. I just can't. It will be humiliating for her, and I don't want to hurt her. As mad as she makes me, I don't want to hurt her. So I don't. "He was just saying all kinds of shit about our family. You don't even know."

She taps a finger on the steering wheel, contemplating. "Oh, I can imagine. Did I not tell you this place was built on a portal to hell? Thought I was clear about that."

"You were," I say weakly.

"Okay, so you got upset, and you didn't tell Evie that you were leaving the party with Lucky Karras? Since when in God's name did you start palling around with him again?"

"I—"

"Didn't I tell you? From the first day we got here, I said don't mess with that kid. Everyone can see he's trouble now, Josie. And he's throwing rocks at windows for you? That's a weird kind of romance—some dark Bonnie and Clyde shit. Feels super intense, and that spells serious to me. I don't like it at all, Josie."

Oh my God. Is that what she thinks?

I mean, what other reason would there be, given the circumstances?

This is awful. I've never felt so guilty in my entire life. One lie is leading to another, and they're all jumbling up together in my stomach and breeding, and now there's a whole litter of Lie Bunnies hopping all over the place and kicking me in the ribs. I don't know what to say to her that isn't just another lie, so I do the only thing I know and twist it back around on her:

"Where were you tonight?" I say accusingly.

"Excuse me?"

"I tried to call you when I first got to the station."

"I was down in the shop."

"Not on a date?"

Sharp eyes meet mine. "You don't get to ask me about that."

"You think I want to? Because I don't. I'm just saying that you implied you'd cool it with the random hookups."

"Hey! My love life is none of your business," she says, slashing her hand through the air. "I'm allowed to have one, you know. I'm not a nun, and when have you ever once seen me on a date? Never. Not once. Because I may fail at motherhood sometimes, but I don't mix home and dating. I make sure it never touches you."

"Oh yeah? You really wanna know why all this happened, huh?" I ask her, lashing out in frustration. "Do you? All this happened because Evie's ex called you 'the Whore of Babylon.' And he said I post nudes on my subscription service online because apparently, I follow in your footsteps from when you used to model for Henry. And all day long at school, people are talking about me and you, and no matter how many times I tell them to keep their mouths shut, it doesn't matter, because how can I stop air leaking out of a balloon if you keep poking holes in it!"

I've shocked her. I can see it all over her face. Hurt her too. And the satisfaction that comes with that win lasts for all of one millisecond, because the thing about being this close to someone is that when you hurt them, you hurt yourself. And now I regret saying it.

"Don't you *dare* blame me for your mistakes!" she snaps, riled and aggrieved. "I'm not the one who got hauled off to jail with our delinquent neighbor for throwing a damn rock at a department store window!" Her face's long and normally graceful planes are now sharp with anger, her freckles burnished by the streetlamps that circle the police station. "I've done a lot of stupid things in my life, but I damn well have never been taken into police custody. *Your* mistake. You own it, not me. What do I always say, Josie? If you're going to break the rules, do it the right way. Now, look me in the eyes and tell me there was *anything* right about destroying someone's property."

I want to fight her. Fight anyone. I want things to make sense again. I want to take it all back, rewind time and start over. But none of that is going to happen, is it? "You're right. I'm sorry for everything," I finally tell her, defeated. "For being such a disappointment."

After a long, strained moment, anger dissipates, and silence fills the space between us. Then she gently bumps my arm with her elbow and says in a softer voice, "Hey. I'm disappointed in your choice of company, not with you."

Eyes on my lap, I fiddle with the closure on the glove compartment, opening and closing it, over and over. "He's the same Lucky he always was, you know." The kind of boy who would lie to protect me, even when I didn't deserve it.

"He's a vandal, Josie. That window was huge and will be expensive to replace. Could be a felony charge. He's likely going to have a criminal record for this."

He is?

A record that should be mine.

I think I'm going to pass out.

"Josie? Are you okay?" She reaches over my lap and quickly rolls down the window, letting in a burst of cool air. "Breathe. Slowly. In through your nose, out through your mouth," she says, lightly stroking the sensitive skin on the inside of my wrist with her thumb. "There you go. It's okay. You weren't drinking tonight, were you?"

I shake my head once. "I'm just . . . tired."

"It was a stressful night." She takes my temperature with the back of her hand on my forehead, my neck. Brushes hair away from my temples. "I'm sorry that moving back here has been . . . more difficult than our usual relocation. And I'm sorry I didn't answer the phone when you needed me."

Sorry I committed a felony and am letting someone else take the fall for me, I think. But I don't say it out loud, because I'm a coward and an awful person.

"We'll talk about it later. Let's just go home right now, okay? Evie will be worried." She squeezes my shoulder before starting up the Pink Panther. The engine roars to life, shaking the seats and the windows.

How can I hold a grudge against my mom for lying when I'm doing exactly the same thing? That makes me just as bad as her. Worse, because I'm not just hurting myself. I'm hurting Lucky, too.

What's going to happen to him?

BEAUTY COURTHOUSE 1857: Chiseled into locally quarried marble, this sign graces the entrance of a historic municipal building on the town common. A disgruntled farmer once dragged the body of a dead sheep inside the lobby and a ship captain shot up the ceiling in protest of taxes. *(Personal photo/Josephine Saint-Martin)*

5

It's after one in the morning when we get back to the Nook and park in a designated spot tucked into a narrow side alley between us and the Revolutionary War–themed Freedom Art Gallery next door. As soon as we climb the rickety stairs to the above-shop apartment, Evie slides up to me in socks and attacks me with questions and apologies. *Why did I leave the party? What was I thinking? Am I okay?*

"I'm fine," I lie.

"She wasn't arrested," Mom reports. "They just took her in with Lucky. He's the one who broke the window, not Josie."

"Lucky broke the window?" Evie says, brow furrowing.

Ugh. I ignore the tightness of my stomach and whisper to Evie, "Don't tell her about the photo. I'm sorry for making everything worse." Then I nearly start crying again.

"Don't be stupid. You didn't do anything," she says, wrapping long arms around me. Then she murmurs in my ear: "I was wrong about everything. We shouldn't have gone to that party. It's the curse. It works in weird ways. I'm sorry you got hurt in the blowback."

While Evie and I lean on each other, clinging, Mom relays the story to Evie about the window, asking me for details occasionally. Like Mom, Evie seems to buy the lie. And I let her. Because I don't know what else to do.

Well. That's not *exactly* true.

I know I could confess. There are, in fact, several moments in the conversation when I think *Right now! Do it now! Just tell them!* But I hesitate, and the moments fall through my fingers like sand. The longer I stay silent, the harder it is to speak up, and the sicker and sicker I feel about it.

So I finally just tell them I'm tired, that I need to sleep. And because they are both better people than me, they don't suspect anything is amiss.

If they only knew.

I'm so confused about the whole thing, and all I can do is go back over what Lucky said in the police station. What we talked about there . . . what we discussed behind the pool house at the party. Our old friendship before I left town. How much had changed.

And the flirting.

I consider what my mom said, the Bonnie and Clyde comment.

And the pit-pattering-panic I felt behind the pool house fills up my chest again. Dear God. I have to stop thinking about that. There's no way he's suddenly filled with amorous longing for his former best friend and because of these feelings, decided to take the fall for her crime.

Correction: *accidental* crime.

Anyway, now we're back to square one.

Why in the world did he do it?

I think before this goes any further, it's best I find out.

Because it's officially summer break now, I'm working *extra* shifts at the Nook along with Evie and a couple of other part-time employees Mom has on staff. Summer season is serious business for the entire town—definitely for our bookshop. Yesterday, I was happy about putting in more time at the Nook. It's Step Two of my three-step plan: Save up enough money for a plane ticket to Los Angeles.

Today, however, I want to bail on my shift and run across the street to Nick's Boatyard, because I can plainly see through our front window that Lucky's red Superhawk motorcycle is parked out there, which means he's working for his dad today.

And I really, really want to talk to him.

But I've already been warned against doing that just this morning.

"I seriously don't want you hanging around Lucky Karras anymore," Mom told me at breakfast. "I'm not going to ask for details about the seriousness of your relationship with him, but all I know is that he's in deep shit, and rumors will be spreading around town like wildfire."

She doesn't know the half of it. "I can handle it."

"Don't care. I don't need our name tangled up in it," she says, getting agitated. "So stay away. Period. Putting my foot down."

That's pretty much Mom's harshest commandment. Putting her proverbial foot down means she's serious and it's final. No arguments. She's assuming parental privileges, a rare event, and that's that.

Only it's *not* that, because I can't just never see him again. Hello! He works across the street, so it's a physical impossibility. And on top of that, I need to find out what's going on with him. Is he going to jail? Juvie? What's going to happen to him?

It's my crime, after all. I have a right to know.

And he's my friend, not hers.

I put it out of my mind for a while and instead concentrate on my morning shift at the Nook, where I try to guess which of our regular customers have seen "my" naked photo or heard the *That's the Girl Who Sells Nudes Online* rumor—only, it's hard to tell from their darting glances which ones may have also heard the *That's the Girl Who Was Hauled to the Police Station Last Night* rumor.

Occasionally, someone walks by our shops and makes it clear by puckering up their lips and making a kissy face at me. Lovely. Just lovely . . .

Around noon, tourists begin heading to pubs and clam shacks

for lunch, and things finally quiet down enough for Evie to read a book at the counter on the Nook's squeaky stool. I prop myself up on my elbows next to her and stare out the window, trying not to stress while watching Nick's Boatyard. Below me is a string of gold-and-green postcards from Nepal: Kathmandu, temples, monkeys, and mountains. Grandma sends one a week with general updates. Regular customers *ooh* and *aah* over her descriptions of yak milk.

"We should get one of the coin-operated telescopes on the Harborwalk moved in here so you can get a better look at the boatyard," Evie says in a bored voice, squeaking the stool.

"I'm just curious."

"Yep. I'm curious too. Curious why a notoriously hardboiled lone wolf like Phantom would suddenly destroy a very public piece of town history in a fit of Hulk-like rage."

Ruh-oh.

"So strange," she says, not looking up from her book. Her eyeliner is extra dark today, and she's rearranged the enamel pins and buttons that line the lanyard of her Siren's Book Nook ID badge—we wear them hanging around our necks—so that the topmost one says *When Doves Cry* and the one beneath it says *Heathcliff, it's me.*

"Lots of things are strange," I say, trying to mimic her cooler-than-cool unbothered tone. "Like how you have been dating the prince of Beauty. I mean, it would have been nice to know we were at a Summers house last night, as in Levi Summers, the king of town?"

"Hey, cuz? We were at Levi Summer's brothers' house last night," she says saucily.

"Oh, were we?"

"Surprise."

"It's just . . ." I sigh. "You know . . . I felt really stupid when Lucky told me that."

Her eyes flick to mine at the mention of Lucky's name. "First of all, I didn't realize it mattered. And second, I had a life here before you showed up and probably will after you're gone."

Lucky said the same thing. I guess everyone thinks I'm just a blip, a twenty-four-hour-long disappearing story, not a permanent part of the town's feed. She's not really being mean about it, just honest, so it's hard to argue.

"You wouldn't happen to have his phone number, would you?" I ask, super casual.

"Levi Summers?"

I give her a faux-catty look. "Lucky's."

"Ah, your old pal *Lucky*," she says, pretending to catch on. "Nope, can't say that I do. No need to call him. He's in here every afternoon after school."

Only, school is out now. And then there's the tiny matter of him taking the fall for me.

Across the street, the boatyard office door opens, and several people exit onto the sidewalk: Lucky's parents, Nick and Kat. An older couple—his grandparents. A few more dark-haired people with the same chiseled builds and smiling faces. Aunts and uncles,

I think. Three kids. And a perky Latina in a professional-looking pantsuit, carrying a briefcase.

Then there's Lucky. I almost didn't recognize him. He's wearing black dress pants and a tie with a button-up shirt.

"Whoa," Evie says, leaning over the counter to peer out the window with me. "Got to admit. Phantom cleans up *real* nice. No wonder he's knocking up girls left and right. He's the male Medusa. Don't look into his eyes. Might get you pregnant."

"Gross, Evie," I mumble. But now I'm curious. "I heard about Bunny Perera. Just how many girls are there?"

"Who really knows? Several? None? Everyone was surprised about Bunny. Certain blond rowers I know that shall not be named ever, ever again because they are dicks, and I can't believe I ever allowed myself to trust them—"

Yikes. Honestly, I'd rather not discuss Adrian Summers ever again either. Ever-ever.

"—these certain people said the whole Bunny and Lucky thing must've been a one-time hookup situation, because they definitely weren't an ongoing item. Maybe it's just a rumor. Or maybe he's a serial dater."

I don't like that. At *all*. It reminds me of my mom's dating habits, all wrapped up in lies and sneaking around, and kids at school whispering "Wild Winona." It makes me a little sick to my stomach, to be honest.

I don't know why I care. Lucky can do what he wants.

"Why is he dressed up like that?" I ask. Irritated that he might be a serial dater. Irritated that it bothers me. That I don't know anything about a boy I used to know, who stuck his neck out for me. "Looks like he's going to church or a funeral."

"Or an arraignment," Evie says. "They're going to the courthouse."

Stomach in knots. *Guilt. Shame. Worry.*

"Entire Karras family en force," Evie notes. "Aunts, uncles, grandparents. I think that's Kat Karras's sister and two of her kids. Damn. They aren't screwing around."

"Is that their lawyer?" I whisper.

"Yeah. Think that's Gina Garcia. She's not cheap. But if anyone's going to fight the Summers family, she's a good choice."

Guilt. Shame. Sickness.

I watch the entire Karras family piling into several cars, patting Lucky on the back for support, looking serious yet positive, ready to fight for him, the boy who didn't even do this thing, and, and—

"It was me," I whisper into Evie's hair.

The stool squeaks as she stiffens. Doesn't say anything.

"I did it," I whisper again. "I threw the rock. I broke the window."

"What?" she mouths back at me, eyes big as moons as she quickly glances around the store to check where my mother is. And then again: *"What?"*

"I didn't mean to break the window!" I whisper into my hands, watching Lucky's head ducking inside his father's truck. "I meant to hit the metal letters above the glass, but I guess my arm isn't all that strong, and I missed. And Lucky had followed me there from the party on his bike. I guess he was worried that I was walking home alone, because we'd talked at the party. We barely even talked! Only for a few minutes. He said he was a bad flirter, and I didn't even know we were flirting, and seriously, why does he have to be so hot now?"

"Oh, *cuz*."

"We barely talked. I swear."

Long enough for me to spill my guts to him about my Los Angeles plans.

But I don't say this, of course.

"And then he followed me, and I was so angry about the photo . . . I threw the rock, and the alarm went off," I tell her. "The security guard caught us, but the cop didn't care who did it—he took us both in. Said they could sort it out at the station. So we got hauled off together. I told Lucky I'd clear things up and make sure they knew I did it. But I guess he told the police he did it, and they let me go free."

"Son of a bitch," Evie murmurs, blinking at me in surprise.

"Mom believed it," I say. "And she said it would be a felony, and I got scared, and I didn't know what to do. But I don't want him to go to jail for me. I don't even know him anymore! Now everything's way out of control, and there he goes, and I can't even talk to him before he gets sent off to death row—"

"He's not going to death row."

"I don't know what to do, Evie. We used to be best friends, but we barely know each other now. I can't let him do this for me. It's too weird, right?"

She looks rattled. She *never* looks rattled. Only two times in the months since we've moved here has she been anything but unflappable and even-keeled: last night when Adrian was fighting with her, and now. This time it's my fault.

"I'm sorry," I tell her. "I just got so mad. The Harvard rower whose name we aren't speaking made you cry at the party, and the photo—"

I can't finish. I'm too upset now. Thankfully, I don't have to, because Evie's eyes are glossy with emotion, and in this moment right now, I know she understands.

"Shit," she murmurs.

"Yeah," I say.

We both stare out the window at the Karrases' caravan of cars. Lucky's dad flips over the CLOSED sign on the office door to the boatyard, locks the door, and heads to his truck, rubbing his hand through his hair as if he's worried and nervous. Guess I would be too, if I were taking my child to an arraignment for a possible felony.

When I was a kid, sometimes I felt like the Karrases were more of a family to me than my own. I can't make these nice people go through this. I just can't.

Adrenaline pumping through my limbs, I race toward the bookshop door with the intention of stopping them.

"Josie?"

I stop in my tracks, hand reaching for the shop door, and turn to look at my mother.

"What's the matter, shutterbug?" she asks, looking puzzled. "You okay?"

"Mom . . . ," I say, unable to finish.

Evie's voice calls out as she jogs up behind me, "Stop! Wait. I was only kidding, cuz. Come back—you don't have to, uh, get my lunch. We can take a break together when Anna clocks in and takes over the register."

Heart racing, I glance at her, then out the window, where the Karrases are driving away. Oh God. I wish Evie wouldn't have stopped me . . . and I'm so thankful she did.

Coward. Liar. Wimp.

I'm a mess. I'm a great big ball of anxiety and anguish. This is all so screwed up.

Mom doesn't seem to notice. Her face softens as she says, "Evie's right. The town will be talking about the broken window, and even if you didn't do it, you were there. Rumors are going to fly about you and Lucky, so maybe it's best you stick around the shop and lay low. Just for a couple of days, until this whole thing dies down."

"Will it die down?"

"Sure," Evie says.

"Absolutely," Mom agrees, nodding enthusiastically.

So why don't I believe them?

NICK'S BOATYARD: A hand-painted warehouse sign hangs over the office doors of a harbor-front business. The two-story brick building was once a historical dry dock to repair cargo ships sailing from Canada and Europe in the early 1800s. *(Personal photo/Josephine Saint-Martin)*

6

Evie and Mom have severely underestimated this town's interest in a broken window, because the hubbub over my crime doesn't quote, unquote die down.

In fact, it's all anyone talks about online for several days.

Photos of the broken window are posted to the Town Crier, Beauty's social media account for town-related activities, tourism, and community-interest items—which this is, apparently. The pictures are recaptioned and spread around by a bunch of kids from Beauty High, and next thing I know, it's being memed and used as ammunition against the Goldens from the private academy, then volleyed back and forth as both a symbol of smashing privilege on one side and proof of blue-collar delinquency on the other, and now I've somehow started a low-key class war?

Only, I'm not in the middle of it.

Lucky is.

This is going to send me to an early grave. I'm bad at lying, bad at secrets, and I'm dying to know what happened with Lucky and the arraignment. So after several queasy, restless nights of no sleep—and Evie being no help whatsoever, telling me over and over that it's too late to confess—I make up my mind to sneak away from the bookshop and talk to Lucky about this whole sordid debacle.

Unfortunately, the only time I ever see his red motorcycle there is when I'm working at the bookshop, and escaping my shift at Siren's Book Nook takes some work, but Evie lets me know when Mom heads out to drop off the shop's daily bank deposit—which always takes extra-long, because of her whole superstitious aversion to Lamplighter Lane.

That's my moment.

After borrowing a floppy sunhat from Evie and a pair of big, dark sunglasses that practically swallow my face, I make a beeline outside and wait for a break in the traffic to jog across the street. The boatyard's office window has the blinds cracked, and it's hard for me to see inside, but I think I spy Lucky's mother at a big desk and one of several mechanics that work for the Karrases. No Lucky, though.

I slink down the sidewalk and head into the side alleyway that leads around to the boat docks and the back of the building, where a couple of large work bays are open. A few small speedboats are inside the bays—there's a welder working in one—and the bigger boats are lifted by a crane into a drydock area off a private pier.

You can see the entire harbor back here, crystal clear and robin's egg blue, and it's so startlingly pretty, with the sun glinting off the waves and the wind blowing through my hair, that I can almost pretend that nothing's wrong.

Shooing away seagulls, I scan the concrete boatyard for either Lucky's dad, Nick, who'd I'd like to avoid, or Lucky, but I see neither Karras. Not until I glance up and spot a pair of crossed legs wearing scuffed black boots. My nerves get a little jangly at the sight of them.

Lucky's lounging on the narrow sundeck of a small boat that's been pulled up onto the concrete and is now parked on wooden blocks like an old car that doesn't run. Making sure no one is looking my way, I approach a rolling ladder at the base of the boat. "Psst. Hey."

He peers down at me over the deck railing, a purple lollipop on a white stick tucked behind one ear. He's wearing a navy button-up mechanic's shirt with his name embroidered in a vintage font on the pocket next to a number thirteen, and he looks startled to see me at first—but that vanishes in a blink.

"You look so familiar," he says, voice full of sarcasm. "I mean, I can tell from your big hat and glasses that you're hiding from the paparazzi, but I can't quite place your face . . . ?"

I frown. "Can we talk? Please?"

"Josie Saint-Martin. The poor, shy little lamb who got hauled into jail with the big, bad wolf by pure accident. What a scandal. However did she get caught up in that? He probably roped her into it against her will. Sounds like something nefarious and sexy went down."

"What? That's not what people are saying!"

Is it . . . ?

"And now she wants to talk to little ol' me? Oh wow. Just wow . . . This is the most exciting day of my life." He snaps his fingers. "Dammit. And I forgot my autograph book."

"Lucky, please!" I beg.

He gives me a withering look before glancing over his shoulder, checking to make sure his father isn't nearby, I think. When he finds the coast clear, he pats the ladder. "Permission to come aboard, Miss Saint-Martin. Escape your adoring fans on the S.S. Fun N Sun—not to be confused with the Sun and Fun, which overheated last week."

"You want me to come up there?"

"Did you develop a fear of heights over the last few years?"

"No. I just mean . . . it's on blocks. Is it safe? Is this, like, a dead boat or something? It doesn't drive?"

He laughs. "Pilot. You pilot a boat and drive a car."

"Oh, yeah. I forgot." When we were kids, we spent most of our time in the apartment above the bookshop or running around town. The Karrases' old boat-repair place was a lot smaller, and it was the last place we wanted to be. This boatyard here? It's huge. And obviously *way* more successful. This is new territory for me.

Lucky taps the side of the boat. "This here is what we in the boat-repair biz like to call a floating death trap out on the water. But right here, it's perfectly fine. It's been sitting on blocks for about a month because the cheapskate who owns it won't pay for the repairs.

I come up here every day. It's not going anywhere, I assure you."

"Fine," I tell him. "I'll come up."

"Whoa, watch your step. Rickety ladder and seagull shit are a dangerous combo."

"You just said it was safe!" I complain, stumbling as I clear the edge of the deck.

"Safe-ish. Sit down before you break your neck and I get blamed for that, too." He gestures to an empty spot next to him on a built-in seat, moving a paperback out of the way.

Jesus. This is not how I thought this would go. My stomach clenches, and I feel a little sick and terrified. Gosh, it's tight quarters up here. "Lucky . . ."

"Josie." He leans back against the boat, legs sprawled, arms tightly crossed over his chest, and he stares at me from under a curved lock of dark hair that's fallen across his brow.

I twist in my seat and try to focus on why I'm here. "What happened at the arraignment?"

He lifts one shoulder, lets it drop, and looks off into the harbor. "Eh, it was bullshit. Whatever. My dad has a lawyer he uses for the boatyard, so she told me what to say—that the whole thing was an accident. That I never intended to break the window or was even aiming for Summers & Co, because I would *never* do anything to hurt my father's best client."

"Oh God," I whisper.

"So I said it ricocheted and hit the glass. Just a stupid mistake. Said I'm sorry, yadda-yadda-yadda. And my dad apologized.

And my mom apologized. It was a disgusting suck-up fest of epic proportions, and Levi Summers said, 'No problem. I won't press charges—'"

"Oh, thank God!" I say.

"'—if Lucky pays for the window to be replaced.'"

"O-o-oh."

"Oh yeah," Lucky says with a tight smile. "Richest man in town. But he didn't get that way by giving it away, right? Oh no. He watches every penny. And he wants me to pay every penny back. Guess how many pennies that is?"

He tells me. I nearly pass out.

"That's . . ." I do a quick calculation in my head. "It would take me a year to earn that at the bookshop, working part-time." Even with my Photo Funder subscriber donations, which are down to an all-time low of sixty-five dollars this month. Guess I'm not providing enough new content for my subscribers, because a couple of them bailed. Or maybe they don't like all my new photos of signs around Beauty.

Maybe I should've given them actual nudes, like Adrian said.

"Well," Lucky says, "your cheap-ass mom needs to give you a raise, because it will take me about six months to pay it off, working for my dad. Our lawyer negotiated that I pay for the glass itself and work off the cost of the repair labor by doing some tasks around the department store. Like tomorrow, I go in before the store opens to vacuum out the window display. I've already done it once, but the store manager wants me to go over it again, just to make sure.

And I get to do other helpful things like"—he ticks off a list on his fingers—"sweep up the sidewalk. Repaint the lines on the parking lot. Wash the windows using the scaffold lift. Clean seagull nests off the roof. You know, fun stuff. All summer long."

"That's awful."

"Don't worry. I didn't have plans or anything," he says, rancor in his tone.

"Hey!" I say, frustrated. "I didn't ask you to do this, you know."

"But you didn't turn it down, did you? You didn't argue. Not even a 'Hey, thanks for having my back, Lucky. That was a swell thing you did for me.'"

"I don't have your phone number!"

He cranes his neck and pretends to peer over the boat in the direction of the bookshop. "Golly gee. Is it just me, or do you live awfully close to our boatyard? What is it . . . an entire two-minute walk away?"

"My mom won't let me see you."

A single brow arches, the one that's missing the tail end, making it look like an apostrophe. "Is that so?" He sounds amused. Like I've told a funny joke. Or a dirty one. Something improper and salacious.

I throw up my hands. "Fine. She thinks there's something going on between us, okay? Are you happy? And I didn't tell her I threw the rock because . . . I just didn't. I was a coward. Is that what you want to hear?"

"That's a start," he says, a little smug.

"Well, there you go. I'm a coward. I chickened out."

"If you tell her you threw the rock, then you'd have to tell her about other things, right? Like that you were trying to get a magazine internship so that you could impress your fancy father."

I stare at him, practically feeling my ribs cracking under the thundering pressure of my heartbeat. In a small voice I admit, "It's easier not to say anything. I don't want to tell her about the photo Adrian flashed around at the party. I don't want to tell her everything Adrian said about our family. And I don't want to explain why I was upset at Adrian's father before the party even started that night. . . ."

"No, you can't do that," he says, and there's an edge to his words. As if he's implying that everything I want—the magazine internship, Los Angeles, apprenticing with my father . . . a real family—is sitting on one side of a scale being measured against his worth, and I'm selfishly choosing my own needs over his.

And, okay, I am. I know I am. *He* knows I am.

And I wish I could change it.

"I'm not that person," I argue. "I'm not just out for myself at whatever cost, damn it all."

"Everyone is," he says matter-of-factly. "Humans are selfish. It's our nature."

"It's not mine. Look. I'll fix this. I'll go back to the police and tell them I did it."

"No, you won't."

I nod, feeling more certain now. "I will."

He leans forward until his face is inches from mine. I move away. He leans forward again to erase the distance again, insistent. The sweet scent of grape candy wafts in my direction. All the hairs on my arms stands up, and a cascade of warm chills races over my skin.

It feels nice. A little too nice.

"No." One word. It falls from his lips, but I'll be damned if I know what it means. He smells like candy, and for the first time in what seems like forever, I'm not filled with panic and dread, and he's *so very close*. . . .

"Hmm?" I murmur.

"I said no."

"No?" *Snap out of it, Saint-Martin!* "So . . . you're telling me I can't go to the police."

"Bingo."

"Why the hell not?"

"Because I didn't put my family through all this expense and trouble for nothing. Do you know what this did to my mom? She's stressed out. My grandparents? They've got to defend my honor at church this weekend when everyone will be talking shit about me again. 'That Lucky, nothing but trouble. Just look at him. He used to be such a sweet little boy. What a shame.'"

He's talking about the fire—the one that gave him all the scars on the side of his face. I see the shadow of that pain lingering behind his eyes.

"I said I was sorry for what you went through," I remind him.

"Yeah, I remember you saying you were sorry back then, too, right before you split town. While I was stuck in the hospital, about to get skin grafts so that I looked a little less like a monster."

This makes something in my chest contract and ache.

"Like I had a choice about leaving?" I argue. "Even though you were still in the hospital, I know you heard what happened—surely everyone in town heard about the domestic disturbance at the Nook. The big Saint-Martin mother-daughter fight . . . ring any bells? I literally was in my pajamas when we left town. It was the middle of the night. I was given no warning. It was well past visiting hours, so I couldn't drop by to tell you goodbye. And besides that, I thought my mom was going to be arrested. Or my grandma. It was a nightmare. So, you know, I'm sorry that my family is screwed up, but I was twelve, and I had no control over that, and I cried all the way out of town."

I texted Lucky from my mom's phone—I remember Mom allowing me to do that—because unlike him, I didn't get my own phone until I turned thirteen. I also tried calling the hospital the next day, but the phone in his room just rang. "And once we got to Boston, I emailed you, but you never replied. Not once."

"Pardon me for being in agony and covered in bandages."

"Do you think I don't remember? My best friend was stuck in the hospital with terrible burns. I was worried sick about you and came to see you in the hospital every day. Remember? I didn't know what was going to happen with your burns, and no one was telling me anything because I was just a kid. And then when my mom and I left town, it was late at night, and I couldn't reach you. Then you didn't answer the next day, or the next—and I thought, okay, maybe he can't reply because he's having surgery or something. Maybe he'll respond when he gets home. So I kept trying to contact you—for weeks. Weeks! But you never replied, Lucky. You just . . . vanished."

"No, Josie. *You* vanished. I was still here. You left."

"My mom left town and took me with her," I repeat. "I wrote you to explain. You didn't write back."

My chest aches, thinking about it again, and I'm surprised how much it still hurts.

"Look, I don't want to dig up the past," he says, suddenly agitated and intense. "The department store window is about *now*. It's about the present. It's about pride."

How did this get so serious, so fast? He's mad now. *Really* mad.

He throws up a hand. "And you don't get to just flounce in here and decide that you're feeling generous today, shutterbug."

"You don't get to call me that," I whisper. "You don't know me anymore."

"Then don't treat me like I'm trash. Don't demean what I did. It wasn't disposable. I didn't do it so you could bide your time and swoop back in to take your licks."

Okay, now *I'm* upset. Angry. Scared. And something else . . . I don't even know what. All I know is that if I want to fight with someone, I can do that with my mom. I don't need Lucky 2.0, aka a complete stranger, to make me feel like I'll never be good enough.

Every molecule of my being is vibrating with energy. "Then why?"

"Why what?"

"Why did you do it?"

He blinks at me, black lashes fluttering. He's so close, I can see the pale network of burn scars on one side of his face. The apostrophe of his marred eyebrow. The deep hollows of his cheeks. The way his sharp eyes are scanning my face . . . and the hesitation behind them.

He's hiding something; I just don't know what.

"Got to get back to work," he says, jaw tightening. "Juggling two jobs now, so time is a little tight."

"*Lucky*," I plead.

"Don't want your pity, Saint-Martin. Keep it. I'm fine."

Part of me wants to scream. He's bitter that he's taking the blame for something he didn't do, yet he doesn't want me to turn myself in to the police. He's mad that I didn't tell him I was grateful, but he doesn't want my pity?

I squeeze my eyes shut and admit, "I've done a lot of stupid things in my life, but I've never screwed anything up this badly. I want to fix this. Let me fix this."

When I open my eyes, he's looking at me. Contemplating. Silent.

"I've really got to get back to work," he says after a moment, in a gentler voice, encouraging me to stand. "And you better go before my parents see you up here and start giving me shit. You aren't the only one who's getting bombarded with questions about us hooking up, and 'no girl is worth ruining your life for,' all that."

My cheeks grow warm. "But that's . . ." I sputter something that sounds nearly like a complete word, but my brain glitches, and I can't quite get it out. I try again. "Ridiculous." There! Got it out. "I mean . . . right? No life-ruining. No hooking up. I mean, obviously." I manage a hollow laugh, suddenly nervous. "We don't even know each other anymore."

Sharp and serious, his eyes dart over me from beneath a fan of dark lashes—the quickest of looks, buried in a blink.

That look makes me want something I shouldn't want.

"Better go now," he says. "Let's not give them a reason to speculate any more than they already have."

"Let's not," I agree. "This disaster is already large enough as it stands."

But as I head back down the ladder and sneak across the boatyard, eager to put both physical and emotional space between me and Lucky and this whole tangled mess, his words drum in my temples along with my pounding pulse. And I realize something.

He's lying too.

His parents don't know that he didn't throw that rock. They don't know that he's covering for me. That seems significant. I just can't figure out why.

But I'm going to.

COAST LIFE IS THE GOOD LIFE: This etched glass sign is posted by the entrance to the lone quarterly magazine headquarters in town. The brick building also houses the local newspaper and sits on the historic town common next to Summers & Co Department Store. *(Personal photo/Josephine Saint-Martin)*

7

Like most of the smaller shops on our block, the Nook traditionally closes early at noon every Wednesday for a half day—something to do with farmers back in the 1800s, I don't know. But the Wednesday after I talk to Lucky, I'm thankful for it. If Lucky won't let me turn myself in to the police and unburden my soul, then I'm going back to my original plan: Los Angeles or bust. I've just got some repair work to do. A teeny, tiny little patch.

And maybe while I'm in the process of patching, I might do a little snooping. I've been cooped up in the Nook too long.

I need to get out and assess the damage. And other things . . .

"You can use your darkroom if you need to develop any film," Mom tells me when I clock out for the afternoon and she's taking the till out of the register. "I won't be receiving books in the back this afternoon."

"That's okay."

"You were begging me to clear it out yesterday."

"I'm going to . . . shoot some signs on the common." Lie.

"Oh? Thought you'd snapped all those."

"Not all of them." Double lie. I've taken a million shots of every sign on the town common. "Maybe I'll head down the Harborwalk. Need new material for my Photo Funder. Losing subscribers left and right."

"Only losers who don't appreciate good art when they see it. You'll get new subscribers. I don't like you walking around town alone, though. If anyone harasses you—"

"I'll record it."

Which is probably what I should have done that night at the party with Adrian; then again, I'd have to look at that nude photo of my mom all the time. She still doesn't know, which is a miracle, considering how small this town is. All I can hope is that it stays in the teen gossip circuit and doesn't make it up to her old friends.

When I'm certain she's taken the till into the stockroom and will be busy for a bit, I race up the rickety back steps to the above-shop apartment and scour my clothes for an outfit that screams Professional and Adult, but not Trying Too Hard: black pants, flats, white blouse. Hair in a simple French braid. Not much I can do about the splotchy freckles that make me look years younger, and after two failed tries, I give up on covering them with makeup.

Satisfied, I grab my big sunglasses and my portfolio—a black leather binder with twenty-five prints zipped up inside—and race out the door. I take the long way through the alley, to avoid being spotted by Mom or anyone else, and cut through a narrow lane with a shop that always smells like Christmas and sells hand-dipped beeswax and bayberry candles, and a darkened door with a bright red FOR RENT sign: It once housed the office of Desmond Banks, Private Investigator. Beauty only has one store that stays open twenty-four hours a day, but we had a need for a PI? Or maybe the point is that we *didn't*, and that's why he's out of business.

Who knows. Beauty is strange.

But strange isn't a bad thing, and it's sunny and warm, a perfect June day without a cloud in the sky, making it easy to lie to myself and pretend that I'm not anxious. As I cross the town common, tourists shade their eyes to stare at the historic town hall and take pictures on their phones of iron hitching posts and red-and-purple pansies under massive beech trees that rich families brought here from Europe in the Gilded Age. I hurry past them, hoping no one recognizes me, and I stride down a long sidewalk to my destination.

The entrance of *Coast Life* magazine's offices.

I'm breathing heavily when I push through the old brass doors and stride into a silent lobby with vaulted ceilings and marble floors. A lone receptionist sits behind a glass desk, guarding a glass door: The actual offices are beyond it.

All is quiet except the sound of my flats on the marble. When I reach the desk, the young woman with short hair holds up a finger until she's finished talking in a low, metered voice on a wireless headset. Then she lifts her head and smiles.

A smile is good. A smile means she doesn't associate me with the police station. Or the broken window at Summers & Co. Or the nude photo of my mother that's circulating around town . . .

"Josie Saint-Martin to see Nina Cox," I say, a little breathless and nervous.

She looks confused. "Did you have an appointment?"

"Not, uh, exactly, but she was considering me for the photography internship—"

Before Levi Summers yanked my application.

"I'm sorry," she says, making a pained face while holding up a hand to stop me, "but Ms. Cox canceled all her appointments this week. Her daughter is in the hospital."

"Oh no," I say.

"Do you have her email address?"

"I think I had her card"—I did not—"but if you could give it to me again . . . ?"

She thumbs through something on her desk and hands me a business card. "There you are. You can just email her and ask her when she wants to reschedule. Give her a bit to respond. She'll be catching up for a while. I'm sure you understand."

"Of course," I say.

The receptionist nods once and smiles. "Good afternoon."

"Good afternoon," I say, feeling weirdly dismissed.

Once I'm outside the building, I feel a little disappointed yet also hopeful. I have a business card and an email address. I'll just wait a few respectable days for this poor woman's child to get out of the hospital, then boom. Email her and request a meeting to talk about reconsidering me for the internship that I'm *definitely* not too young to get.

No one got anything by not asking for it. Right?

Unless this Nina Cox woman has seen the nude photo. Or heard that I was taken to the police station, *ugh* . . . Feeling 50 percent less confident, I pocket the business card and head around the corner of the *Coast Life* offices.

I could go back home. That's what I tell myself . . . another lie. I feel my nerves get a little twitchy, and I slow my gait in an attempt to calm myself as I pass by a pair of tourists on a park bench, spooning frozen lemonade into their mouths.

Right now? I'm just a narrow private parking lot away from the scene of my crime.

Summers & Co.

There it is, all boarded up with plywood. My stomach plunges several stories and churns sickeningly.

The side parking lot has been taped off and closed to the public. I think it's normally where the store valet-parks cars, but right now a lone person in jeans and a tight black T-shirt crouches over freshly painted white parking-space lines, paintbrush in hand. I'd recognize that dark, messy hair and aura of unapproachability anywhere.

Churn. Churn. Churn . . .

Clutching my portfolio, I pick my sick stomach off the ground and drag my feet over to the taped-off parking lot, then I stand there for a moment and watch Lucky. He's swearing to himself—or to the paintbrush. Saying really foul, blasphemous things. I only catch half of what he's mumbling, but wow. It's remarkably profane—a skill I always admired about him, but right now, I'm intimidated. He's not in a good mood. I should go. Like, now.

Midbrushstroke, his arm stills. He stops swearing, and before I can take my portfolio and run for the hills, his head slowly lifts.

I raise one hand. "Hi."

"You know," he says, sticking the paintbrush into a can and pushing to his feet. "I thought to myself, hey Lucky? What could make this worse? And the answer is, an audience. But not just any audience. Josie Saint-Martin, looking all fancy. Did you dress up for me?"

"I should leave," I say, pointing vaguely the way I came.

"Don't go. You'll miss the best part of the show. Any minute now, the store manager will walk out here to judge my work and find me wanting." He approaches me and stops in front of the line of yellow tape, brushing dirty hands on his jeans. His black T-shirt is splattered with white paint and even tighter up close. I didn't realize he was so muscular these days. I mean, good *God*. Is that from working in the boatyard? I'm not sure why that bothers me so much . . . why I'm even noticing it. I wish I wouldn't.

"Never mind," I tell him, a little agitated. "I don't want to get you in trouble."

"Oh no. Stay. The loss of my dignity in a public space is so very special," he says, kissing his fingers like a cartoon chef. "Must-see. You'll love it. Which is, I assume, why you're here, to wallow in my misery."

Anger heats my chest. "You know what?" I say, pointing a finger at him. "You're kind of a jackass."

He's surprised by my outburst. Then his mouth turns upward, dimpling at both corners. "You're just figuring that out now?"

Huh. Hold on. He's *smiling*? Like, not sarcastic-smiling. Okay, maybe a little sarcastic, because he's definitely smirking at me. But it's more playful than mean. And there's something else there . . . something different that I haven't really seen since I've been back in town.

I think he's . . . happy.

Like, the tiniest sliver of happiness. It fades quickly, but I know I saw it. Like a sighting of Bigfoot in the woods, or a UFO in the skies at night. It's exciting . . . and a little bit sexy.

"I should've brought a camera and taken photos," I say, pushing my luck a little.

"Definitely should have," he says. "Could post those online and get all the likes and hearts and re-likes and re-hearts."

"True. You're famous now. Working-class hero, smashing a town elder's window as a symbolic protest against privilege and colonial pedigree? Well done. I think all of Beauty High's going to rise up and stage a march for you."

"Very funny."

"Shepard Fairey will create poster art with your face on it. People will wear it on T-shirts and paint murals of it on sides of buildings."

"And you'd rather it be *your* face?" he says. "You want all the fame and attention?"

"Attention, no. The cold, hard cash that comes with fame? Maybe. Film is expensive, and as you've pointed out, the Nook isn't a high-paying gig."

He laughs. "All right, respect. Seeing as I'm all out of cash these days myself . . ."

Yeah, that. I glance at the boarded-up window that he's working to pay off.

He glances at my portfolio.

We look at each other.

"Actually, I'm glad I saw you," I say, as if it was pure accident that I came over here and not like I was scoping out the scene of my crime, hoping he would be here. "I had an idea I wanted to run by you, if you were interested in hearing it. It's not perfect, but it's something."

He throws a look over his shoulder. "I'm done here in half an hour, and I can spare a little time before I head back to the boatyard for the rest of the afternoon. You want to meet me someplace?"

The Quarterdeck is a coffeehouse off the Harborwalk between my family's neighborhood in the South Harbor and the heart of the historic district. But it's not just any old coffeehouse: It's a docked replica of a French ship from 1778's Battle of Rhode Island. Patrons cross a plank-like bridge and board the main deck of the ship, where tables sit under masts and rigging, flags fluttering in the harbor breeze.

To order, you head down into the belly of the ship—there are tables and small booths down here, too—and Lucky has given me a very specific, very irritating drink order: Fill the cup exactly one-quarter-full of cream, then add plain cold brew coffee to the brim, no ice. The barista gives me an apathetic look when I repeat this but doesn't question it, so I tip her extra.

Nearly spilling Lucky's stupid extra-full drink, which threatens to slosh out of the straw like a whale spewing water from a blowhole, I climb back up to the upper deck and find an empty table between two cannons that overlooks the harbor. When I'm halfway finished drinking my normally filled but not-so-great latte, Lucky slides into the seat across from me. He's wearing his leather jacket over the paint-splattered tight T-shirt, so at least I don't have to stare at the pornographic outline of his chest.

He inspects the cup sitting on his side of the table. "You got it right."

"Don't sound so surprised. I can order a drink in a coffee shop . . . even ridiculous ones. You forget that my mom's managed half the bookstores in New England and a good chunk of them had coffee shops inside. I've done most of my homework in below-average coffee shops."

"Don't drink coffee in bookstores? That's what you're saying?"

"Oh-ho-ho, the health code violations I've seen."

"Well, you left town before the Quarterdeck opened, so I should've warned you that the only thing good here is the cold brew. Because I'll take coffee in a bookstore over coffee in a tourist ship any day of the week," he says, peeling off the top of his plastic cup to drink without a straw, like he can't even be bothered. He downs half of it in three swallows. "What's that?" he says, nodding toward my portfolio. "Is this the big idea you wanted to talk about?"

"This is nothing." I cover it up.

"Weird, because it looks like a portfolio. And *you* look dressed up."

"So?"

"Come on, Saint-Martin," he says, stretching out long legs under the table. "Thought we already agreed you're still a terrible liar."

"Don't think we *agreed*."

"You said you were going to try to weasel your way into a magazine internship." His eyes crinkle at the corners; he's teasing me and clearly enjoying himself.

"Hustle my way in. Not weasel."

"Because when people tell you no, you can't have something, that's when Josie Saint-Martin digs in her heels and tries harder. You haven't changed one bit."

"I resent that. But okay, yes . . ." I glance around to make sure no one is listening to us and briefly explain what happened at *Coast Life*. ". . . and that's when I saw you."

"Now *that*, I believe."

"It's the truth."

"You never used to lie to me, you know."

I nod, a little heat creeping up my chest, both embarrassed and pleased. "I remember."

"I like it when you are teeth-gratingly honest. That's part of your charm. When you're honest, then *I* can be honest, and it feels like . . . I don't know. It feels like there's this invisible wall that comes down between us? The wall is kind of electric, or lasers, or something—"

"An electric, invisible wall."

"And you're the only one with the key to switch it off. When you're honest, whoosh! It comes down, and we both can cross over freely and talk." He squints, smiling with his eyes. "Does that make any sense?"

I'm not sure how to respond to this divulgement. It feels like tasting a wedge of lemon on a dare: unexpectedly bracing, too much all at once. But . . . I quickly get accustomed to the foreignness of it and am surprised to find myself craving more.

"I think so," I finally admit, still a little uncomfortable but fighting it. "In a weird way?"

"Just don't hold back with me, okay? Otherwise, we've got this wall between us and it's hard to communicate." He gestures toward my photography case. "Can I?"

"My portfolio?"

"Yeah. Unless it's private or something."

Something inside me shrivels up, and all the good will we've been kindling nearly dies.

"A joke," he amends. "I wasn't—"

"Oh, sure. It's been all of a week since I've heard that one," I say. "How does it go again? The one about me selling nudes online because my mother modeled in college, so I'm easy prey?"

"Whoa," he says, brow lowering. "Hold on a minute—"

"If you think just because I told you personal stuff about me in a moment of weakness at the police station, you can just fly into my life like some kind of superhero and rescue me, and I'll be so grateful that I'll do *anything* to thank you, well—you can think again, buddy."

He holds up both hands. "Hey, I made a dumb joke. I wasn't thinking about what Adrian said that night at the party. My bad. But thanks for assuming I'm a dirtbag who 'rescued' you just for a chance to get in your pants." His shoulders are rigid, eyes tight with insult. "I know you've been going through a tough time, but maybe have a little faith in me?"

"W-well," I stammer, caught off guard and scrambling for a defense. "I *have* heard stuff about you."

He snorts. "I'll bet you have."

"Never mind."

"Oh no. Go on. What have you heard, pray tell?"

I can feel my cheeks warming to the same color as the basket of geraniums that hangs off the side of the ship near our table. "You and that Bunny Perera girl from Golden Academy. That you . . ." I can't make myself finish: *That you knocked her up.* "And maybe some other girls?"

His laugh is dry and humorless as he leans back in his chair and shakes his head slowly. "Of *course.* Why am I even surprised? You realize you just did exactly the same thing, right? Only I was joking, and you're not. You're repeating gossip that you actually believe."

"I didn't say I believed it!"

"Don't you, though?"

"Is it true?" I ask.

"Why do you care?"

"I don't."

He shrugs one shoulder. "Well, then . . . ?"

"Well?" I repeat.

"Well, what?" he asks, a flare of anger behind his eyes. Or maybe a challenge.

"Truce," I suggest. "I'll ignore gossip about you if you ignore it about me. And if you promise not to tell other people what I told you about me."

"Your Los Angeles plans?"

"And the other thing I told you in the police station."

"What other thing?"

Oh no. I'm not saying *I'M A VIRGIN* out loud on a coffee-house ship. Absolutely not.

A couple of teen boys murmur as they walk past our table, and I hear Lucky's name. Then the taller one looks at me and elbows his buddy, who makes a puckered-up kissy face at me.

Oh no.

"Do that *one more time*," Lucky challenges, standing up from the table and pointing in their direction, his face lined with anger.

The two boys look back at him, surprised, but keep walking.

Lucky sits down, and after a few moments, the anger drains from his features.

"You didn't have to do that," I tell him in a quiet voice. "But thank you."

"Don't mention it." He stares across the harbor, watching a sailboat. "And as to what we were discussing before we were interrupted by the scum of the earth . . . I agree to your truce. And don't worry about the other thing. It's already forgotten. It also didn't have anything to do with my decision at the police station that night."

Okay. I don't know what to say to that.

"Now," he says, holding out a hand, "can I please see your work? It's the least you can do, since I'm painting parking spaces at Summers & Co. You pretty much owe me forever, and I *will* milk that favor."

"Thought you weren't a dirtbag."

And there's the smile again. Barely, but there. It flicks on a switch inside my chest and makes me feel like I'm glowing from the inside out.

"But I *am* a jackass, remember?" he says.

I pass him my portfolio. "How can I forget, when you keep reminding me?"

He chuckles briefly and unzips the leather binder to browse the pages of photographs. It's obviously only a selection of my work, and I've included a smattering of things outside my wheelhouse to show range—a black-and-white portrait of my mom, a cityscape at night, a bookstore cat, and an action shot of traffic. But the bulk of the prints are photos of my signs. Two years' worth. And watching Lucky pore over them, his paint-flecked fingers gingerly holding the page corners, the black cat tattoo staring back at me from his hand . . . It makes me feel self-conscious and expectant. Exposed. As if he's stripping off layers of my clothes with each turn of the page.

I want him to say something. I want him to give it back to me. I want him to like what I've done. I don't know what I want.

"Wow. These are . . ." He nods silently. "Really, *really* good."

Oh. I exhale, relieved and spinning like a top. "Yeah?"

"These are all shot on film? Like, real film? Is that why they look this way?"

I'm *so* happy he asked. I wasn't doing any of this work when we knew each other. I was barely interested in photography back then. All of this is new stuff to share with him, and suddenly it feels like I've only been away on a long trip, and we're just catching up.

"No. Some of them are digital." I wipe nervous palm sweat on my jeans and flip pages to show him which ones. "Digital is easier, but the best cameras cost thousands. Film has more character, and I like the control of developing it. I like knowing I did it from beginning to end. No auto settings. No fake filters. My eye, my vision, my hands . . . . I guess that sounds arrogant or artsy, or whatever, I don't know."

I'm a little self-conscious now.

But he just nods. "Respect. Absolutely understand that. Doing something with your own hands is satisfying. It's a skill. And at the rate this world's going, one day we're going to wake up to find our electrical grid down and all our technology's been hacked. What are we going to do when we can't just ask a computer what the answer is? You know who'll survive? The people who can think, and the people with skills. I'm not a great thinker, but I intend on surviving."

That's weird. When we were kids, he was super smart. "Bleak and dark. Very on-brand for you," I say with a smile. "But I doubt photography will be a much-needed skill in the coming apocalypse. No one who's struggling will give a damn about what I can do."

"We need art to remind us that the struggle is worth something. That will never change."

"Sure you're not a thinker?"

"No one in this town would accuse me of being a brain," he says, a little humor behind his eyes as he flips back through my portfolio. "I'm surprised how funny some of your photos are. And sad." He points to a picture I took of a yard sale sign in

Pennsylvania: THREE DAYS BEFORE WE'RE HOMELESS. PLEASE BUY SOMETHING. "That's heartbreaking."

"Yeah," I say, scratching my arm. "Mom bought a bunch of stuff from that woman just because—how could you not? No one plans to be evicted. That's not part of the dream."

"No," he says soberly. "A lot of stuff in life isn't. They don't tell you that part, do they?"

I shake my head.

"You should shoot people next to the signs," he says. "That would be interesting."

"I hate shooting people. People are complicated. The lighting . . . the baggage." I laugh a little, but I'm sort of serious, too. "Maybe my father could give me more experience with portrait photography."

He hands me my portfolio. "Definitely see why you'd want to apprentice with him, for lots of reasons. He's become a big deal over the last few years, yeah? But . . ."

"But what?"

"I've read stuff about him online. My opinion? He sounds a little bit like an asshole."

"Oh, he is," I say, smiling.

"But he's the king, yeah? Guess that's his prerogative."

"Right," I say, and then more firmly, "Right."

"He's probably a decent guy underneath all the gruff . . . right? All that talk about him evading child support and stuff is just gossip."

"Of course." Why is he questioning this? It's making me

117

uncomfortable. And he knows all this stuff, anyway. Mom didn't ask for child support. She didn't want him to have anything to do with me for years. I think the first time I met him was when I was three? But that doesn't mean he's a bad person.

I guess he realizes he's being weird, because he backs off a little and says, "Hey, you gotta trust your gut. Don't listen to me. I don't know anything."

"He's my father," I say.

"He's your father," he repeats with a shrug. "Bet you going out to LA will send your mom through the roof, though, right? Two birds, one stone."

"That's not the point," I argue. "I'm not trying to stick it to my mom. This is just about me improving my craft. Photography is everything to me, and—" And of course it's more than that, but I feel funny spilling my guts to Lucky about my yearning for a real family, so I change my mind and simply repeat, "It's everything."

He raises both hands in surrender. "Listen. If I had that opportunity and your talent, I would be dreaming up the same plan as you. A good teacher is important. There's stuff you just can't learn from watching videos online. I can tell you that from personal experience."

"That's all I want."

"Then follow your dreams. Go big or go home. I mean it. All jokes aside. Even the bad ones."

I don't know what to say to that. He's actually being nice to me? I don't think I trust it.

There's too much of a mess between us for niceness.

I can't think about it too much, how good it makes me feel, so I don't. I just zip up my portfolio and jump to safer subjects. "I want to help pay for the window."

"Already told you—"

"You told me not to go to the police and turn myself in, but right now I'm talking about giving you money to help pay off the window faster. Two can pay it off faster than one, right? And I've got a subscription service online for my photos, and my patrons are a little down right now, but I'll be getting some money from that in a few days. And I'm making money at the bookstore. I mean, it's not *boat-mechanic* money, apparently," I say, teasing.

He laughs and does an imitation of his father, using dramatic air quotes. "'It's good fucking money, Lucky. No matter what happens, people will always need their boats repaired, and none of these pretty boys want to get their hands dirty.'"

"'There's always money in the banana stand,'" I say using air quotes back at him.

We both laugh.

Then Lucky says, "Really. You don't have to."

"But *I do*," I say, looking him straight in the eye so that he understands. He may have pride, but so do I. And I can't let him do this for me. "I'm losing sleep. I'm not a good liar, as you keep pointing out, and I'm terrible at keeping secrets. It's literally making me sick."

He doesn't say anything.

"We used to be friends," I add. "I'm assuming that's why you took the fall for me. So if you care anything at all for me, then let me help pay it off. For old time's sake."

He stares at me, watchful eyes slowly blinking as his fingers lightly trace the bottom of his empty coffee cup. My pulse speeds wildly, and for a moment, and I'm not sure if I can hold his intense gaze. A wary part of me wants to look away, as if he's some sort of dark sorcerer, casting a wicked spell on me with the power of his mind.

My phone buzzes against my hip, breaking the spell. I dig it out of my pocket. It's Evie.

"Hey," I say, grateful for the distraction. "What's up?"

"Aunt Winona isn't answering," she says, frazzled. "I need you to come get me."

"What's happened?"

"I'm at the hospital. I've been in a wreck."

MEMORIAL COUNTY HEALTH CENTER: An ultra-boring white-and-blue sign is situated near the entrance of the main rural hospital in Beauty County, Rhode Island. The cookie-cutter building looks like every other new American hospital. *(Personal photo/Josephine Saint-Martin)*

Panic spreads through my chest. Without thinking, I stand up before pulling out my chair and painfully bump my thighs on the underside of the coffeehouse café table. "Evie?" I say, massaging my leg. "Are you hurt?"

"I'm okay," she insists. "Just scraped up. Nothing broken."

She's okay! Oh, thank God. "Wait . . . You wrecked the Pink Panther?"

"No. Aunt Winona took it when we closed the shop. No idea where. She said she had to run some errand this afternoon. Can you try to call her? Maybe she'll answer you. If not, can you call a car to take you here and pick me up? I'm at Memorial, the hospital north of town? I don't want to be here anymore, cuz. Please. You know I hate hospitals, and the nurse keeps asking when my mom is coming to pick me up, and I already told them she's in Nepal, and I just . . . I want to go home." She sounds as if she's on the verge of tears.

"Stay there. I'll come get you one way or another, fast as I can," I assure her, hanging up.

"What is it?" Lucky says.

"Evie's been in a wreck," I tell him, dialing my mom's number. "I don't know how. She doesn't have a car. She said Mom took the Pink Panther on an errand—"

Is it wrong to want to strangle your own mother? I mean . . .

"—and she can't get her to answer. Evie's okay, I think?" I continue telling him. "She says she's just scraped up. But her dad died in a hospital, you know? And she gets really freaked out about them, like super phobic, so I need to go get her, or at least calm her down—what the hell? Why isn't my mom answering her phone? Now I'm going to have to call a taxi or a car or something?"

"Hey," Lucky says in a calm, firm voice. "Evie's okay?"

I nod. I'm out of breath. Gotta relax. Gotta slow down and breathe.

"All right. That's the most important thing. My bike's parked right there," he says, pointing. He pulls out a ring of keys from his pocket. "I'll take you."

I blink at him, still holding my phone. "I don't have a helmet."

"You can wear mine. Don't argue. This is a onetime emergency, and your head is more important than mine."

I don't see how that's true. "How will we get her home?"

"She's freaked out, yeah? Then she needs you there. Get there, calm her down, call a car or get in touch with your mom. But you'll get to her faster this way. Come on."

Sounds logical. And I'm too worried to question it. I grab my portfolio and follow Lucky across the deck of the creaking ship while he makes a phone call. I think it must be to his father, because while we're heading down the plank back to shore, he briefly explains what's transpiring in a hushed voice and says he'll call back after we get there.

Once we cross the Harborwalk, I spot the red Superhawk a few yards away, parked on the street. He retrieves his helmet from a locked compartment behind the seat that has the same decal—LUCKY 13—and hands it to me, offering to stow my portfolio in its place. The helmet is ill-fitting, and I have trouble with the strap under my chin—my hands are shaking a little—until he helps me adjust it.

"All right?" he asks.

When I nod, he throws a leg over his bike and gestures for me to straddle behind him. The seat barely accommodates two, so I'm forced to fit my legs around his. I try to lightly hold on to his arms, but he moves my hands to his waist. "Keep your feet on the pegs—yep, that's right. Steer clear of the wheel and exhaust. It gets hot. I'll hold up a hand to signal when I'm stopping. Don't fight curves. We won't fall over. Lean on me if it makes it easier. Got it?"

"Have you carried, uh, passengers before?"

"Many," he says, slipping on a pair of narrow sunglasses that fit like goggles around his eyes. "If you get freaked out, tell me. Try to relax."

I've never ridden on the back of a motorcycle. I don't even know how to ride a regular old *bicycle*, for the love of Pete! But it's too late now. He twists the handle, and we lurch onto the street. I hold on like grim death, hugging him as we speed away from the Quarterdeck Coffeehouse.

The hospital isn't all that far away. Lucky takes side roads out of the harbor area, avoiding the tourist traffic and picking his way over to the main highway out of town. It's so unsettling and strange on a bike, surrounded by bigger cars and trucks. It's as if they all have armor and we're naked as fools, dangerously exposed to the air and the sun and the thunderous sounds of the road.

We glide over hilly asphalt, and my stomach dips as if I'm on a carnival ride. I loosen my death grip on his torso and give in to the impulse to lean against his back. He's solid and steady, and the sun warms the leather of his jacket, which is somehow a comforting scent.

We cross a multilane bridge over a river outside of town, and the motorcycle's tires bump rhythmically over the bridge's seams as the landscape changes to trees and flat countryside. After a couple of miles, Lucky slows as we round a sharp curve and approach black skid marks that lead off the road.

Was this where the wreck happened? A metal road sign is flattened, but there's no sign of a car. I wonder if it was hauled away or if this is some other accident. I forgot to ask who she was riding with when she wrecked. Maybe that Vanessa girl from Barcelona.

Everything feels surreal. The skid marks. This bike. The solid feel of Lucky's body under my arms . . . similar to the boy I used to know when we were younger, but very different now. Familiar, but strange. I hold on a little more tightly.

The landscape changes again as we approach an unincorporated community outside of Beauty, and after we pass a gas station and a couple of strip malls, a rural hospital comes into view. Lucky pulls into the ER parking entrance, slides the bike into an empty spot near the door, and shuts of the motor while I release my death grip on his waist. I can't get off fast enough.

"Whoa, now," he says as I wobble off the bike. My legs feel numb, and he's gripping my shoulders to help me stay vertical. "Get your sea legs under you before you try to walk."

"I'm okay," I tell him, tearing off the helmet.

"Sure?" he says, retrieving my portfolio from his bike's storage compartment, which I immediately grip to my chest as if it's a security blanket.

"My pants are hot, and all my bones are still shaking. . . ."

He nods. "You get used to it."

"I'm never getting on that thing again."

"Never say never, Saint-Martin."

"Oh, I'm saying it. Never."

He stows his helmet without comment and says, "Come on. Let's find Evie."

The hospital is shiny and quiet. From the looks of things, it must have been built recently. The ER waiting room is practically empty, just a scattered few people, and most of them seem to be in the flu/cold group of emergencies, rather than the I-sawed-off-a-finger group. A nice man at the check-in desk looks up Evie's name in his computer and, after making a phone call and logging our IDs, directs us to the second floor of a different wing.

Honestly, I'm utterly thankful to have Lucky with me. It strikes me that he was in the hospital five years ago when I left Beauty, getting skin grafts and healing from all his burns. For a moment, I worry that Evie's not the only person who may have a hospital phobia, but when I try to catch his gaze, he seems to be okay.

Maybe he's not thinking about it. Maybe it's just my guilt.

After walking in circles, we finally find the right area; however, a nurse has to question two other staff members to track down where they've put Evie.

"I thought she wasn't hurt?" I tell the nurse.

"She's fine. Her friend is another story. Who are you? I thought she said she was calling her guardian to pick her up."

Of course my mom is MIA. . . . *Strangle, strangle, strangle.* "I'm her cousin."

"All right. Let me get you to her." The nurse leads us to a private hospital room and turns to Lucky. "You all know one another, right? Family and close friends only."

Lucky shoots me a questioning look, asking me with his eyes if I want him to bail.

I really don't want him to leave. "We're friends," I say, hoping he'll stay.

"Yes," Lucky says. "We all know one another."

Good. I'm relieved.

The nurse nods and tells me, "I'll get the paperwork to release your cousin. In the meantime, keep it quiet in here, because her friend needs rest. Doped up pretty good, so you may hear some wild things. Fair warning."

What friend? Vanessa? Her other friend from the party?

I look at Lucky. He looks at me. And as we step inside, I suddenly understand.

On the far side of the room, Evie sits under a bank of windows. Her eyes are closed as if she's catnapping in a beam of sunlight, Cleopatra eyeliner smeared, and she's curled up in a ball in a visitor's chair—the kind that a spouse would sleep in while keeping vigil over their sick loved one. One of her forearms has been wrapped in a narrow, light gauze, and it looks as if a small cut on her face has been taped up.

Next to her is the person we were warned about.

Hooked up to a monitor and bolstered by pillows, Adrian Summers reclines with his eyes closed on a hospital bed surrounded by IV stands. Lacerations cover one side of his face. One arm is heavily bandaged. His left ankle is wrapped in stretchy green bandages; it's propped up by a couple of pillows.

"*What the actual fuuu—*" Lucky whispers.

Evie's eyes blink open. "Josie," she says, leaping up.

I race to her, and we embrace. She clings to me as if the world is falling apart. From the looks of things in here, maybe it is. "Are you sure you're okay?" I whisper. "Is anything broken?"

"I'm okay, I'm okay," she mumbles into my neck near my ear. "Just cuts and scrapes. Thank God you came. I couldn't call Vanessa. She's going to kill me when she finds out. . . ."

I pull back to look at her and ask, "What happened?"

"Nature. That's what," Adrian says in a scratchy voice.

I release my cousin to look at him. His eyes are bloodshot and swollen, and it's pretty clear that he's been medicated to the moon and back. "Deer ran out in the road. Swerved. But the bastard ran into my side. Luckily Evelyn got out okay."

"I tried to help him out, but . . . ," Evie says, still gripping my hand tightly.

"Stop," he tells her. "It was a big ass deer. I couldn't have lifted it myself, and the paramedics got there fast, so it's all good. Well. Except for the broken ankle, five stitches on my arm, and all this glass in my face. But I'm in Morphine City right now, so it's hard to care about that too much."

"He will," Evie says. "When it really hits him that he can't row at Harvard."

"Just for summer practice."

"Maybe not for fall, either. You heard the doctor," she argues. "Six weeks on crutches."

"There's more to Harvard than rowing. I just need to convince my dad of that. . . ." He pauses, frowning, and I follow his gaze behind me. "What the hell are you doing here?"

Lucky stares at Adrian, arms crossed. "Visiting a dumbass."

"He drove me here," I say.

"Well, he can drive himself back home," Adrian says. "He's a felonious deadbeat who threw a rock at my family's business. I don't want him here."

Lucky snorts. "That makes two of us, bucko. Though it's a little entertaining to see you on your back."

"Screw you."

"Like you screwed yourself?" Lucky says. "Guess you'll have to wait a little longer for that Olympic medal."

"Bet I get one before you finish vocational school, grease monkey."

"Oh-ho-ho, that cuts!" Lucky clutches his chest dramatically. "It's so tragic that I actually have to work for money instead of paddling a canoe for gold medals or waving at the Victory Day flotilla crowds from the deck of the largest yacht in the harbor while good ol' Daddy Warbucks buys me Italian sports cars that I wreck."

"Hey, the first car I totaled was German."

"You totaled another car?" I say, stunned.

Lucky laughs darkly. "This is Wreck-It Ralph's third accident. The second one at that exact same spot."

"None were my fault," Adrian assures me. "A truck veered into my lane last time, and the first one was when I was fifteen—I wasn't even on a public road."

"He smashed his father's Porsche," Lucky says. "But it doesn't matter at Summers & Co, because a world-class surgeon and a replacement car are always on the horizon."

Adrian groans and shifts his shoulder into a different position. "At least I didn't have to scour junkyards for parts to rebuild a shitty motorcycle," Adrian says as the numbers on the blood pressure section of the screen near his bed begin climbing. "I know I'm living a charmed life. I'm fucking happy about it. Zero shame. And I know that if you had the choice, you'd be sitting where I am right now too."

"Enjoy sitting," Lucky says. "Because I don't think you'll be doing much walking anytime soon."

"That's fine. I don't need to throw rocks at windows for kicks. Is that how you show your lady friends a good time? Property destruction? By the way, I've been meaning to ask, Karras . . . What is it with your family and these Saint-Martins, huh? Just can't stay away?"

What?

"I think the morphine has addled your brain," Lucky mumbles.

"Stop it," Evie says, dropping my hand. "Both of you!"

She's upset. She was just in a wreck. She's in a hospital, and she hates hospitals. I get all that. But right now, I'm really confused. "Can you just explain," I say to her in a quiet voice, shielding my face with one hand in a poor attempt at privacy, "why in God's name you were riding in the car of an ex-boyfriend who was drunkenly embarrassing us at a party a couple of weeks ago?"

"Josie," Evie pleads.

"An ex who said horrible things about our entire family,

including basically calling me and my mother whores in front of whole bunch of people."

"Not my proudest moment," Adrian calls out from the hospital bed. "But I don't remember everything I said that night."

"Well, I'm not going repeat what you said about me," I mumble, refusing to look at his face. *Or mention what you showed everyone.* "Though maybe you don't remember that, either."

"Seem to recall being called an asshole by certain parties in the room," Adrian says, directing this toward Lucky. He turns back to me to say something else, but Lucky quickly cuts him off.

"Whoa, whoa! Hey," Lucky says, holding up his hands. "That nurse will come in here if they hear us, and you need to rest. Maybe we should do this another time?"

I start to argue, but Evie interrupts and looks at me as she says, "I asked Adrian to talk with me today, okay? He apologized for . . . his behavior the night of the party, and I was *trying* to ask him if he could talk to his father and get him to drop the whole window thing with Lucky. There. Are you happy? Is it not enough that everything he's worked for at Harvard next semester has just been lost? You two aren't the only people going through shit, you know."

I'm too shocked to respond. I guess everyone is, because for a strained moment, there's nothing but the sound of Adrian's monitors. While I'm picking my jaw up off the floor, the nurse comes into the room with a wheelchair and Evie's release papers. Evie signs them in a huff, ignores the wheelchair, and storms out of the room.

"Thanks for stopping by. A pleasure," Adrian says, closing his eyes. "Now I'd advise you to leave before my father comes back and catches you in here. He's likely to make you pay to replace all the windows in the store to match the new one, just out of spite."

Lucky doesn't bother to say goodbye. He just leaves the room, heading in the same direction that Evie went, and stops when he sees her striding into the ladies' restroom. "Welp, that was fun," Lucky mumbles. "Guess we took her mind off her hospital phobia."

Yeah. Not happy about our methods. Upsetting Evie is the last thing I wanted. And now that I'm out of Adrian's hospital room, I'm a little embarrassed we had an argument with a guy who just wrecked his car and broke his ankle, asshole or not.

I didn't handle any of that well. At all.

"Sorry," Lucky says. "But after what he did to you . . . If I'd known he was in there, I wouldn't have gone in. Hope Evie's okay."

Me too. Exhaling a couple of times to rally my courage, I start to tell Lucky that I'll go check on her, but movement through a pair of doors near the restroom snags my attention.

Cat-eye glasses, bright retro-red lipstick. Mom.

She strides toward us, handbag tucked under her arm and face lined with worry. She's walking alongside some guy I don't recognize.

Lucky spies her too, and I can practically feel all the energy around him withdrawing like a turtle on the side of a highway sensing an out-of-control semitruck headed its way. "I'm gonna take off. Your mom doesn't seem to like me much."

"*Yeah,*" I say on a long exhale, "I'm going to be in *so* much trouble for being here with you."

"Not sticking around for that. I've already filled my drama quotient for the day."

"Wait!" I whisper loudly to his back as he turns to leave. "What about our payment arrangement? This doesn't change anything."

He turns his head toward me briefly, eyes cast downward. "I need to think about it."

Before I can respond, he shoves his hands in his jacket pockets and takes off down the hall. When he passes my mom and the young ginger-haired guy she's with, he says something briefly, a stiff nod of his head, and then he's gone, disappearing around a corner.

Dammit. None of this is going right.

Now I have to deal with my Mom, strutting in here on the arm of some young-and-pretty dude in topsiders and a pastel polo shirt, in front of God and everyone. . . . It doesn't take a rocket scientist to know he's the reason she wasn't answering her phone this afternoon.

So, yeah. Think I've filled my drama quotient too. Unfortunately, I don't have the luxury of walking away from my supremely messed-up family.

Not yet, anyway.

NO SENIOR DISCOUNTS—YOU SHOULD HAVE THE MONEY BY NOW: Handwritten sign in the window of the kitschy and beloved Revolutionary Doughnuts in the South Harbor district. The always-packed doughnut shop is popular with both locals and tourists. *(Personal photo/Josephine Saint-Martin)*

9

My mom's ginger-haired boy toy turned out to be a real estate agent named Hayden Harwood. After Lucky left the hospital, Mom was too worried about extracting Evie from the public restrooms to question pesky details, like why I was dressed up and carrying my portfolio. Or why the person I was specifically forbidden to hang around was very much hanging around the hospital when she arrived. You know . . . stuff like that.

When we got ourselves sorted, Hayden carted us girls all back into town in his insanely big, insanely expensive SUV and dropped us off at Mom's car . . . which was stuck in a hotel parking garage, because Mom couldn't find her parking ticket?

Okay . . .

Their story was patchy, at best. Hayden's a *whole* lot younger than Mom, cockier than he should be, and not at all uncomfortable with the elephant in the room—the fact that he was Mom's so-called "afternoon errand." Honestly, I don't even care. Evie's not speaking to me, and I'm too stressed about that. So when we finally get the Pink Panther out of the garage and end up going our separate ways at home—Evie to rest in her room and me to develop film in the bookshop's stockroom—I'm happy not to discuss the matter with Mom. I'm sure she's relieved too, because every time she tries to talk to me, I politely find a way to excuse myself and thereby avoid any kind of *Hey, kid. Sorry I wasn't there when you girls needed me* speech.

What's the point of apologizing if you're just going to keep doing it? Besides, if she apologizes to me, then she'll be able to ask me about *my* elephant in the room: Lucky Karras.

And I can lie about why he was at the hospital. I guess I'll have to. But if she doesn't ask me, then I won't have to say anything. Which would be easiest for both us. I mean, after all, that's what she's taught me, right? If you pretend it never happened, it's not really a lie.

That's what she tells herself.

So that's what I tell myself, too.

The next day, the mood at *la Maison de Saint-Martin* is still strained but getting better. Evie is talking to me, but she's prickly and a little reserved. Not her usual *I'd Like to Haunt a Gothic Castle* reserved; she's definitely still holding a grudge. For the first time, I realize that maybe it's not just me that she's mad at. I think Evie and her friend Vanessa are fighting about the wreck. Maybe Vanessa hates Adrian too; if so, I like her a little more.

Mom puts on an extra-bright pink lipstick and a fake cheery

face, trying to ignore the weird vibes. I can't do that. I know what Evie tried to do for Lucky in going to talk to Adrian. What she tried to do *for me*. Now she's not only physically bruised from a car accident, Adrian has messed up his rowing season at Harvard and totaled an expensive car. I mean, just look at the cost of this lie. I'm leaving a path of total destruction around my family and this community.

I'm a walking tornado.

I can't repair that damage right now. But I *can* try to make up with Evie.

Revolutionary Doughnuts sits across the street from us, about a block down. I definitely don't need to pass by Nick's Boatyard to get there, but when I check the usual spots for signs of Lucky's red Superhawk motorcycle and don't see it parked—he must be working at the department store—I find my feet heading in that direction anyway and slowly stroll down the sidewalk in front of the boatyard's front offices.

I'm not even sure why. From the sidewalk, I see his mom working at the front desk, smiling and talking with another dark-haired girl. A cousin, maybe? A toddler is running around the desk, chasing a tiny black dog, who is chasing the black cat—the one that sleeps in the window and that's tattooed on Lucky's hand—and they're all laughing as both the cat and dog make a break for a door that leads into the bays out back facing the harbor. Their laughter is so boisterous, I can hear it through the window.

Sometimes when I was little, I used to fantasize about what things would have been like if Mom and Henry had stayed together, and we'd been a family—pipe dreams that every kid has. Funny, but I never once imagined us laughing like that. Now I'm almost sorry I witnessed that scene with the dog and cat and cousins, because it's one more thing I'll never have.

It's easier when you don't know.

A short walk away from the laughter of the boatyard, the doughnut shop comes into view. It's known for having a lot of special flavors—toffee butter crunch, apple cider angels, and some puffy Greek doughnuts they call honey dippers, which are Evie's favorite thing in the world . . . and the reason I'm here.

The shop is also *super* popular with locals, so it's always busy, especially now, when everyone's scrambling to buy up what remains. Once they sell out, it's gone. They don't keep making them all day like a chain. Hopefully I'm not too late. I head around a wooden clapboard sign painted with cartoon Revolutionary War figures fighting a battle with doughnuts instead of guns and cannons, and step inside.

I inhale the intoxicating scents of yeasty dough and sweet lemon zest as I queue up in a long line that snakes around the tiny shop. Quite a few folks stand ahead of me, so I scroll through articles about photography gear on my phone, and as I shuffle along, a girl in sandals and white shorts backs into me.

"Oops, sorry," she says, turning around while flipping dark hair over a shoulder.

Holy crap. I know her—or who she is, anyway. Bunny Perera. The Golden Academy girl that Lucky is rumored to have knocked up a few months ago. If she ever was pregnant, she's not anymore. The sliver of brown skin that peeks beneath her summery shirt is far flatter and fitter than mine.

I smile, a little nervous. Bunny's not just the Girl Who Got Pregnant. Her father is ambassador to Sri Lanka, and her mother's family owns a chain of hotels in South Asia. They helped finance a big renovation of the Beauty Yacht Club last year.

"Um, hi . . . Bunny?" I say.

"Evie's cousin, right?" she says, cradling her phone.

I nod, unsure of what to say. "Josie. Saint-Martin. My mom is, uh, managing Siren's Book Nook while my grandma's in Nepal with, uh, Evie's mom." Ugh. So awkward.

"Yeah, I heard about that. And about your trip to the police station with Lucky after Adrian's party," she says, gold bracelets clinking as she languidly swipes on her phone, watching the screen between glances at me. "Definitely started the summer off with a bang."

I manage a weak smile. "Uh, yeah. You could say that."

"Hey, I've been where you are right now," she says, smiling back sympathetically.

"Umm . . . ?"

"The town gossiping about you."

"Oh," I say. "It's fine. I think Lucky got the brunt of it."

"He's got a habit of doing that. Sometimes I think he's got

a savior complex or something. By the way, I hope it works out between you two. He deserves some happiness."

Wait, what? I glance around, shuffling forward when the line moves, and say in a low voice, "Um, think you have the wrong idea. Lucky and I aren't a thing. In case you still had, uh, feelings or an attachment, or, I mean, I don't know what your situation is. . . ."

Her brow furrows, then she says, "No, no. *You've* got the wrong idea. I guess he didn't tell you, huh? He's just a friend. We were never together."

"You and Lucky . . . ?"

"It wasn't his," she says simply, shaking her head. "Lucky's dad does upkeep on my family's yacht, and that's how I know him. That's the thing about this town and rumors. They may be based on things people have witnessed, but assumptions get made, and sometimes those assumptions are dead wrong. Like, for instance, you say that you and Lucky aren't a thing, but everyone saw you getting arrested together—"

"That was coincidence," I insist. "He just happened to be at that party, and when I left . . . It's a long story."

"See? Same. Lucky's been nothing but kind to me, which is more than I can say for other people."

She steps forward when the line moves, then says, "Lucky is flat-out one of the sweetest guys I know. People have said shit about him for years, and I'm not saying he's an angel, but for what it's worth, he's a genuinely decent guy and a good friend."

I'm a little bowled over by her earnest endorsement . . . and by everything she's just told me. Not sure if relief is the right word, but I mull it over as Bunny steps up to the counter, orders, and leaves with a bag of green apple fritters, mouthing words of encouragement that I initially mistake as "Good Lucky."

And was he? *Good*, I mean? She made him sound as if he's a paragon of manners—a cherubic choirboy, humble and full of grace. *Savior complex.* Maybe that's the only reason he took the fall for me . . . because he's addicted to helping old ladies cross the street, and I'm just another person for him to save.

Nope. Don't buy it. He's hiding something, and he's lying to his family about saving my ass. He let them think he broke the window, just like I let my mom think he did it.

I did it to avoid trouble.

Maybe he did it to *attract* trouble. . . .

Because, now that I'm thinking about it, Bunny's whole rainbows-and-glitter endorsement of Lucky's overall wholesome goodness *does* make me question all the other rumors about him. Like, *all* of them. If he isn't the reprobate that I once assumed him to be, and if our trip to the police station wasn't just another notch in his notoriety . . .

Then maybe he isn't really the bad boy.

What if he's only *trying* to be bad?

What if he's ruining his reputation on purpose?

SUNSET CHARTERS! FISHING—SIGHTSEEING—HISTORIC HARBOR TOURS—ROMANTIC CRUISES—CASH UPFRONT— NO REFUNDS: Metal sign by Goodly Pier advertising a pay-by-the-hour boat charter service that ferries tourists around the harbor. *(Personal photo/ Josephine Saint-Martin)*

10

My trip to the doughnut shop was both a revelation and a restorative. A restorative, because Evie accepted my peace offering of the honey dippers, and we're officially now speaking again. A revelation, because now I can't stop obsessing over my new Lucky theory.

And I have plenty of time to ponder over it at work the next couple of days at the Nook, where we are steadily busy but not so slammed that I can't think. Evie and I do pretty much everything in the shop except the detail-y management stuff. We ring up customers. Cash out drawers. Pull returns. Yell at stupid punk kids to stop trying to steal graphic novels. Find books for customers who only have a vague idea what color the cover is, but they know for sure they saw it mentioned on a morning news show last week. Threaten to call the cops when elderly "Tugs" McHenry comes into the store, before he can try to masturbate on books in our restroom.

Again.

"I need to know everything you know about Lucky 2.0," I

tell Evie as I stand next to the Nook's printing press while she's bent over a rolling metal book cart near the romance bays in the Nook's fiction section. "I'm interested in everything that happened to Lucky after we left town."

"Aren't we the curious cat. . . ." Cradling two books against a T-shirt emblazoned with a design of two mummies kissing, she still wears the gauze wrap around her arm from her car accident, matching fashion to injury.

"Basically, fill me in on ages thirteen to seventeen, but mostly the last year or so," I continue, trying not to look out the window toward Nick's Boatyard. "Who his friends are. What he reads when he comes in here. Why he's been in detention so much. Who you know for a fact he's dated. No rumors. Only first-hand knowledge."

A slow smile spreads over her face. "My, *this* is interesting. Perhaps the Saint-Martin curse is racing through your veins? Are you having erotic dreams that end in bloodshed?"

I hold up one finger. "No. Stop this. Don't even joke, Evie."

"We did warn you, cuz. Did you not just witness what happened to me? Accident. Hospital. Ex-boyfriend, who is now recuperating at home for the rest of the summer when he should be in Cambridge. *That* was the curse in action."

Talk about the curse almost shakes me for a moment, but then I realize she's teasing me. I think. I hope. . . .

"My interest in Lucky 2.0 isn't for romantic reasons," I insist. "It's research."

"For seduction purposes."

"Exactly. I mean, no!" I look around the books displayed on the printing press to make sure Mom is still at the register and not listening to us. "Just for research purposes."

"I've got some books you can read . . . for research purposes. Hold on one second. Erotica section, let's see . . . Anaïs Nin is always a classic. Hmm . . . Did I already get you to read *Fanny Hill*?"

"It was sort of ridiculous," I admit. "Too many plump, fleshy thighs and large machines."

"Ha!"

"Stop," I plead, laughing when she pokes my side to tickle me. "And no erotica. This is serious research."

"Fi-i-i-ne," she says, picking up a book to shelve. "But I don't really know anything. I missed Lucky's early teen years. We were in Boston for my dad's job."

That's right. I forget she missed some of the same Beauty years that I missed when her parents relocated to the neighboring state.

"Plus, you guys are two grades behind me," she says, reaching above her head to straighten a section of falling-over books. "I only really knew him as the kid across the street that I'd sometimes see when I came to visit Grandma. I was a junior when he was a freshman. He hung with a different crowd."

"What crowd?"

"Let's see . . . he hung out with a guy from Argentina named Tomas. But he moved to Toronto last year. Oh, and he dated Kasia

Painter right after Tomas left. For a few weeks, maybe? I used to see them eating lunch together my senior year. I think there were a few other girls—just like casual dates, here and there."

"So you don't know for a fact that he's knocked anyone up?" I ask, squatting down next to the metal book cart to look for any romance books that need to be shelved.

"The Bunny thing?"

"Besides that. The Bunny thing has been disproven."

"Interesting," she says, thoughtful. "No. I don't know for a fact about anyone else."

I pull out two paperbacks from the cart and hand them to Evie. "What else do you know about Lucky? Like maybe why he's had so much detention?"

She thinks for a moment. "I know for sure that he's been in trouble for spouting off in the classroom. Saying smart-ass things. Correcting teachers in class, that kind of thing."

My mind wanders back to when he borrowed my notes in class and corrected everything I'd written down wrong. "He's always been kind of a smart-ass." And I always kind of liked it.

"No, he's just plain smart. Like, I remember Adrian saying he would've killed to have his test scores. And okay, this isn't exactly firsthand, but . . . I heard that Lucky scored really, really high on his SAT this spring. Maybe perfect? Or so close to perfect that it doesn't matter. One of the rare narrow percent of test takers that hits the top."

No one in this town would accuse me of being a brain.

I *knew* it. He was always smart when we were kids. That little liar!

I feel like I'm onto something. I'm just not sure what. When Evie's not looking, I peer through the Nook's display window, and as traffic speeds past, I catch a glimpse of what *might* be Lucky's red Superhawk parked across the street. "Okay, what else? When did he get his motorcycle?"

"God, I don't know. He fixed it up for months. A year ago, maybe? Before that, he rode an actual bicycle around town. Weird to think about that now. He sort of transitioned from the nerdy loner in the bookstore to Phantom."

"Oh, *really*? You don't say . . . ?"

She frowns. "What's this all about, anyway?"

"I'm just thinking about something Mom told me once," I say, staring out the window at Nick's Boatyard.

"Which is?"

"Even little trees cast big shadows when the sun is setting."

I think about everything Evie told me. I think about it a lot, in fact. And I wait for Lucky to get back to me about letting me help him pay for the window.

He finally does.

A small envelope mysteriously appears, mixed in along with the shop's business mail—no stamp, no postmark, no return address. It's simply addressed to me in tight, neat script, and when I unearth it, I stare at it as if it's some strange archaeological discovery before ripping it open to find a short note scribbled on what appears to be a blank invoice sheet from Nick's Boatyard. It says oh-so-politely:

> *Dear Josephine,*
> *Though I do appreciate your offer, I can't accept*
> *it. This is something I need to do alone.*
> *Thanks anyway.*
> *Your old friend,*
> *Lucky*

I reread it several times. So formal . . . so familiar. Then it hits me. It's basically the same email I sent him two months after I left town when I was twelve, after Mom had heard through Aunt Franny that Lucky was out of the hospital, healing up from surgery, and back in school. I still have the email in the Sent file of a free, virtually dead email account that I barely use or check:

> *Dear Lucky,*
> *Though I've tried in vain to contact you multiple*
> *times about my current family situation, you have*
> *not responded. We're now in Boston, staying at*
> *a Motel 6. Guess this is something I have to do*
> *alone now. Thanks for nothing.*
> *Your former friend,*
> *Josephine*

I'm not sure whether I want to laugh at how obnoxious I was back then, or cringe at how callous it was. Okay—cringe. I'm definitely cringing. I wrote that email before Mom found a decent job and after most of our money had run out. We were days away from getting booted from the motel . . . and from sleeping in our car for a short stint. It was a really scary time for me.

It's just that now, with some distance, I realize that even though my extended family was broken, and Mom and I bounced from motels to family shelters to cheap apartments . . . we still had each other.

Lucky and I, however, were torn apart.

Relationship cut short. Communication ended, over and out.

As I reread Lucky's short note to me now, I sense a little of his dark humor, but I'm not fully certain about the meaning behind his words. Everything aside, I'm not letting him have the final say in this. My broken window. My mistake. He doesn't get to take credit for it, pay for it, and play martyr.

I see you, Lucky 2.0. . . . Mr. Not-So-Bad Boy, casting a big shadow. With your beautiful, normal family, and all those cousins running around the boatyard offices, playing with that cute black dog and the black cat in the window, the symbol of your survival. With your dad, who is probably still the nicest guy in town. And Kat, who I always secretly wished was my mother, because she didn't do things like fight with my grandmother until the police were called.

I think about all this, about Lucky's polite letter, and begin hatching a scheme.

A strategy. A plot. A plan.

Sure, my plan has a couple of hurdles, the first being Mom

and her insistence that I stay away from Lucky. However, since she hasn't chastised me for his being at the hospital that day when she showed up with her "ride," and since that whole parking garage experience was so supremely humiliating for all of us, I believe it nullifies her right to have a say-so about who I can or can't hang around. Therefore, I decide to use my own judgment in this matter. After all, if I'm going to leave her next year, what's the point in obeying her now?

So one afternoon after my talk with Evie, I don't tell Mom where I'm going when it's time for my break. I just quietly walk out the door and head to the other side of Freedom Art Gallery next door, where I withdraw a hundred and fifty dollars from my savings account out of an ATM, and I march across the street to Nick's Boatyard.

Ignoring the fact that my pulse is racing because Lucky's red motorcycle is parked in the side alley, I head through the front door, into the boatyard's offices.

It's cool inside, quiet, and I have to push up my sunglasses and adjust my eyes to the wood-paneled walls. It smells of engine oil, fiberglass resin, and my childhood.

A filing cabinet shuts, and I swing to face the sound. Kat Karras stares at me with sharp brown eyes. Dark hair curls around the collar of her shirt as she leans on the filing cabinet, crossing her arms in front of her.

"Why, hello there," she says plainly.

"Mrs. Karras," I say formally, approaching a long, narrow

counter that separates a small waiting-room area with boating magazines and coffee from her desk. "Long time."

"Very long time." Discerning eyes look me over. "Wow. You look just like your mother did in high school."

I think of the photograph on Adrian's phone and wince.

Lucky's mom seems confused. A tense silence hangs between us.

"I came by the Nook to see you . . . ," she says.

"I'm sorry," I blurt, but I'm not sure what I'm apologizing for. Oh God. This was a terrible mistake. I forgot how intense Kat Karras can be. Sharp, dark eyes . . . sharp cheekbones. "I wanted to see you. I'm sorry I missed you. I mean . . . I'm sorry I wasn't there when you came by the shop—not that I missed you." I let out a nervous laugh, and it sounds awkward and hollow. Maybe because it's a lie. I lick dry lips and try again, this time with something closer to the truth. "Actually . . . I *have* missed you, and I'm sorry I haven't come by to see you sooner."

Her brows' rigid angles ease. "I've missed you too. And it's okay. Everyone's busy."

"It's been weird . . . being back. Everyone talks. I wasn't expecting that. I thought it would be the same. Things change, though, don't they?"

"Things change," she agrees in a soft voice.

Behind Lucky's mom, framed photographs of boats crowd the walls like a Hollywood restaurant sporting signed headshots of stars. Big boats. Small boats. Black-and-white photos from the mid-twentieth century. Lucky's grandparents. The old boat-repair businesses across town and the one down the block. They didn't used to repair super yachts.

"There a reason you're here, *koukla*?" she asks, drawing my attention back to her face. I forgot how pretty she was. And intimidating. More intimidating than Lucky, really. Maybe this was a terrible idea. . . .

Is it too late to just leave?

"Uh, yes," I say, straightening my shoulders. "So, um, I want to charter a boat so I can take photographs of the harbor?"

She looks taken aback. Confused. "We aren't a charter company. We repair and build boats."

"But you do *own* boats," I say, gesturing toward the kajillion framed photos on the wall.

"Not luxury yachts, but yes."

"Well, things have changed, but not *that* much—I'm not used to luxury, so it's okay by me," I say, forcing a soft laugh as I tug at the neckline of my shirt. "It's just, um, this is definitely different than the old place down the block, right? And I noticed on Mr. Karras's truck outside, it says, 'Ask us. No job too small.'"

She chuckles. "It does say that, sure. But—"

"This is a really small job," I assure her. "I just want to charter a ride around the harbor for one hour to take pictures. I know you guys are busy, but I was wondering if Lucky could take me? Maybe?"

"Oh?"

"Preferably the hour before twilight, because that's when I can get the ideal light. For photography." I plunk down my cash on the counter and get the rest of my practiced spiel out before I lose my nerve. "I checked the rates with the other charter companies in town, and this should be enough. I think?"

She stares at the money.

Heavily lashed eyes flick up to meet my gaze. One dark brow lifts.

I take a deep breath and keep going. "After the police station, my mom told me to stay out of your business, because she was worried about town gossip. She actually doesn't know I'm here. . . ."

The look on her face is sharp but unreadable. Whew. This woman is tough.

Somewhere in the back of my mind, I think about Evie teasing me, and Mom calling us Bonnie and Clyde. Now I'm worried Lucky's mom might think I'm here to ask him out on a date. "Um, in case it matters, I want to assure you that Lucky and I are still just old friends, if you could even call it that. Old acquaintances? He's been nothing but nice to me—a perfect gentleman, really."

She makes a surprised noise in the back of her throat. I hope I didn't make things worse. I keep going before I either run out of adrenaline or pass out.

"Anyway, I'm working on my portfolio, like, for internships or maybe college one day, or whatever—"

"Your pictures," she says, pointing a manicured nail at me, as if things are making sense to her now. "All the photographs of signs."

I nod several times. "That's right."

"And you want Lucky to take you around the harbor?"

"Yes!" I say, relived. Maybe she's finally understanding, and this request doesn't sound so strange after all. "Lots of signs around the harbor."

Her nose wrinkles. "Water level signs? Pier signs . . . nothing special."

"I like all kinds," I assure her. "And I don't want to add to your son's workload. I know Lucky is super busy, working here and at the department store," I tell her. "And I'm not trying to stir up gossip, believe me. I've had about all the gossip I can handle. But I also have to live in this town like everyone else, and I just want to take some photos of signs, that's all."

She blinks at me.

I clear my throat. Is it hot in here? I think I'm starting to feel sweat run down my back.

I push the money toward her before I can chicken out and race through the front door. "So that is why I'd like to charter a boat. Strictly a business transaction. For my portfolio."

She leans over an old microphone that stands on her desk, presses a button, and shouts, "LUCKY."

Oops. I seem to have gotten him in trouble.

Or maybe both of us.

I think I've made a huge mistake.

His mother holds up a finger, walks around the counter in impressively high heels, and storms through the back door. For a brief moment, I catch a glimpse of one of the work bays and a mechanic soldering something onto a small speedboat that's sitting up on a lift. Classic rock music. Laughter. Hammering. The blue harbor. The door shuts behind her.

Okay, I could leave now. Make an excuse later. Only, she might walk over to the Nook, and then it would be—not good. Nope. I'm stuck here. Gotta wait it out.

It only takes a minute before the door flings open again. This time, his mother returns with Lucky in tow . . . and a few pairs of curious eyes gawking in the background.

A smear of oil marks both the bridge of Lucky's nose and high on one cheek like the eye black grease paint of a professional quarterback. He looks wide-eyed and off-balance. Maybe a little bit furious. Maybe a *lot* bit furious. I forgot about his muscular arms and hands. The intimidating swagger.

Right now, he's looking a lot more like Actual Bad Boy than Wannabe Bad Boy.

Maybe I should've thought this through.

So hot in here . . . so, *so* hot.

"Saint-Martin," he says in a tight voice.

"Karras," I answer, discreetly pulling my sweat-logged shirt away from my sticky skin. Then I turn away from him and smile at his mother, who's sort of jog-walking in heels around the counter, her shoes making a mesmerizing *click-click-click* sound on the tile floor.

"Okay, we're all up to speed now," she says, "Let me look at the calendar, sweetie."

"Mom," he complains.

"You're going to help Miss Josie," she says, holding up my cash and waving it.

My scheme actually worked? It worked! YES!

"Jesus Christ," he mumbles.

"No swearing in front of customers," she says.

"She's not a customer, Mama. She's just Josie." Whee! I'm *just Josie*! That probably shouldn't make me so gleeful, but it does. "And I'm not a boat prostitute for hire."

"A job is a job," she says.

"No job is too small," I remind him.

His mom huffs out a laugh. "Maybe things haven't changed after all. Forgot that you inherited Diedre's dry sense of humor." Don't tell my mom that; to her, Grandma Diedre is a humorless sack of unbending rules and wrong about everything. "How is your grandmother, by the way? She's supposed to bring me back a souvenir from Nepal."

I shrug. "Drinking yak milk and teaching ten-year-old girls to read English. She hasn't had a hot shower since February."

"That woman will *not* make it a year out there," Ms. Karras murmurs. "No offense."

Ugh. *Tick, tick, tick* . . . Ticking time bomb.

I try not to let that scary thought ruin my good mood.

When she holds up a hand to quiet us and answers a ringing phone, Lucky speaks in a hushed, exasperate voice near the side of my head. "What the hell do you think you're doing?"

"Renting your services," I whisper back, feeling a little powerful. Feeling . . . seductive.

Not in a sexy way. Just a powerful way. I think?

"I'm not for rent."

"My money says otherwise."

"Why can't you just let things be?"

I swing around, and we're *way* too close, both of us too stubborn to move. "You shouldn't have rejected my offer to let me pay you back the normal way. Now I'm renting you out. By the way, I ran into Bunny Perera. She says you're the sweetest guy in the entire world and a complete angel. Just super-duper wholesome and respectable." I boop him on the nose where the oil streaks his skin and wipe my finger on his shirt.

His eyes narrow. Oh, he's *mad*. Seething. Maybe something else.

I should probably be careful. The curse. All that.

But I tell you what. If this *is* seduction in a non-sexy way—I repeat, in a *non-sexy* way—it's blissfully sweet. Okay, and it could be *ju-u-u-st* a little bit wrong, because he's my childhood best friend. The tiniest, teeniest bit. Even if it's not sexy.

Because it's not. Probably.

But I try not to think about that too much. . . .

I just smile up at him. "Think I was listening to the wrong gossip about you before. Don't worry. I'm on the right track now. See you at twilight, captain."

CAUTION! DEEP WATER. NO SWIMMING OR DIVING: Sign
posted in the harbor. The waterline stops at the bottom edge of the sign, making
it nearly unreadable from a distance when waves crash. *(Personal photo/Josephine
Saint-Martin)*

11

Boy-oh-boy, do I love golden hour. It's the time either right after
sunrise or before sunset when the light outside is great for photography. Everything looks nice and warm, the light is diffused,
no harsh shadows. It's kind of when the planet says, *Go on: Take
my picture. Right now. Let's remember this moment together.*

During a particularly excellent golden hour, while Evie is
attending class at community college and Mom is nowhere to be
found, I head out to meet Lucky behind his parents' boatyard. All
of the Karrases' workers are gone for the day, so it's deserted and
quiet back here. And when I spot Lucky on the main dock, his
back is to me, shoulders all lined in gold as he stares out over the
shimmering harbor water; my pulse goes a little wild.

In a moment of weakness, I give in to the temptation of
spectacularly good light, uncap the lens of the camera around
my neck, quickly get Lucky in focus, and photograph him. Only
a few pictures—just to get warmed up. He's wearing shorts. So
am I, but I haven't seen Lucky 2.0 in shorts. Or in anything but

leather boots, to be honest. But the black low-tops he's wearing right now sans socks are showing an *awful* lot of ankle, and I can see those ankles through the lens . . . and also that his legs are long and leanly muscled like his arms.

But before I can lower my camera, he turns and catches me.

Crap! *Noooooo.*

Not good.

I try to play it cool by quickly photographing a couple of other things as I walk over to meet him. The boatyard crane. A rusted chain. Don't think I'm fooling him, though. Ugh. See? I should never take photos of people; it only gets me in trouble.

"You know . . . I didn't realize modeling was part of this job or I would've asked for extra," he says as I approach.

"Just doing some warm-up shots to test the light," I tell him, seeming relaxed. Sounds good. Maybe he believes me. "Don't get excited."

"I don't like my picture taken."

"You used to."

"Well, I don't anymore, so don't waste film on me."

"It's not film. I brought the digital," I say, holding it up to show him. "I figure I'll be taking a lot of motion shots, and besides, I can't afford film right now, since I spent all my savings on chartering a fancy boat."

"Sounds like a problem, all right. Just so you know, the boat is *definitely* not fancy, and we don't give refunds. So your money is g-o-n-e," he spells out.

I shrug. "The things we do for art."

"Is that what this is? For art?" He steps closer, scowling down at me in a dark T-shirt printed with a fierce wolf and anvil design—an advertisement for some local business on Lamplighter Lane. For a moment, my mom's stupid superstitious mumbo jumbo about that bedeviled street floods my brain. She'd definitely take it as a sign. *Warning! Stay away from this guy!*

"U-uh . . . ," I stammer, trying to recover my wits. "You know I'm serious about my photography. In fact, you know lots about me. But I don't know all that much about you. I mean, the *new and improved* you."

"Sounds to me like you've been snooping around if you're talking to Bunny . . . ," he murmurs.

I ignore that and crane my neck to see around him. "Which boat are we taking? I don't want to lose the light."

He mumbles some mildly foul things under his breath and nods with his head, leading me down a short wooden dock to an ugly orange boat. Not a yacht. Not a houseboat. Not even one with a tarp to keep out the sun. Just a little boat with four seats, a motor, and a steering wheel.

"This is your boat?"

"Not mine," he says. "It's *a* boat. I would not name my boat '*Big-Enough.*'"

He's not kidding. I take a second look at the peeling letters on the side.

"Okay, wow. It's making the *Fun N Sun* look pretty good," I say, glancing back at the boat sitting up on blocks, upon which we had our little tête-à-tête. "This is a family boat?"

"'Family' isn't a word I'd choose to describe it. But hey. It's the boat my dad said I could use," he says, holding up a key ring and shrugging as his mouth curls up into something I'd call a smirk. Yep. He's smirking. What a jerk. A *cute* jerk, but . . . "We dock a lot of boats here. There's a system. It's complicated. It's not like you can just put keys in a car and drive it out."

"I'll bet it's not," I say.

Smirk.

"Besides. This one had a leak. We're testing it out. So it's a double-duty thing."

"A leak?"

"We repaired it. It's fine. We do good work. But it's smart to test it."

Smirk.

"Fine," I say.

"Okay?"

I nod. "Let's go. It's 'big enough,' right? I'm just taking photos."

He holds out a hand to help me inside. "Ladies first. Careful now. Don't want to tip the boat over. Your choice of four seats here. Care to sit in the captain's chair?"

"Is that a nautical pick-up line?"

"No. 'Want to go for a ride on my dinghy?' is a nautical pick-up line."

I pretend to gag. "A bad pickup line for a badly named boat—which, by the way, I refuse to say again during our outing today."

He laughs. "It's *so* bad," he admits. "The dude who owns it is a total dumbass. He doesn't know anything about storing boats for

159

winter. Remember that old rusted boat near the North Star with the holes in the bottom? It was almost that bad."

"Is the North Star still at the end of the Harborwalk, or has Beauty torn it down to make way for a new colonial museum?"

"Think it's still standing. I haven't been out there in years. Not since . . . well, since you left, I guess. Hanging out in an abandoned boatshed is fine when you're twelve and have company, but it's a little depressing when you're seventeen and all by your lonesome. People might mistake me for a meth addict or a prostitute."

I snort a laugh as I sit in a plastic seat, trying not to freak out that the boat doesn't feel all that stable or that the water is . . . so close. I tuck my arms close to my body and peer over the edge. "What's that smell?"

"Fish. Or sealant. Fish and sealant," he guesses, untying a rope from the dock and throwing it into the back. "The sealant was us. Fish was the owner."

The boat dips with Lucky's weight as he plops down on the seat next to me, long golden legs stretching out near mine. He puts on a pair of dark sunglasses and starts the engine—it takes a couple of tries. When he backs up the boat, his arm grazes my shoulder as he turns in his seat to look behind us, but he doesn't apologize. He just maneuvers the boat around without a word . . . and we're off.

For several moments, all I'm aware of is the purpled setting sun and the feel of the wind on my face. The salty harbor air in my lungs as Lucky navigates past sailboats and yachts darting around the coast, heading home or flicking on lights to stay out in the harbor for Saturday night booze-cruise parties. And we're in the middle of everything. It's thrilling and warm and wonderful, and the water ripples around us like lace as Lucky turns the boat sharply and—

My stomach lurches. I slam my hand on the side of the boat, clutching for balance.

"O-oh dear," I say.

"You okay?"

"Just a little dizzy."

He glances at me. "You've been on boats, right?"

"Sure. The swan paddleboats at Witch Lake across town, which I vomited on, if you'll remember."

Lucky laughs. "Are you serious? When we were, what? Ten? Wait . . . we never went on boat rides? That's not possible."

"You were at the old boat-repair shop. We used to sit in that little fishing boat and pretend to fish off the pier until . . ."

"Until you said the waves made you sick."

I moan. "You made fun of me."

"Oh shit," he says, chuckling a little. "Josie . . . is this seriously your first time on a real boat?"

"Maybe?"

He slows down and looks at me, grinning under his sunglasses. "Really?"

"Shut up! I don't even know how to swim, okay?"

"Of course you do. We used to go over to Leah's pool every summer."

"And I sat on the steps while you splashed around in the deep end!"

"How is that possible?"

"No one ever taught me—that's how! I can't ride a bike, either. I haven't had a normal family life like you. Latchkey Josie, remember? That's what that stupid Golden called me when we were in sixth grade, and then everyone at school picked it up, even though no one knew what it meant. I didn't even know! Mom had to come talk to the principal about it."

"I remember."

"So go ahead and laugh at me, I don't care."

"I'm not laughing, jeez. Who said swimming and riding bikes had anything to do with normal families?"

"Because that's what normal families do! You see it on TV!"

"You see pigs surfing on TV too. That doesn't make it real! Jeez, Josie. If you've never been on a boat, why did you want to do this today?"

I can't answer. I'm too busy trying not to inhale the nauseating scents of old fish and new sealant, and everything is haywire and prickly. Cold sweat spreads over my skin.

No, no, no . . . I can't vomit. Not in front of Lucky. Not here. That would be humiliating. I shut my eyes and try to stop my stomach from revolting against me, curling up around my camera as I lean over my lap. "Gonna be sick."

The boat slows and comes to a stop. The engine shuts off. Waves lap against the boat.

"Throw up over the side," Lucky says in a calm voice, warm hand on my back between my shoulder blades. "I've got you. I won't let you fall in."

I don't say anything for a long time. Minutes. Longer. I just wait for the terrible clammy feeling to subside and the boat to stop bobbing in the water. His hand feels nice on my back, a gentle circular rub. Very soothing. I concentrate on that until my balance rights itself and the dizziness slows.

"I'm okay," I finally say toward my feet in a voice that sounds strange. "Mostly."

"You're seasick. It's an inner ear thing. Your brain is getting conflicting signals from your ears and eyes and sensory receptors, so everything's scrambled inside. Some people get really scrambled, and that makes them feel sick."

"I'm scrambled, all right."

"It might help if you sit up and look at the horizon."

"Can't."

"Seriously, Josie."

"I said no."

"Fine. What do I know? I've only been on boats all my life, born into an immigrant seafaring family that goes back for generations. We don't get scrambled. But go on. You do what you'd like."

I groan. "Give me a minute, okay?"

"Okay, okay." He exhales dramatically. The soothing circles on my back slow and then come to a stop, as if he's just realizing he's been doing it.

"That helps," I tell him in small voice.

"All right," he says gruffly. But he begins rubbing my back again, and his hand is gentle.

"Josie?"

"Yes?" I say into my arms, cradling my camera.

"Why did you arrange this boat charter if you get seasick?"

"Clearly I didn't know that," I complain. "I wanted to help pay for the window. You refused. So I came up with this plan."

"A good, old-fashioned Josie scheme. Missed those."

"I thought I could take pictures," I explain, hoping it sounds less . . . weird. "I didn't know I got seasick."

He chuckles.

"Are you laughing at me?"

"No, no. Just picturing you interning at that magazine during Regatta Week, that's all."

Oh my good God. "Is this a one-time thing, or are people genetically prone to it?"

"You get used to boats. Usually. Some people never do."

Seagulls squawk as they fly near the Harborwalk. A small fishing boat motors past us. I finally dare to lift my head, and Lucky jerks his hand away. After a sickening moment when blood rushes back to where it belongs, I sit back in my seat and breathe. I'm okay. Not sick. Where's the horizon? There. Okay. Not sure that really helps, because too many boats keep speeding past it, but at least we're not moving.

I shift my focus to a nearby sign that warns of deep water.

People need a sign to tell them not to swim here? I swear, people will post a sign for anything. People are strange. Thank God for strangeness.

Wish Lucky's hand was still on my back.

His sunglasses rest atop his head, and he's twisted in his seat, one bare knee up between us, elbows resting behind him on the edge of the boat. He squints at me and says bluntly, "So . . . you talked to Bunny."

Right. That. "I ran into her. Your name came up, I didn't—"

"It's fine."

"I wasn't gossiping about you."

"No?" He studies my face with a curious kind of enjoyment in his gaze. "That's disappointing to hear."

"She was telling me that some things I heard were wrong . . . and that you apparently are not the father of her child."

"No, I am not. Not hers, not anyone's."

"Okay, that's good. Not that there's anything . . ." Ugh. Awkward. "I mean, if you . . ." One more time. "I guess I don't know why people ever said that about you and Bunny to begin with?"

"People say that because I drove her to an abortion clinic."

Oh.

He shrugs lightly. "I found her crying. She needed someone to drive her and couldn't tell her family. None of her friends would help, and the jackass who should have been helping had ghosted her. So I went with her and waited, and then I drove her back home in her car. We're friends, that's all."

I nod. "I see."

"Someone saw us coming out of the clinic. That's how the rumor started."

"Assumptions aren't facts," I murmur, remembering things Bunny said.

"No, but people sure do love to make them."

"They make a lot of them about you," I note.

"Yep."

"You don't seem to mind. I think you want people to talk."

"That's absurd. Why would I want that?"

"I don't know," I say in a quiet voice. "Why would you?"

He stares at me.

I stare at him.

And something hangs in the air between us. Something unsaid that I almost understand, but not quite. Something he *wants* me to understand. He's looking at me as if he's stranded alone on a deserted island and I've found his message in a bottle. Like he wants me to rescue him.

But that can't be right, can it? Because he's the one with the savior complex—as Bunny said. He's the one who rescued her . . . who took the fall for me. Why would *he* need help?

Our boat bobs in the water, threatening another wave of wooziness and joggling my arm into Lucky's leg that's propped up between the seats. I look down. The skin-to-skin contact is a shock. He's so feverishly warm in the cool breeze blowing off the harbor. It feels . . . too intimate. As if I've crossed the line somehow by accidently touching him—which is ridiculous. It's just a shin. Just my forearm. Nothing sexy. For the love of Pete, he was rubbing my back a second ago, practically a massage, which everyone knows is a million times more risqué, if we're racking up steam points. Right . . . ?

But when I tear my gaze away from where our bodies are pressed together oh-so-casually and look up into his eyes, I see something unmistakably different there. He feels it too. Not casual. Not casual at all. Not friendly. Not old pals catching up.

What is this? What's happening?

I move my arm away, heart beating wildly against my ribs, and I pretend that nothing has happened. Because nothing has.

I think the seasickness has seeped into my brain and caused a temporary malfunction. That's probably all it is, right? Just need to breathe and stop thinking about it. I'll be fine.

Lucky clears his throat. "You know, you could've just asked to meet me at the Quarterdeck again. Less nausea. More coffee. No mothers involved in the meetup."

"Ah, well. I didn't want to stalk you around the department store or creep around the boatyard, and I didn't have your phone number."

"Tell me yours."

"What?"

He lifts his chin, encouraging. "Go on. Tell me yours."

"Now?"

"Right now."

I recite my number. "You'll remember that without writing it down?"

"Yep. Mind like a steel trap. Remember? I used to help you cheat on math tests."

God. He totally did. "Is that because you've turned into a genius?"

He groans.

"Evie said you got a perfect score on the SAT," I say.

"Gossip," he says, dismissive.

"Really?"

"Near perfect."

"Shut up! Then it's true?"

"Who cares?" he says, shrugging. "Test scores don't measure intellect. They just prove you're good at taking tests. And who cares if you can get into an Ivy League school if you can't afford it? None of them offer scholarships. You still have to pay. All the rest of the colleges offering full rides want extracurriculars and students 'of character.' I think we can all agree that's not me."

"But—"

"It's not even what I want to do. No one stops to ask me that. My mom wants me in college. My dad wants me to take over the boatyard. . . ."

"What *do* you want?"

He hesitates. "Maybe I'll show you sometime. If you're interested . . ."

"I'm interested."

"Yeah?"

"Yeah."

"Hey," he says. "Did you ever call the woman at the magazine?"

"Oh, her. Uh, she hasn't gotten back to me," I lie.

He squints at me, and I remember his talk about the invisible wall and honesty.

"Okay, fine. I haven't emailed her yet. What if she's heard about the police station? Or . . ."

"I'm sure she hasn't seen your mom's nude photo," he says after a moment.

"Now I've got seasickness to add to the mix. Regatta Week . . . ugh."

"You can beat that with practice. Email her," he insists, "if that's what you want to do. I wish you wouldn't, because I personally don't think you should go to Malibu, but that's just my stubborn and ill-informed opinion."

"Did I tell you about the ticking time bomb that is my grandmother returning from Nepal next year? I can't stay in Beauty forever, even if I wanted to. You want me to be teeth-gratingly honest? Well . . . there you go."

He looks hurt for a moment but sighs deeply. "I get it, okay? You should do what you want, and that's the important thing. Email the magazine."

"Yeah?"

"Yes. Do it. Weasel your way in there, Saint-Martin."

"Hustle."

He smiles. "Hustle."

We blink at each other, and . . . there it is again. A little thrill that wasn't there before. Nothing that I can point to definitively, but it makes every tiny hair on my body flutter as if an unseen breeze has gusted inside my clothes.

"The sun makes your freckles darker," he says in low, raspy voice as his gaze trails over my cheeks and nose where the wind is blowing loose tendrils of hair.

He reaches out for me. Fingers splayed. Slowly. He's going to touch my face, right now, right here. I hold my breath, waiting to feel that shocking warmth again. . . .

But.

His hand stops midair and flexes, hanging there for a moment as if all his muscles have been turned to stone. He blinks rapidly and then withdraws his arm, mumbling an apology under his breath that I barely catch. And the disappointment that rolls over me is fast and intense and completely unexpected.

I look away, rattled, bewildered, and pretend to stare out at the water. The sun's falling out of sight, making the sky all purple, casting long shadows. Too long. Golden hour is gone.

"Stomach back to normal?" he asks in a quiet voice.

"Think so."

"Good." He turns in his seat to switch on the engine. "Your hour's up."

Oh, thank God. I need some space. To process what's happened here today.

Or maybe to forget.

He takes it slow getting me back to the boatyard. Even still, I cling tightly to the boat and keep my eyes on the horizon. It helps. I really hate that he was right.

When we get back to the dock and he maneuvers *Big-Enough* into place, I practically tumble over myself and nearly fall on my face trying to get back onto shore. He offers a hand, but I refuse it. Unhelpfully, he tells me I need to practice being out on the water until I can get over my seasickness. Short, slow trips.

I've got another cure: never going out on the water again. And maybe staying away from him until I figure out what happened out there . . .

"Hope you enjoyed your charter, Saint-Martin," he says, sounding like the boy I've come to know over the last couple of weeks, sarcastic and dark and slightly distant. Not someone who makes all the hairs stand up on my body.

"The views were a ten," I say, pretending I'm my normal self too. "The captain was kind of a jackass who drove like a maniac—"

"You drive cars, not boats."

"—and nearly made me puke my guts out."

"Sounds like a personal problem."

"I'll be filing a complaint."

"No refunds, remember."

"You really should post a sign."

The corners of his mouth curl. "I'll bring that up to management."

I turn to leave and hold up a hand over my shoulder, trying to seem cool and unfazed. Definitely not someone who's completely confused by what just happened and wants to get out of here ASAP. "Adieu, Captain Lucky. If that *is* your real name."

"Goodbye, shutterbug."

I ignore that.

When I'm halfway down the boatyard, he calls out behind me, "Hey, Josie?"

"Yes?" I say, stopping again.

"You never took any pictures," he points out.

Ugh. I was hoping he didn't notice that. "Guess I'm in the wrong town if I'm not good on boats, huh?"

"Don't give up just yet," he says, tying up the boat. "After all, you *could* acclimate. Might surprise yourself one day."

Maybe I'm surprised already.

WELCOME TO BEAUTIFUL GREEKTOWN: A white neighborhood sign sits at the junction of Battery Street and Atlantic Avenue. The earliest Greek immigrants to settle in Beauty were fishermen who worked in the South Harbor in the late 1800s. *(Personal photo/Josephine Saint-Martin)*

12

Nothing happened.

Not really.

But if that's true, why do I still feel like this? How come, now that I've been back on shore for a couple of hours, no trace of seasickness, all I can think about is Lucky?

And the way he looked at me. The way his hand flexed when he reached out to touch me.

The way it made me ache when he didn't.

Because that's the worst part of it. I *wanted* him to touch me.

I think about that. I think about his hand on my back when I was in the middle of that dizzy spell, and the way his thumb circled the bones in my spine. How shockingly warm his skin was when we bumped into each other. The way he stared at me. The way everything felt different between us.

The way we talked when we left each other, like nothing had changed.

Maybe I'm still seasick after all. . . .

"School is boring, Mom. I want to hear about Nepal," Evie says to Aunt Franny on her laptop as she lies sprawled across her bed.

I'm sitting below her on the floor, out of sight from the screen, on a braided Amish rag rug that's leaving marks on the backs of my thighs. It's just after eleven p.m., and Mom left the apartment an hour ago because she needed to "take a drive around the harbor" and "get some fresh air." Hard for me to argue with that, seeing how I took a forbidden boat cruise earlier tonight. Anyway, I was giving Evie the lowdown about said boat outing when her mom Skyped; it's morning in Nepal.

I don't really want to be here, listening in to their private mother-daughter convo, but Evie made me stay. They don't talk long, and she wants to hear the rest of my juicy boating story. I'm not sure I want to give her *all* the details. It feels too raw right now. And how do I explain it? He "looked" at me in a different way? Sounds ridiculous. Maybe because it is?

I've got to stop thinking about him.

Aunt Franny looks thin and tired—I caught a glimpse of her on the screen before I ducked down here. She's only five years older than my mom, but I don't think Nepal agrees with her. Guess it wouldn't be a surprise to anyone if my grandma's *Having a Great Time!* postcards are all one big fat lie. It's the Saint-Martin way, after all.

While listening to Aunt Franny tell Evie about the school in

Nepal that she and Grandma are teaching at, trying to get my mind off Lucky and the boat ride, I stare at a shelf of Evie's weird taxidermy collection—a mouse wearing a tiny wizard outfit is the only one I truly like—and space out momentarily.

Until I hear Aunt Franny say something.

"—surprised she has the guts to move back to Beauty, frankly, since whatshisname is out of the navy and back in town."

Hold up a minute. What's this all about, now?

I look up at Evie on the bed.

She looks down at me with wide eyes.

Aunt Franny is talking about my mom . . . and some guy. Some navy guy.

"Who's 'whatshisname,' Mom?" Evie asks when I prompt her by yanking at her pajama pants leg and mouth the question. "Who are you talking about?"

"I can't remember his name. It was high school."

"High school? Why would Aunt Winona care about someone from high school?" Evie says. "What's up with this mystery man? Spill the beans, Mom."

Her mom is silent for a moment. "No one, baby. I shouldn't have said anything. That's all in the past, and not our business."

"Mom—"

"Evie," her mom says over the laptop screen, "that's enough. If Winona wanted us to gossip about her, she'd tell us herself. End of story."

Great. Mom will never tell me, and I definitely won't be asking.

Mom will shut that down faster than a food inspector visiting a rat-infested pizza parlor. But now I'm super curious about Navy Man, who was possibly some boy in high school . . . who would have been reason enough to stop my mom from coming back to Beauty?

Now I'm remembering when we first came into town and how nervous she was, and I thought it was all the town gossip or possibly the Saint-Martin curse. But now I wonder if it's something more. . . .

I ponder this while Evie asks her mom about Grandma Diedre, who refuses to participate in these calls—they have no Wi-Fi in their living quarters, and she hates having to walk down to a local internet café. And just when I'm thinking of leaving Evie's room to give them some privacy, my phone buzzes inside the pocket of my shorts. A text from a local number. Not in my contacts.

Have you recovered from our excursion on the SS Too Big?

My heart skips as I smile at the screen. Well, then . . . Guess he wasn't lying about memorizing numbers. I quickly add him to my contacts and make sure Evie can't see my phone before typing a response.

Me: I see what you did there, funny man. Def should have used Sunset Charters. They promised champagne + smooth jazz.

Lucky: U would have yacked that up. I gave u old fish and sealant. Where's the love?

Me: It's at the bottom of my empty bank account.

Lucky: Told u a million times, you don't need to pay me back

Me: Told you a million times, I do.

Lucky: Next time, I'll bring smooth jazz and a barf bag.

Me: Next time, we sit on the dock.

Lucky: How about dinner, instead?

I stare at the screen, hot and cold chills running up and down my arms. Is he . . . asking me out on a date? That can't be right. Can it? Smashing my hopes, he rapidly types another text before I can reply.

Lucky: Remember Sunday dinners? Cousins. Uncles and aunts. Neighbors. Backyard cookout? My mom asked me to invite u.

Oh. Not a date.

But that was silly of me, duh. He's my friend.

Friends don't date.

Regardless, dinner with his family might be . . . good. I used to love Sunday dinners at Lucky's house. I looked forward to it all week, like a big nerd.

Me: Not sure how to respond to "my mom made me ask you."

Lucky: Didn't say she MADE me. Give me a little credit. I'm exercising free will.

Lucky: But if it's too weird, I'll tell her you're busy.

Me: I'm not opposed to weird. Did you tell your mom I nearly upchucked in your boat?

Lucky: Again, not MY boat. And yes. *steeples fingers*

Me: Oh God.

Lucky: You work at the Nook tomorrow?

Me: Until 7.

Lucky: Meet me in the boatyard side alley at 7:15.

Me: I didn't say yes yet.

Lucky: I hate begging.

Me: Knowing that is its own reward. See you at 7:15.

Okay, then. Sunday dinner. At the Karrases. I just agreed to that. Not intimating at all. I'm not feeling like my insides are melting. No sirree, Bob! Not me. Guess I'm gonna need to find another excuse to give Mom for tomorrow night, since I'm *technically* not supposed to be seeing Lucky, as Mom put her foot down—forbidden territory, stay away from that boy. *He's a vandal, Josie.* Him. Not me. At this point, I'll need a garbage truck to haul away all the lies I've been accumulating.

I also need to remind myself that I don't want to get too attached, so I leave Evie, retreating to my room, where I pull out my father's fashion photo book. And I lay on the rug, turning the slick, glossy pages, re-memorizing the details of each photograph, reminding myself that there are other things out there in the world. Brighter, shinier things. And if I want them badly enough, I can have them. I just have to stick to my plan.

Lucky 2.0 might be a mirage.

I should be careful with him.

I should be careful with my heart.

* * *

It's easier than I expected to come up with a suitable lie for Sunday dinner. I just tell Mom that I ran into Bunny Perera at the doughnut shop—true—and that I'm meeting her at the Quarterdeck for coffee . . . not true.

See? Only a half lie. Half the guilt.

The Nook is having computer issues, and Mom is so consumed with trying to get the end-of-the-day totals to process that I could've told her I was going to have one of Evie's taxidermy bat wings surgically attached to my back, and she would've said, *Okay, babe. Be careful.*

Leaving her and Evie to close the store, I take the long way past the Freedom Art Gallery and weave my way through tourists to make sure I'm not spotted. When I sneak into the boatyard side alley, I'm a minute late. And I find Lucky pacing around his bike, a black-and-white striped shirt under his leather jacket. The moment he looks up and sees me, I forget all about guilt and my garbage truck of lies. I forget about everything.

His eyes light up as if I'm a winning lottery ticket, and we smile at each other like we're splitting the jackpot fifty-fifty.

"Sorry I'm late," I finally say.

"One minute, but I'm not counting."

I laugh.

The corners of his mouth curl. "Got a surprise for you."

"O-oh. Hope it's a vomit bag for my seasick stomach."

"Even better. It's an air freshener that smells like old fish and

179

sealant. Here," he says, handing me a small, rainbow-striped helmet with a flying white horse on the side. "Safety first. Didn't want to risk my head twice. Now we'll both be covered."

"Uh, wow," I say. "It's . . . sparkly?"

"My cousin Gabe uses it," he explains. "Sometimes I take him for a ride on the weekends to our grandmother's condo on the harbor."

I point to the winged horse. It has three unicorn horns. "Tricorn?"

He shrugs. "He's really into horses right now, and he wanted it to have three horns."

"Correct me if I'm wrong, but I remember another boy who loved sea monsters. The kraken?"

"The kraken," he says excitedly. "Yes."

"Giant octopus that takes down ships."

"Badass, right? So much better than a flying horse. Still a fan of the kraken, actually. But Gabe is scared of anything with tentacles."

"I see. . . . Don't remember your cousin Gabe."

"He moved here after you left. He's nine, but he's got a big head for a kid—this is actually an adult helmet that I tricked out for him, so it should fit, I think? Better than my brain bucket." He helps me slip the helmet on my head. "Yeah. See? Your dome is protected by the power of Trig-asus. Hop on, shutterbug. You're street legal now. And you get to reintroduce yourself to my big Greek family. This is what happens when you walk into the boatyard and chat with my mother."

"Sort of regretting that now."

"As well you should. Too late to turn back now. May God save you."

Following his reminders about how to ride, I straddle the Superhawk's seat behind Lucky and put my arms around him, pretending it's no big deal. I did it before when we went to the hospital. It's practical, *not* sexy, and I should not be enjoying the smell of his leather jacket or how solid he feels under my arms. . . . Wait. Oh God. He can probably feel my breasts pressing against his back.

How can he not?

Oh God. I think I'm going to have a nervous breakdown.

Right. That's it, then. Should probably just bail now. Jump off the bike and run. No one would blame me. But he's right. It's way too late now. With a rev of the engine, we're pulling out of the alleyway, and me and my boobs and my anxieties will just have to cling to him and pray he doesn't notice any of us.

The motorcycle bounces on setts and cobblestones as we turn down the boulevard and head west, away from the harbor. We pass a slew of eighteenth century houses with historic-registry signs like the one on our house, two Revolutionary War statues, and a white church with a grand steeple. And after several blocks, when the tourist traffic clears and the streets widen, I spot the familiar sign for Greektown.

No turning back.

The Karrases' house is a pale blue Cape Cod and not unlike most of the others on the quiet, tree-lined block—simple New

England homes with small, neat yards framed in white picket fences. Cars line the curb on both sides of the street, and more are driving around the block, looking for a place to park. Lucky squeezes his bike between two Nick's Boatyard trucks in the driveway and stops in front of the detached garage that's painted the same pale blue as their house.

I've been here a hundred times before. Hundreds. Literally.

It feels like the first.

And when we get off his bike and remove our helmets, he doesn't seem to be anxious or showing signs that he's been going through the same mental gymnastics I've been experiencing on the ride over here. He's not even looking at my face. It's like night and day from the smiling guy who met me in the alley.

I try to forget about it and focus on my surroundings. I can already see across the sidewalk between the house and the garage that the fenced-in backyard is packed with people.

"Come on," he says, urging me forward with a hand guiding me behind my back—behind, but not quite touching me. "Remember the drill? Nothing much has changed. It's a serve-yourself kind of deal. People come and go. It's casual. It's not usually this many people, so don't freak out."

"I'm not freaked out."

"No?"

I glance at his tight eyes, and I remember what he's said about me being a terrible liar. No point, really. Plus, it's a relief not to pretend around him. "I'm terrified. Sunday dinners were some of my favorite times of the week when we were young. I love your family. I've missed them. But everything has changed, and I'm afraid they won't accept me anymore. I'm afraid . . . What if they've seen my mom's photo?"

His face softens. "They haven't. You think my working-class aunts and uncles move in the same circles as the Goldens across town? They couldn't care less about anything a dink like Adrian Summers has to say."

I laugh a little, still mildly nervous but improving.

He knocks his shoulder gently against mine. "Don't worry. They accept you, because I do. Nothing's changed."

That's not entirely true. The first minute in the backyard is a blur: white fairy lights strung across the top of a wooden pergola; the scent of smoke, grilled meat, and garlic, and my stomach growling with hunger despite my rattled nerves; people joyfully shouting *"Yiamas!"* while toasting with plastic wine glasses; kids running underfoot. And between all this is Lucky's name being called out repeatedly as he puts his hand lightly on the small of my back and weaves us between several picnic tables and too many patio chairs to count. He waves at people, nods his chin, laughs at a joke, but keeps leading me past pair after pair of curious eyes until we get to the boss.

Kat Karras.

Sitting at a table, she lifts her head to him the same way he does, a tiny nod of the chin. "Finally. What, you aren't answering texts anymore? Was afraid you might skip out."

"I don't text while I'm driving. And I said it would be after seven."

"Fair enough. You did." She smiles and reaches up to pat his chest. "And you brought Miss Josie. Thank you for coming, *koukla*," she says to me.

"Thank you . . . uh, for inviting me."

"Things may change, but you're always welcome here," she says, sounding as if she means it. "Over the last couple of years, Diedre's been eating with us on Sundays every once in a while."

She has? Wow. Usually my grandmother will only allow herself time enough to microwave takeout and eat at the kitchen counter. The surprises never end.

"You'll have to tell her you came next time you email her," Kat says.

Hate to break the news to her, but Grandma and I don't enjoy an email-friendly kind of rapport. Or a communication-friendly rapport of any kind, really. She hates texting. I only see her every year or so, and we barely hug. I guess Grandma and Mom's relationship issues are like the flu, and they've infected me with it too; now we're all sick.

"Where's Dad?" Lucky asks.

"Minding the grill," she says, pointing. "Hope you're hungry, Josie. Drinks are over there. A million side dishes. Save room for ice cream. Oh, and steer clear of the blue casserole dish. Aunt Helen's been cooking with her cats," she whispers, making a face.

"Oh *shit*," he says. "Thanks for the warning."

She pokes him the stomach, making him grunt. "No swearing in front of family."

"She's not family, Mama."

"Of course she is."

I'm caught off guard by her words. She probably doesn't mean anything by it—just something that rolls off the tongue. But it makes me long for something I don't have, and now I'm more emotional than I want to be.

She waves a hand to her son. "Go. Say hello to your grandparents. Find your father. And Lucky?"

"Yep?"

"Love you."

"Mmm."

"My son, the poet," she says, winking and grinning at him with obvious affection.

Over by the biggest grill I've ever seen, standing in smoke rising from hardwood and ash, we locate the shoulder-length, curly hair and bushy eyebrows of Lucky's dad, who pauses grilling long enough to hug my neck but is too busy chasing flames with a water bottle to chat. Then it takes us a while to wind our way through the boisterous crowd to the food. I'm reintroduced to Kat's sister. One set of grandparents. Three of Lucky's male cousins. An uncle on his father's side. His neighbors, Mr. and Mrs. Wong, from across the street. Two kids flying paper airplanes. And the tiny black dog that I saw running around the boatyard office that day I walked by their window . . .

"This is Bean the Magic Pup," Lucky tells me as he crouches near the small ball of fluff and scratches him behind one ear.

"Why is he magic?"

"We found him roaming around the boatyard, and no one claimed him, and my mom kept feeding him. . . . Go on—pet him. He doesn't bite, but he is *super* gassy. That's his magic power."

"Ah, pass," I say, holding up my hands and chuckling.

"Still scared of dogs?"

"Not scared."

"Ever since that Doberman, when we were nine. The one by the school."

"I hated that dog," I admit. "It's not that. I don't know . . . I've just never been around any. Not up close and personal."

His nose crinkles. "I don't remember that. Are you sure? Never?"

"A few cats at some of the small bookstores that my mom's managed, but no dogs. I've never really had a pet. Never been anywhere long enough, I guess."

"Well, if you ever want to practice dog ownership, Bean is happy to oblige. And the good thing is, he's got a short attention span," he says as the dog scampers off, tongue lolling as he chases a paper airplane. "Come on. Let's eat before someone else corners us."

We pile plates with food—a mishmash of everything from spanakopita and moussaka, to pork egg rolls from Mr. and Mrs. Wong, and not one, but *three* kinds of potato salad—and find an unoccupied table. It's a little awkward between us while we eat. We don't have much to say, and it's so noisy . . . so much going on in the small backyard. Conversations. Laughter. And it continues like this until one of his uncles—George, who is a little tipsy—trips over a water sprinkler. Thank God, because it attracts everyone's attention, and Lucky finally breaks the awkward silence between us, reminding me of funny stories about Uncle George embarrassing himself at other Sunday dinners.

"You hate this," Lucky suddenly says, toying with the tab on top of a can of grape soda. "Being here. You were worried about being here today, and I said it would be okay, but now you're not talking, so I'm pretty sure you hate it."

I think for a moment. "You know what? I actually don't. It's just that I forgot what it's like. I've been used to just me and Mom. It's been weird since we've moved back here for Evie to be added into the mix. Not bad-weird. Just . . ."

"An adjustment."

"Yeah."

"This is my normal," he says, gesturing toward the yard. "Always loud, always people coming and going. At home. At the boatyard . . . You may remember that my dad also has two sisters and a brother, and they all moved into town two years ago, so I have a million cousins. Someone's always needing something. Money. Help. Attention. Sleeping on our couch. Dinners. Errands. Favors. Drama. Babysitting . . . I get so tired of all the chaos. I would kill to have the kind of refuge you have there. That's my dream—living above the Nook? That seems amazing."

"Seriously?"

"Hell yeah. Why do you think I love coming in there? One of the few places I can enjoy some peace and quiet and get away from my family."

"You haven't recently, you know. Been in the bookshop. Not since . . ."

"Well," he says, shrugging as he pushes his plate away. "Been a little busy, chartering boats and whatnot."

"And whatnot," I say, smiling. I'm just happy that we're talking, and it's not awkward like it was when we first sat down to eat.

He glances over his shoulder, then says, "Hey. Wanna see something?"

"Are you going to show me where the bodies are buried?"

"I'd be surprised if there weren't at least one." He gestures with his head, and I silently follow him around the edge of the yard, through a pair of tall bushes, and into a side door that leads into the detached garage, where he flicks on an overhead light that takes a second to illuminate the dark space.

I look around while he closes the door behind us, shutting out the din of the backyard. It's a one-car garage with no car parked inside, same as it always was when we came in here to play games on rainy days. But that's all that's the same. Next to the door is a beat-up couch and a tiny dorm-sized fridge being used as a side table, a stack of books and a lamp on top. But that's not the bulk of what's taking up the room in here.

Salvaged metal parts.

Everywhere.

Spokes. Wheels. Bars. Fenders. Pipes. Sheets. The walls are lined with industrial shelves that are packed with metal parts of all shapes and sizes. Metal hangs from the rafters. It's stacked in the corner next to a large rotary machine that looks like it cuts or grinds—both, maybe. A large table in the center room stands near welding equipment; I recognize the small orange machine and nearby mask from seeing a similar one in use at the boatyard.

At the end of the garage, opposite the door, Lucky flips on a lamp over a workbench. Hammers and saws and a variety of strange tools hang from a pegboard. Rows of tiny drawers.

I look around in amazement, feeling his eyes on me. He doesn't say a single word. Which is kind of weird. That's when it hits me.

"This is your thing," I say. "This is your photography."

He nods.

"Metalwork."

"Yep." He pulls out the steel stool from under his workbench. "I made this."

It's not fancy. Simple, clean lines. And I can see where it was welded together at the joints. But it's beautiful. And it doesn't squeak like the stool behind the counter at the Nook.

Before I can open my mouth to say anything, he points to other things and explains what each is for and how they came to be: A basket-shaped dome around a light fixture that was once a tin can. A cage he salvaged from a crab trap that holds more scrap parts. A set of drawers from a 1950s paint shop that he cut up and reassembled. He melts down metal. Cuts it up. Joins it. Makes it into something new.

"You're an artist," I finally say, stunned. "Like me."

"Craftsperson," he corrects. "Small difference. I need things I make to have a practical purpose."

"For the coming apocalypse," I say, remembering our talk on the Quarterdeck.

He chuckles. "Hey, I like art, too. A lot. But this . . . is my thing. It's just a personal choice. Like your photographs of signs. This is what speaks to me, I guess."

"Hey, I get that." I look around. "You rebuilt your motorcycle here."

"Yep."

"You weld."

"I do," he says, nodding.

I blink up at all the scraps of metal hanging from the rafters. There's something else up there too. A sword. "What about that?"

"That," he says, taking it down to unsheathe a rustic black blade, "is what I'm learning. The forge."

"Wow," I say, touching the pommel. "So cool. You can fight off zombie hordes."

"Maybe slice off an arm or two before it goes dull," he says with a shy smile. "Not that great at forging yet. It's hard work. But really cool. You can hammer iron into anything you want, if you're patient. Not sure I am, but I've got a good teacher. I just haven't had time to take lessons from him lately, what with everything going on."

Iron. Hammer. Forge. Anvil.

Blacksmith.

"Your shirt—the one you were wearing when you took me out on the boat . . ."

He nods and looks at me a little funny. Like maybe he's surprised I remembered it?

"The blacksmith," I say. "There's a blacksmith on Lamplighter Lane with a wrought-iron wolf hanging above the shop. That's what was on your shirt. That's your teacher?"

"Mr. Sideris," he says, nodding slowly. Squinting at me.

Why is he looking at me so strangely?

He's making me nervous, so I scratch my arm and yammer. "My mom has this weird hang-up about Lamplighter Lane. Like, I sort of remember her mentioning it once or twice when I was kid, but she definitely freaks about it now. Anywho, she thinks there's a black cloud over that street, or a portal to hell. It's haunted? Something, I don't know. She hasn't stepped foot there since we came back."

"Really?" he says, making a face and chuckling.

"You know how superstitious we Saint-Martins are. The whole romance curse and all."

He sheaths the sword and hangs it back up on its hooks. "I'll definitely have to tell Mr. Sideris about Lamplighter Lane. He'll get a kick out of that. Maybe he unwittingly opened up the portal inside his forge. Hot enough, that's for sure."

Hot enough to burn someone. I glance at the burn scars on his forehead. "There's actual fire in the forge, right? I mean, I don't know anything about how it works, but it seems intense after what you've been through with the fire at the lake house that you'd . . ."

"Want to stick my face over a screaming hot inferno again?"

I laugh a little nervously. "Yeah, I guess so."

"For a long time after the lake house, I wouldn't go near an open flame. Totally petrified of my dad's grill out in the backyard. Old Man Leary, who owns the store at the end of the block and always smokes those stinky cigars out on the corner? I nearly had a heart attack one day when I was walking past while he flicked a lighter."

"Oh God," I mumble.

"Yeah. Anyway, I was seeing a counselor at the children's hospital in Providence a couple times a month, and she suggested I confront my fears head-on. What could be scarier than a red-hot forge that heats up to two thousand five hundred degrees? Surprisingly, it worked. Took a couple of tries, and I may have sobbed like a baby the first time. Don't tell anyone."

Little tree, big shadow.

"Your secret is safe with me," I say, smiling softly. Then I glance at his scars. "I'm sure you get tired of people staring. They were all bandaged up when I left. It's weird to see them now." I scratch my arm and look at the floor. "I worried about you for a long time after we left town. Everyone kept telling us it wasn't that serious, but I knew they were lying."

He's silent for a moment, then says in a quiet voice, "I'm okay now. They're just scars."

I doubt that's true. I don't want him to have to think about it again, so I shake my head. "I didn't mean to dredge up bad memories or anything."

But I realize as soon as I say it that they're already there for him—he doesn't have to dredge them up. It's me who's inconvenienced by the uncomfortable emotion of it all. It's *me* who feels guilty that I wasn't here for him to lean on when he needed a friend most.

I wasn't the one who was on a lake vacation in Massachusetts with my family—who was supposed to be watching my younger cousin Chloe while my parents drove to the store. Who, when all the cousins wanted to go swimming in the lake, said it was okay that she stay in the little lake house . . .

Who couldn't swim fast enough, when there was a gas leak in the stove and an explosion.

He thought she was still inside. She wasn't—she was fine, safe outside. But when he finally got to the other side of the lake, he rushed inside anyway . . . and he found nothing but a frightened, trapped black cat.

The same black cat that now lives in the boatyard.

The tattoo on his hand.

Lucky was traumatized. I think he couldn't decide if what he'd done had been completely pointless or if the black cat was the most important thing in the world. Maybe both. He was confused and in a lot of pain. But I was a kid, and I didn't know what to do or say to make it better.

And then came the Big Fight between Mom and Grandma.

Then we were gone. And Lucky and I were ripped apart. And I was alone.

"I'm so sorry," I whisper. I know that's not nearly enough, but it's all I have right now.

Unsure, I reach for him and catch his forearm. Maybe that's too intimate for former childhood friends? How we touched on the boat seems a thousand lifetimes ago, and perhaps all the meaning I attached to it was in my head.

I start to let go of him, but as my hand falls away, he catches the tips of my fingers with his and oh-so-gently holds on to them. I don't stop him. Not when he runs his thumb over my knuckle, sending shivers over my skin so intense, I have to shut my eyes for a moment. And not when he dips his head lower, and I can feel warm breath tickling the hair near my temple, and it makes my own breath come faster.

I don't stop him.

He's the one who lets go.

And when he does . . . when he drops my hand and turns away from me, I feel an awful, hollow ache inside. But now he's shut down completely, as if he's pressed a button and erected some kind of electric barrier between us that I can't cross. He's turning off the light on his workbench, putting everything as it was, tidying up. . . .

"Better get back out there," he says in a husky voice that sounds lost and cold. A voice that thinks he's made a terrible mistake and is now overcompensating to correct it.

No! I open my mouth to be teeth-gratingly honest, but one of his little cousins bursts through the garage door, bringing with him the noise of the backyard and the little black dog . . . and all my honest words stay stuck inside my head.

I want to tell him that I'm glad he brought me in here to show me his work and be reunited with his stupidly nice, wonderfully loud family. That he's not a monster. That he's actually wonderful and kind and funny, and I never realized how much I missed my best friend until right this minute.

No, I don't just miss him. I want my best friend back. My boy.

But I think I *also* want Lucky 2.0.

I *also* want to ask him if he would please hold my hand again.

I *also* want to be a lot more than friends.

I'm greedy: *I want it all.*

Tick, tick, tick.

What in the world do I do now?

DRIVE LIKE IT'S YOUR NEIGHBORHOOD: Obnoxious red paper sign posted in the shop window of Regal Cosmetics in the South Harbor district. The shop's owner has made multiple complaints to the police and during town hall meetings about speeding cars and loud music. *(Personal photo/Josephine Saint-Martin)*

13

Of all the things I've inherited from my mother—the secret-keeping, my inability to communicate in a healthy manner, love for fried food, and intense loathing of the word "y'all"—the one thing I wish she'd passed down was her ability to chitchat in uncomfortable situations. She's very good at it, and even when she's putting her foot in her mouth, she's usually able to laugh it off and talk her way out of things. Gift of gab.

I could use a little gab when Lucky takes me home from Sunday dinner and—after I text Evie and find out that Mom is out of the apartment on another one of her "night drives" around the harbor—drops me off in front of the bookshop. I just don't know what to say to him, not when he's all clammed up and pushing me away.

He's back to being intimidating and distant, and as I hand him back the sparkly tri-corn horse helmet, I'm weighing whether I should try to be gabby, like Mom, or serious, and tell him about all the things I realized in his garage.

But before I can speak up, a bright blue sports car with an obnoxious, thundering racing engine screeches its brakes in front of the shop. Hypnotic music thumps from the interior, and three pale, male faces look out at us. I don't know the two in the front, but the boy with his arm hanging out the back window is more than recognizable.

"What do we have here?" Adrian Summers drunkenly says. His face is still bandaged from the wreck with Evie, and he's got terrible bruises under both eyes. Two crutches are propped on the seat next to him. "It's the littlest Saint-Martin and Beauty's only one-man motorcycle gang. I smell collusion."

"And I smell vodka," Lucky says with feigned cheerfulness. "Do you have a liquor license for your bar-on-wheels? Gonna have to report you to town hall if you don't."

Adrian makes a sloppy shooing gesture to Lucky and points a water bottle at me, the contents of which aren't *quite* clear. "You. Is Wild Winona home?"

All my muscles tense. "Go away, Adrian."

"I need you to do me a favor. Go upstairs and tell Evelyn to come down here. She's not answering my texts, and I need to see her."

No way in hell am I doing that. The two guys in the front seat are staring out at us, chuckling, and they look as inebriated as Adrian. Not sure if they're Goldens or some of his Harvard buds, home for the summer.

"She's probably in class," I say.

"On Sunday?" Adrian says.

"She has a test," I tell him. Ugh, Lucky's right. I'm a terrible liar. She's only taking one class this summer, and Adrian probably knows it.

"It'll only take a minute. Tell her to come down now," he says, slapping the car door with his open palm twice. "Chop-chop."

"No one's telling Evie anything," Lucky says.

"Stay out of this," Adrian warns. "Not your fight."

"Not anyone's fight," I say. "I'll tell her you came by."

"But I'm here right now, and I came all this way. Come on," he says, "Go fetch Evie."

"I'm asking you nicely to please leave."

"What if I say no?"

Lucky swings off his bike. "Get the hell out of here, Summers."

"Or what? You'll punch me? Call the cops and get thrown in jail again? And why are the two of you always together? Methinks you got a little something going on."

"Not your business, is it?" Lucky says.

Adrian grins. "I mean, sure, she looks nice with her clothes off, but we've all seen it. Not worth it, man."

Adrian's buddies in the car laugh along with him.

Lucky swears profusely and starts to lunge for the car, but I grab his arm.

"Keep talking like that," I tell Adrian, hoping I sound braver than I feel, "and I'll make sure to remind Evie what kind of an asshole you are, and how she made the absolute right decision to stay away from you."

Adrian glares at me for a moment and then lazily points his water bottle at Lucky. "Haven't forgotten about you. Gonna get you back for that window, grease monkey. Eye for an eye . . ."

Signaling his buddies in the front seat, Adrian gives up on us, and the car peels away from the curb—causing a lone SUV on the otherwise empty road to slam on its brakes and honk when they cut in front of it without looking. Then they speed down the block and disappear into the night.

"Goldens . . . entitled pricks," Lucky grumbles. "You okay?"

I nod, feeling mildly creeped out. It was probably just boozy talk, nothing more. He won't remember it tomorrow. Still. It weirds me out that we're here alone. Maybe it shows on my face, because Lucky asks, "Hey. Do you want me to stick around, or . . . ?"

I shake my head. "We've got a security alarm. I'll lock the door and set it. And I'll text Mom. She'll come home."

"You sure?" he asks, wavering.

"Yeah," I say, hoping I sound more confident than I feel. "She could be on her way back any minute, so I should probably head up."

I need to check on Evie. Make sure Adrian isn't harassing her via texts.

"I'm only a few minutes away, if you get freaked out or need backup, or whatever. Not that you can't handle it yourself. But . . . you know."

"Thanks," I say, meaning it and hoping he knows it.

"And maybe you could let me know when your mom gets home? I'll be up for a while."

"Yeah, no problem. I will," I say, then gesture upstairs. "I'm gonna . . ."

"Yep."

"Good night."

"G'night," he says, still sounding concerned.

Everything I wanted to tell him from earlier gets lost under all this new worry. For a moment, I even worry that some of this is my fault—that maybe Adrian wouldn't have even stopped and threatened us right now if it weren't for me breaking the Summers & Co Department Store window. But I guess that's not true; he would've come to see Evie regardless.

After Lucky revs his Superhawk's engine a few times—his eyes on the street, as if he really wasn't quite sure Adrian was gone—he finally straps on his helmet and drives away from the curb.

Letting out a sigh, I head around the bookshop to the back of the building and jog up the steps. It's quiet now. Thank God. When I get to the top and stick my key in the door, I hear something in the distance that interrupts the quiet and gives me pause.

Racing engine. Thump of loud music.

They're coming back.

My pulse rockets. I take the key out of the lock when the brakes squeal.

Then I hear something worse. A terrible sound I know too well.

Glass shattering.

Oh God. No, no, no . . .

Taking the steps two at a time, I race back down and sail around the bookshop to find the sports car speeding off in the opposite direction on the dark street, its red taillights two glowing eyes. And across the road, the boatyard office window is gone. Shattered. Smashed. Glass tinkling from the open window frame onto the sidewalk.

What did Adrian say? An eye for an eye?

Problem is, he took out the wrong one.

It's like Summers & Co all over again, only this time it feels so much worse, because it—

Wasn't an accident.

And it's the boatyard window.

Not some retail object that showcases luxury goods, that can be replaced by the richest man in town with the snap of his fingers. No. The simple warehouse office window through which a big, happy family laughs.

This is personal.

An old man in a truck slows as he sees the damage.

"Hit and run!" I shout.

He pulls over at the curb, confused. I know the feeling. And that's when I remember the black cat.

Oh no!

I race across the street, holding up my hand to stop another approaching car, and crunch over broken glass, peering into the boatyard offices. I can't see! There are too many ambient street-lights making too many shadows. My heart's in my stomach, thinking about the poor animal. Lucky will be devastated if anything bad has happened to it.

One of the shadows shifts—above. On a tall filing cabinet.

Thank God.

I reach through the broken window and coax it into my open arms, snatching the warm body as it tries to lurch past me in a panic. Claws dig into my shoulders, but I don't care. "I've got you," I tell it, quickly moving to the side alley where it's less chaotic. "You're okay. Let's call your big brother."

I'm shaking as I pull out my phone and scroll to Lucky. He answers on the first ring, and I bluntly say, "Come back. Adrian broke the front boatyard window and drove away. Call your parents. I'll call the police. I've got your cat."

I don't even have to, though, as I already hear the wail of a siren competing with the shrill boatyard security alarm. I stand numbly in the dark alley, petting the twitchy black cat as scattered people begin jogging toward the dark, gaping hole in the building. And then it's:

Evie, racing down from the apartment.

Police lights.

Lucky's Superhawk.

His parents.

My mom.

An ambulance, which isn't needed, but sticks around—just in case.

A city clean-up crew.

And crowds of gawking people, well past midnight.

Mom opens up the bookstore and makes coffee for the Karrases and the police. Kat is furious. The black cat is relieved to be allowed to retreat into one of the boat-repair bays, away from all the chaos. And for the first time, I learn that it has a name. Saint Boo. Boo for short. The cat with seven lives at this point.

"I was twelve," Lucky explains when I question his name choice, the only chance I get to talk to him alone amongst the chaos for a few minutes. "And I swear to God, if Boo had been hurt by a flying piece of glass or ran out into traffic, I would've killed someone."

I believe him, and we both know who that someone is.

But now that the shock of it all is fading away, there's another emotion that's settling in, especially for Lucky's father: worry.

"Is it the money?" I ask. "To repair all this?"

He shakes his head. "I think it's more about being in a fight with Levi Summers. It's just a window, but a war with him could ruin our business."

My stomach twists.

It should have been our window.

It should have been our war.

I don't know what to do, but I'm a little scared, and I think maybe it's time to reevaluate my part in all this. No way can I let my original mistake cause an entire war that ruins a family business. Everything was so easy when we stepped into town. I had the three-step Los Angeles plan. Graduate from high school before my grandmother comes back from Nepal. Save up money. Prove to my father that I'm worthy of being his apprentice. . . .

Now I've already dipped into my savings to start helping Lucky pay for the window. And I can't even get up the nerve to email the stupid magazine about the internship because I'm a secret vandal and the nude photo of my mom, and, and—

Tick, tick, tick.

Breathe.

I'm going to figure this out. I will find a way to fix things somehow. But I know one thing. Whatever happens, I will not allow the Karrases to lose their business.

Los Angeles or not . . .

Mom doesn't know that I was coming back from Lucky's house when the boatyard window was broken. But she knows that I was outside the bookshop when Adrian drove up and demanded to talk to Evie. And Mom is *pissed*. And a little scared.

"If that really was Adrian who did it . . . ," she says a day later, when we watch four people installing a new window across the street.

"Of course it was him! Who else would it be?" Who else would hurl a crowbar at a window after drunkenly threatening people with that eye-for-an-eye speech? I don't understand how the police can't get fingerprints off it, but apparently they can't. He must have wiped it before he threw it.

Or someone in the police department is covering for him. . . .

"Why would an Olympic rower from Harvard be vandalizing windows in Beauty?" Mom says. "Evie? Would he really do that?"

"I couldn't really say," Evie murmurs.

Oh, but she could. She could say, all right. Evie doesn't want me to tell Mom—I think because she's so embarrassed that Adrian's such a toxic stalker, even though it's no reflection on her, duh—but she swore me to secrecy when she showed me all the drunken texts he sent her that night. Forty-three. Forty-three! And that's on top of eleven phone calls. Who does that? A maniac, that's who.

Then again, who throws a rock through a historic department store window?

Maybe I'm a maniac too.

Which maniac came first, the chicken or the egg?

After I insist again and again that it was Adrian, begging her to trust me on this one, Mom relents and tries to call up Adrian's father through his business number—just to talk—but he's not taking calls. And he's not the kind of guy to whom you can march up and demand justice. You can't just ring his doorbell. Guess when he's the one whose property is destroyed, he's available. When it's his son who's doing the destroying . . . well, he's a busy man.

Take a number.

When Wednesday rolls around, Mom locks up the store at noon for our half-day closing and walks next door to Freedom Art Gallery, where several neighborhood shop owners are gathering to talk about security. Hate to break it to them, but they are in zero danger from Wreck-It Ralph. Adrian doesn't care about their windows.

Evie is remarkably quiet about all of this. Pretty sure she's *far* more upset than she's letting on, but she says she needs time to think about things. So I'm giving her space. But I'm also thinking about those forty-three texts.

Maybe we've all got our ticking time bombs.

While Evie closes out the accounting up front, I pull all the empty book carts to the stockroom and line them up for receiving tomorrow, when we're supposed to be getting a big shipment from a distributor. At least that's what I *start* to do, until someone knocks on the stockroom door—the one that opens to the side of the house between the street and the alley.

Delivery people don't knock. They ring the bell.

Cautious, I unlock the door and peek through the crack to find Lucky's face staring back at me over a deep-red T-shirt. My heartbeat quickens.

"Hey," he says, one side of his mouth quirking upward. "Saw Winona heading to the neighborhood meeting next door. My mom's there too. Not sure if I'm still banned from these premises . . . ?"

"In Winona's eyes? I don't know; in this time of crisis, it's hard to tell. Would you like to risk it all and come inside for a minute?" *Please.*

"Isn't it *you* who's taking the risk? I'm not banned from seeing you."

I shrug, attempting to look casual, and open the door. "And I'm not good at following rules. Welcome to the stockroom."

"Sorry to disappoint, but I've been back here. Lots."

"You have?" I say, shutting the door behind him.

"Your grandmother lets me browse the new stuff before it goes out on the shelves."

She never let us come back here when we were kids. *Never*. Honestly, I'm surprised she allowed kids in the bookshop. She dislikes noise and disorganization.

"She also lets Saint Boo sleep in here sometimes when we go out of town."

Mouth open. Jaw on floor. "Beginning to have some serious suspicions that the Diedre Saint-Martin you've been acquainted with over the last few years is some kind of pod person," I tell him. "The grandma *I* know and love dislikes pets. She's also a rule-obsessed harpy who ruined my mom's life, and mine by extension, and listens to too much fiddle music."

"She *does* have a disturbing preoccupation with fiddling. Wonder if they fiddle in Nepal?"

"You must've missed her weekly postcards on the singing bowls and the flutes."

"Maybe she'll like that more than the fiddling and decide to stay. Never know . . ."

No chance.

"So . . ." I'm relieved he's standing here, an arm's length away. And anxious. And oddly fluttery. It's the first time I've been alone with him since Sunday dinner—minus broken glass and police cars—and I'm trying to hide all those feelings that are now tangled up in the new worries that have descended with Adrian's drunken stunt, so I busy myself with the empty carts. "How *is* Saint Boo? And what's the update on the window? I saw them calking it yesterday afternoon. Is it costing your parents a fortune?" *Should I be completely sick to my stomach? Because I am.*

"Boo is fine. As for the window . . ." He squeezes one eye closed.

"Oh boy. That's what I thought. I'm already downing expired Benadryl I found in my grandmother's medicine cabinet to make me drowsy enough to sleep at night."

"That sounds super not good," he says, frowning. "Don't do that."

"Evie says it's safe for cats and dogs and babies, so I figure it's okay for Josies."

"Look, the window is mostly installed and should be finished up by tomorrow. It wasn't cheap, but it was no Summers & Co by a long shot, so stop taking expired allergy medicine. Seriously. Okay?"

"Okay." I tap my fingers on the receiving table, a little nervous. "Any word from the Summers or the police?"

"There isn't such a thing as CCTV in Beauty, and no private security cameras caught them. The lady who owns Regal Cosmetics on the corner said she's willing to testify that she saw a blue car drive through here at that time, but she didn't see the actual crime. And neither did we. . . ."

"But we *know* he did it. And they never had me breaking the window on camera either."

"But they had my confession," he says. "And Adrian will flay the skin from his body before he confesses."

"Then what happens next?"

"I don't know, honestly. My dad's a little worried. I think some of the damage is covered by our insurance, but mostly he's concerned about Levi Summers and how it affects us long term, businesswise."

"He's your father's biggest customer?"

"Pretty much. But it's more than the actual dollars he pays us. If he takes his business away and tells other people to do the same . . ."

I nod. "Yeah, I get it. He can have you guys blacklisted."

"That's one way of putting it. He's got a lot of influence in this town. Owns a bunch of property. The department store. The newspaper."

The magazine, I think, but I definitely don't say it out loud.

"What are your parents going to do about it?" I ask.

He scrubs the back of his neck and shakes his head, shrugging with one shoulder. "They're just waiting to see how things shake out."

"Lucky?" I ask in small voice. "Do you think I should tell them that I broke the department store window? Would that help?"

His brow lowers. "Absolutely not. You said you wouldn't, Josie."

"But—"

"We already talked about this."

"Why, though? Wouldn't it be better for your parents if Levi Summers knew I did it? I don't want to ruin their business—this is my fault."

"What about LA? What about your father not taking you in if you have a police record? What about your mom putting you in a car and dragging you out of town before your grandmother even comes back—what about that, huh?"

Oh. Did I say that in the police station? Wait . . .

Is he worried I'm going to leave town again before Grandma comes back from Nepal? I try to catch his gaze with mine, but he won't look at me. His eyes light everywhere but on my face, and that's how I know for certain.

He's worried I'm going to leave.

Well.

To be honest, so am I.

"Okay, hey," I say. "I won't tell them I smashed the department store window."

His shoulders relax. "Okay."

"It's going to be fine."

"It's going to be fine," he repeats.

I'm not sure either of us believe that one hundred percent, but we're trying.

He taps his fingers on one of the book carts and looks around the stockroom at shelving filled with boxes of supplies and fixture parts—pegs and old signage and book stands—until his gaze pauses on the open door near the receiving desk. "That's new. Used to be sitting off its hinges and the inside overflowing with junk."

"Mom and I put it back on and I cleaned it out." I brush off my hands and walk to the walk-in closet. "Darkroom. See? A very rudimentary, very tiny one."

"You develop film in here?"

"Yep."

"How does it work?"

"Like this . . ."

He follows me inside. "Wow. Close quarters."

Man, he's not kidding. I should've thought this through. "Uh, well. It's normally just me in here."

"Right, yeah. Cool clock," he says, pointing to the wall. "Analog?"

"That's my timer." I try not to bump into his arm as I shuffle around him to flip on a lamp that sits on a makeshift plywood desk under the slanted part of the ceiling in the corner. Then I scoot past him, shut the door, and close a floor-length curtain over it.

"Cozy," he says.

"That's to ensure no light leaks in here from cracks," I tell him, a little nervous.

"Ah."

Best to stick to the technical details. "It already had ventilation, because someone started to turn this into a restroom at some point. So that's my fan going outside. Shelves below the desk for all my pans. Tools here. And I've kind of got things divided into a dry side here, and a wet side here, for my chemicals, see?"

"Looks dangerous."

"Only if you stick your face in it, so don't do that." I flip on the safelight bulb that's installed in the overhead socket, and the closet glows red. "Ta-da! That's what I use when I'm developing. Magic."

"Whoa," he says, turning his head to look around. His red shirt blends in with the walls. "It's like we're in a strip club."

"Uh . . ."

"Obviously I've never been in a strip club."

"Makes two of us. Does Beauty even have one?"

He snorts. "We still have strict bathing suit laws on the books. Technically, I think the town has the right to put you on trial for being a witch if you show your stomach on a public beach."

"Beauty, Where Modern is Just a Word We Use for Our Furniture."

"Beauty, Where IKEA is a Little *Too* Progressive," he says.

I chuckle and try another one. "Beauty, Where Tabasco Sauce is Sort of Unnecessary, Really?"

Then he says: "I've been one of your anonymous Photo Funder subscribers since you started the account."

I open my mouth, but nothing comes out.

"I'm sorry I didn't tell you," he says, lashes covering eyes that stare at the floor between us. "I wanted to, but I was worried you'd think it was weird. Especially after what Adrian said about nudes at the party and him flashing that pic of your mom."

My brain tries to make sense of it. "I started that account last summer. I was living in . . ." Where? I can't even remember where Mom and I were. "Massachusetts."

"Your grandmother told me about it."

I stare at his shirt, the color of it disappearing in the safelight's eerie glow. My pulse swishes inside my temples so loudly that I can't think straight. "She told you about my photography subscription account? You've been following me online for . . . a year?"

"Well, your photos. You don't really say anything personal— just the photo descriptions. You don't even have a recent selfie posted, so it's not like I've been spying on you."

"I don't care about that. I care about the fact that you've been there all this time and haven't said anything to me. This whole time? We could have been talking *all this time*? Why didn't you say anything?"

"I don't know. . . ." His brow furrows like he's a little unsure, and he finally admits, "I wanted to get back in touch with you somehow, but I didn't know how to go about doing it. When I found out about your website, at first, I thought it was the perfect way to reconnect. But then I lost my nerve to speak up, so I just sort of stayed in the shadows. I'm sorry. I should have told you sooner."

"You should have told me!"

"You're mad."

"I'm not mad, I'm . . ."

"What?"

"I don't know. I guess I'm hurt that you didn't reach out to me and say hello," I say, getting flustered. "No one in my family communicates normally, so I was led to believe . . . I thought your family moved away from Beauty, okay? I didn't even know you were still here. We could have been friends online. Mom and I have come to visit every year or so—were you at Evie's dad's funeral?"

"We were out of town that weekend. We went to the wake the night before—"

Oh. Mom and I didn't make it into town until late that night, after the wake.

I shake my head, "It doesn't matter now. You should've told me it was you online."

"I'm sorry, okay?" he says, a little angry . . . a little desperate.

We were so close, yet so far. Connected by my photos but separated by his anonymity. The sorrow of this catches me off guard and tightens inside my chest.

"I checked that old email account of mine for years, hoping you'd reply to my last email. You don't know how lonely I was, Lucky."

"About the same as me?" he challenges, dark eyes narrowing. "Or maybe a little less, seeing as how you got to leave, and I was stuck here, all alone. You were off seeing the world, but I was trapped."

"Lucky, Mom and I were *literally* living in Section 8 housing before we moved to Beauty. Do you know what that is?"

"So? You haven't been trapped. You've traveled. You've seen things."

Oh, I've seen things, all right.

But . . . But. I guess I never thought about it that way. Maybe he has a point.

He lifts a hand. "Now look at you. Don't even want to be here anymore. All you think about is running off to Malibu to live with a man you don't even know—that's how much you hate it here?"

"Hey!" I snap. "You may remember that people are circulating nude photos of my mother around town and saying that it's me, making kissy faces at me when I walk down the street—okay? And this jet-setter life of mine that you're painting in your mind has been gossiped about and criticized at Beauty High since the day I walked through the doors. So don't make it sound like I've had the red carpet rolled out for me."

"And don't make it sound like you haven't had anyone to help you fix that. Because both me and my family are now shouldering the load for you."

"Didn't ask you to. Have said a million times that I will turn myself in."

"If you do, I'll never forgive you."

Breath comes faster through my nostrils.

He wants honesty from me? Fine. Let's do this.

"Is that why you did it?" I ask.

"Did what?"

"Is that why you took the fall for me? For the department store window? Because you're scared my mom's going to take me away again, and you're trying to keep me here?"

Surprise widens his eyes—just for a moment. It's quickly replaced by anger.

"I did it for a lot of reasons."

"Oh really?"

"Really."

"Name one," I challenge.

"Okay, fine. You want to know one reason why?"

"Yes."

"One reason I did it is because what happened at the party that night was shitty, and you were upset, and that made me upset, and Adrian Summer is obviously a complete asshole, so, yeah. It was unfair that you were going to get dragged through the mud for a stupid window that his dad can afford to replace a million times over. So I thought, what did it matter if I got dirty? Because unlike you, I actually *do* deserve to get punished. I'm not good. I'm a scarred-up monster who nearly got his little cousin killed because I wasn't watching her when I should've been, so what does it matter? That's one reason why I did it," he says, his face a rocky cliff being thrashed by a sea of dark emotions. "Because I deserve it."

I blink.

The red safelight glows above our heads in the cramped

darkroom, but the light inside my head is clear and bright: Lucky hasn't gotten over the fire at the lake house. The rumors. The bad reputation. The sullen attitude. The detention. I watch the turbulent emotions swirling around his face until they change into something else that I can't quite identify.

"I should go," he says in a rough voice, eyes on the floor, trying to move around me.

I block the door with my body.

He looks shocked.

I'm surprised, myself.

"You can't live in the past, always thinking about the lake house fire," I tell him. "You're not a monster, and you don't deserve to be punished for something that happened years ago. Your cousin survived. *You* survived."

"Some days it feels like it just happened yesterday, and everyone still blames me for not watching her."

"You can't really believe that."

His chest rises and falls as he gazes down at me, blinking in tremolo. "Oh, okay. So I guess you're going to tell me what I can and can't believe now?" he says, as if he desperately, secretly wants me to but is far too proud to ask.

"If you're going to believe stupid things, then, yes. That's my duty as your friend."

He snorts softly. "Oh, you mean like your stupid love curse?"

"Hey, tell it to my mom. She's the one who says it's ruined all the Saint-Martins' love lives."

"Has it, though?" he asks as if he's eager not to talk about himself anymore.

"I've never been in love, so don't have any firsthand experience." I try to make a lighthearted joke. "Guess I was too busy traveling the world—and I guess *you* were just plain busy. Maybe not with Bunny, but I know there have been other girls. Come on."

He frowns. "Are you accusing me of something, here, or . . . ?"

"No. I don't—" I huff out a breath. Wow. I sound like a jealous girlfriend, accusing him of cheating. That went in a weird direction, and he's still upset, and I'm doing this all wrong . . . and I wish I could take it back.

"I don't know why I said that," I finally admit.

But I do. I wish it would have been me and not those other girls.

I can't say it, though. Not that. I can't be that teeth-gratingly honest.

It's quiet. Still. Almost stifling. We've been in here too long, breathing all the air in the small space.

"I need to go," he says softly. "Move."

"No."

He's surprised by that.

He exhales a hard breath through his nostrils. Silent. Studying my face. The longer he stares at me, not saying anything, the faster my heart races. I try to look anywhere but his eyes. The sharp shadow under his jaw. The bob of his Adam's apple when he swallows. The line of his collarbone against his T-shirt.

Warm fingers graze mine.

My hand trembles as if it's a rabbit caught in a snare. I know he can feel it, because I'm looking between us, and I can see the tremor as our fingers twine. I'm a little bit terrified. But I don't move away.

"Josie," he whispers near the top of my head.

No choice now.

When I tilt my face upward, he's right there. So close. Sharing the last of the air in the tiny room. Both of our faces lit up like we're at the last subway stop at midnight; both of us gripping each other like we don't want to get off.

"Move," he whispers.

I shake my head slowly.

His eyes are hooded and lazy as they survey my face. He leans closer, closer, and says against my lips, "Move . . . Josie."

And when I open my mouth to tell him no, he kisses me.

Softly, once.

Again.

Then I kiss him back.

And that's the tipping point, right there. He lets go of my fingers to cup my face, and we're kissing each other like there truly is no air left in the tiny closet. As if we're locked in some kind of escape room and fighting for our lives—our very survival depends on the maximum amount of pleasure we can derive from one deep, long kiss, and *my God*, are we going to endure.

A hurricane could hit. Tectonic plates could grind and shift below our feet. A legendary sea monster could rise from the harbor and wrap its tentacles around ships, trying to drown the people of this town, and we wouldn't care.

We would endure.

I wrap my arms around him like I do when I'm on the back of his bike, only it's a hundred times better holding him from the front, especially when he presses his weight against me and we both fall into the door together. I lose my balance and grab the darkroom curtain, but one of the curtain rings pops open where it's attached to the rod above the door—then another. One, two, three . . . And the fabric starts to fall down on our heads.

"Oh shit," he says, untangling us from the falling fabric, one hand on my lower back, pulling me away with him.

"It's okay," I whisper. "I can fix it. Not broken."

He's breathing heavily. So am I. And for a moment, I think he's going to let go of me, and I'm about to shout that I really do not care about the stupid curtain, and then—

Then he's pulling me closer. Good lord, he feels nice. I feel nice.

We both feel nice.

He's nuzzling my neck, close to my ear, and I really, *really* want him to kiss me again. The tremble in my hand is gone. It's been hijacked by a wave of warm tingles that spreads all the way up my arms and lights up each one of my cells from the inside out, and—

"Josie?"

Muffled voice. Stockroom. Evie.

We push away from each other in a panic, breathing like marathon runners. Seems we've failed the escape room and must now face the consequences.

I wipe my mouth with the back of my hand.

He pulls down his T-shirt to cover the front of his jeans.

Well.

Evie calls my name again, and there's no way in hell we're sneaking out of this darkroom. No. Way.

She's going to know what we've been doing in here, and—

Oh my God.

I just made out with Lucky.

My best friend.

And you know what? I'd do it again.

Maybe I am cursed, after all.

REBEL ALLEY 1768: Historic marker sign posted in the cobblestone alley behind Siren's Book Nook. The alley was used to transport illegal seditious material from the printer during the Revolutionary War. *(Personal photo/ Josephine Saint-Martin)*

14

The tingly good feelings we cooked up together in the darkroom linger long after Lucky coolly raises his hand to Evie in greeting and slinks out of the stockroom the same way he came in, like it was no big deal.

Like he's used to kissing his childhood best friend until her legs are wobbly.

And see, I know that Lucky and I must have done something shocking, because Evie says not one word to me after Lucky leaves—*not one word*. She just stares, mouth open and shaped like the full moon, as I hurriedly try to hide the evidence of our crime by stuffing the broken curtain inside my darkroom and shutting off my red safelight.

"Do *not* tell my mom" is the only thing I tell her.

And thankfully, she doesn't give me away when Mom soon returns from the neighborhood meeting. And Mom, oblivious as ever, doesn't notice anything amiss.

"Well, ladies, that was a waste of time," she announces.

"Oh?" I say, pretending like I care as I fiddle with the CLOSED sign on the front door of the Nook, eyes darting across the street toward the boatyard, heart racing.

He kissed me.

Mom throws her keys on the counter and sits on the squeaky stool. "The business owners on our block have decided that there is no possible way Adrian Summers—handsome, talented, Olympic-hopeful, son of a prominent member of our community—could have possibly destroyed the boatyard window in retribution against Lucky. He's too mature for that. He wouldn't endanger his career at Harvard. He's on crutches, poor thing."

Evie groans and rubs her temples with the tips of her fingers, careful to avoid the whirls of heavy black makeup framing her eyes.

I'm just trying to focus on the words Mom's saying, because all I heard was "Lucky."

He kissed me, and I kissed him.

I feel like maybe I need to lie down. Or something.

"I'm sorry," Evie says.

"Never apologize," Mom tells her. "Women do that too much for things that aren't our fault. And this is definitely not your fault."

Mom tried to argue with the rest of the shop owners. Tried to tell them what Adrian said to me and Lucky. That he was in the blue car with the other boys, drinking and speeding down the street. The car that the old woman from Regal Cosmetics spied from her window.

"Even Kat Karras backed me up," Mom says, "if you can believe that."

We had our hands all over each other.

I laugh nervously.

"You okay, shutterbug?"

"I'm *so good*," I tell her, and immediately regret saying it that way, ugh.

She makes a weird face at me and then shakes her head, as if to say, *Whatever, kid.*

"Anyway," she says, "Kat and I were shot down. Mob rules, and the mob supports the Summers family. No one saw Adrian do it, and everyone loves Adrian. Therefore, it must have been some tourist hooligans that broke the boatyard window. Unrelated to the department store window. One person suggested Lucky might have done it himself—that maybe he's got a thing about breaking windows now. Some kind of gang initiation."

"What?" Evie and I both say in unison.

"That's ridiculous," I add.

Mom cleans her cat-eye glasses on the front of her shirt, then squints in the light to check the lens. "Yep. That's when Kat and Nick stormed out of the meeting," Mom says. "Hard to blame them. This town is what happens when puritans and greedy rich people breed."

"What happened to all our revolutionary resistance fighters who fought for freedom and justice?" I ask. "Beauty wasn't always bad . . . right?"

"Our revolutionary spirit got stamped out of the town when people like the Summers family figured out they could use it to make a profit out of tourism," Mom says.

"Well, what do we do now?"

Mom shrugs. "I don't know, babe. I'm hoping Adrian will stay away and let this thing die down now. But Evie, maybe you shouldn't engage with him anymore if he texts?"

"Trying," she says.

Seeing as how Lucky and I are pretty much the epicenter of the event that sparked the neighborhood meeting—broken windows, all that—you'd think he'd be interested in discussing what happened at that meeting, kiss or no kiss. I expect he'll have a sarcastic opinion about it, and it will come via text any second now.

Any second.

I mean, maybe he's busy.

He's still trying to balance working at Summers & Co and the boatyard. And I don't see his Superhawk parked outside, so he could be doing something with his family. I don't know what he does every single minute of his day.

I'm sure he'll text when he gets a chance.

But I don't hear from Lucky that night . . . or the next day.

Or the next.

Two days . . .

Okay. Two days is definitely a long time, and that's when I'm suddenly filled with a strange kind of panic that feels like thin ice forming over my skin, cracking, and re-forming . . . over and over again.

I go over everything in my head again—the entire conversation we had in the darkroom before everything happened. I worry I said something wrong, or I didn't say enough. I worry about his state of mind regarding what he went through in the fire at the lake house, and that maybe we should have talked about that more.

God. I hope I didn't pressure him into kissing me. I mean, I blocked the door. He asked me to move. Was all of it one-sided? Did I read the signals wrong? I don't think so. . . . At least, I didn't at the time.

Or maybe it was none of that. Maybe he just changed his mind and decided that kissing his best friend was too weird and squicky. *Please, please, please don't let that be it.*

I could just ask him. That would clear things up.

Be upfront and honest: Are you awash in strange, new feelings for me? Because I can't stop thinking about you, and you're messing up all my plans, and now I need to know if I'm under a dark generational curse, or if you feel the same way, because I've never done this before, and I don't know what I'm doing.

I think about texting him several times. I even compose a practice message, but before I hit Send, Evie walks behind the bookshop counter and catches me in the act.

"Want a little advice from Madame Evie the Great?" she says, dark circles under her eyes. "The spirits would tell you not to send that. Let him come to you. Or even better, just let him go. Chasing

Adrian when he ghosted me after our first date got me where I am now, and I regret it completely."

I'm a little insulted she'd even lump Lucky and Adrian into the same group; then again, she's got more experience in these matters. Maybe she's right and I should just wait. The more I hesitate, the more unsure I become . . . until all I end up doing is watching Lucky come and go, wondering what I did wrong, from the bookshop window.

I try not to think about it. When I'm not working, I load a fresh roll of film into my Nikon F3 and stroll through the historic district, snapping some interesting closeup shots of the horse-drawn carriages and one of the drivers, dressed in colonial costume. I'm concentrating so hard on my work, I'm able to ignore a kissy-face gesture thrown my way by a random Golden across the Harborwalk. *Don't know you, don't care.* But when I spy someone familiar eating at a café—my teacher, Mr. Phillips, his round Harry Potter glasses glinting in the afternoon sun—I get nervous that he's heard about me trying to hustle my way back into the magazine offices, and that's just too much; I cap the lens of my camera and head back home before he sees me.

At lunch on the third day of radio silence, I'm *still* wondering about Lucky while shelving books in the psychology section when I hear a couple of noises that catch my attention. The first is a dog barking outside the shop. Not out of the ordinary. Lots of dog owners on our street.

The second thing is Mom talking at the register. Again, nothing unusual. It's the tone of her voice that's alarming. She's using her Not Friendly tone. And when I peer around the antique printing machine in the middle of the shop to see who she's talking to—when I see the tiny black dog on the leash that's tied up outside our steps—I understand why.

I stride around the Nook's printing machine, heart racing.

"Of course you can. It's a free country," Mom is telling Lucky, who is standing in front of the counter with his back to me, black leather jacket stretched across his broad shoulders and jeans hanging low on his hips like he's a walking, talking advertisement for sexy rebel-without-a-cause teenage dreams. "Not going to kick you out of the store. I'm just asking why it is you're here, is all. If you're not buying anything. And why is that dog yapping?"

"He's Bean the Magic Pup, and he's trying to tell you that he wants to come inside. He hates being outside when he can see people inside."

"I hate dogs," Mom says, making a face. "They pee on things."

"He's house-trained. Mostly."

"Nope. He's not coming inside. Why are you here?"

"Trying to tell you," he says, sliding something across the counter.

She frowns. "What is this?"

"Looks like cash," he says. "A hundred and fifty dollars, to be exact."

Mother of God.

"Hi, uh. Hi. H-hi," I say in the most awkward way possible,

sliding around the side of the counter. A tiny earthquake shakes me from the inside out at the sight of his long black lashes and the playful swoop of his hair. I'm not prepared for this. I can't see him here—not in front of my mom. She's going to know something happened between us. Isn't it obvious? Every molecule in my body remembers. They're practically shouting.

LUCKY. LUCKY. LUCKY.

I've got a tangle of weird emotions about why he hasn't texted me, and I'm very panicked right now, but . . .

But I still want him.

The worst part is that *he knows*. He sees it all over my face, the wanting, and he lights up like a city skyscraper at midnight.

His scarred eyebrow lifts. And *oh*, the evil look behind his eyes. In the history of the world, no one has smirked like he's smirking. This smirk of his is sly. It's full of knowing. It says, *Why yes, I kissed your face off, and we both know it was damn good, but here I am, turning the tables on you. And there's nothing you can do about it.*

Dead. Me. Go ahead and call an ambulance, because I'm going to have a heart attack right now, right here. Goodbye.

"Good afternoon," he says, like he's a Jehovah's Witness, come to save my soul with a pamphlet and a smile. "I was just asking your mother here about hiring out your services."

"Were you, really?"

"I was, yes. Need a photographer."

"Is that right?"

"Yep."

"Quick job. Need some photos of the boatyard."

"The boatyard."

"The front window, back bays. The crane. The docks."

Bean the Magic Pup sees me and scratches at the glass on our door to come inside, pink tongue hanging out of his mouth.

"Why?" Mom asks.

Lucky lifts his face to hers. "We just got the new window put in, and the trim and paint is different. You may have noticed."

We both stare at him.

"Anyway," he continues, "My parents want to update our website photo of the front of the business. So might as well update the others while we're at it. We've just got standard phone photos up there now. Would be nice to have more professional shots. If that was something Josie could do?"

"Of course she could," Mom says, like he just insulted both of us. Like it was a challenge, and she just fell for it.

Wait a minute. She's actually buying into his scheme? Correction: *my* scheme. Because I thought of it first. I think I'm actually a little miffed at him now. I don't care how pretty he is, or how much I want to stick my hands deep inside his leather jacket. Why is he even wearing that thing? It's hot outside, for the love of Pete.

"She's really good," she tells him. "Don't know if you've seen her work online, but she has a website you can browse. One of those subscriber things?"

"Mom," I say weakly. Ambulance. 911. Emergency. Dying.

"Yes, I have seen it," he says, suppressing a smile as I discreetly try to step on the toe of his boot. It's got some kind of reinforced steel thing inside it. Won't budge. He shifts his boot to the side and says, "All the sign photos. Really cool."

Mom crosses her arms and nods. "It *is* really cool. She's got a good eye. But as for this job . . . It's for your parents?"

"It is," he says.

"They know about it?"

"They do. You want to call my mom?"

She doesn't answer. Just considers it for a moment while she shifts on the squeaky chair and says, "Suppose it's up to Josie, not me."

I blink at her. I blink at him.

"I've got work here in the Nook right now," I tell him.

"That's okay," he says. "I'm on a break. Just finished up at the department store, and I'm about to start a shift with my dad. It would probably be better to do the photography after the boatyard's closed, so you wouldn't have everyone in the way. And isn't there something about the light being better right before twilight . . . ?"

"Golden hour," I say, smiling tightly. *You bastard.*

He snaps his fingers. "That's it."

"It's a real thing," Mom says, completely clueless. "Right, shutterbug?"

Oh my God. Lucky is eating this up. I want to kick him in the shin.

He clears his throat and says in a cheery voice, "So, golden hour? I can meet you in front of the boatyard office. I'll show you which things to shoot. Shouldn't take all that long, I wouldn't think? But if that's not enough money—?"

Kick him in the shin, strangle him . . . Maybe he's the one who needs the ambulance, not me. "Oh, it'll be enough."

"Hey," Mom says. "If you do this, I want to make it clear that I'd be right across the street, and I will not be picking up anyone at the police station again. You have to earn my trust back, Lucky."

"Understood," he says. "Zero police stations."

"You're not in contact with Adrian Summers, are you?" she asks. "Because I know our neighborhood is filled with buffoons, and I'm not saying I don't believe that Adrian wasn't the one who smashed the boatyard window. But whatever's going on, I have to ask—this hasn't turned into a turf war or anything, has it?"

"Turf war? Jesus, Mom. There's no turf in Beauty. This isn't a football rivalry."

"I *have* heard there's bad blood between the clam shacks," Lucky says.

Mom has a low tolerance for smartass-ery, so I expect her to give him the ol' Saint-Martin glare, but she just patiently tells him, "You know what I mean. I don't want my daughter caught up in the crossfire of anything."

What about your daughter *causing* the crossfire? How would you feel about that, huh? My stomach twists around the old lie of the department store window, and I try not to look at Lucky's face, because it only makes me feel worse.

"No ma'am, there's no contact between me and Adrian Summers," he tells her. "However, I did hear through the grapevine today that his father sent him to Providence to stay with his aunt for a while. Mom says his father's trying to keep him out of town until the dust settles."

Okay, that's actual real news. Out of the corner of my eye, I spy Evie's worried face peering out from behind a rack of local postcards. She's been listening, and apparently she didn't know this either, because she speaks up and says, "Adrian went to his aunt Cynthia's house?"

"Yeah," he tells her. "My mother found out through someone in our family."

"Probably for the best," Mom says. "Well, I guess this photography project at the boatyard is all right, then. If Josie has time . . ."

I straighten a stack of bookmarks on the counter, keeping my eyes down. "I have time."

There's nothing more we can say in front of my mom, so he just thanks us and leaves the store, fetching Bean the Magic Pup on his way.

Mom watches him go, a look of confusion on her face. "I'll never understand why people choose to own pets. They just die and break your heart."

"Jesus, Mom. Way to look at the world. Bean is actually kind of cute."

"You're scared of dogs."

"I know," I grumble.

She sighs. "Wonder if I should walk across the street and talk to Kat about this."

Um, no. Disaster! Absolutely not. Then she might find out I went to their house for Sunday dinner, or that I hired Lucky to give me seasickness, piloting me around the harbor.

"I don't think that's necessary," I tell her.

Her eyes dart toward mine. "Still not sure about you hanging around that boy."

Yeah, well.

She'd be even less sure if she knew what we did in the darkroom.

I braid my hair. Unbraid it. Brush it a thousand times. Dark makeup. Light makeup. Wash it all off. Try again. Okay, this is stupid, because the only thing I need is my best jeans—the one pair of jeans that fits so absolutely perfectly, I can completely relax when I'm wearing them. Those jeans. I'm wearing them and my perfect black flats, and the rest doesn't matter.

It's just Lucky.

It was just a kiss.

After the Nook closes, I use my digital camera to get some experimental shots of the Karrases' new window from the across the street between breaks in the traffic. They're a bit more *Art* than the Karrases would probably prefer. They just want pictures for a website; any monkey with a DSLR could take them. But I'm a little wired and anxious right now, and everything in my lens is hyper saturated and full of odd angles.

It's just Lucky.

It was just a kiss.

Lucky and his leather jacket are waiting for me—no Bean this time—when I cross the street and make it over to him, super cool, my camera hanging around my neck, best jeans and perfect flats. . . . You can do this, everything is fine . . .

"Hey."

One word. That's all he says. And all at once, my body suddenly turns into a dark cave filled with a thousand bats that are all trying to escape in a panic, flapping their batty wings and gnawing at my insides with their tiny vampire teeth.

O-o-o-h, what is happening to me?

Must calm down.

Maybe he doesn't notice, because his gaze swings from me to the windows above the Nook. "So . . . is that your mom watching us from your apartment?"

"Yes, indeed-y," I say, moving around him to get a better angle of the boatyard's sign.

"Wow. Okay. I didn't think she meant it *that* literally. About watching us."

"She did."

"What's wrong?" he asks.

Tiny bat wings. So nervous.

"Nothing. Can you move? You're blocking . . ."

"Oh, sorry. Is that better?"

"Yep. Thanks."

"Josie?"

"Are these real photos that your parents want, or is this just a ruse?"

"No," he says as early evening traffic speeds past us, bumping along the setts. "I mean, yes. I told my mom about this. She said it would be nice to have better photos on the website. They need to print new catalogs, so she'll use them there, too. It's legit."

"I just didn't want to waste my time if this is fake."

"You mean, fake like when you hired me to pilot you around the harbor?"

"That was a completely real scam to pay you back for the department store window. And just when I'd scrimped and saved up enough dough to hire Captain Lucky again—"

"Puke buckets will cost you extra, by the way."

"—you went and pulled this stunt, and now I'm back where I was before. So thanks?"

"You're most welcome."

"Thanking you most unkindly."

He chuckles and leans against an iron hitching post with a molded horse head—one of a hundred that dot the old streets around town. "So, hey . . . How have you been?"

I adjust a setting on my camera. "Fine, fine. Working at the Nook, makin' that *cash*," I say in a ridiculous voice, immediately regretting it. I sound nervous. But Lucky looks completely calm and cool, as usual, so now I'm wondering if this is a one-sided nervousness, and that only makes the bats in my chest flutter faster.

"And you . . . You've been busy, I take it," I say. It comes out sounding more agitated than I intend, but I'm just so. Unbelievably. Palm-sweatingly. Anxious.

It's jUsT LuCky.

It wAs jUsT a kIsS.

He frowns and scratches the back of his neck. "Yeah. It's been weird around here lately."

"The boatyard window, you mean?"

"That's definitely been a big point of stress. You heard about what happened at the neighborhood meeting right? Nobody believes Adrian did it."

"I heard."

"Wow," he mumbles, turning his head. "She's really watching us like a hawk."

I glance across the street at our apartment window.

"Does she know?"

"What?" My eyes flick to his. "Know what?"

He lightly kicks the iron hitching post with the heel of his boot. "Never mind."

Wait, wait, wait—we *almost* made it to The Topic. Then he backed down.

"Of course she doesn't know," I say, adjusting my lens. "I haven't even told her I went to Sunday dinner at your house. You think I'm going to tell her about . . . ?"

"The darkroom," he finishes, voice deep and husky.

"The darkroom," I repeat, feeling a little lightheaded. "She'd only say I've activated the curse. Nope. She can never know. Ever. I'll bury her first. It's the Saint-Martin way. She keeps her love life secret, so that's exactly what I'll be . . ." I trail off. I realize as soon as it's out of my mouth that I said "love life."

It's only supposed to be Lucky. My friend. *Friend* life, not love life! Can I get a do-over?

I snap five photos in row. All unnecessary. All poorly framed.

Lucky. Kiss. Uncertainty. Good jeans not helping. Bats! Bat escaping!

I can't hold it in any longer, so here comes the honesty. I'm lifting the invisible wall.

Hope he's happy.

"Look," I say in a low voice, as if my mother can somehow hear us all the way through a closed window and across a street filled with traffic. "I don't know if you regret what we did, or maybe it was no big deal to you, but it meant something to me, and I've been really confused that you've just sort of ghosted me over the last few days. I don't know what we're doing, but I really hate not talking to you."

"Wow, okay."

"Or we can make small talk."

"No, stop," he says, holding up a hand. "Don't do that. Don't put the wall back up—please. Just . . . give me a second. I'm trying to sort it all out. Why would you think it didn't mean something to me?"

I lower my camera and look at him. "Did it?"

"You first."

"I already went first."

One corner of his mouth lifts. He shoves his hands into the pockets of his jeans and glances across the street at the half-timbered historical houses that face the harbor. "Okay. Maybe it did. Yes. It did . . . unless we're talking about different kinds of 'something' that it meant, in which case I'd like to change my answer."

A swell of emotion catches me off guard, and I'm surprised to feel my eyes welling up. Oh no—Temper Tears. Those stupid, out-of-control, I-want-to-punch-something tears.

"Josie! Hey, I was just joking."

"These are tears of frustration," I say, swiping at my eyes and getting myself under control. Ugh. I turn my head away and pray my mother doesn't see this.

"Are you mad at me?" he asks in a softer voice.

"I'm not—" My voice breaks. I clear my throat and blow out a hard breath. There. Better. "I'm not mad. I'm confused," I explain. "You kissed me, and then you left me hanging in the breeze, and I didn't know what was happening. I didn't know if you'd changed your mind, or if you'd hated it, or felt guilty or if it was terrible—how am I supposed to know? I've never kissed anyone before . . . not really. Not like that."

"What? Come on." His face is contorting into strange expressions. He makes a sound that's almost a laugh, but not quite. Then he blinks at me. "You're serious."

I hesitate and glance across the street at our apartment windows. Mom's silhouette is gone, but then reappears. She's still checking on us. Lucky sees it too and swears colorfully under his breath.

"This is ridiculous. Listen to me," he says in a calm voice. "You're taking photos—that's all. Now we're going around back to finish the job. Okay? Come on."

I follow him through the alley, his heavy boots crunching the occasional piece of loose gravel, until the harbor comes into sight, and we turn the corner into the back of the boatyard.

"Do you want a picture of the bays open or closed?" I ask, trying in vain to put the invisible wall back up now that we're alone, because I'm suddenly very scared of what we're going to say to each other.

"That was just to get away from Winona. Forget the damn pictures," he says in exasperation, standing in front of me on the stained concrete as gulls squawk in the distance. "Just talk to me, okay? Were you serious?"

"About what?"

"What you just said."

Oh. That. I lean back against a short brick wall that sticks out between the mechanic bays and the alley, tapping my camera against the leg of my jeans. "Why do you want to know? Because it's weird that I'm seventeen and you're the first person I've made out with?"

He pushes hair out of his eyes and says, "It's not weird."

"Then why? Because it was bad."

"It wasn't."

"*I* was bad."

"No." Dark eyes meet mine. "Definitely no. All the noes in the world baked into a giant cake and covered in no frosting."

I smile and scrunch up my face. "Okay."

"It was amazing," he says.

I exhale. "Okay, good, because I thought so too. I mean, I have nothing to compare it to, but I've had some really tempting offers—like, Big Dave on a daily basis."

"Don't make me serve time for murder, because I would chop him up into pieces."

"That sounds super protective."

"Too protective?"

"No." I shake my head. Then I whisper, "What are we doing, Lucky? If it was so good, then why didn't you text me? Is it because we've made a terrible mistake?"

"Because—" He scrubs the back of his neck furiously. Turns around, paces a couple of steps, and then returns. "Because of Los Angeles. You aren't staying here in Beauty, Josie. I've known that since I saw you looking at flight schedules in the Nook when you first came back into town. I can't go through it again. I can't . . . I can't lose you all over again."

"I don't want to lose you, either."

"And what we're doing now? Josie . . . this is adding a whole other level to things. It's going to hurt."

"I know that," I say, my voice getting smaller.

"But . . . ?"

I frown. "Why did you say it that way?"

"Because I know there's a 'but' coming. You're about to tell me about that ticking time bomb, and your grandmother coming back, and how your mom can't live in the same house with her."

I wilt against the wall. Well? Those things are true. "I can't make my mom and my grandmother magically get along. I'm seventeen, broke, and the only resource I have is Henry Zabka. That's it. That's my only card to play."

"That can't be the only solution."

"Name a better one," I challenge. "Go on. Name one. Stick around with my mom? Because I love her to pieces, but you have no idea what it's like to be dragged around from town to town—no idea, Lucky. I can't keep living like that. There's no future in that for me. I feel lost all the time, and scared. And completely unstable. I wake up in the middle of the night and can't find my way to the bathroom because I can't remember which apartment I'm in—I can't remember which town I'm in!"

"Let me help you."

"How?"

"I don't know."

I huff out a hard breath.

"I really don't," he admits, gesturing openly with both hands. "I'm sorry. I haven't figured that part out. But there's got to be another viable solution."

If there was, he'd be offering it up. Mister genius. Perfect SAT score.

"I came up with this plan before I knew you were here," I say. "It wasn't perfect, but it was a way out. Now it's all completely messed up, and that's before I even consider any of . . . whatever this is," I say, gesturing between us. "So you don't have to tell me that it's flawed, because I already know that, okay? If it wasn't flawed, I'd be knocking down the door of *Coast Life* magazine, begging them to reconsider me for the internship."

"Hey. If you still want to go for that magazine internship, fine. Go for it—I mean, yes, you'd be working for a magazine that's owned by a man who spawned Adrian Summers, but that's your business."

"Not fair," I say, pouting.

"But seriously," he says, holding up a hand, "if you want it, go for it. And if you want to be with your dad, if that is your one true dream, I would *never* stand in your way. But if it's not? If it's just a means to an end? If it's just a place to run to? Then let me help you figure out an alternate route."

"Why would my dad be a place to run to? He's rich and famous, and he's one of the most talented photographers working right now."

Lucky sighs heavily. "Come on, Josie. It's me."

"I need to think about all this."

He nods several times. "That's fair."

A terrible sadness falls upon me, draining all my energy. He's right about a lot of things. I know better than anyone: Making attachments with people that you're going to have to leave hurts. It's why I never do. Ever. But here I am, breaking my own rules. Rushing back into old habits with him—and worse. Trying to make new habits with him.

"Maybe we should stay away from each other until this gets sorted out," I say, a little dazed. "I guess that's what you were trying to do over the last few days." Detachment.

"No."

"No?"

He shakes his head, pries my fingers away from my camera, and sets it atop the brick wall. Then he wraps his arms around me and pulls me against him.

"Dammit," I whisper into his shirt.

"I know," he says against my head. "I know."

"If this is a pity hug . . ."

"Shut up. It's not a pity hug. Let me hold you, okay? You could try holding me back. If it won't kill me, then it won't kill you."

My arms are folded up between us. My last line of defense. "You don't know that. It might. I'm cursed, remember?"

"Told you already, I don't believe in curses."

"Doubt they care if you believe or not," I tell him, allowing myself to loll against his shoulder and chest—just a little. But I keep my arms folded up like a bird's wings. I can hear his heart thumping, steady and strong, faster than I'd expect. I try to concentrate on it until my muscles relax a little more. He smells really good. I'd forgotten already.

"We're going to figure this out, okay?" His deep voice reverberates through his chest and into my bones. "Your grandmother doesn't come back for a year. A year is a long time."

"A year is a long time," I repeat.

His hand strokes a path up my back. He shifts my hair out of the way and holds me tighter, tucking his chin better into my neck, where he speaks in a soft voice against my skin. "I knew when you walked into the bookshop that day that my life was about to change."

"You did?"

"I did. Maybe it was the curse," he says, lightness in his voice, "Or . . . I don't know."

"What?"

"Because I saw you, and it just felt like everything that had gone wrong in my life just magically healed . . . like I'd been walking around all broken, and all my broken pieces suddenly reconnected."

"*Oh,*" I whisper on a soft exhale.

He groans. "That sounds stupid."

"Not at all. I'm magic," I tease. "That's what you're saying."

"Maybe we're magic together."

"It does feel that way, doesn't it?"

"It really does."

"Oh, Lucky," I whisper against him. "What are we going to do?"

"I don't know, but we have to try."

I unfold my wings to be able to get my hands around his back. He sighs against me when I do, and we melt into each other for a long moment. Then he kisses me softly on the neck.

"Sorry," he whispers, smiling against my skin. "I couldn't help it."

"You couldn't?"

"Nope." He kisses my neck again, tickling me. "Oops. Sorry again."

I laugh, shoulder reflexively jerking upward to push his face away from the crook of neck. Or trap him there. I'm not sure which. "Lucky Karras. I don't believe you're sorry at all."

"Well . . . not about that."

"Me neither."

I pull back and smile up at him. Was he always this beautiful, when we were kids? The way he looks now, with the light gilding his skin, and his dark hair all mussed up and windblown. And the way he's looking at *me* now, like I'm the only thing standing for miles that matters . . . I don't know.

Maybe it's just the magic of golden hour.

"Hey, Josie?"

"What?"

"Can we agree to not talk about the ticking time bomb that is your grandmother returning from Nepal for the moment, until we figure some things out?"

"Most definitely," I agree. "Let's not."

"And in the meantime, there's one thing I want to do together."

My pulse races. "What's that?"

He shakes his head. "Nope. You're just going to have to trust me. And meet me Saturday night. Same time, same place—after we both get off work. Deal?"

"I guess you've got yourself a deal."

"Oh, almost forgot." I dig in my pants pocket until my fingers find the folded-up hundred and fifty dollars he left on the counter in the Nook. *My* hundred and fifty dollars . . . along with another hundred and fifty that I added for our payment plan arrangement. I quickly stuff it all inside the front pocket of his jeans before he can stop me.

"Hey now—"

"This photography session is free."

"Josie, Josie, *Josie*," he says, sucking in a quick breath. "You can't just go around sticking your hand down guys' pockets like that without a warning."

"Consider this a warning then. I might even do it again one day when my mom's not watching us."

"Saturday night."

"Saturday night," I repeat, grabbing my camera off the brick wall as I smile back at him. I feel warm and hopeful for the first time since he left me that afternoon in the darkroom. And I want to keep feeling that way. I want to believe that if we try hard enough, we can figure out a way to diffuse the ticking time bomb . . . or keep what we have if I go to California.

A year is a long time.

Is it long enough?

OLD FISHERMEN NEVER DIE, THEY JUST SMELL THAT WAY:
Yellow-and-black sign attached to the cabin of a geriatric fishing boat docked
behind Nick's Boatyard. *(Personal photo/Josephine Saint-Martin)*

15

I find out what Lucky has in store for me when I meet him behind
the boatyard again. It's early evening, but summer heat is still
warming the dock boards when Lucky coaxes me down a couple
of steps into the belly of a beast.

And by "beast," I mean the *Nimble Narwhal.*

And by *Narwhal,* I mean a cabin cruiser fishing boat, circa
before I was born.

Maybe even before my mom was born, if the carrot-orange
color scheme of the boat's interior is any indication. Below the
main part of the boat, it has an underdeck living space big enough
for a hermit serial killer, with a teeny, tiny kitchenette, built-in
sofa, and a matchbox bathroom that's pretty much the same as
an airline toilet.

The boatyard and the Nook are both closed, and I pretend like
I'm interested in the tour he's giving me, pointing out all the boat's
features, but honestly, my mind is halfway between the gutter and

a sliver of golden skin I keep seeing above the waistband of his charcoal board shorts when he reaches to switch on lights in the boat's low ceiling. He's wearing a shirt with the sleeves rolled up high enough to show off his bronze arms, and his shorts aren't just low, they also have a bonus strategic rip exposing one muscular thigh. I mean, come on. He switches the lights on. Off . . . I signal for him to show me again. He gladly complies. His hips have that weird boy muscle that makes a V shape on either side of his stomach, pointing toward greener pastures.

Kind of hard not to look.

And we haven't been alone since that day my mom watched me take pictures of the boatyard. Some of them turned out pretty good. Kat is happy, so that's what's important.

"So that's the *Narwhal* tour," Lucky says. "How's your queasy factor so far?"

"Ugh. Don't say that word, p-wease," I say around a ginger-flavored lollipop that I've been sucking for several minutes in preparation for boarding. I also have a tin of candied ginger in the pocket of my shorts.

"Ginger is proven to help with seasickness," he assures me. "So does getting back on the water. Practice and practice again. I researched this thoroughly and asked a bunch of hardened, salty old boaters. You're going to beat this. Mind over matter. We'll make a sea-loving lass of you yet."

I pluck my lollipop out of my mouth with a soft pop. "Really don't know how you talked my mom into letting us do this."

He shrugs "Just pointed out where she could see us from your apartment window through one of your camera lenses," he says casually, and sounds like he means it.

"Uh, *what*?"

"Look," he says, ignoring me. "If you want to get past this seasickness—"

"I could just stay on land forever."

"—a bigger boat is a good place to start. That's why I thought we'd try out the *Nimble Narwhal*, here. My dad acquired it in a trade earlier this year. Impressed?"

"If by 'impressed' you mean 'is it giving off Cape Fear vibes,' then yes. Are you sure there aren't bodies stuffed inside the sofa?"

"You insult me, Saint-Martin. I'll have you know I spent hours scrubbing everything down here until my fingers bled."

"Don't believe you." God, he's adorable.

"Maybe not *bled*. I did clean it, though. And it's body-free. And rodent-free. I also threw away a lot of insect carcasses. You're welcome."

"What is all this for, if I may ask?"

"This is how I'm going to turn you into a water rat."

"Why?"

He taps the side of his head with his finger and waggles his brows. "I have a plan."

"Hey! That's my thing," I insist. "I'm the person with the plans and schemes."

"Tough," he says, shrugging. "It's upside-down day. You ready?"

"No, I'm not ready in the least bit! I don't want to get sick again," I say, clinging to the carrot-colored kitchenette counter. "Especially not in that bathroom."

"Told you before, seasickness is an inner ear problem. It's sort of a battle between your senses, right? Your body is used to being on solid ground, and once you're on a boat, your eyes are seeing one thing, and your inner ears are detecting another, and it's one big sensory overload, and kablam! You're sick."

"Terrific for science. Let's not do any kablamming."

"Nope. We're going to kablam until your body gets used to the water. The ginger helps your inner ear. So does antihistamine. That's all motion-sickness pills are, really. And I've got them in case you need them." He pats his pocket. "Remember last time, with the old fish and the sealant smells? I think that was a big factor. Strong smells make it worse."

"It definitely didn't help," I agree.

"That's why I cleaned, see? And I aired everything out. No smells. So today let's start small. We're just going to sail out for about a nautical mile, then I'll stop the boat. Got it?"

Okay, adorable or not, I'm really unsure about all this and moan a protest.

"Mind over matter," he says, gesturing to the deck above.

"I'm going to crack open *your* mind for making me do this, Lucky Karras." The only thing saving him is that even though I can't see his spectacular hips at the moment, he's smiling down at me with that beautiful smile of his, and his hair is a particularly floppy mess today, and it's all driving me a little wild. All of it. All of him: the adorable parts, the sexy parts, and the parts that did all this research.

This is a much bigger boat than *Big-Enough*. I wouldn't call it a party boat, but it's big enough for several people to take out fishing. I just wish it was someone else instead of me. Especially when Lucky forces me to strap on an ugly orange life jacket—"them's the rules"—and leads me up four steps to a covered cabin with the boat's controls and two seats. From here, I can see the deserted boatyard and the backs of all the brick warehouses that line the South Harbor. I can even see the Quarterdeck Coffeehouse, which is where I'd rather be right now.

"Deep breath," he tells me. "And watch the horizon."

That's exactly what I do as Lucky starts up the rumbling engine of the *Narwhal*. Abandoning the lollipop in a wrapper inside my shorts pocket, I go for the stronger ginger gum, chewing down on it like a camel as Lucky maneuvers the boat around the Karrases' small dock. Then we motor through the harbor.

I try not to look at anything, but I can tell we're going the opposite direction from where we went in the smaller boat that first evening. Every once in a while, I allow my eyes to dart away from the horizon—toward the disappearing Harborwalk, cobbled streets, and bright flags blowing in the bay breeze. We're up so much higher in this boat. It's strange to be out here, to see it all from this point of view.

"You okay?" he asks.

"Don't talk to me. I'm trying to concentrate on the horizon."

"We're almost there. You're doing great."

A few bigger yachts cut through the water near us, a few sailboats, too, but Lucky veers around them gracefully. At least I thought. When I watch the last turn, I feel the queasiness begin to rise up in me—it starts in the back of my cheeks and with a cold sort of sweat that sweeps over my brow.

"Oh no," I tell Lucky.

"Okay, okay," he says. "We're just about where I wanted to be. Yep. Okay. I'm shutting the engine off. Look at the horizon. Are you focused on that?"

"Ugh."

I feel the boat sway, then it goes quiet. Then it stops. After some loud grinding noise, Lucky puts a hand on the back of my neck. "You all right?"

"Think so."

"You want to lay down on the deck?"

I think about it for a second. The queasiness is subsiding. Not gone, but better. "I'm managing. If the water would stop moving, that would be great."

"I can help with that. It's why I brought you out here."

I blow out a hard breath and dare to turn in my seat to look up at him. "To kill me and throw my body in the water? I *knew* this was a Cape Fear situation."

"Nope. I'm going to teach you to swim."

I stare at him. "Um, what?"

"Swim," he says, paddling like a dog. "Me, you."

"In the harbor?"

"Prudence Beach," he says, pointing behind us.

I look out over the harbor water, and sure enough, there's a sandy beach stretching around the southern tip of the coast. No surprise. Lots of beaches around Beauty. One right near the center of the historic district by Goodly Pier, in fact. It's littered with tourists and bright umbrellas as we speak. This beach, however, is sort of rocky and windy. South of town. Not the pretty beach. Practically deserted.

There's another problem. Well, there are about a hundred of them, but another big one: "It's, like, a half a mile from us or something," I say. "There's no dock."

"Nope," he says. "We aren't going to the beach. We're swimming right here."

Here, he means. In the harbor.

"This is where my dad taught me to swim. It's completely safe," he assures me.

"I don't have a swimsuit."

"Don't need one. You can swim in your clothes. The world won't end. There are clean towels downstairs."

"You said my mom could watch us."

"Can she really, though? I said I *thought* she could. I don't know anything about your cameras."

I glance back at the town's jagged buildings, crowded along the shore in the distance. I've got a cheap telephoto lens with a serious zoom for my digital camera, but there's no way it could get detail this far. She could probably see the boat through it, but not us. What am I even talking about? My mom couldn't switch out a camera lens if her life depended on it. Bet him telling her that she'd be able to see us made her *feel* better, though, sneaky bastard.

"But, why?" I ask.

"I told you already, I'm turning you into a water rat."

"Not following."

He sighs dramatically and explains. "You were upset about not knowing how to do things like ride bikes and swim, because that's what real families do, you said. Therefore, my plan is to help you beat your seasickness by getting you used to the water in this boat. And when you're used to the water, I teach you to swim. When you learn to swim, you love the water. Once you love the water, then you'll love Beauty. Once you love Beauty, then you'll forget about your dad's fancy house in Malibu and start thinking of alternate ways to diffuse the ticking time bomb of your grandmother's impending return from Nepal."

I stare at him, awed. It's a plan, all right. A scheme. A strategy. A plot. I'm both touched and impressed. "That, sir, is conniving and beautiful," I say, hand on my heart. "You're basically trying to ruin my dreams, though?"

"Sort of a bad person, remember?"

"Liar."

"I'm seriously not trying to ruin your dreams, so please don't joke about that. I'm still supportive of your dreams, from one artist to another."

"Thought you were a craftsperson, not an artist."

He feigns annoyance. "However," he says, holding up a finger, "if you *are* going to live with your dad, which I still support, for the record, I want you to know that there are lots of boats in coastal California—like *so* many. It's a beach, Josie."

"Point taken," I say, smiling. "Oops?"

"So you should be prepared. I'm doing you a favor, really."

I chuckle. "Okay, fine. Favor accepted."

Grinning, he pops the latches on his life jacket. Ditches it. Then pulls off his shirt and tosses it on the deck. If I thought his arms were nice, I was a fool. Because there it is, his entire naked torso, all lined with muscles that I don't know the names of, and the color of warm sand. His stomach is bisected by a dark slash that leads into his shorts, which hang far too low and provocatively on those spectacular hips of his. It's all too much. If the seasickness doesn't take me, I'm definitely going to faint from all this titillation.

"Let's learn to swim, Saint-Martin," he says, squinting down at me from under black lashes, as if he's completely unaware of the power he's radiating. Or is he doing this on purpose?

Am I being seduced?

With . . . swimming? Is that a thing?

I CAN'T TELL.

One by one, he tugs off my sneakers while I remove my life

jacket. We both empty our pockets. Then he urges me off the chair and leads me to the back of the boat, where we step down onto a half-moon deck that curves around the tail. We sit side by side on the inner edge of the moon, legs dangling into the warm water. It . . . feels really nice, actually.

"How's your seasickness?"

"Huh?"

A smile splits his face. "See? Your signals aren't scrambled. Baby steps, Josie. Baby steps."

Before I can respond, he slides off into the harbor, feet first. A seal slipping off a rock into the ocean. He holds his nose and disappears under the surface for a moment. And when he reemerges, he's glistening, hair slicked back, lashes blinking away water.

"Feels fantastic today," he says, kicking in place with his feet. "You ready?"

"For what?" I say, terrified.

He swims below me and reaches up to grip my hips with sun-kissed arms. "Just hold on to the deck with your hands and slide on in, feet first. I'll catch you, don't worry. I won't let you drown. Lifeguard training with the Red Cross when I was fifteen. Totally certified."

"Seriously?"

"Yep."

"You have those super tight lifeguard trunks and everything?"

"Nope. Mom wanted me to do it, but I started working on the motorcycle instead," he says, grinning and a little breathless. He playfully slaps my hip with a firm hand. "Come on, Saint-Martin. On three, two, one."

"I'm not ready!" I shout, but I slip into the water anyway with a terrible splash.

Warm, briny water engulfs me and soaks my clothes as gravity pulls me down. For a shocking moment, I'm terrified that I'll plunge right through the surface. That I'll keep going. The harbor is endless and deep, and I accidently suck in salty water, but—

Steady hands snag under my arms.

"I've got you," he says. "Stop fighting me. Put your arms around my neck. There you go. Okay, okay."

I only put one arm around his neck. The other I use to grip the deck of the boat. "I can't do this!" I tell him. "I'll pull us both under."

"Nope, you won't. Look at my face. Hey, hey. Look at me."

I look at him, and he smiles at me, head just above the water's surface. I can feel his legs kicking below. And after I stop panicking, he tells me how he's doing it, like an eggbeater. And how I can do it too, if I hold on to his shoulders from a little farther away. The funny thing is, I actually am able to.

"I'm doing it!"

"You are."

"I'm kicking."

"You're treading water."

"I'm treading!"

"Kablam."

I laugh, but it makes me lose my rhythm, and I nearly choke him to death when I panic all over again and try to cling to him like a monkey. He's not deterred by my loss of progress. "Let's see if you can float."

Patiently, he shows me how to grip the half-moon deck with both hands and let my body gently float out behind me while he keeps guard, one hand on my stomach in case I slip.

"See? This isn't hard," he tells me after a few false starts.

"Famous last words."

"Just hang there and try to relax," he says. "Talk to me. Talking keeps your mind off what you're doing."

"Talk about what?"

"How about the obvious . . . Heard from your dad lately?"

"Uh, no. We don't talk on the regular, though. I was sort of waiting until I had something to tell him before I called him. . . . You know, like the internship. Only I'm still too chicken to write my contact. I composed the email, but I haven't sent it yet, because of the naked photo of my mother circulating around town and whatnot."

"I don't think that's the reason."

"Oh, really? I don't see a naked photo of your dad floating around town, so how would you know what it feels like?"

"Hey. My dad struts down our hallway from the shower to my parents' bedroom every day without a stitch on, because 'it's only a body, Lucky, and we all have them,'" he says, imitating his father. "Trust me, if that hairy body floated around town, it might trigger an actual apocalypse. Buildings would collapse. The portal to hell would open up and swallow the entire town."

"Shut up," I say, laughing. "I can't balance!"

"You're doing great. Keep it up," he says. "Okay, what else? How about . . . tell me everywhere you've lived."

"Oh, good God."

"Come on," he says in a teasing voice.

"Too many places to name. Everywhere in New England, pretty much. Easier to tell you where I haven't."

"Okay, what was the most favorite place you lived?"

My hands are starting to cramp on the deck. I stretch them out one at time. "Vermont. It snowed so much in the winter, and there was nothing to do, so mom and I would play board games all night. We lived in this kooky apartment that had chalkboard paint on everything—like, the previous tenant went overboard, you know? And we kept a tally of all our games on a cabinet that was painted like a chalkboard, who was winning which games. Only, she would sneak into the living room and erase my wins, and I had to catch her cheating. . . ." I laugh and nearly choke in the water. "You had to be there, I guess. It was just a fun winter."

"Your mom was always fun."

"She can be."

"Can I ask you something about her? If you don't want to answer, you don't have to. Don't get mad."

"Kinda have me in a precarious position here," I tell him.

He laughs, holding on to the boat deck beside me, and then

goes serious. "Does your mom really date . . . a lot of people?"

"Is my mom the giant slut that everyone says she is?"

"Whoa. I didn't say that. I'm not the morality police. No judgment."

"It's fine," I say, a little weary in both my arms and my mind. "Honestly? I don't know what's normal and what's not. She says she's not interested in relationships, and she just likes men. But I don't even know if that's true, because she's never happy about it."

Last year, when Mom was managing a bookstore up the coast, one of her assistant managers, a woman in her late twenties, had a similar dating philosophy: new guys every weekend. Marianne was loud and proud about it, and all her online dates met her for the first time at the store, were introduced to all the booksellers on shift, and they gave the thumbs up or down—it was all boisterous and funny, and even though I felt sorry for the men she dumped, at least Marianne was honest about it. At least I believed her when she said that's what she wanted.

But, see, I don't think it's what Mom wants. She's not *happy*. Sometimes I think there are other reasons why she's only interested in random encounters—she's escaping something, hiding something. I tell Lucky, "It almost feels like . . . I don't know. An addiction? A gambling problem? Something she does to stop feeling depressed? I don't even know."

"Is she depressed?"

"I don't *think* so? She doesn't act like it. She's just a very private person, weirdly enough. I think everyone in my family is. Like, that's just the Saint-Martin way. We all keep a part of ourselves locked up. She's kind of hinted that my grandma was the same way, and I guess I do the same thing to her, because I haven't told her about my plans to go to Los Angeles."

"Yeah," he says, sounding a little forlorn.

"Anyway, it's none of my business, I guess. I just want her to be okay, you know?"

And that's true, I realize. Even if I don't want to keep moving around the country with her, being dragged from town to town, it doesn't mean I don't love her. I want her to be okay. I want her to be happy. It makes me feel bad that I can't help her.

That I'm not enough for her.

"I wish she'd talk to me about it," I tell Lucky, "but it's kind of a forbidden topic. Everything about her relationships and her past is. So it's hard for me to help if she won't let me know what's wrong," I tell him, kicking my legs in the water. "I used to think maybe my dad could make her happy. Like maybe she was doing all this as a way of punishing him somehow? Like a cry for help? I don't know. That sounds stupid."

"No it doesn't."

"Anyway, she really, truly couldn't care less about my father. So I don't think it has anything to do with him. It's something else. I just wish I knew *what*."

"Maybe you should just ask her."

"You think I haven't?"

He doesn't say anything. I don't say anything. I just lie in the

262

water, thinking about why he's asking all these questions. Then I remember something I'd forgotten in all the recent drama. "Hey. You wouldn't happen to know about anyone who was in the navy and recently came back to town, would you?"

He squints at me in the sun. "That's an odd question."

"Evie's mom mentioned something when she called, but she clammed up and wouldn't tell Evie who it was. Gave us the impression that it was someone from high school my mom would want to avoid so badly, she may have had second thoughts about moving back here."

"I see," he says. "Sounds dramatic."

"Right?"

"Maybe you should ask your mom."

"Have you not been listening? She'll never tell me."

"What about your grandma?"

"We're not close like you are, apparently," I tease. "So you really don't know any navy dudes? No one in town? Anyone your parents might know?"

His face squinches up. "You think this has something to do with your mom's depression?"

Wow. I don't know. That's a weird way of looking at it. I also get the strange feeling that he's avoiding answering my question. I'm probably being paranoid. Regardless, I'm afraid if I keep thinking about all this, it's going to ruin our lovely day. Because it *is* lovely. And I'm not letting my mom and all the question marks in her past take it away from me.

This is mine.

"Think you're ready to try floating on your back?" he asks. "Last swimming trial of the day before we go home."

"No. Yes. No. Do I have to?"

"Completely up to you. It's fun, though."

"Okay. Let's try."

The back float is much harder than on my stomach. So hard, I'm almost positive I can't do it, and I think he's getting frustrated with me? Or maybe I'm getting frustrated with myself. Because once I completely give in, stop worrying about water getting into my ears . . . then it happens.

I'm weightless.

I float on my back, looking up at the blue sky, feeling my body being buoyed by the warm harbor water, gently rocked. I float while Lucky paddles beside me. While he lets go and swims around me. I float while he smiles and slyly peels up my wet shirt from where it sticks to my skin and kisses my belly button where water pools. I float while he swims beneath me like a shark, pretending to bite my thigh and upsetting my balance—then swimming back around and catching me when my legs sink.

"Hey!" I shout, laughing and splashing as I grasp his neck.

"Scared of a little ol' fish nibble?"

"Scared of drowning, you jerk!"

But it strikes me that's not true.

I'm not half as wary of the water as I was before we came out here. And when he wraps his arms around me, legs treading water around mine, and kisses me, mouth wet, chest pumping up and down with the exertion of swimming and holding me up, I'm not thinking about the horizon or the possibility of drowning. I'm not thinking about town gossip or whether my mom is happy. I'm not thinking about Adrian Summers or the broken windows, or the ticking time bombs in my life.

I'm not thinking about anything but the two of us.

About this.

This joy.

Right now.

Maybe, just maybe, I *could* be a water rat, after all.

Kablam.

KNOCK BEFORE ENTERING: Doorknob hotel sign placed inside a plastic picture frame and mounted with wall-hanging putty on the outside of the bedroom door of Evie Saint-Martin. *(Personal photo/Josephine Saint-Martin)*

16

Lucky and I take the *Narwhal* out almost every evening for a couple of weeks to the same spot. Turns out there're these wristbands that Lucky found. You wear them on your pressure points, and they help stop nausea caused by seasickness. Well, that and the antihistamine that I'm now taking before we set sail.

I'm unscrambled, and I can be on the water without wanting to die.

Strangely, I actually like being on the boat now. It feels like we're escaping the world for a couple of hours. A safe place. Just ours. And yes, we go out in the *Narwhal* to practice my swimming in the new bathing suit I've bought. But often we do a lot of other things, like:

Talk about the difference between art and craft.

Take photos.

Put our hands all over each other.

Play with Bean the Magic Pup, who sometimes rides
    along and barks at passing boats.
Trash talk Adrian Summers.
Plot revenge that we'll never enact.
Put our hands all over each other.
Talk about our failed D&D campaigns from childhood.
Consider a trip out to our old secret North Star boatshed
    to test out a new campaign.
Decide the boatshed might be inhabited by ghosts or
    spiders and change our minds.
Watch the Fourth of July fireworks.
Eat iced lemonade.
Put our hands all over each other.

Here's what we don't do on the boat:
    Talk about me going to California to live with my dad
        next year.
That subject is off-limits. Maybe if we pretend like it doesn't
exist, it will never happen.
Here's what we also don't do:
    We don't tell anyone that we're more than friends.
I mean, sure. Half the town is probably talking about us. My
mom has made the Bonnie and Clyde comments, and Lucky's
parents have been nosy too. And then there's Evie, who definitely
knows something happened in the darkroom . . . but I don't even
tell her.

It's not because I don't want people to know or because I'm ashamed of what I'm doing with my childhood best friend. I'm not doing anything wrong. It's just no one's business, that's all. And this town has proven that they can't be trusted to handle delicate information with grace. My name's already being whispered; I don't need to give the rumor mill any more fuel.

One evening, when Lucky and I were supposed to be heading out on the *Narwhal* to practice my backstroke, or some kind of more salacious stroke, I find him in the boatyard with his father, working late on a last-minute engine problem for a customer.

"Sorry," he tells me. "They're paying us overtime rates, and it's the kind of favor that my dad can't turn down. Shouldn't take more than an hour but might be too close to dark for us to take the boat out. Maybe we could stay in? Order pizza? Watch a movie on TV? My house is overrun with toddler cousins at the moment. What about yours?"

"Evie's home. My mom's, uh . . . out. But she might come back by the time you're done." I squint at him. "Would that be okay? Or too weird?"

"I'm fine with it, if she is."

Mom's definitely warming up to him, and he's been in and out of the Nook. But he's never been inside our apartment. I think she'd be cool with it.

Lucky in our apartment. Whoa. I'm a little fluttery just thinking about it. Another first for us. It's one thing for us to be on our own private boat together, but in public, around other people . . . that's new territory. *Good* territory. It's just new. And exciting.

"I'll double-check to make sure it's all okay," I tell him. "But I'm pretty sure it is. Just text me when you're done?"

He checks to make sure no one's watching and quickly kisses my forehead, holding oil-stained hands away from my shirt. "Sounds like a plan. Mushrooms and olives on my side, by the way. No cheese."

"That's not even pizza anymore," I say, making a face.

"If they have clams—"

"NO."

He grins. "See you in an hour."

I cross back over to the Nook and head around back, up the steps, and into our apartment. Looks clean. Okay. At least I don't have to freak out about that. I text Mom but when she doesn't reply right away, I'm not surprised. Hopefully she'll see it before he comes over.

Heading through the living room past our 1950s pinup girl lamp, I make a beeline to Evie's room and knock briefly on her door. I know she's there, because the sounds of grungy 1980s post-punk music rattle the walls. She's probably studying for class and can't hear me, so I knock louder and then crack open the door and stick my head through.

"Hey," I shout over the music.

Then I freeze.

Evie's there, all right. She's not alone.

A dark head of hair rises from the covers like a mermaid from the water, and for a moment, there's a jumble of limbs, and I'm seeing *way* more of my cousin's skin than I want to see. But when

I blink, most of that skin is quickly covered up with a quilt, and a face I never wanted to see again is staring back at me.

Adrian Summers.

He looks at me.

I look at him.

Evie looks at me.

What do I do now? I know I shouldn't be here, but it's too late. They're both staring at me in horror. And I'm staring back. It's all super uncomfortable, and the music's still blasting like it doesn't realize that it's underscoring a really awkward moment for all of us.

Oh, Evie. Cuz.

Whyyyyyyy?

She blinks at me with big eyes that say: *I couldn't help it. 'Twas the Saint-Martin curse!*

And I glare back at her with narrowed eyes that say: *All the disappointment.*

Adrian's crutches are propped up against her bed. Some dark part of me would like to race over to them, snatch them up, and beat him over the head with them until he's got a concussion. But of course, I can't do that.

Too late to pretend I haven't seen this. What do I do here? WHAT DO I DO? My thoughts race and tumble. It's Adrian. *Adrian.*

Anger builds the longer I look at his stupid face. "Thought you were at your aunt's."

"I was," he says, one shoulder shrugging as he props himself up on Evie's pillows while she tugs the quilt up higher. "Now I'm here."

"You should be in jail. You could have killed an animal. Did you know that? Their pet was inside the offices when you threw that crowbar."

He looks momentarily taken aback. "I don't know what you're talking about. I didn't throw anything."

"I should call the cops right now."

"Josie!" my cousin pleads.

"You have no proof," Adrian says. "Who's to say it wasn't another car? Or maybe it was Jam or Crandall?"

I have no idea who those people are, but I'm guessing they're his Golden buddies who were in the car with him.

"Besides," he says. "What if there were actual people inside my dad's store when grease monkey threw the rock into our window? Ever think about that? Not animals, but real people. He could have murdered someone when he threw the rock."

"It was an accident," I say. "I don't how many times I have to keep saying it."

Adrian looks at me funny. "Why did you say it that way?"

"What way?"

He points in my direction. "*That* way."

Oh god. How did I say it? My heart races when I glance at Evie's face. She shakes her head—almost imperceptible, but a shake. A warning. "I just meant that I was there with Lucky that night," I explain to Adrian. "I was there when it happened, and it was an accident. He wasn't trying to hit the window. He was aiming for the sign. It wasn't intentional."

Adrian looks at me for a second too long. . . . Finally he frowns and sighs. "Whatever, kid. Let's just agree that both incidents were misguided. Best for all of us if we forget it and move on. Why are you here, anyway? You need something from Evie? Otherwise, we're kind of busy. . . ."

Wow. This guy just doesn't give a damn. No damns. One minute he's breaking windows, and the next, he's up here in my cousin's room—

Nope. Don't want to think about it.

I look at Evie and say, "We'll be having company in about an hour, just so you know. . . . Might want to clear out." *I strongly suggest you do.*

My cousin nods at me, understanding, Cleopatra makeup slightly askew.

"Right. Well, then . . ." *Have a good evening? Enjoy sleeping with the enemy—literally? Please, continue your toxic relationship that is clearly ruining your life?* "I don't know," I mumble while I exit the room. "Whatever, Evie."

As I'm pulling the door handle, the second Evie's head turns away, Adrian puckers up and makes a kissy face at me.

Just for a second, I consider sticking my phone back inside the door and taking a quick photo of him as revenge for what he's done to me, but my mind quickly sobers to what that photo would entail: *He's on Evie's bed.* Besides. I'm not sinking down to his muck. Screw him.

I slam the door behind me.

At first, I head into my room, but it's next to hers, and I can hear them arguing through the walls. That's too weird, so I quickly head to Mom's room and shut the door, listening for sounds that Adrian's clearing out of the apartment.

They're definitely fighting. Good.

I'm not sure whether to be mad at Evie or disappointed. Hurt? It was one thing for her to go to him that first time after the party, when they were in the wreck together, if she was genuinely trying to get him to talk his dad into dropping the department store window settlement against Lucky. But now?

He broke the Karrases' window.

He showed everyone a nude photo of my mother—thinking it was me.

That's not okay. And I'm furious that she'd disregard all that like it wasn't a big deal. Because it is. But even if none of that had happened, he's still a dick. He still treated her like shit at that party. He humiliated her. He harassed her, sending all those demanding texts. And if he's going to show everyone nude pictures of "me"— someone he doesn't even know or care about—then what's to stop him from doing the same to her if he gets mad enough?

He's got warning signs written all over him.

Why can't she see that?

I don't know what to do about it. Talk to her, I guess. Maybe it's time to talk to my mom—which is a weird thing to think about. We're such terrific communicators and fine examples of piety. Ugh.

When I'm pretty sure he's not sticking around, I glance at the closet door in Mom's room. Grandma's old closet. Locked. Personal stuff that she didn't want to move into storage when she left for Nepal.

Maybe old family stuff.

Maybe old photos.

Secrets.

Ever since Lucky and I had that talk about my mom, when he took me out for my first swimming lesson, I haven't been able to get the navy guy out of my mind. I also haven't been able to ask her about it, despite Lucky suggesting I do so. My mom doesn't handle confrontation well. Especially not about her past. Our biggest fights have been about Henry and Grandma—and questions that I've asked. About why she never wanted to try to be a family with Henry. About why she doesn't get along with Grandma.

Asking those things got me nothing but tears. We don't talk about stuff in the past.

So if I want to know about my mom and the mystery navy guy, then I need to either ask my grandmother—who isn't here to ask— or try the next best thing.

Snoop in my grandmother's things.

I know.

I know.

But maybe I can just peek inside and see if there's anything I can skim without being too invasive.

Maybe?

I dare to jump a few times to reach the top of the closet door, and I'm rewarded with the sight of tarnished metal falling with a ping onto the floorboards.

Well. Bingo. If nothing else, this will get my mind off Adrian's stupid blond head inside my cousin's bed. One less secret in the Saint-Martin household . . .

The key I've found is old-fashioned, one that was probably new when they renovated this apartment in the 1940s, and it snicks satisfactorily when I turn it inside the closet door's lock.

The door creaks open. Scents of must and mothballs float out.

I turn on the overhead light by pulling a string. The closet is packed to the gills. A fur coat that nearly gives me a heart attack because it looks like an animal cowering in the corner. A couple of dresses zipped up in plastic. Stacks of boxes that are all labeled in my grandmother's cursive handwriting. Documents. Paystubs. Nothing interesting, really . . . A lockbox certainly doesn't seem boring, but I don't have the combination. I put it aside and look through the boxes on the top shelf until I find what I'm looking for.

A box labeled *Winnie.*

No one calls my mom that. No one but Grandma.

I dig out the box, sit on the floor with it between my knees, and open up the flaps that are folded over one another. There's not much inside. A baby blanket and a silver rattle with my mother's initials engraved on it. A tiny photo album—baby pictures, mostly. A few of my mom as an adorable toddler, laughing at the camera on a strange man's shoulders—my grandfather. So weird to see a man I never met.

At the bottom of the box, under a pile of birthday cards and school records, I find some things from my mom's teen years. A worn felt high school pennant with a big Breakers wave design on it. A photo of my mother when she was voted Best Dressed. And there. The coveted prize.

Beauty High School Yearbook.

My mom's senior year.

Pulse racing, I crack it open and have to pry the endpapers apart—there's an old strawberry candy wrapper here, one that still faintly holds the sweet scent, and its sugar has crystalized on the paper.

My eyes scan over the signatures and scribbled notes from classmates. Rainbows and hearts. *Love yous*. *Go Breakers! Have a great summer. It's finally over!* And sillier things—*Party hard?* People said that? So weird.

I look through the pages of the yearbook and find my mom's class photo. God, she was pretty. So strange to see her without her glasses. Stranger still to see her in casual shots around campus. But when I flip to the endpapers at the back of the book, I find a couple more handwritten notes that catch my attention.

Note one: *We've been through it all together, Winn. From the top of the pyramid to the boys next door. Here's to getting out of this place.* —*Chloe*

Top of the pyramid: a cheerleading reference, perhaps. My mom is no cheerleader, that's for sure. Who are the "boys next door," though? Is that a metaphor, or the actual boys next door?

Note two: *It's finally over. Only palm trees and white, sandy beaches on the horizon now. Our future is bright and sunny, and I can't wait for the two of us to start it together.* —*Drew*

I sit with the yearbook open on my lap, stunned.

Palm trees and white, sandy beaches? I've heard this exact phrase a hundred times out of my mother's mouth. It's her dream. Florida. The reason she agreed to come back to Beauty and save up money—so we could finally get out of New England and move where it's warm and sunny.

Now I'm convinced this "Drew" is the mystery man I've been looking for.

The navy man that Evie's mom said came back into town.

In the yearbook, he's talking about starting a future together with my mom. I wonder if that's just another saccharine yearbook salutation, or if he meant it literally. If he *did* mean it, obviously it didn't happen. She didn't start any kind of future with someone named Drew from high school.

She went to art school. Met my dad. Got pregnant. Dropped out of college. Moved back in with my grandma and had me. Lived here until I was twelve, then the time bomb exploded with Mom and Grandma.

End of story. At least, that's what I always thought.

What really happened to my mom in Beauty?

PREVENT BOAT THEFT—LOCK YOUR CABIN: Sign posted on an unnamed boating pier between historic district and South Harbor. Though Beauty prides itself on a low crime rate, boat theft remains a problem. *(Personal photo/Josephine Saint-Martin)*

17

"Air. I need . . . fresh air," Lucky says as we exit my apartment and step onto the rickety back stairs, closing the door behind us. Moths flutter around a bulb that shines a spotlight of yellow on the steps leading down into the dark alley behind the Nook. "I mean, is it just me, or was that the most awkward, tensest movie night of your entire life?"

"I thought *Parasite* was amazing," I say, feigning innocence. "Bong Joon Ho is a brilliant director and the cinematography was excellent."

He gives me a pointed look.

Yeah, *that*. Not a great movie night in *la Maison de Saint-Martin*.

Pizza: not good.

Evie: not good.

Mom and Lucky . . . well, remarkably okay, actually.

But everything else was tense. Very tense. "There is a reason for Evie's mood, and it had nothing to do with a fast-paced plot of revenge," I tell Lucky. "I'm sorry, but there was no good point to tell you this, because Mom kept hogging the conversation, so I could never get you alone—"

"She's warming up to my dark charms," he says, one side of his mouth curling.

"This is serious."

"Clearly. Got a serious vibe between you and Evie, for sure."

"That's because before you showed up," I say in a low voice, just in case Mom is listening in the kitchen, "I caught Adrian Summers in Evie's bed."

Black lashes slowly blink at me. "Um . . . as in—"

"Yeah," I say, hugging myself. "Like, half naked. And we had a short argument, during which he basically denied throwing the crowbar at the boatyard window, but in one of those wink-wink kinds of ways? And Evie was completely embarrassed. And I nearly told him that I'm the one who threw the rock at the department store window—"

"You better be joking right now," he says, brow lowering.

"But I caught myself in time! It's okay. I covered it up." I think.

"Josie."

"It's fine."

He swears under his breath and shakes his head. "What is she doing with drunky dipshit, anyway? Is it not enough that he nearly killed both of them in a car accident?"

"On top of everything else. What should I do? Does she need an intervention? Am I the messenger that's got to deliver the bad news that she's in a toxic relationship? Or is this none of my business?"

He blows out a hard breath. "Wow, I don't know. On one hand, I've known him awhile. On the other hand, I am the last person to ask, because when it comes to Adrian Summers, I do not have any goodwill. I fantasize about building one of those pagan wicker-type effigies out of his rowing boats and oars, a la Burning Man, and setting it ablaze with him inside it, begging for his life."

He's joking. I *think*.

"If you end up in actual jail, I will never forgive you, Lucky Karras," I warn him.

"Just a harmless fantasy," he says, holding up both hands innocently. "And as far as what to do about Evie . . . I honestly don't know. She's nineteen. In college. An adult. And I don't know if Adrian is seriously dangerous, or just an entitled asshole who makes terrible decisions when he drinks too much."

Me neither. But I'm a little weary of my family right now. Sometimes having to solve everyone else's problems feels as if it's a load I'm not built to carry. Like, I'm just a tiny elevator made for transporting one or two people, max—but every floor, someone's dinging my buttons, and suddenly I'm crammed with people and now my doors won't shut.

"Maybe I'll talk to her over the next couple days. Once things have stopped being weird between us." I squint at Lucky under the porch light. "Got any plans for this weekend?"

He cracks his knuckles over his black cat tattoo. "Perhaps plans for both of us, if you're interested. Two words—Rapture Island. Know it?"

"Afraid I do not."

"Few miles outside of the harbor mouth. Used to be a colony, now it's a bird sanctuary."

"Bird sanctuary, eh? That sounds . . . positively riveting."

"Now, hold on. I wasn't finished."

"Is there golfing, too? Because bird watching and golfing are the two things I definitely do not want to do with my weekend. Top two things."

He holds up a finger. "First, birds are cool, so screw you."

I laugh. "Wow. Didn't know you were such a bird-o-phile."

"Or maybe even ornithophile."

"Potato, tomato."

He ignores that. "And second, the island is only accessible by boat, and I'm not sure if anyone lives out there besides the lighthouse keeper and a handful of scientists during certain times of the year, but it's got"—he leans closer and says in a spooky voice—"the ruins of an entire colonial ghost town."

"Okay, sounding better and better. I didn't know we had a colonial ghost town."

"Ha! Taught you something new," he says, smiling at me with tired eyes.

"Look, I just learned that there are now two clam shacks in our neighborhood, not one."

"Manny's and Clam No. 5. Manny's is still better."

"Good to know. So, you think we should visit Rapture Island for the ghost town?"

"And because there's a really cool sign there. You would love it."

"Yeah?"

"Very unique. Your portfolio would thank you. And you'd thank me."

"Okay. Liking this . . ."

"And you've been seasick-free for a couple weeks now, so I was thinking, you know. It's *not* that far. We could take the *Narwhal* out there. Get you some good practice out on the water." He runs the back of his index finger over the inside of my wrist. Barely a touch at all. I hold my breath as waves of shivers cascade over my skin.

"That's true," I say.

"Just a minute ago, your mom was joking about letting you off at noon on Sunday, saying you'd better be good while she was working her ass off for the rest of the day, but I was thinking, I don't know . . . maybe we don't be good. Maybe we sneak away on the *Narwhal*."

My heart skips a couple of beats and then stumbles all over itself, trying to catch back up.

"What about Sunday dinner with your family?" I remind him.

He waggles his brows at me. "Maybe we skip Sunday dinner."

"Lucky," I say, feigning shock.

"We could have our own Sunday dinner on Rapture Island. Just the two of us. Picnic lunch. Picnic dinner. What's between lunch and dinner? Linner? Picnic linner?"

"I think it's called 'your mom getting mad at us for skipping a family function just so I can take a photograph of a cool sign'?"

"The things I do for art," he says, stealing a quick kiss before my mother spies us through the kitchen window. "It will be our little secret," he says, heading backwards down the steps and speaking in a low voice. "We'll be back before anyone misses us. Before the Nook closes. And before my mom gets too mad about Sunday dinner. Run away with me?"

"Okay," I whisper. "I'll run away with you."

Feeling giddy, I watch him race down the steps and head off to the Superhawk. It's not until he's speeding off down the road that I realize I never had the chance to tell him about what I found in my mother's closet. I'm definitely not telling her. I'd have to tell her how I came by the information, and that wouldn't go over well.

And as I catch Evie's silhouette moving across the kitchen window, I remember that there are more pressing relationship matters in the Saint-Martin family that probably need more attention than ones buried in literal closets. Maybe I should try to talk to her now. Not tomorrow.

I slip back inside the apartment and have no problem avoiding Mom, who is buried deep in her phone, a TV commercial on in the background, and I head straight for Evie's room. But when I rap on her door with my knuckles, she doesn't answer. Not verbally. She just sends me a text.

Evie: Tired. Don't want to talk. Please leave me alone.

Well. Classic Saint-Martin move. Communication severed.

Can't help people who won't listen. Can't talk to people who isolate themselves.

But who's responsible for getting things back online, me or her?

Lucky stands on the dock behind the deserted boatyard in shorts and a lightweight navy hoodie, a cooler sitting at his feet.

"Ready to set sail for the high seas?" he asks, smiling at me.

"Took my antihistamine pill half an hour ago," I say, and then flash him my wristbands. "Got these babies on and a pocket full of ginger. Ready as I'll ever be. I come seekin' adventure and salty old pirates."

He shakes his head. "Nope. You're not doing a Disney pirate voice the entire trip."

"Can I at least shout 'anchors away' when we set sail?"

"It's actually 'anchor is aweigh,' as in, off the sea floor. Never mind. You can shout whatever you'd like once we're out on the water as long as you're not vomiting."

Adrenaline zips through me. I've got my bathing suit on beneath my clothes, which is exactly the same as a bra and panties, but somehow it always feels a little naughty. Like why is one kind of fabric only for underneath clothes, but another kind of fabric totally okay for flashing around in public? One of the mysteries of life.

"What did you tell Winona?"

"That we're taking the boat out to the same spot we always do."

"Good," he says. "I told my mom the same. Said we may be late for Sunday dinner, so not to wait for us."

"Ugh. Now she's going to text you, asking where we are."

"Who cares? I'll tell her we lost track of time. It's fine."

I groan. "Definitely don't like lying to Kat Karras."

"You lie to your mom on the regular," he points out. "It's the same."

"But it *feels* wrong." He has the traditional family with the big backyard. That makes it worse somehow. I just have Winona, who doesn't keep track of where I am half the time.

He squints at me. "Got a feeling there's something else that's bugging you. What's wrong?"

"I don't want anything to spoil our perfect getaway."

"If there's another broken window, I swear—"

"Stop."

"Come on, shutterbug," he teases. "Talk to me."

I squeeze my eyes shut and let my head loll backwards. "It's Evie. She hates me. I tried to talk to her." Several times, in fact. She's now taken to locking her bedroom door. And okay, fair enough. But she refuses to look at me in the Nook. "This is the last communication I got from her. Look at this."

I pull out my phone and show him the single text she's sent me since the *I don't want to talk* one from movie night—

Evie: I broke it off. It's over for good. Don't want to talk about it, so don't ask.

"Over? Between her and the scumbag?" Lucky asks, squinting at my screen. "That's what she means? She and Adrian broke up."

I nod. "Yeah. I also heard Evie Skyping her mom a couple

285

days ago and crying. It wasn't their normal day to talk, so I definitely think Evie's upset about this. I wish she'd talk to me about it, but . . . nope. Now I'm worried."

"At least she and Adrian broke up," he says. "That's good, right?"

Is he serious? "Lucky, the last time she broke up with him, Adrian showed up at a party he wasn't supposed to be at, drunkenly shouted at her, and humiliated my family. What if he does something horrible this time? He threw a crowbar."

"He wouldn't hurt her. He's an asshole, but he's not a psychopath."

"Are you sure about that?"

"Pretty sure? But I can absolutely understand why you'd be worried. I can't even imagine what it would be like to even have to consider that. It's messed up." He frowns. "Should you tell your mom to watch out for Evie today?"

"Then Mom will know I'm up to no good. Besides, Evie's studying with her friend Vanessa and some other people today, so she's not alone."

"Good," he says. Then he squints at me, sensing there's more. "Or . . . not good?"

"It's good. But that's not the only thing. Evie is now pissed at me, and how is their breakup *my* fault? I didn't know he'd be in her room that day. Why am I the bad guy for pointing out something she wasn't seeing herself?"

"The messenger always gets shot. No one wants to hear about their failings. But once she has some time to think about it, she'll realize the messenger is not your enemy. The messenger is there to help you. Messenger *good*," he enunciates broadly. "Josie *good*."

"Josie's always good, but Josie has zip to show for it," I mutter.

"Well, guess what," he says, putting his hands on my shoulders. "That's what today is for."

"Is that so?" I say, wanting to believe him.

"Absolutely. Forget all that. Forget about trying to solve everyone's problems, and all your plotting and scheming. Evie is safe with Vanessa. You said so yourself. Today is just about us. Let's be a little bad together."

"Okay . . . fine. You and me," I say, giving in to his seductive speech of temporary freedom and smiling up at him. "Let's be a little bad."

We board the *Narwhal* and stow the cooler in the below-deck apartment. Then Lucky quickly unmoors the boat, and while I chew on ginger and don my life jacket, the sky above begins to look overcast. And then more than overcast.

Definitely not a perfect summer day. But I guess it's still okay to sail.

"Chance of rain," Lucky reports. "We need to keep an eye on the weather. Hopefully it will stay south of us. I'm not too worried."

The darkening skies make me nervous, but I know zilch about navigating a boat. So I just nod and take a deep breath.

"Let's get out of here before anyone catches us," he tells me, "and find out what it's like to be free of Beauty for an afternoon."

Sure. Let's be a little bad.

Let's just not get caught.

NO OVERNIGHT DOCKING: Sign posted on dock at northern end of Rapture Island, several miles south of Beauty. There are more than thirty islands in Narragansett Bay, and Rapture, though uninhabited, is one of the largest. *(Personal photo/Josephine Saint-Martin)*

18

Lucky was right: Rapture Island is small. Very small.

It's a little rocky on both ends, with trees in the middle. Among those trees, I can make out a few old buildings—or what remains of them. Just stones, really. And at one end of the island, near a weathered pier, a white-and-red lighthouse beckons like a finger into the water.

Not a single human being in sight.

Just the two of us.

Our own private getaway.

Lucky pilots us to the pier by the lighthouse, shutting off the motor to startling silence. And as he moors the boat, I exit it and tread onto old, gray boards stippled with white bird droppings. The boards bounce like rubber with each step.

It smells good out here, like saltwater and cedar, and as I approach a boxy, gray clapboard dock house on the sandy land at the end of the pier, the sweet scent of shrubby beach roses drifts from beneath its dusty windows.

A painted sign stands between the empty dock house and a footpath that splits between the lighthouse and farther into the island. It reads:

RAPTURE ISLAND

FIRST SETTLED BY THE NARRAGANSETT TRIBES.

SOLD TO EARLY AMERICAN PATRIOT, ROBERT HART.

HAS BEEN: TRADING POST, PIG FARM, RELIGIOUS COLONY.

RAIDED BY THE BRITISH IN 1776.

DESTROYED BY THREE HURRICANES.

SETTLED BY FORK-TAIL ROCK SWALLOWS IN 1969.

MINDFUL HUMANS MAY VISIT THE RAPTURE BIRD SANCTUARY FROM APRIL THROUGH OCTOBER. PLEASE PAY FEE TO TOUR THE ISLAND INDEPENDENTLY TO THE LIGHTHOUSE KEEPER.

NO OVERNIGHT STAYS. NO FIRES. PICK UP YOUR TRASH. DON'T PICK ANY VEGETATION OR FEED ANIMALS. STAY ON THE DESIGNATED TRAILS.

PEACE BE WITH YOU.

"Oh my God," I whisper as Lucky trudges up behind me. "How did I not know this was out here? This should be a huge tourist attraction for Beauty. This is . . . amazing."

"Yeah?" he says, hefting the strap of the cooler across his chest.

"Yes." I swing around, trying to take it all in. "Look at all this. Everything."

"Everything?"

"Like, okay, first of all—I love beach roses. They're better than garden roses, because they're the outcasts of the rose kingdom, and wherever we've lived up and down New England, there they are, like a good luck sign that smells amazing," I say, smiling.

"Never thought about them that way. My mom calls them trash roses."

"My mom says they're magnets for bugs. See? Outcasts of the rose kingdom."

He nods. "I can get behind an outcast."

"And second, the website for the island isn't half as weird as this sign, so now I'm totally intrigued about what's here. But, oh my God. *This sign!* Wow!"

He shrugs. "Told you."

"Lucky."

"Was I right, or what?"

"You were *so* right. Hold on a second. I need to set up some shots from different angles," I tell him, and he agrees, cheerful and patient, watching me work as I capture the strange sign. He even helps boost me up by my waist, letting me stand on his bent knee, so that I can get a better shot from above.

How could all of these things exist on one tiny island—the Narragansetts' settlement, the religious colony, the pig farming, wars, hurricanes . . . all of that, only to be deserted and forgotten? It's as if it's one big time capsule of humanity's successes and fail-ures, and all that's left is a marker of what happened. A marker, a sign, one last communication: *Don't forget us.*

The best sign in all of Beauty.

Maybe the best sign in my entire collection.

"It's so weird and beautiful," I tell Lucky after I change out my film.

"Just you wait. This place gets weirder, if you're interested in exploring?"

"Well, I didn't come all the way out here to get back on the stupid *Narwhal*, I'll tell you that. You promised me a colonial ghost town. . . ."

"Did indeed," he says, looking upward. "Wish the sky looked a little better. The forecast said the storm passing over Connecticut should miss us, but those clouds are starting to worry me. Should probably ask the lighthouse keeper about them. No one knows weather patterns like sailors and lighthouse keepers."

"And meteorologists, maybe."

"I suppose," he says, smiling. "Come on. Let's check in."

Problem is, we can't. When we hike to the lighthouse, there's a sign on the door that cheerfully informs us where the keeper is: GONE FISHIN'. It doesn't say when this person will return, or even what to do about the fee. So Lucky runs back to the boat and finds a pen and paper, writes a note with our names and the time, and sticks it under the door with money for our fee.

"Hope that's good enough," he says gruffly. "Would it kill them to have someone on duty here during the summer? I mean, come on. This is peak tourist season. Not to mention that the pier is about to collapse. They need to put some damn money into this place. Why isn't anyone here?"

Wow. Bad mood descending and fast. What's up with that?

"Well, we did just sort of show up here without telling anyone," I remind him. "They had registration online."

"Fair point," he concedes, still gruff.

"Should we walk around the island? We don't need a lighthouse keeper to give us permission for that, right?"

"Guess not," he says, looking a little less grumpy.

"Besides, we're supposed to be being a little bad. At least, that's what someone told me, I don't know."

His shoulders relax. "All right, Saint-Martin. You win. We're outlaws today. We do as we please."

Whew. Crisis averted.

Inside a little plexiglass holder that squeals when I lift the lid, there's a small stack of tri-folded maps. They show a walking path around the island and point out several colonial buildings, including a church and a "burying ground."

I crane my neck to kiss him lightly on his lips. "Take me to the burying ground. I want to snap a million pictures."

"What about the haunted trading post?"

"It's hard to decide. But wait. You didn't even notice something."

"What?"

"I didn't get sick once on the way out here. Does that make me an official water rat, or what?"

"Well, damn. It certainly does." He fist-bumps my hand and then grabs me around the waist and half-kisses, half-tickles my neck, making me shout out in surprise. And after I nearly fall over laughing, we settle down and stop fooling around, and he takes over map duties. Then we begin exploring the island.

Under gray skies, we hike down a sandy path bounded by tall grasses and more beach roses to the first historical site, set away from the coast at the edge of the woods. The settlement of Rapture—religious colony, pig farm, trading post—was torn apart by war and weather, so what remain are merely the outlines of where buildings once stood, stone labyrinths in the dirt that hint at rooms and the spines of fallen fireplaces.

As the skies darken, we loop around the other end of the island—pausing to take pictures of gravestones—and when we're halfway down the opposite coast, we stop to eat a late afternoon snack at something called the Stonehenge of New England. It's a mysterious standing stone circle—rather, what was lauded as one in the 1920s, before the last hurricane wiped out several grand summer homes that had been built here by a few pioneering rich people who thought Beauty was too crowded. Those were the last people to live on Rapture Island: One of those survivors admitted later that he built the stone circle as a hoax.

"It's a pretty good hoax, you have to admit. I would've been fooled," Lucky says. He's picking up the remainders of our picnic near one of the stones that's less *standing* and more leaning while I finish snapping another roll of film. "I think the fact that he built it inside an actual stone wall that's hundreds of years old added to its veracity. Sort of a fool-the-eye thing. He shouldn't have told anyone and let the mystery stand."

"I wonder if guilt finally ate away at him," I murmur from behind my Nikon. I'm getting a lot of spooky shots out of this trip. It's getting darker out here, though, with the line of storms veering closer. Not sure how this roll will turn out. I bump up the ISO as far as it'll go and say, "Speaking of guilt . . . I broke into my grandmother's closet."

"Whoa. Really? You did?"

"I found something. My mom's old yearbook. And I think I found an inscription from her mystery navy lover. It said, 'It's finally over. Only palm trees and white, sandy beaches on the horizon now. Our future is bright and sunny, and I can't wait for the two of us start it together.'"

"Interesting . . ." He says this like someone who knows way more than he's letting on, and that frustrates me to no end.

"Know anyone in town named Drew who was once in the navy?"

"Drew . . ." He scrunches up his face, and I can't tell if he's actually thinking about this or pretending to. That's weird. He wouldn't be lying to me . . . right? The one person in my life that I trust not to lie to me for any reason. Especially for no reason. And some random guy from my mom's past definitely seems like a silly reason to lie.

So maybe it's just my imagination.

Maybe I'm projecting all my mom's lies onto him. It's getting confusing.

The wind's blowing pretty hard, and I can hear waves break-ing just over a shrubby line of pink beach roses past the circle. "See, that's always been her big dream, to move to Florida. The endgame. Everything's better in Florida—that's what she's told me constantly for the past few years. That's why we're here right now in Beauty, in fact. So she can save money and we can move to Florida."

"But you aren't going with her," he points out. "LA is a long way from Florida."

My chest squeezes as I lower my camera. "A very long way."

"If your mom is convinced that she's going to settle down in Florida and stay put there, then why don't you just go with her instead of moving to LA? Do you not trust that she'll stay in Florida?"

It takes me a long time to answer. "Remember how the Summers & Co store window was before I broke it?"

"Much the same as it is now, only it was a lot filthier back then."

I huff in frustration. "What I mean is, remember how they had all the beautiful Christmas displays, and people would stand outside on the sidewalk and press their faces against the glass and stare at the pretty, sparkly things inside the display window that were *just* on the other side of the glass, *just* out of reach, but they couldn't touch?"

"Sure?"

"That's what it's like, living with my mom."

He shakes his head, confused.

"She's beautiful and sparkly, but just out of reach. I'm just a stupid bird that sometimes flies into the glass and gets hurt."

His brow lifts. "Ah . . . She's got an invisible wall up."

"You know," I say, peering at him thoughtfully, "I think she really might. And if I had to guess, it went up after the big fight with Grandma, when we left Beauty five years ago. And to tell you the truth, I'm not sure it will ever come down. Not for me, not for anyone."

"You never told me what that fight was about. What caused the neighbors to call the police all those years ago?"

I shrug. "The funny thing is, I don't even know most of it. Some of it, I think I've blocked out, and some of it, I just couldn't hear clearly. I was in my bedroom—they wouldn't let me come out—and they were in the kitchen. I heard a lot of swearing and shouting. I heard my name, so I know some of it was about me. About Mom getting pregnant with me in college and decisions she made. Maybe she regrets keeping me, I don't know."

"Aw, come on," Lucky chastises. "Winona adores you. Anyone can see it. She brags about you nonstop to every customer that walks in the shop."

This surprises me. So much so, that I'm not sure I believe him. "Well, I didn't say the *entire* fight was about me, but like everything else, Mom won't talk about it. Forbidden subject. And if we can't talk about it, how can we get past it? So maybe you're right about the invisible wall theory. You and I, we're okay now, because we let down the wall. But Mom and me? I'm not sure we can ever be fixed. If there's a permanent wall up between us, blocking any communication, the only way it's coming down is with a bomb—see? That's why that fight with Grandma happened."

"Which is why you won't go to Florida with her," he says, finally understanding.

"It would be like flying smack into the Summers & Co window. Only pain and heartbreak for us little birds, not palm trees and sand."

The skies darken dramatically. It smells like rain. It almost feels as if I could have conjured it with my guilt.

"Did you hear that?" Lucky asks, head tilted.

I still, listening. I hear nothing. Wind? Waves? What happened to the birds? The dark sky lights up blinding white and a terrible crack strikes the island—so loud, it startles me. My foot slips on the rocky ground, and I drop my Nikon.

"My camera . . ." I check it quickly, but it seems to be fine. I quickly close the lens and stow it away in its leather case as Lucky brushes dirt off my shirt. "That was lightning?"

"Yeah, and it definitely hit something nearby," he confirms. "Maybe a tree or the lighthouse. It's the tallest thing around. That's what it'll go for."

"What about us? Will it go for us?"

The skies darken again as if it's midnight, not four in the afternoon.

Thunder rumbles, and it's loud. More lightning strikes. White.

Bright. Close. Very, very scary. But this time, it doesn't crack the sky open. It just brings rain. Sudden, surprising, steady.

"Shit!" Lucky says. "Let's go to the boat and head back to town."

"Is it safe to be out on the water in this weather?"

"It's not windy, and the lightning's passed. Yeah. We'll keep an eye on it."

He seems remarkably unfazed. He knows what's he's doing. Everything's fine.

We quickly pack my camera case inside the cooler bag because it's fairly water resistant, and then we make a run for it, jogging down the muddying path through a gentle but steady rain. It's light enough to see, but not as well as I'd prefer. I spy the lighthouse up ahead, and Lucky says that's a promising sign that it wasn't hit by the strike—especially when we jog out of the woods and spot the little dock house with the fabulously weird Rapture Island sign and the fragrant beach roses.

Lightning flashes again.

I jump, startled. Lucky, pulls me toward the dock house, under the modest cover that the door's overhang provides. "We need to stay here until the lightning passes," he says, pointing to a metal stick jutting at an angle from the top of the dock house's utility pole. "Nice, fat lightning rod. Better to let it strike that than us."

"Yes, please," I say as the rain comes down harder.

He pulls me closer and looks behind us. "In fact, maybe we should go inside."

"Is that legal?"

"Do you see a sign, Miss Sign Lady?"

I . . . do not. The island will probably curse us, but what do I care? I'm already cursed.

The windows are dark, and the door's barred, but it's just a latch on the outside—no lock. I lift it, and the door pushes open easily. No light switch inside, but the utility light shines through the window in a slant, and it's enough illumination to see one big, empty room. Wood floors. Wood ceiling. Wood walls with a few shelves and a built-in desk that looks as if it was once a ticket-window, maybe for a ferry that ran here at one time or another. A dinosaur landline telephone sits there, the rotary kind with a dial, but it's not even plugged in; its cord is wrapped around it like a noose, and the panel where it fits into the wall is missing. The only other things in the small room are a wooden chair, a few old manuals, some mooring rope, and a multipack of lightbulbs—presumably for the utility light outside.

Most important: It's dry, and there's no lightning.

All the winning.

"Hey, sort of reminds me of the North Star," I say.

He makes an amused noise. "Sort of does . . . only, there are four walls and no gnarly tree growing through the roof."

"True. More like North Star's luxury annex, then."

"And look at us, breaking and entering it," Lucky says, pushing wet hair that's gone wildly curly out of his eyes as he throws our cooler on the floor to keep the door propped open.

"Oh dear . . . What will people say?"

"There go those darn vandals again, being wicked."

"Better call the cops."

He slings an arm around my waist. "I could make a citizen's arrest, if it will clear your conscience."

"Do you have the power to arrest me out here? I think we're in international waters, or something. We could probably gamble and trade arms. Transport bricks of strange drugs. Something about maritime laws . . ."

"You really don't pay attention in class, do you?"

"I definitely won't in the fall, now that I've got me a perfect-SAT boyfriend," I joke.

He lowers his face near mine, eyes glittering. "Am I?"

"Are you . . . ?"

"Your boyfriend?"

I still, heart racing, as rain pounds on the metal roof above us.

"Don't do that," he says in a raspy voice, sliding a hand behind my neck. "Don't put up the invisible wall. Please, Josie. If you don't want to answer the question, then I'll go first. . . . So here's the truth. You're my friend. The only person I can talk to without censoring myself. You laugh at my jokes."

"That's because your sense of humor is as bad as mine."

"Worse," he confirms, pushing damp hair away from my eyes. "And when I see your face, it makes me feel like everything is going to be okay. Like maybe . . . like, sure I might be a little bit of a monster—"

"Lucky."

"—but here's this beautiful, talented, glowing person who obviously likes me, because she smiles at me and laughs at my jokes, and she's all I can think about, and sometimes I even dream about her, and I love the way her freckles scrunch together when she gets mad at me, which is sort of sexy, and I love how she blushes when I stare at her a little too long—"

He swipes his thumb over my cheek, and I shiver.

"—but most of all, I think . . . if this person likes me, *this* person . . . then I must not be *too* much of a monster. I must be okay. So to answer the question, yes. In my mind, you're absolutely, unquestionably, categorically my girlfriend."

"Don't change your answer," I say, trapping his hand against my cheek with my fingers.

He whispers, "Don't break my heart. Don't go to California."

I close my eyes and inhale sharply. Exhale shakily. Rain hits the roof above us.

I don't want to hear the time bomb ticking.

But there it is in my head, *tick, tick, tick . . .*

Before I open my eyes again, Lucky kisses me softly, until goose bumps spread over my skin, and deeply, until all my bones soften like rubber. Then his mouth is all over my neck, trailing kisses over my skin like tiny blessings, murmuring soft devotions in my ear.

Tick, tick, tick . . .

Beneath his damp shirt, my fingers trace the jagged shape of his spine, and I marvel at the surrounding muscle. A thousand warm chills rush across my skin until my knees get wobbly, and I don't want to stand. He pulls me down with him to the dry floor.

Tick, tick . . .

I kiss the scars around his face until he shivers beneath me. He molds the ditch of my back, urging my hips toward his, and I'm achingly aware of the hard outline pressing against the place in my jeans where my seams converge. I think we should take more clothes off.

Tick . . .

"Josie," he says to me, "what you told me that night in the police station?"

I already have skin exposed. I don't want to talk about any of that. I don't want to change my mind. "I want this."

"Good. Me too." He holds my face in both hands. "Just so you know, none of the rumors about me are true. We're the same, Josie."

My heart races. What is he saying? All the blood from my brain has shifted southward.

Oh.

Wait.

Lucky is a virgin?

LUCKY IS A VIRGIN TOO.

I listen for the ticking inside my head:

Silence.

"Do you have a condom?" I ask, a little shaky and awash in emotion.

He nods slowly, eyes hooded and lazy as he stares at me.

I'm not blushing now. . . .

As lightning flashes, we peel off the rest of our clothes as if we're trying to race the storm, hungry and afraid we'll lose each other. But we don't, and it doesn't take us long to figure out that losing your virginity isn't a thing that happens all at once. It's not part A inserted into part B equals done. It's more of a multi-part triathlon than a continuous sprint, and there's no camera to hide behind, no program to digitally edit out the details I don't like.

Everything's there, for better or worse. Lucky can see all of me.

But it's okay, because I can see all of him, too. Lucky 2.0 and every Lucky I've known.

I can see the scars on his forehead, and the way his hands tremble because he doesn't want to hurt me. In his eyes, I can see the years of solitude, the resentment and bitterness, the scars from the fire, every rumor around town. I see it all. The good, the bad, and the lonely.

But the thing that surprises me most is the commentary.

The conversation.

All the honest communication that happens when there isn't even a *chance* at an invisible wall . . .

The heated whispers—"Here." Explicit directions, "Not like that—Jesus! *Don't ever do that.*" Quick apologies, "Sorry-sorry-sorry." And simple assurances: "You're perfect. This is perfect. We're perfect."

And for one beautiful, gasping moment, we truly are.

The scent of beach roses drifts through the dock house on a warm breeze. Flush with pleasure, I listen to the rain on the roof and the strong, otherworldly thudding of his heart against mine, our limbs intertwined, feeling weightless and filled with bliss and hope.

I don't feel cursed at all.

For the first time in years, I don't feel alone.

I want to stay here. I want it to last forever.

I know it can't.

But when the doorway of the dock house lights up, and an apocalyptic crash thunders beneath our bodies, I'm genuinely surprised that we don't even get five stinking minutes.

FOR EMERGENCIES, SEE LIGHTHOUSE KEEPER: Sign posted inside small dock house at northern end of Rapture Island in Narragansett Bay. The rugged building doesn't appear to have been in use for many years. *(Personal photo/ Josephine Saint-Martin)*

19

A howling gust of wind roars through the door, driving rain into the dock house. Our cooler shifts across the floor, and the door slams shut, leaving us in darkness.

"What . . . was that?" I shout over the driving rain. It sounds like a war hitting the metal roof. I'm scrambling to get up in a panic, but my legs don't work. Knees jelly.

Naked Lucky is already on his feet, taking all his warmth away, and yanking the door open to peer outside.

Can't see much of anything—it's raining too hard—but I think the dock house got struck by lightning. The gods are smiting us for our wickedness.

"Did we get hit?" I shout, holding a hand up to my face as rain comes through the crack in the door that Lucky peers through. "The lightning rod worked?"

It must have, because we're still standing. "Can't see anything," Lucky says, coming back to hurriedly slip his clothes on, and I do the same, a little panicked. After a minute or so, when the rain slows enough for us to open the door all the way and prop it back with the cooler, we both stick our heads outside to assess the damage. I notice that a utility light is now shining down on the sign. It's probably automatic, one that has a sensor that detects when it's dark and triggers it to turn on. I'm so busy thinking about this that I don't notice that Lucky is frozen.

He's staring agog at the pier.

What's that funny smell?

Oh God.

He's not staring at the pier, because there is no pier. There's only a single wooden pole where it was once attached to the land, and it's scorched black and smoking. Pieces of wood drift on the surface of the dark water in every direction as if they were hit by a bomb. And the *Narwhal* . . .

Our boat is currently unmoored, afloat on the horizon, a good quarter mile away from the island, dragging half the pier behind it.

The dock house wasn't struck by lightning.

The pier was.

We're both too dumbfounded to react for several moments. Then thunder rumbles again in the distance, and Lucky shakes himself roughly, scattering rain droplets over both of us.

We're stranded on an island.

Nobody knows we're here.

And I just had sex for the first time.

With my best friend.

Oh my dear lord . . . I think I'm going to pass out. I snap my seasickness wristbands over and over, as if that will magically help the situation somehow.

"Okay," Lucky says, voice strained. "Let's just be rational here."

"Rational," I agree.

"I could swim out and get it . . . ?" he says, voice going up an octave, as if he can't believe he's suggesting it himself, but he can't think of anything else to do.

Panic fires through my limbs. "Out there? Out *there*?"

"Well? It looks like the pier was hit, not the boat."

I point emphatically. "Who cares? It's already God-only-knows-how-far out in the ocean. You can't swim that! You could drown. Die. There are sharks in the bay!"

"Only dogfish and sandbars."

"At the rate we're going, your mythical kraken is probably down there!"

"Josie—"

"No, Lucky—absolutely not. You aren't Saint Boo. You don't have extra cat lives to risk on stupid feats of machismo—so forget it. We'll just call your dad, and he'll come get us. He's got a tugboat thing-y, right? So even if the *Narwhal* is dead in the water, he can tow it. That's what he does."

"No signal."

"There must be."

Lucky pushes wet hair out of his eyes. "Already checked, back in the stone circle when you were taking photos. There's no signal out here. Usually isn't, once you clear a certain point in the harbor. That's why you need Wi-Fi onboard."

I quickly dig out my phone and shield the screen with one hand. Have I really not checked it the entire time I've been out here? That must be some kind of record. But he's right. No signal. Shit! I swing around wildly, trying to figure out what we can do. Surely there's an emergency call box out here? A rowboat?

"What about the lighthouse? These lights weren't on before?"

"Automatic, probably."

That's what I thought too, but *probably* isn't good enough. What if the lighthouse keeper has returned? We run off toward the lighthouse to double-check, but it's still locked up as tight as it was before. No side door, either. No call box, no nothing.

"Oh, fuck me," Lucky moans over my shoulder as we slosh our way back to the dock house. "How is this happening? Why does everything I do turn to shit?"

I blow out a hard breath and try to think. Can't use our phones. No landline. Lighthouse locked up. Lighthouse keeper nowhere to be found. *Narwhal* too far out to swim to.

Lucky's thinking the same. I can see it in his long face. "Bound to be another boat that comes by here when the storm passes. Barring that, my parents will notice when we don't show up for Sunday dinner. They know we're on the boat.

"They'll notify the Harbormaster," he assures me. "My dad knows the harbor like the back of his hand. He'll find us. And the *Narwhal* can't float away that far. I think?" He shakes his head as if he's not sure but trying to convince himself. "People around here aren't going to steal a boat."

"We pretty much did! What if your parents decide to press charges against us?"

He rolls his eyes. "They aren't going to press charges."

"Sorry, I'm just . . . freaking out."

"Someone will find it floating at sea. It's registered to us, and everyone knows my family. They'll return it."

I try not to let him know how panicked I feel as we enter the dock house. "You're right. It's going to be fine. The *Narwhal* will be fine, you'll get it back, and our parents can't be too mad about lightning. That wasn't our fault."

"Lots of things aren't my fault, but it's funny how I'm always stumbling my way into them," he says, miserable. "Maybe you're not the one who's cursed. Maybe it's me."

"Hey," I say after a quiet moment. "I'd rather be cursed with you than with anyone else right now. In case you care."

He looks up from the floor and gives me a weary smile. "I care."

"We'll get through this. We're outlaws, remember? A couple of desperados."

Lucky snorts. "Oh, that's us, all right. Hardened criminals."

"I can't even drink milk past the expiration date," I admit.

"I take the blame for crimes that aren't even my fault."

I whimper and check my phone again, just to be sure there

isn't a signal. There's really not. Technology: great until it's useless. I pocket my phone and try not to cry.

"Josie?" he says in a low, unguarded voice.

"Yes?"

"Whatever happens, I regret nothing."

I reach for his face and gently run my hand over his scars, pushing back his hair. Awash in emotion. "Whatever happens, I wouldn't change a thing."

DANGER FROM ROUGH SEAS DURING STRONG WINDS: Broken sign posted on a South Harbor public pier near Nick's Boatyard. *(Personal photo/ Josephine Saint-Martin)*

20

By eight o'clock, the hellish rain is only a drizzle, and the island is swarming with five boats: the lighthouse keeper's fishing boat, two harbor patrols, one coast guard, and Lucky's parents, who brought my mom along in their tugboat.

We are rescued.

There's no place for anyone to dock except for the returned lighthouse keeper—who was *actually* "gone fishin'," spotted our boat adrift, and radioed the harbormaster. He's tied up his small fishing vessel somewhere on the other side of the lighthouse, so all the responder boats are bobbing in the water, shining blinding lights onto the shore, talking to us on megaphones and rowing in on smaller rescue boats.

It's a complete shitshow, to be honest.

After we've explained what's happened with the lightning strike and the pier and the *Narwhal* to the lighthouse keeper, harbor patrol, and coast guard—*can this get any worse?*—and when we finally, *finally* make it onboard the Karrases' tugboat, Lucky's father is shouting instructions to Lucky about circling the island to go get the *Narwhal*, and Mom hugs me.

She hugs me way too hard for way too long, telling me that we scared her half to death, and joking that I'm never leaving the house again. She holds me by the shoulders and looks at me a little strangely. Then she reaches for my hair, trying to fuss it back into place.

"Stop," I complain, pushing her hand away.

Her eyes go wide, and she inhales sharply. And that's when I realize: She knows.

She knows what Lucky and I have done.

"Oh, good God," she says. "You've got to be joking. Your best friend?"

"Mom, please," I hiss, using my body as a shield to block her as I lean over the railing and look into the dark water below.

She snorts and mumbles near my ear, "Hope it was worth it."

I don't respond. Of all the times for her to want to communicate openly with me, she chooses *this* moment? Invisible wall button . . . where are you? Pressing button now. *Press-press.*

But she doesn't get the hint and instead uses it as an excuse to scoot up closer to me on the tugboat's railing, shoulder to shoulder, before tossing a glance behind us to ensure no one's listening. "I hope you were safe. Please, Josie. Tell me you were safe."

Ugh. "We were."

Her shoulders relax. "Okay, but I also hope it was worth throwing your life away."

"I didn't throw my life away. Please don't be dramatic."

"Sex can ruin your life, you know."

"That's . . . super healthy, Mom." Especially for someone who does it on the regular. I mean, come on. Is she trying to ruin her own life with sex? That makes no sense.

"I'm just saying, it's not something you should just do with the first warm body that comes along. It's a big step. I hope it was worth it," she repeats.

Seriously? Now she wants to mother me? Oh, the irony. *Oh,* the snarky comebacks I want to hurl back at her. But all I say is, "It was."

"Always seems that way in the moment," she murmurs, glancing toward the other side of the tugboat. "Trust me. Been there."

"What do you want from me?" I say. "I mean, do you think we should have waited until we were married or something?"

She doesn't answer, but the lines of her body are rigid. She's upset. And I don't understand. Lucky isn't a "warm body." He's my friend. Why is she trying to spoil this for me? It's almost like she's jealous that I had a moment of joy with him.

But that can't be right.

Maybe it's what I've suspected before about her sex life: that it's a casino machine that she feeds money into but it never pays out. Something that she does to try to make herself happy, or to distract her from the fact that her life isn't everything she planned. I'm not sure if her plans went wrong when she got pregnant with me in college or when she had the fight with Grandma five years ago.

Or maybe the fight with Grandma was when she had another realization that everything in her life was messed up.

Whatever it is, I don't want to argue with her. Because I look at her now, with her arms crossed tightly across her chest, and I'm just sad.

I'm sad that she's been so unhappy, she's spent the last few years resenting her own mother, dragging her burden of a daughter with her, moving up and down the coast from cars to motels to cheap apartments. And I'm sad that she can't commit to a job or a person, or even a stupid pet.

Maybe it's best that I just shut her out completely going forward, because whatever happens next year with my grandmother and Nepal, I've got to get away from her.

If I'm the reason her life didn't go as planned—

The reason she keeps playing casino games and losing.

The reason she has big blow-out fights with Grandma.

If I'm the reason she's not happy . . .

I've got to leave.

For both our sakes.

Before long, the *Narwhal* comes into view. We chug up alongside it, and I pull myself together while Lucky jumps over to check if it's taking on water (it's not) and if the engine starts (it does). And Mr. Karras is shouting out commands about cutting away the mooring lines attached to the scorched pier. Then

Lucky's piloting the *Narwhal* back to the harbor with his mother, and I'm stuck following behind them on the tugboat with Mr. Karras and my mother, Medusa: bitter woman-turned-monster.

Night falls as we motor into the harbor, its twinkling lights reflected on the dark water. And when we reach the Karrases' boatyard, mooring the tugboat on one side of their small pier, and I'm finally able to step foot on civilized ground again, I'm hurting from the things Mom and I didn't say to each other, and I'm anxious because Lucky and I went from being as close as we could possibly be to completely separated without any closure.

"Maybe it's best that everyone cools off right now," Kat suggests to my mom as we all drag ourselves across the creaking boards of the boatyard pier. "Everyone's tired and stressed. We can talk about all of this tomorrow after we've had some rest."

"Agreed," Mom says.

I glance at Lucky. A few of hours ago, we were blissed out in each other's arms. Now he looks as if he's been swimming in the harbor for hours. Bone-weary. Defeated. Lost.

That's how I feel too. I want to reach out and hold him, tell him everything will be okay—and for him to tell me the same. But all I can do is watch his beleaguered face over my shoulder as my mother escorts me out of the boatyard, away from the Karrases.

Through the dark side alley, past his vintage Superhawk.

Across the bumpy street, setts steaming and slick with the recent rain.

But when we get to our historic building, instead of heading around back to the rickety staircase to our apartment, we both stop in front of the Nook and stare at the front door.

It's dark inside the bookshop—it's been closed for a couple of hours. But there's always a light on Salty Sally the bookish mermaid that can be seen from the street. Right now, it's also shining on a large poster that's been plastered over our shop's door.

A photograph I'd recognize anywhere.

I'm sure Mom does too.

It's a life-size enlargement of my mother's nude photo.

My pulse lurches and pounds in my temples.

Mom's cry is anguished and broken. She slaps a hand over her mouth before quickly looking around the sidewalk. It's empty now, but a car slows as it passes and the driver gawks.

And that's what snaps me into action. A little fury rises up in me. I quickly dig out my phone and flick on the camera.

"What are you doing?" Mom says, horrified. "You're taking a picture of this?"

"We'll need evidence when we sue."

She raises her hands then drops them, utterly confused. Raindrops dot her cat-eye lenses. "Josie? Sue who?"

"Adrian Summers. Or maybe his father?" I don't know how it works.

A strange sound burrs from Mom's mouth. She just shakes her head in disbelief, ignores me, and races to the Nook's door to snatch at the damp paper. It's been plastered on with some kind of thick glue, and the recent rain has made the paper one big sticker. "It's not coming off!"

I scoot her over and reach for a corner of the poster, using my fingernail to scratch. She's right. It's fixed fast. It rips in places, but it's not coming off in one piece. "It's like wallpaper," I tell I her. "Maybe that's what was used. Wallpaper paste?"

"You might be right." She's able to peel off most of her nipples. "That's a little better. What about the sticker remover gunk in the stockroom?"

"We're almost out, but there's a little left in one of the boxes under the counter. There's a metal scraper, too, I'm pretty sure." Maybe some of the chemicals I use to develop my photos . . . "We'll find something. Come on."

Her hands are shaking so badly, she drops her store keys, so I pick them up and unlock the door, punching in the security code when we step inside. Then I grab some sticky notes from the register, quickly stick as many of them as I can over the remainder of the poster, and shut off the outside light. A temporary fix, but it buys us some time.

Mom turns on a tiny work lamp near the register; the only other illumination comes from the red EXIT sign above the stockroom and streetlights shining through the windows, along with the occasional car headlights. She pulls out a box and slams it on the counter, then proceeds to rifle through it angrily.

"Why would Adrian Summers have one of my modeling photos from college?" she asks in a tight voice.

"No clue," I say. "But he had it on his phone at the party that night Lucky and I got taken to the police station. He thinks it's me."

"What?"

I nod slowly. "Doesn't show your full face . . . only enough of your face that it could be mistaken for mine. And I don't know where he got it. I don't know how many people have seen it, but he flashed it around at the party."

"Oh my God," she whimpers, abandoning her search inside the box. "That photo is all over town? Why didn't you tell me?"

"I didn't want you to worry about it," I say.

"Oh, Josie."

"Anyway, Adrian's the one who did this, probably to get back at Evie because she broke up with him again. And . . ."

And to get back at me.

This is his crowbar through our window.

I didn't cover my tracks well enough—when I caught him in Evie's bed, and I slipped up, talking about throwing the rock.

He knows it wasn't Lucky.

"I can't believe it," Mom says, a stunned look on her face as she stands at the counter, taking off her glasses to wipe them on her shirt. "All these years, and those stupid photos are finally coming back to haunt me now. Unbelievable. I'll tell you who I should sue, and it's not the Summers family. I should sue Henry Zabka."

Umm . . . "Excuse me?"

"They're his photos. I should sue him for releasing them without my permission. I never signed anything that said he could."

Now I'm confused. "You never signed a release?"

"Nope."

"But weren't they for class or whatever?"

"It was a private session on campus, but after he showed them in class as examples, I later found out that no current students are allowed to model, and definitely no one under twenty-one. He pretended to be ignorant about it, like it was an honest mistake. But he knew all along what he was doing. I wouldn't be surprised if he distributed the photos online somewhere."

"Whoa," I say. "Let's not go flinging accusations. You don't know how Adrian got this photo. Maybe Henry donated them to the school?"

"Without my permission?

Yikes. Yeah, even I know that's not legit. "I'm sure it's just a mix-up. Maybe they were stolen—off the cloud, or something? That happens all the time."

"You're defending him?"

"Someone has to," I say. "Everyone is always attacking him, and no one here knows him. Maybe give him the benefit of the doubt, okay? He's a family man now. Why would he suddenly release nude photos of you for revenge?"

She chuckles darkly. "A family man. Oh, you know him so well, do you? Those yearly phone calls that last for all of five minutes? Because he can't be bothered to come visit you anymore. The last time he saw you in person was for half an hour at Thirtieth Street

Station in Philadelphia two years ago when he was waiting for a train. You were fifteen."

"He's busy! And we text."

"Oh really?"

"I send him photos to show him what I've been working on."

"And he comments on those photos?"

"He did once . . . a few months ago." He told me to work on my negative space.

"That's what I thought," she says, sneering. "He's a rat, and I'm going to sue him."

This is ridiculous! Why is she going after my father when Adrian is clearly the enemy here? *He's* the bad guy.

Something rises up in my chest, and I think of the invisible wall between me and Lucky. And how Lucky said there's one between me and Mom, too. Maybe I have more control over it than I thought.

After all, communication doesn't run one way.

"You want to know the truth?" I ask her in a low voice, feeling the need to divulge bubble up inside me, dark and angry and wanting to be free. "The absolute shocking truth?"

"Babe," she says in a tight voice, "my naked body is out on the door of my mother's bookshop for all of Beauty to see. Nothing you can say to me will shock me right now."

"Are you sure?"

"Positive."

"Okay . . ." I warn her one last time.

She puts her glasses back on angrily. "Just say it, Josie."

"Fine! I don't want to move to Florida with you. I've been planning to go live with Henry in Los Angeles when I graduate."

Mom stills. Then she inhales sharply through her nostrils. Like I've slugged her in the gut.

"Look," I tell her, "I think it's clear that something is broken between us, because you don't talk to me about anything. The last few years have been hard, and I can't handle moving around the country with you anymore. I don't even know if you'll end up in Florida at this point, and I need stability. On top of that, it's not fair that you kept me away from an entire side of my family. That's so selfish, Mom. He's an award-winning photographer. I could be learning things from him. I could have grandparents who aren't running around Nepal. I could have a normal life in Los Angeles! And . . . and . . ."

I try to plow on with my angry tirade, but everything Mom just told me flashes through my head along with the poster on the shop's door. It's muddling things, and I'm getting rattled.

"And *now* . . ." I continue, though not as surefooted. "Now it almost sounds like you're accusing him of things, and I don't know what to believe, but it's confusing, because I haven't heard his side of the story, and . . . it's not fair. It's not fair that you've kept me from him all these years."

"I haven't kept you from Henry Zabka," she says, biting out every word as if she's barely able to control the anger in her voice. "You want to be a part of his family? It's bigger than you think. Your so-called father has three kids in three states. I wasn't the first teen-age girl to model for Henry Zabka, okay? He was a creep, Josie."

"What?" I say, blinking away shock.

"He may be a genius, but that doesn't mean he's not a goddamn loser. He preyed on me—I didn't know it until years later that there were others, okay? That's why he lost his teaching job. Because he was an asshole who had a thing for college students. So he doesn't want you because he never wanted to be a father."

"That can't be true," I say, tears slipping down my cheeks.

"That's what I thought too, back then. He didn't want his name on your birth certificate. He said he'd make my life a living hell if I tried to get child support out of him—because he had nude photos of me, and what kind of mother does that?

"Josie," she says, eyes glossy with unshed tears. "What do you think your grandmother and I were fighting about when we left Beauty five years ago?"

"I—I . . ." My breath comes faster. Thinking about that terrible night is the last thing I want to do, but it comes back to me now, unbidden. Waking up in the middle of their argument. Grandma shouting. Mom crying . . . Red and blue lights flashing outside the window on the street below.

Mom told me to pack as fast as I could. Only my favorite clothes and the stuff I'd need for a week. A short trip, until we figured things out. That's what she told me. She said not to listen to what I heard—that none of it was true.

She told me to hurry.

Not to bother to get to dressed.

Grandma was having a breakdown.

No one was getting arrested.

Everything was going to be okay.

We'd call Lucky from the road.

We were coming back when things cooled off.

A week.

Two weeks.

A month.

Five years.

Mom stares at me now over the bookshop counter. "Five years ago, Henry Zabka was still working at the university. Your grandmother was trying to pressure me to get child support out of him, and when I refused, she went behind my back and hired a private detective to look into him."

A private detective . . . Briefly, my head fills up with the scent of Christmas that always wafts from the hand-dipped colonial candle store down the alley—and the empty door next to it with the bright red FOR RENT sign. Former office of Desmond Banks, private investigator.

"A detective? Like a PI?" I ask.

She nods. "And he uncovered . . . all kinds of nasty things about Henry Zabka."

The argument.

The big blowup that sent us fleeing Beauty in the middle of the night.

The argument was a little bit about me, yes.

But it was really about my father.

I shake my head as tears fall. "No, no, no."

"I tried to keep you away from it," she says, taking off her glasses again to wipe at her eyes. "I tried so hard. I didn't want you to hate him like I hated him. I didn't even want to believe it myself. I thought it was just your grandmother trying to be controlling. She's done that before with my life. This wasn't the first time the meddlesome old bat tried to ruin my relationship with someone—"

Her voice breaks.

She swallows and starts again.

"However, I took a second look at what her private detective uncovered, and . . . it was pretty damning. A few months later, I contacted the university and got him fired. Well. Quietly dismissed—that's what they called it. They promised he'd never know it was me who came forward, if I agreed not to sue. That's when he went back to LA and his career *really* took off. Which was depressing, honestly. It felt like he was being rewarded, and we were . . . left behind to fend for ourselves."

"Mom—"

"So screw him. If you're talented in any way, then I choose to think that you inherited that from me, not from him. Because once upon a time, I was talented too."

I'm shocked.

Devasted.

I don't know what to say.

The lines on my mom's face harden. "So yes, I may be a terrible mother. And I know I haven't been present. I hate myself for that—I hate being depressed, and I hate that you notice it, because more than anything, I wish I could keep you in a bubble, nice and safe, so you'd never have to know any of these things, and you'd never be hurt or unhappy. If I could have one wish in life, I would spend it on that."

"I'm not a child, Mom!" I say, exasperated. "I haven't been for a long time. You could have told me this years ago!"

"Maybe so, but you're wrong about one thing," she says, pointing a finger in my direction. "You'll *always* be my child, and I'll always be your parent. And see, that's the difference between me and Henry Zabka. No matter how badly I've screwed up sometimes, I'm here for you, right now, and I've always wanted you, every single day you've drawn breath. So I'm sorry if that's disappointing—I'm sorry I've dragged you around from town to town, and I'm sorry I wasn't the parent you wanted. I'm sorry I wasn't the famous photographer and just plain old cursed Winona Saint-Martin. But for better or worse, you're stuck with me, aren't you? Because if you try to leave me, I swear to all things holy, I will chase you down, Josie. You're not an adult yet, and I'm still your mother, even if you hate my guts."

Shaking and upset, she tosses the box of supplies back beneath the counter and yanks out another one, plopping it down by the register with a loud thud to angrily search through its motley contents. One of Grandma's Nepalese postcards falls off its taped anchor and flutters to the floor.

All I can do is watch her in a daze, rocked to my core.

Heartbroken. It feels as if she's taken a rock and smashed all my dreams like I smashed the Summers & Co window. Only, no one can bail me out this time. Not even Lucky.

Funny that I thought once he might be a mirage. The real mirage was Henry Zabka.

I don't have a father.

I don't have a mentor.

Los Angeles is just a city, not a utopian place where all my troubles will fall away.

Nothing's real. I'm stuck here with no exit strategy when the ticking time bomb goes off.

It was all a lie.

Neither of us speaks for a long moment while she tears through the box of supplies, making a racket inside the quiet, dark shop. Then I remember something she said, and it aligns with a puzzle piece that's stuck inside the back of my head.

The invisible wall isn't just down between us, it's collapsed for good. Might as well put it all out there now. So I ask in a soft voice, "Who's Drew?"

Her hands still inside the box. But she says nothing.

"I saw his inscription inside your high school yearbook," I say. "And I'm pretty sure he was in the navy and came back to town. I know Aunt Franny was surprised you were willing to come back to Beauty with him here. Who's Drew, Mom?" I ask again.

She exhales heavily and rests against the stool behind the counter. It takes her a long time to answer, but she finally says,

"Drew was the love of my life. We were going to run away together after we graduated from high school. Your grandmother caught us and put a stop to it. Told his parents. They were furious. Made him enlist in the navy, and he got shipped off to the Persian Gulf almost immediately. That was that. One day he was there, and the next, he was just . . . gone."

"Oh my God," I murmur. Like me and Lucky.

She sighs. "Oh, in retrospect, maybe she was right. Maybe we were too young to get married. I don't know. I wasn't sensible like you are. I was 'Wild Winona,' who made a lot of mistakes and did a lot of impulsive things. Running off to Florida with no plan seemed like something fun to do, so I'm not even sure if I was in it for the right reason. But then I went to college, where I met your father, and the rest is history."

Right. Everything went to shit after that. Now I'm starting to see the root of the problems between Mom and Grandma.

"Still, I think about him a lot," she says, wistful.

"Have you kept in touch with him?"

"Not a peep. I saw him once, at your uncle's funeral last year. We didn't speak. I was shocked to see his face again, honestly. I think he was shocked to see me, too. I know he was married to a woman when he was stationed on a naval base in Japan, but they later divorced. I don't know what's going on with him now. I've made an effort to steer clear of him since we've been back in town. The Saint-Martin curse . . . ," she says weakly.

A little tingle starts in my fingers and races up my arms.

"Mom . . . what does Drew do now that he's retired from the navy?"

"He took over his family's business." She gives me an uncomfortable, awkward look. "On Lamplighter Lane."

The portal to hell. The place mom avoids. It's not the root of all evil in town—it's the place where she left her broken heart.

And I know exactly one business on Lamplighter Lane.

The blacksmith where Lucky is apprenticing.

"Drew . . . Sideris," I guess.

She nods. "Lucky told you?"

"No," I say. "Actually not. He's apprenticing for him, though, and I think he must know, because he's been cagey about it."

"The night of the boatyard window breaking, Kat told me that Lucky was learning metallurgy, so I kind of figured . . ." She shrugs, face pulling to one side. "Drew's parents live down the street from the Karrases. They've done a lot of the ironwork around Beauty. His father made Salty Sally out front," she says, gesturing toward the bookshop door. Then she crosses her arms and sighs. "Beauty's a small town. Everyone's trees are growing over each other's fences."

Maybe knocking a few fences down.

"So . . . Lucky got lucky, huh?" she says.

"Mom."

"Sorry," she says, turning her head to give me a soft smile. "Do you need to . . . talk about anything? He for sure used a condom, right?"

"Yes, and no, I don't need to talk about anything. I'm perfectly fine."

"I mean, I know you were angry when you said it on the tugboat, but I guess I kinda did hope you'd wait until you were married, or whatever the right way to do things is."

"Is there a right way?"

She throws up her hands. "You're asking me? How would I know? I'll tell you what, though—there's *definitely* a wrong way. That, I know. The wrong way is when you immediately think, 'Oh crap. I've made a *huge* mistake.' Did you think that afterward?"

I shake my head. "Nope. Not a bit."

"That's good." After a long moment she admits, "To be honest, I'm glad it was him. He's a good kid. I like him."

"Pfft. You do not."

"He's funny and smart. And he's hardworking, which I like. Plus, he was also good to you, even when you were kids. Guess I misjudged him when we first came back to Beauty."

"Rough exterior, soft on the inside," I tell her. "I like him, Mom. A lot."

She nods slowly. "Maybe I was being overprotective of you because I don't want you making the same mistakes I've made. I don't want you to get hurt."

I stare at my mother, silhouetted in the window, golden headlights from the road shifting shadows across her, and it's as if I'm seeing her for the first time. As if I've spent the last few years only looking at her through a camera lens that was smudged with grease and dirt, and now I've wiped it clean and can finally see her clearly.

A mama bird with a broken wing, trying to find a safe nest.

Swiping right, trying to find something she lost, or maybe to forget.

A car pulls up to the curb outside the bookshop. I turned off the light on the shop to get the spotlight off the stupid nude poster of Mom, so between that and the display of Revolutionary War sailing books, it's hard to make out what's going on . . . but it looks like a taxi.

"What's that?" I ask, coming up behind Mom as she stands on tiptoes to peer out the shop window.

"Oh no. *No, no, no . . .*"

"Mom? You're scaring me."

"Shit! The poster—it's still on the door."

"It's fine. I covered it up." Sort of.

She cradles the sides of her face. "What have I done to deserve this?"

Panic flicks to life inside my chest and trickles into my limbs, making them go numb. My throat goes dry. I should do something, but what that is, I don't know. So I just stand there, stock still, side by side with Mom, watching in horror as the bookshop door darkens, rattles, and then finally, after a set of keys is inserted into the lock, *oh-so-slowly* creaks open.

The ticking time bomb walks into the bookshop.

BEAUTY REGIONAL AIRPORT: Small, private airport mainly used by people who can afford to own their own planes or charter private jets and can't be bothered driving for less than an hour to get to the closest international airport in Providence, Rhode Island. *(Personal photo/Josephine Saint-Martin)*

21

Diedre Saint-Martin stands in the open door of the Nook, silver hair in a long, tight braid that's tucked into the front of a lightweight gray jacket, and drops a colorful, bulging backpack on the floor in front of her near a pair of worn hiking boots.

"What in the living hell is that?" she says, pointing a thin finger behind her at the door, where my Aunt Franny is cautiously entering, along with the taxi driver, who is helping to lug several pieces of luggage labeled with white airport tags.

"Hello, Mother," my mom says through tight lips. "It's nice to see you. Been a year since we've breathed the same air? Here's your granddaughter, by the way."

"Josephine," Grandma says, gesturing for me with outstretched arms. "Come here. I'm too tired to walk. The drive from the airport was complete and utter misery, and I haven't slept for an entire day. Come hug your poor grandmama while your mother tells me why her naked body is plastered all over my shop like we're a brothel in Amsterdam."

Aunt Franny, who is a several years older than my mom and quite a bit lankier—or maybe Nepal has taken a toll on her—pretends to strangle my grandmother behind her back. I don't know how to react to that. Aunt Franny is prim and proper. Most definitely not Wild Winona. What the hell happened in Nepal?

I'm torn. I want to hug my grandmother, but my head's full of things I need to sort out. Plus she may have come back from the airport, but did she get stranded on an island and rescued? I think not. And that's on top of the fact that I HAD SEX FOR THE FIRST TIME.

The bookshop door opens again, and Evie races inside. "Mama!"

Aunt Franny pulls Evie into her arms, and they embrace tightly. "You smell funny," Evie says.

"Cold showers and yak milk," Aunt Franny says. "I just want my bed back."

"Your bed is occupied," Mom reminds her sister. "Your house is still being rented by a family of four. Where is everyone staying?"

"Here, of course," Grandma says.

One, two, three, four, five. Five people, three bedrooms.

And half of us aren't on speaking terms.

"We don't fit," Mom points out.

"We'll find a way. Franny, pay the driver," Grandma says bluntly.

Aunt Franny grumbles under her breath.

"For the last time, and before we do anything else," Grandma says in a louder voice, "why is there a naked photo of my daughter on the front of my shop?"

"Adrian Summers put it there!" I shout.

Everyone looks at me.

"Adrian Summers?" Grandma says. "Levi's boy? Why in the world would he do that? He's at Harvard. That's preposterous."

I look at Evie. She broke up with Adrian, and this isn't her problem anymore. It's mine. It's always been mine. Now it's time to own up to it.

"Because," I tell Grandma, exhaling deeply, "he somehow got that photo online and thinks it's me."

"Why would he think that?" she asks.

"I don't know," I tell her. "But he showed that photo to a bunch of Goldens at a party and bad-mouthed all the Saint-Martins, and I got mad, so . . ." I turn to my Mom. "So I threw a rock and smashed his father's department store window."

"You what?" Grandma says.

"I got taken into the police station, but not arrested," I tell Grandma. "Lucky took the fall for me. His family's lawyer negotiated with Levi Summers to pay for the window. I've been paying him back out of my paycheck every week." And to my Mom I say, "I'm sorry. I should have told you the truth from the start."

Mom's shoulders slump, as if there's a physical weight to what I've just told her. "Dammit," she mumbles. Not mad. Just defeated. "Josie . . ."

"What in the world is happening here?" Grandma asks. "Police?"

"Mom, stay out of this," my mother warns.

"I wanted to tell you," I say to her in a low voice. "Lucky asked me to keep it secret, because he thought if you knew I was the one who threw the rock, that you'd be furious at me, and you'd make us leave town like before. I think—I think he was afraid we'd be separated again."

"Winnie," my grandmother says to my mother. "I'd like an explanation, please."

Mom curses under her breath.

At least I was honest. At least I communicated. But I may have also just lit the fuse on the ticking time bomb, and I don't have a plan to run for cover. No plans whatsoever.

"I leave for six months, and this entire place just goes to hell?" Grandma says, her face pinched. "Six months! That's all it took for the two of you to turn my life's work upside down? Nude photos . . . vandalism? Police station?" Grandma says, throwing a hand in my direction. "And now Levi Summers is involved, the pillar of our community? His son is going to the Olympics. He wouldn't have done this."

Oh my God. Et tu, Grandma?

"He did it," Evie confirms, Cleopatra-rimmed eyes on mine in solidarity.

Thank you, cuz.

"I was at the party with Josie when he flashed the picture around," she continues. "He definitely is trashing our family name around town and spreading gossip, and I know because we've been seeing each other off and on for months."

"Then he got mad at Lucky when he was drunk, and he broke

the boatyard window with a crowbar," I tell Grandma. "No one in town believes he did it, but he threatened Lucky, and I saw him drive past. He's all but admitted it, and he doesn't care because his dad owns this town."

Evie concludes, "And I think the poster outside is revenge because I won't sleep with him anymore. He's an asshole. I just didn't see it soon enough."

"Hey, it happens," Mom says.

My grandmother puts a hand over her heart. "What in the world . . . ? What is happening to you girls? Franny. Did you know about this?"

"It's why I wanted to come home, Mom," Aunt Franny admits. "I want to be with my daughter."

"Well, bully for you." Grandma looks around at all of us, stunned. "I can't believe any of this. Everything was fine until we left." She narrows her gaze at Mom. "Until you came back."

Whoa. Hey now. Okay, wait. If anyone's to blame here, it's Adrian Summers. Did we not just explain? WHY DOES NO ONE UNDERSTAND THIS, FOR THE LOVE OF PETE?

Mom turns to me and a calmness sweeps over her features. "Shutterbug? I'm going to tape a piece of butcher paper over the door to cover up the poster. You go upstairs and pack. We need to find a motel before it gets too late."

Everything inside my head empties at once.

Nothing but blank, empty space. Shiny and bright to match the empty cavern inside my chest. The only thing I feel is a strange buzzing all through my body—one that's so loud, it drowns out the sounds of the shouting in the shop. I half-hear what's being said, but I don't really feel it.

"You're leaving?" Grandma shouts. "Like cowards? Is that what you're doing? Tucking your tails and running, like you did before?"

"Run the shop tomorrow by yourself, Mother," my mom says. "I'll text you the new safe combination. Great seeing you again."

My chest feels too hot. Is it warm in here? Why is there no air conditioning in this stupid store? I'm going to pass out. I thought Mom and I were finally on the same page. I did the right thing and admitted my guilt. I told the truth about the window. It's all out in the open. No invisible walls.

But here we are.

I soldier past the rest of the Saint-Martins, Evie clinging to Aunt Franny, Grandma shouting at Mom, and I head outside the Nook. I walk around the building and head up the rickety staircase to the above-shop apartment, through the living room of our stuff mixed with Grandma's things, and I enter my bedroom.

I can pack in ten minutes. I've done it before. In the middle of the night, even. Just like this. But I can't seem to make my legs move. I can't quite put my adrenaline to work. The panic is there, but it's not fueling anything. My body is just spinning in place. Empty. Bright.

My gaze lights on the Nikon F3 sitting on my bookshelf.

Prized possession. Gift from my father.

What a goddamned joke.

I don't think—I can't. My head is empty. I just stride to the bookshelf, snatch up the camera, and smash it against the wall.

Over.

And over.

And over.

Until the metal and plastic and glass break and shatter.

Until shrapnel flies off and scatters around me.

Until footfalls pound the floorboards, and my mother pries what's left of it from my shaking fingers.

"No, baby, no," she says, pulling me into her arms as she drops the broken camera on the floor. "Why did you do that? I didn't want you to do that. I don't want you to hate him."

I squeeze my eyes shut, but there's no stopping the deluge.

"These aren't sad tears," I tell her. "These are angry tears."

"I know . . . I know."

She holds me for a minute, until we both pull ourselves together. Then she clears her throat, looks around at the mess I've made, and says, "Okay. Look. Get your purse and leave the rest. We'll figure this out later. Let's just go find someplace to sleep tonight, okay?"

It takes me a second to realize what that means. And then I do.

Leave the rest.

If we leave our stuff, we're coming back.

"What are we going to do?" I ask.

"Shutterbug, I honestly don't have a damn clue."

Fair enough. I'll take it.

I grab my purse, and we head back outside into the night air. Aunt Franny and Evie are huddled near the Pink Panther with two large pieces of luggage. "Can we come with you?" my mom's sister asks. "I can't spend another night with our mother, and my car's in storage."

Mom holds out her arms to Franny and hugs her, and I reach for Evie's hand. I don't have to say anything, and she doesn't either. We're all good. She squeezes my fingers, and like magic, everything is healed between us, all the tension from her breakup with Adrian is erased.

Family is funny that way.

"Pile in, ladies," Mom says. "Don't know where we'll go . . ."

"I do," Aunt Franny says. "Marblecliff."

"Marblecliff?" the rest of us say in chorus. That's an old-school posh resort in the historic part of town. Suites for wealthy tourists who think the yacht club is too gauche.

"Jeez, Franny," Mom says. "Talk about a town scandal if we show up there."

Evie snorts. "Who cares anymore. We're already the town hags. Cursed, remember?"

"After what I've been through, if there's one thing my late husband would want, it's for me to have a hot shower and a feather bed right now," Aunt Franny says, voice quivering. "I've slept on dirt floors, I've climbed literal mountains, and I've had to tolerate my mother's never-ending petty demands for the last six months. So tonight, I will spend my savings how I see fit, and none of you will argue with me. We're going to Marblecliff."

Mom looks half surprised, half impressed. "You heard her, ladies. Let's hit the road."

We're barely able to fit in the cramped car, but we somehow manage. And as Mom pulls onto the bumpy setts—the only vehicle on the quiet night road—none of us look toward the Nook, but I can feel Grandma watching us from the window. And it makes me . . . sad. How's that for irony? I think I should hate her right now, but I don't, and I can't figure out why.

Before the Pink Panther can pick up speed, someone shouts at us from the sidewalk. Not from the Nook, but from the other side. For the first time, I realize that the boatyard's office lights are still on, and I catch movement on the sidewalk, running toward us.

"Stop the car!" I shout at my mom.

"What?" she says in panic, slamming on the brakes. "Why?"

I roll down my window as Lucky races up to the Pink Panther, breathless.

"You're leaving town?" he shouts into the car, slamming both hands on the window before I can get it down all the way. His eyes jump around the faces in the car, and I know it doesn't escape him that Evie's mother is sitting behind me—maybe he's even watched what's been happening from across the street.

"My grandmother came back—" I try to explain.

"No!" he shouts. "You promised, Josie. You can't leave."

"Hey, Lucky?" Mom lowers her head to peer across me while she speaks to him. "I appreciate that you were trying to help, but we're going to have sort out this window thing with your parents. Josie's told me the truth about what happened the night of the party."

He looks astonished. All the color drains from his face. "Please don't make her leave."

"Whoa, Lucky—" she starts.

And then in the distance, his mom calls out to him, leaning from the boatyard office doorway. "Lucky! Get inside. Let them be."

A car behind us beeps their horn and swerves around us.

"We need to go," Mom says.

"Hey," I tell him quickly, covering his fingers with mine. "Look at me. We don't know what's going to happen, but we're not leaving town tonight. You have to trust me. Please, Lucky. Trust me."

He stares at me intently, face lined with worry and dark shadows.

Then he sticks his head through the window and kisses me. Firmly. In front of both my mom and his . . . our relationship now boldly out in the open. He kisses me like it might be the last time. Like he wants to trust me, but he's filled with doubt, because how do you do that when you've got scars and a history of being left behind?

And the worst thing is, I'm not sure I blame him for worrying.

MARBLECLIFF RESORT: Snootiest and oldest resort in Beauty. Rude people at desk. Walls paper-thin. Best breakfast in town, though, I'll give them that. *(Personal photo/Josephine Saint-Martin)*

22

I didn't think I'd sleep that night. Not with the gilded antique furniture, mounted butterfly collection, a nineteenth century portrait with eyes that seemed to watch me in the darkness, and a fireplace big enough to burn all four of us at once.

But just add that to the ever-growing list of Josie Was Wrong about These Things.

Take, for instance, time bombs. I was *so* certain of an explosion when Grandma Diedre entered town, but I was wrong. Granted, something crouches in the back of my head, still waiting for my grandmother's presence to blow my life to smithereens; maybe she's one of those buried bombs from WWII that you suddenly walk across in a field and it detonates after years of being lost. Or your ship runs into one at sea, and *kablam*! The worst of the bombs.

Or maybe the ticking time bomb of Grandma doesn't matter anymore because the real bombs were the other things I was wrong about all along. Like my mom. And my father . . . Because I'm still struggling to reconcile the image I have of him from all the interviews I've read online—from the few times I've met him. Our scattered phone conversations. His cool life. His perfect family. His house in Malibu.

Wrong. Wrong. Wrong.

God, that stupid magazine internship that I fretted over—that got me so angry at Levi Summers for rejecting me . . . All of it goes back to wanting my father's approval.

And it was all for nothing.

It's hard to accept something's wrong when you once felt *deep in your soul* it was right.

I once felt deep in my soul that Los Angeles was my way forward.

That my father was my ticket out.

That my grandmother was going to tear my family apart.

That my mother didn't want me.

But I was so wrong about all of it.

What else am I wrong about?

What else . . . ?

But I try not to think of it now, here in our suite at the Marblecliff, where not only did I sleep like the dead last night, I did it with Mom curled up next to me in the same bed, because there was only the one room with two queens available when we arrived, bedraggled, at midnight. Evie and Franny took one bed, Mom and I took the other.

One fractured and very strange family.

And I don't know. Maybe Marblecliff's mattresses are stuffed with drugs as well as feathers, or maybe it was the sound of the harbor waves crashing against the rocky cliffs below that lulled us to sleep. Or maybe it was that my entire life was turned upside down in one day, and my body just said, *Forget it, I've had enough*. Regardless, after we deplete all the hot water and luxury hair products in the newly remodeled bathroom, we gather in the suite's cozy sitting area in front of the enormous fireplace, lounging in crested bathrobes.

"I feel like I've just returned from a really bad weekend in Las Vegas," Mom says, looking out over a stunning view of the blue harbor, where the mid-morning sun is glinting across boats dotting the Beauty Yacht Club's waters.

Franny laughs darkly, looking *very* jet-lagged. "Try living in the worst pollution you can imagine with no toilets, electricity, or showers. The people were wonderful, and once you got out of the smog of the city, it was beautiful. But I was trying to juggle grief and Mom, and an entirely different culture, and now . . ." She shakes her head. "Now I think I need a dewormer, because our cheapskate mother forced me to eat some bargain biscuits from the Beauty Supersaver Market that she'd been hoarding in her luggage, and they smelled a little off—and now my stomach hasn't been right for months."

"Wow," Mom says. "We'll take you to a vet today."

"Thanks," Aunt Franny says, smiling for the first time since last night. "I'm okay right now. I've always loved this resort. Softest beds in town. I could live here. . . ."

"You know who owns it now, right?" Evie says, glancing at me. "Bunny Perera's father."

"Seriously?" I say. "This town is small."

"And that family knows their way around some fine, luxury linen," Aunt Franny purrs, pulling her robe around her.

"Hey, Mom?" Evie asks. "Hate to spoil your hotel fantasy vibes, but I'm just wondering. . . . Where are we going to live?"

"No fair," I say. "I was going to ask that first. Aren't we all sort of homeless now?"

Mom sighs heavily. "Yeah, Franny. Glad to see you, but we've got to iron out some kinks. Because Josie and I cannot live with the old bat."

Three quick raps sound on our suite's door. We all turn our heads, and as if summoned by magic, my grandmother's voice slithers through the wood. "Girls? It's Diedre. Are you up? I brought a late breakfast."

Frantic and wide-eyed, Mom motions for everyone to stay silent, but Franny shakes her head. "She knows we're here, sis. The jig is up."

Evie opens the door, and in sashays my grandmother . . . along with three golden carts of breakfast foods, ferried by uniformed servers. I keep my robe pulled closed, watching as a series of cloches are uncovered and fragrant steam fills up the small suite.

Seduction through freshly made patisserie and hot coffee?

This smells like a big old stinkin' trap. I don't trust it.

Mom doesn't either. The entire room is tense. I don't want a fight. I don't want the time bomb to start ticking again in the middle of the pastries and freshly squeezed orange juice.

"Mother . . . what are you doing here?" Mom asks my grandmother in a strained voice. "It's ten-thirty. Don't you have a store to run? Or have you come to ask for my keys back?"

Grandma swings a single gray braid over one shoulder. I need to stop wearing my hair the same way. *Seriously*. It's giving me the creeps. "Why would I do that? Sales are sky-high since you took over. I'm old, but I'm not a half-wit. I've been looking at the P&L reports, Winnie. You're better at managing inventory than I am."

"Did we just enter the Twilight Zone?" Mom asks, looking around the room, squinting. "I didn't see a logo or a sign. . . ."

"I'm closing the shop today," Grandma informs us.

A collective gasp circles the room.

The Nook doesn't close. *Ever*. Only on holidays. Only when it's supposed to. The Nook doesn't close unexpectedly.

"Until I can get some things squared away. Beauty can survive one day without books. We'll reopen tomorrow . . . if we feel like it." Then she inspects her nails and adds, "I put an announcement sign on the door over the nudie of Winnie. Bucky at the art gallery says there's an industrial-strength solvent he'll loan us to get that off later today, by the way."

"Lord, give me strength," Mom says to the ceiling.

Grandma turns to me. "Josephine, do you have something decent to wear? I need you to walk me to my taxi."

I look around, as if there might be another Josephine in the room. "Me?"

"Mother, no," my mom says sharply.

No fighting, no fighting . . .

"I just need to speak with my granddaughter in private for five minutes. I don't bite, and she doesn't look breakable."

My mom starts to protest, but I speak up. "Let me put on my jeans. I'll meet you in the lobby."

After I hurriedly yank on yesterday's clothes, listening through a cracked bathroom door to make sure no spats are breaking out in my absence, I jog through the suite, and Aunt Franny says, "Don't be ashamed to use the panic button on your phone. I used it in Kathmandu. Zero regrets."

Think that's the jet lag talking.

"Be careful" is all Mom warns me, very seriously.

I've got this. It's only a grandmother. Not an actual weapon of war.

That's what I repeat over and over as I stride across plush hotel carpet and head down an elevator to the lobby, which is covered in framed paintings of Beauty in the 1800s and lit by a tasteful chandelier. Marble floors, the pride of our coastal town, gleam in the sunlight as I straighten my shoulders and catch up with Diedre Saint-Martin.

"You're looking lovely," she says. "Too bad about the freckles, but you can cover them up with makeup."

"Thanks?"

"Walk with me," she encourages, nodding toward a set of doors that leads to the back of the resort. Outside, a wide, empty porch winds around the bottom floor of the hotel. I think they have a lot of events out here—wedding photos, things like that. Massive rocks below. Blue water. The Harborwalk, where people the size of bunny rabbits stroll toward the main pier.

A placid scene. Good place for an ambush.

My stomach twists.

"Do you know why I went to Nepal?" Grandma asks, leaning against the railing of the porch to look out over the harbor.

Strange question. "To help Aunt Franny get over Uncle Ed's death."

"That's one reason. But I did it for Winona, too."

"You went to Nepal for my mom?" I say scrunching up my nose.

"That's right," she says, glancing at my face. "See, it took me a few years to figure it out, but I finally did. I wanted my daughter—Winona—and my granddaughter, you, to come home. But the problem was, my daughter hates my guts. You don't know how that feels, because you don't have a daughter yet. But you might one day. And let me tell you, it's the worst feeling in the world."

"She doesn't hate you," I say.

"She does," Grandma says diplomatically. "But I'd like to

change that. And the only way I can do that is if she's home. And the only way to get my daughter home was to leave."

I blink at her. "You went to Nepal . . ."

Grandma nods. "So that Winnie would come home. And bring you home. But hey—I'm no fool. I know relationships take time. And I know everything that's happened was not part of the plan. I like a good plan, see."

"Me too," I say.

"But my plan got screwed up when Franny insisted on coming back early. So here we are. And we can't all live together, of course. There would be five corpses before sundown."

She's not wrong. . . .

"So now we're on to plan B. You have to have a backup plan. It's as important as the main plan. That's what people never understand. It's two plans, really. Two equal plans."

"Two equal plans," I say, realizing immediately that I have failed miserably on this account. Damn. She's good—evil, but good. Tenacious. Wily as a fox, even.

"So, here's my backup plan," she says. "You and Winnie? You take the apartment. I'm moving out."

"Wait—hold on. It's your apartment."

"Yours just as much as mine. We're just stewards. It belongs to all of us. And if we're getting technical, then what I want is to start a conversation with your mother about her taking legal ownership of the apartment. But I thought I'd talk to you first, to make sure that's something you'd want."

"Me?"

"You and your mother."

"But . . . where will you go?"

"I bought a condo before we left for Nepal." She points over the railing, down toward the main pier. There's a little white building past the yacht club. "See that? Robin's Nest Condos. Nick Karras's parents have one there too, which is how I found out about it, at one of Kat's backyard barbecues after church on Sundays—"

What. Is. Happening.

"They've got stair access to the Harborwalk," she says, "and I can walk anywhere, including the Shanty Pub, where there's a group called Yankee Fiddler that plays live traditional New England music every weekend through the fall, and they serve spiked iced lemonade on the patio."

That sounds like a waking nightmare.

"Also," she says brightly, "I can bike to the Nook. Or walk. It's less than a mile. Or I could buy a little boat and dock it at Nick and Kat's, who knows. Maybe I don't need to work as much, anyway. Once a week? I like storytime on Saturdays." She shrugs. "Your mother and I can work out something, I'm sure. And you can keep your darkroom where it's at—as long as you aren't taking nudies like your mother. That's where I put my foot down."

Ugh. Hearing this now makes me ashamed. Why was I so quick to believe Henry Zabka, a man I didn't know, over my own mother? My grandmother did the same thing, believing Adrian Summers to be a perfect golden boy who could do no wrong. Seems as if a lot of women are quick to judge other women, and quicker to forgive men.

"You'll like my condo, though," Grandma says, as if we're making casual conversation and not changing lives. "It's got three bedrooms, and I already furnished it with the basics, so if Franny and Evie need to live with me until we can kick their tenants out, we'll do that."

Aunt Franny won't like that. Doubt Evie will be all that keen on it either.

My head is reeling. Too much information. Too good to be true. Something feels off.

"Now, as far as this situation you've gotten yourself in . . . ," she says.

Okay, I should have known. This is it; the trap is set. My twisting stomach drops to the bottom of the porch and falls into the harbor.

"Grandma—" I start, but she cuts me off with a wave of her hand.

"I already talked to Kat Karras and Levi Summers this morning," she says matter-of-factly. "I told Levi if he doesn't drop the settlement against the Karrases, then I will band together with Kat and sue him for what his boy has done to our neighborhood. I also told him I was on my way to the courthouse to file a restraining order against Adrian for harassing my granddaughters, and that gossip about everything Adrian's done would be all over town by the afternoon. That did the trick, all right."

I try to speak, but nothing comes out of my mouth.

She folds her arms and gives me a smug look. "It wasn't difficult. I've known Levi all my life, and I just told him how it was—that was that. I'm sorry I didn't believe you about his son. I guess I didn't want to. To tell you the truth, Levi Summers is a decent man, and not many are who have the money and power he does, at least in my experience."

"He's dropping the settlement? The window . . ."

"Forgotten. His lawyer's going to talk to Kat's lawyer and work out an agreeable compensation for anything their insurance didn't cover on their broken window. It's done. Forget the window."

I blink at her. "No."

"What do you mean, no?"

"No. That's not right, Grandma. You can't just swoop in here and fix everything. I mean, in regard to the Karrases, I'm one-hundred-percent grateful," I say, hand over heart. "But the window is my problem. I broke it. And because of me, Lucky has not only endured gossip around town, he's been working two jobs to cover the costs. Hard work. Sweaty, demeaning work. All my savings has gone to pay him back—all the cash I earned from my photos online. You just made everything we did this summer completely meaningless. It can't just be for nothing."

She stares at me for a long moment. "You sound just like your mother, you know that?"

"Good. Proud to."

Her head nods once. "Proud that you do too, kid." She exhales. "Okay, I see your point. You're thinking that Diedre Saint-Martin meddled in your life, right? That's what you're thinking. That's what Winnie always says."

Well, yeah. But now I understand why. "You could've asked me first. There wasn't a rush. I haven't eaten breakfast yet!"

"I haven't slept," she admits. "My schedule is all messed up from the flight. But okay. Maybe you have a point. Sometimes I make mistakes and trip over my own feet. If I screwed up, I'm sorry. Nothing is set in stone, though."

Who *is* this woman? Not the grandmother I know. Maybe this is the Diedre Saint-Martin that Lucky keeps telling me about—Grandma 2.0. Or perhaps Grandma 1.5 with some bugs that need updating. She's not perfect, by a long shot, but we all have a little growing to do, so I guess this is a start, anyway.

"I need to pay off the window, Grandma."

"You feel like you still owe a debt? Then pay it back by sticking around and finishing school. Maybe go to college, too? There's a great art school just up the road. Your mother dropped out, but I think she'd like to see you go all the way."

"I don't think so. Mom told me the truth about Henry Zabka—all of it. So I don't know if that's the place for me."

She shakes her head firmly and puts two slender, cool hands on my shoulders. "Listen to me. Don't let that bastard ruin your dreams. He didn't invent the camera. You're talented, kid. If you don't want to go to that college, then study somewhere else. Find a mentor. Hell, be your own mentor—you can learn anything online these days. Like I've told Evie . . . *just do something*. Whatever you decide, don't waste what you've got, okay?"

"I'm trying. It's just hard."

"I know, baby. If it was easy, any clown would do it. But the Saint-Martins were never scared of a little hard work." She pats my shoulders and releases me on a long exhale. It's clear by her body language that this conversation is coming to an end, and suddenly I feel as though this is the longest private conversation we've had in years—and yet somehow, she's not given me nearly enough information.

"Hey, Grandma?" I say. "Was Kat mad? About Lucky taking the fall for me . . . about smashing the department store window?"

"She's . . . confused."

I groan and put both hands on my hips to keep myself steady, frowning at the picture-postcard view in front of us. "Think I better talk to Lucky."

"Probably wise."

"Before the curse has time to sink its teeth into us," I murmur.

Grandma waves a dismissive hand. "That's a load of bull. The Saint-Martins aren't cursed. We just need to stop shutting one another out, that's all. And this is a start, don't you think?" She winks at me and heads toward Marblecliff's lobby, then puts her hand on the doorknob. "Think about the window and tell your mom about staying in the apartment. I'll text you my condo address. We can have dinner there tonight and discuss what to do about the Nook after I try to kick Franny's tenants out of their lease."

"Grandma?" I say, emotions suddenly rising into my throat. "I've missed you."

"Missed you, too," she says, looking surprised. "Welcome home."

She steps into the lobby, and I watch her leave, a woman with too much pep in her step, especially for someone who just flew across the world and managed to meddle in her family's business before breakfast.

Maybe *that's* what bombs feel like when they explode.

I think I've had her all wrong too.

Right now, I'm too muddled to know for sure. Muddled, a little shaky inside, and a lot numb. I guess I'm not sure how I feel about everything she just dropped on me. My phone is buzzing madly in my pocket, the screen filled with texts from my mother, who's upstairs, worrying about what Grandma has said and wanting updates.

I'm okay, but we need to talk.

That's all I text back.

I don't know how else to explain what just happened. I walk around Marblecliff's porch in a daze, trying to sort through it all, looking down at my grandmother's white condo building.

Another text buzzes my phone. *For the love of Pete. Give me a minute to catch my breath, Mom.* But when I glance at the screen, it's not her. In fact, it's not any number I have in my contacts. Unknown. And all the text says is: Low move, even for a Saint-Martin.

I stare at the screen, confused. Then I type a quick response: Who is this?

The reply comes almost immediately: Just the person who is now being hung out to dry by my father because you hid behind your grandmother. Low fucking move.

Oh my God.

Adrian.

Adrian is texting me. How he got my number, I don't know. Maybe I don't want to. I try to decide if I want to engage with him or not, and curiosity gets the better of me. . . .

Me: What do you want?

Adrian: Nothing from you. Evie's blocked my number, so I want you to tell her I'm backing off for now, but I still love her.

Adrian: Tell her I love her, and that I'm sorry.

Adrian: And that when she's ready to talk, I'll be waiting.

Me: I'm not telling her that. You plastered that photo on our shop door, you maniac.

Several seconds tick by, and I start to think that could be it. But just when I'm about to do what Evie did and block his number, he sends one last text.

Adrian: Just FYI, the person who first sent me that photo was your little grease monkey.

LUCKY 13: Black cat decal on sides of motorcycle helmet and matching compartment on back of Superhawk parked in alley near Nick's Boatyard. *(Personal photo/Josephine Saint-Martin)*

23

Adrian's lying.

He has to be. He's a liar and a scumbag, and I have no reason to believe the person who plastered my mother's naked photo over our shop door for revenge. Who threw a crowbar through the Karrases' window. Who said all those horrible things about my family in front of a room of people at that party. Who's basically stalked my cousin since she broke up with him.

Adrian Summers is not a nice person.

So why am I sick to my stomach right now?

Why would I even entertain *any single thing* he told me about Lucky?

He must be lying.

I just don't know *why*.

And that's what's eating away at me while Mom and I leave the Marblecliff with Evie. The three of us are heading back to the above-shop apartment while Aunt Franny keeps the resort suite for a few days, until she can catch up on her jet-lagged sleep and figure out what to do about her rented-out house.

I should be happier to be going back to the apartment. And I am. Relieved, utterly and completely. But I'm also stressed by Grandma's meddling and trying to figure out a counter plan for what she did about the window.

And.

I can't get Adrian's stupid text unstuck from my brain.

A horse-drawn carriage carting two tourists clops past the Pink Panther as we idle by a brick building covered in vines of blooming flowers. Early August heat is making me crankier, and even with all the windows rolled down, we still can't catch a breeze.

"Victory Day is next week," Mom says, ducking her head to see the vertical banners on the gas streetlamps. That means one big last influx of tourists before the end of summer. "Guess they didn't have flotilla celebrations in Nepal."

Bet they didn't have copy shops to print giant nude photos, either. Ugh. I'm just sick with worry and having a low-level panic attack because I just can't stop thinking about why Adrian would say that Lucky gave him my mother's photo.

Why?

Because my grandmother talked to his father and told him to back off the Karrases and rein in his boy. That's the logical reason, right? One last act of revenge against me.

But the thing is, he didn't sound mad. He wasn't threatening me or angry. I look back over the texts to be sure, and yeah. He sounds sad about Evie. And he said he's sorry. I can't tell if that's genuine regret or one of those warning signs from an abusive partner the day after they did something terrible. It's a text, so I can't read his body language or pick up on some of the clues he might leave if I talked to him in person. When it's a text, it's hard to tell . . . I think. I'm not sure. I wish I was more certain.

And here's what else is bothering me: *I've been wrong about everything*. What makes me so sure I haven't been wrong about this, too?

Because now that I'm thinking about it . . . Lucky was really curious about my father. He mentioned that he'd read things about him. He knew things from articles online. Gossip about child support—he definitely had kept up with my father.

If he was poking around online, looking up things about my father, it's not outrageous to think that perhaps, just maybe, he might have come across one of my mom's photos in some kind of photography forum somewhere.

Maybe it started innocently enough, poking around online. How it got to Adrian, I don't know. Macho stupid drunken boys' night? He was at the Golden party that night, after all.

Did he feel bad about it?

Guilty.

Guilty enough to take the fall for me about the window.

No.

That's impossible. I'm mad at myself for even thinking it. And yet . . .

Mom and Evie are talking about the upcoming Victory Day

flotilla across the front seat of the Pink Panther as we head into the South Harbor, passing a line of people waiting to get inside a Revolutionary War–themed wax museum. But I can barely hear them over the rapid thump of my heart. I clutch my purse in my lap so hard, I feel the contents shift inside and have to force my fingers to unclench.

Guilty enough to take the fall.

We turn on our street. Pass Manny's clam shack and the dough-nut shop. Evie is talking about Grandma's surprise condo.

Guilty, guilty, guilty.

"Stop the car!" I shout.

Mom slams on the brakes. A truck behind us honks, and my mother steers toward the curb, narrowly avoiding being rear-ended. "Josie—what the hell?"

"I have to take care of something," I say, jumping out of the car and looking for a break in the traffic to cross over to the boatyard. "I'll meet you at home later. I'm sorry. It's important. It's-or-death relationship important."

Ignoring my mom's complaints, I race across the bumpy street when I get the chance and stride down the sidewalk. The boatyard office is empty, so I head through the side alley. His Superhawk is parked. My pulse goes jangly. I try not to have a complete break-down and continue on until the back concrete of the boatyard spreads out before me.

I spy his father working with two other men on a large docked boat that's being hauled up on a crane. But it's not until I follow a loud noise and peer into the warehouse bays that I see literal sparks flying—arc welding . . . and Lucky's back bent over an engine block.

He's alone. I wait until the bright light stops, and then I approach the work bay as Lucky lifts a metal welder's mask from his face and turns a dial on an orange machine. The thunderous noise it was making goes quiet.

He looks up with wide eyes, startled to see me. But that's quickly ousted by relief.

Nothing but peace on his face. Shoulders dropping, brow easing.

"Thank *God*," he mumbles, head lolling backward for a moment. Then he yanks thick gloves off his hands and starts to come toward me as a machine cools near his knees. "Is everything okay? What's going on? Why didn't you text me? I've been dying over here."

"I'm okay," I say quickly.

He stops and holds both gloves in one hand. His eyes crinkle as he squints at me. "Are you wearing the same clothes as yesterday? Where did you stay last night?"

I don't answer him. I can't get any words out. Because for a moment, it feels as if I'm not one whole person but a fractured being. There's Wary Josie who's trying to decide if Adrian could have been telling the truth, and there's also a childlike Josie who would never in a million years even consider that Lucky could betray us. Trusting Josie melts at the sight of him. Trusting Josie feels joy seeing his grease-smudged face—*my face . . . my boy*—and wants to run to him and fling her arms around his neck.

Trusting Josie is remembering all the things he whispered in the dark when we were tangled together in the dock house back on the island.

Before everything in my life fell apart.

He knows something's amiss. I see the change ripple through him as if he's a dog whose hackles are raising in defense. "Josie? What's wrong?" he asks in a low, measured voice.

Glancing over my shoulder to make sure no one's listening, I scan both the boatyard and the blue harbor for a moment, gathering my courage, and then turn back to him and ask, "Did you send the photo?"

He wasn't expecting that. "Did I . . . what now?"

"The photo," I say, feeling impatient. "Did you send it to Adrian?"

"Huh?" His face squinches up, and he shakes his head tightly. "Feels like I'm missing something. Gonna need more information . . . ?"

I can't tell if he's been intentionally obtuse or if he's confused; either way, it's frustrating. All this time, I just assumed he'd never lie to me, because it was Lucky. It's so strange to stand here and try to judge whether he's telling the truth—as if we're on some kind of game show, and my ability to pick up on tiny clues is the key to my winning a million dollars or losing my sanity and happiness. It's too much pressure, and I'm not good at it.

"Please don't play dumb," I tell him. "I think I've earned that much, at least. Some respect?"

His brows knit together. "What in the world are you talking about?"

"Talking about the nude photo of my mother. You know, the one my father took of my mom in college?"

"Hard to forget it," he says impatiently.

"All this time, I've never been able to figure out where Adrian got it. He finally enlightened me."

Lucky goes very still. "He told you where he got the photo from?"

"Adrian said he got the photo from *you*."

His face puckers. Jaw clicks to one side. He pushes the welding helmet off the back of his head and tosses it across the work bay where it lands on the concrete floor with a loud bang. "Adrian Summers . . . the drunken dirtbag who threw a crowbar into my family's offices, who could have killed my cat—" he says, pointing toward a black shape that lounges in the rafters of the bay, tail hanging low. "Who harassed your cousin and injured her in a car accident, and who told everyone your Photo Funder site was a secret trove of softcore pictures. *That* Adrian."

"Well?"

"Well, what?"

"What do you have to say to that?"

He squints at me as if I've asked him what's at the bottom of the ocean or why the sky doesn't fall down.

Then I realize something I'd forgotten since the night I threw the rock at the Summers & Co department store window. "You thought that photo was of me."

His eyes narrow. "Um . . . ?"

"When Adrian was flashing the photo around at the party, you thought it was a picture of me like everyone else did. You called him an asshole for showing it around. And then in the hospital after Evie's wreck, when you and Adrian were snapping at each other, and he brought up the fact that you called him an asshole, you cut him off and told us all to stop arguing or the nurse would come in and kick us out."

"So?"

"So, maybe you were more concerned that Adrian was high on painkillers, and that he might spill the beans about where he got the photo from—so you were trying to cut him off before he could spit it out!"

"Josie, that's . . ."

"That's what?" I say, feeling delirious and a little unstable.

He shakes his head. "Ludicrous."

"Is it?" I say, voice sounding funny. "Because I also got to thinking about other little white lies you've told me."

"Like what?"

"Like that you knew that *your* Drew Sideris the blacksmith was my mom's Drew Sideris from high school—the same Drew who later joined the navy because my grandmother wouldn't let them be together. The same Drew that I asked you if you knew, and you claimed that you didn't!"

Lucky points a finger at me and opens his mouth, but nothing comes out.

"Ah-ha!" I say. "You lied."

"I never lied . . . exactly."

"You *knew*."

"What was I supposed to do, Josie?" he says, throwing up both hands. "I was caught in the middle. He specifically asked me not to say anything as a favor to him—said that the past was the past and asked me to stay out of it."

I'm confused now, because that *sounds* sensible. But it also hurts, because this Drew person feels like someone he's close to, and he's someone my mom was going to elope with, and I barely know anything about this guy! Meanwhile, Lucky and I are supposed to be as close as two people can get—I mean, we definitely were on the island—and I feel like that should override whatever loyalty he has to some random blacksmith mentor. Shouldn't it?

I don't know, but I don't like how frantic I feel. "I pushed the button! You told me to lift the invisible wall and be teeth-gratingly honest with you. That's supposed to go both ways."

He stares at me, silent, the lines of his face sharp as glass.

"When I asked you if you knew a retired navy guy named Drew, and you *knew* who I was talking about, you should have told me," I insist, but I'm feeling less sure about it.

"It *wasn't my business*, okay? Try to understand my point of view, here, Josie. I'm just trying to do right by everyone. And I was kind of hoping I wouldn't have to keep anyone's secrets for long, because I can't see how Drew and your mom can live in the same town and avoid each other forever, frankly." He shakes that thought away and then says, "But what does it even have to do with Adrian and the photo?"

"Because if you lied about that—"

"Again, I *didn't* lie. I stayed out of someone's business."

"Did you or did you not send Adrian that photo of my mother?"

"The fact that you would even think I would do it . . . that you would even *question* it for one second is so goddamn hurtful," he says. "I would never think that about you—I would *never* doubt you like that."

"Then just say you didn't do it. Swear it."

"No, I won't. You just have to trust me. Like I trusted you."

My chest suddenly feels as if a mixing truck has backed up to it and is dumping ten tons of wet cement inside my ribcage. I press a fist into my breastbone to loosen the sickening tightness. Because the worst thing is, he's right. I *do* have doubts. I'm ashamed that I do, and I'm confused that I do, and I just want him to assure me that he didn't do it.

"You can't do it, can you?" Lucky says in a dark, rough voice.

"It's easier for you!" I say, feeling hot tears filling up my eyes. "Trust is simple for you because your life is stable in Beauty, and you've got a normal family who loves you and makes you feel safe and secure."

"So do you!"

"That's where you're wrong."

"Oh, really? Your mom doesn't count? Your grandmother doesn't count? Evie doesn't count? You've got just as much of a family here as me. You've got roots here, too—Jesus, Josie. You're always going on about that stupid curse. Your family's been here longer than mine has. This is your home as much as it is mine."

"It may be my home, but my family isn't like yours—it's fractured and screwed up!"

"Right, okay," he says, eyes glossy and dark . . . cheeks hollow, "is this where you're going to tell me that you're going to run off to California now? That what we did yesterday is all in the past, and you're just going to head off into the sunset to your superstar father to be part of his perfect family?"

"No!"

"Find that hard to believe."

"Well, believe it, because I found out last night that my father is basically a Humbert who likes to play the Lolita game with college girls!"

A little concern bends his brows. "What?"

"There were other Winonas and Josies in his life, and he got fired from the university over it. He's a loser, okay? So I don't have a father or an apprenticeship, and I'm not going anywhere. I'm staying here. How's that for irony? Huh? The man who took that stupid picture has ruined my mom's life *and* mine. So thanks, Henry Zabka, for building a coffin for my dreams. And thanks, Adrian Summers, for digging the hole. And thank you, Lucky, for kicking dirt on top of it."

"Hey! Don't you dare lump me in with them," he says, getting in my face, eyes flicking back and forth over mine. "Don't—"

"Shut up! Just shut your mouth." I shove at his chest, pushing him back as tears slide down my cheeks. "I didn't put you anywhere. You put yourself there when you decided to share my mom's photo."

I don't even know what I'm saying anymore. Foolishness—that's what.

Because I don't *really* believe he did it. Somewhere in the back of my mind, a small voice is telling me that I'm just angry and raw over all the revelations about my father, and I'm taking it out on Lucky. But I've forgotten all my swimming lessons—forgotten how to kick and float. Now I'm going under the surface.

Now I'm drowning in my own despair.

"If you—" he starts.

"Deny it, then!" I sob loudly. "Tell me you didn't do it!"

"You gonna let me answer?"

"No! You don't get an answer. Because my best friend would never do that . . . and no boyfriend of mine will, either."

He sucks in a quick breath through his nostrils and backs away. Staring at me. Dazed. Horrified. And then, in a blink—

Nothing. All his emotions are wiped, and his expression goes cool and distant.

I can't move. All the wet concrete in my chest is seizing up. I'm going to turn to stone any second now. Going to shatter into a million pieces.

Don't need a ticking time bomb for that.

This is far worse. Somehow, when I wasn't paying attention, the invisible wall went back up. And I wasn't the one who pressed the button.

I'm no longer in control.

I've been shut out.

BEDECK YOUR DECKS: Signs posted in shopfront windows reminding locals to outfit their boats with white lights for the upcoming Victory Day flotilla celebration. *(Personal photo/Josephine Saint-Martin)*

24

It's funny how life keeps going after something monumental happens—or even a lot of monumental things. Life doesn't seem to care or even notice. A war could end a thousand lives in one day, but across the globe, a family still sits down together to eat dinner.

A relationship can end in the boatyard of the South Harbor, but across the street, a mother is reopening the bookstore, because it's never been closed unexpectedly in her lifetime, and she's not about to let it happen on her watch.

Life keeps going, even when what I shared with Lucky doesn't. Even when he's right across the street. Even when I see his red Superhawk parked there, day after day . . .

After day.

Even when I stare out the bookshop window, hoping to catch a glimpse of his dark head walking through the boatyard office door, day after day . . .

After day.

There's nothing between us. No texts. No coffee on the Quarterdeck. No visits to the Nook or getting handsy in my darkroom. No bad pizza or swimming lessons or Sunday dinners.

He's back to being the outsider. All the beautiful closeness we shared has dried in the August heat. And I miss him. The old Lucky and Lucky 2.0 and all the Luckys I've known.

I wish they were here right now.

Wish I hadn't ruined everything.

"Maybe you should try to talk to him," Mom says when we're coming out of the stockroom after totaling the cash, closing up the Nook later that week. It's Victory Day, and as the shadows lengthen down the street and twilight approaches, everyone's migrating toward the historic district. "I hate seeing you unhappy. There's a lot going on right now, and you've been friends for so long, shutterbug. Maybe if you just started the conversation?"

I shake my head, but I can't explain to her why that's not possible. I haven't even told her fully why Lucky and I aren't a thing anymore, because that would involve more talk about that stupid photo. And Adrian. And maybe we've all had enough of this summer.

Maybe it's best I just let it go and move on.

The funny thing is that I think I *could* tell her. As far as invisible walls go, things are better between me and Mom since that night after the island when everything came out about my father. Knowing that we're staying here for now helps. Mom and

Grandma have been talking about ways to make things work for all of us. There have been a few tense moments, but Rome wasn't built in a day.

It's a process.

"Our breakup was mutual," I say, and it's not precisely a lie. I was an absolute dramatic dumbass to Lucky and he shut me out: mutual. So now I'm back to my original No-Romance stance that I took when we first arrived in Beauty. Straying from that policy was my mistake, but it's not too late to correct it. Probably . . .

"I don't like Mopey Josie," Mom says. "She's the worst of Snow White's dwarves."

"I'm not *trying* to bring down the flotilla," I tell her, grabbing the trash bag out of the waste can behind the register.

She rolls her eyes. "I couldn't care less about the stupid flotilla."

"Oh, please. You love the flotilla."

"I love you being happy more."

"I'm fine," I tell her. Then I think of Lucky telling me to be honest. "Okay, I'm not fine yet, exactly, but I'll be fine eventually. It's getting a little better . . . sort of. I miss him. But I'm trying?"

"I still don't understand . . . who broke up with whom?"

"Mom," I plead.

"Okay, okay. Backing off," she says, giving me a gentle smile. "It's just that you haven't taken any photos in a week, and that makes me worry."

"That's not about Lucky," I say, tying up the trash bag.

"Right. I was afraid of that." Mom exhales heavily and folds up the end-of-day paperwork. "Sometimes I wish I hadn't told you the truth about Henry Zabka."

"Nope. That's the best thing you've told me in years." It's just not the easiest hurdle to jump. I wake up thinking I'm past it, then I realize I'm still bitter.

Evie emerges from the stockroom with a handful of mermaid pens and says, "You know what? My dad was a good man, and I miss him every day. If Josie needs to miss the idea of a father that she thought she had, then I think that's okay. Mourn away. But eventually, you're going to have to make peace with it." She shrugs loosely. "That's a little free advice from Madame Evie the Great, straight from the beyond. The spirits say give yourself a break, lady."

Mom and I stare at her. Madame Evie's been giving out a lot of free advice lately. Maybe getting rid of Adrian unburdened her.

"What's wrong with the stool?" Evie says, frowning as she balances over it to refill the mermaid pens near the register. "Something's different. Wait . . . where's the squeak?"

Mom laughs. "It's a different stool."

Evie leans down to peer between her legs, a cascade of dark hair flipping over and back as she pops back up. Her freckles darken around her Cleopatra makeup. "What the hell? When did this happen?"

"This morning. It was a gift."

I take a second look at the stool. Clean lines. Simple construction . . .

Lucky.

Mom feigns innocence, and I don't say anything. I can't. What's this weird fluttering feeling in my ribcage? Oh, right. The bats are back. Hundreds of emotional bats flapping inside the hollow cave of my chest. I don't know why Lucky would make a piece of furniture for the store, but it feels overly generous. Too personal. Like a bandage being ripped off a wound *way* too soon.

Or maybe I've just contracted rabies.

"You okay?" Mom asks.

"Am I up to date on my vaccinations?"

Mom's face scrunches up "What?"

"Never mind," I mumble.

I try to ignore Lucky's gift—just a simple gesture of good faith, not a grand gesture of love—as best I can as we finish up closing the shop. And I keep ignoring it as we walk over to the historic district to meet Grandma and Aunt Franny. I shouldn't be thinking about Lucky at all. After all, Victory Day in Beauty is a holiday bigger than Fourth of July. All our town's fireworks budget is saved up for this, the last big hurrah of the summer. The waterfront in the historic district is completely jammed with tourists and locals. Everything smells of sugar and barbecue smoke, and there's a really loud, really white, really *annoying* jazz band playing in a grandstand stage at the end of Goodly Pier.

"This will be good to get your mind off things, shutterbug," Mom says as we stop to survey the crowds by the pier and wait for Grandma and Aunt Franny, who are supposed to meet us here by the food truck area.

Oh, sure. It's easy to tell myself I'm not nursing a broken heart of my own making and carting around a chest filled with fluttering rabid bats when I'm surrounded by throngs of garishly dressed, smiling strangers, baking in the summer heat and waving patriotic sparklers.

Forget Lamplighter's Lane. This is the true portal to hell, right here.

Below us, Redemption Beach is crammed, and the crowds in this area are only going to get worse, because the beach and the Harborwalk are the prime viewing spots for tonight's main event.

The annual flotilla.

Anyone with a boat to show off has it lined up in front of the Yacht Club right now. The big yachts from Regatta Week are leading things off—irony of ironies, *Coast Life* magazine is one of the festival sponsors, and their logo is on every banner down here. Regardless, fancy or plain, all the boats are awaiting things to get dark enough for the grandmaster to fire the signal, releasing the flotilla of boats into the harbor, all of them decked out in thousands of white fairy lights, where they'll parade around massive torches.

Torches. Lit on fire. On the water.

Why? Who even knows, but people seem to love it. I'm not sure when this tradition started, but Beauty has been doing some version of it since my mom was a child. Evie says the chief of police's boat crashed into a torch and caught on fire two years ago. Really wish I could've seen that.

Right now, though, I wish I could turn around and go home. The sun is setting, but it's still so warm out that I'm sweating in shorts and a navy-and-white striped shirt. Just when I'm as miserable as I can possibly get, I spot an interesting group of people sitting around an outdoor café table at the worst-named best casual seafood restaurant on the edge of Goodly Pier: the Juicy Clam.

And inside my head, rusty wheels begin turning.

"What's happening here?" Evie says, wiggling a finger in front of my face.

I glance at Mom, who has wandered off to convince the egg roll truck and the cookie truck to join forces and deep fry cookies wrapped in egg roll skins while we wait for Grandma and Aunt Franny to show up.

"Stay here," I tell Evie. "I'll be right back. I need five minutes, tops."

Before she can argue, I push through the crowd and race up the ascending walkway onto Goodly Pier, maneuvering sideways on the outside of the ropes that section off the café area of the Juicy Clam. Stacks of wooden crab traps and fat dock ropes decorate the patio that overlooks the harbor, and everything smells of garlic butter. A couple of diners glance up at me sidling past their tables, surprised. Yeah, I know. Not supposed to be here. Super rude. But I have a backup plan.

A strategy. A plot. A scheme.

"Mr. Phillips," I say, stopping at the table I'd seen from the walkway below.

"Josie? Why, hello." He looks confused. "Ready to get back to school?"

"Just about. It's been a strange summer," I admit. Two other men are dining with him. One I don't know—an old man with a balding crown and a long ponytail in the back—but the other I know vaguely from childhood and most certainly after he was the cause of me losing the magazine internship at the beginning of the summer.

I most definitely am acquainted with his son.

Levi Summers, the king of Beauty.

Extraordinarily tan, piercing blue eyes, dark hair and beard shot through with a healthy amount of white and gray. I think he'd be what people would call a silver fox. He's also pretty much my enemy right now. But that's okay. I try to remind myself that he isn't Adrian.

And this isn't about either one of them, anyway.

It's about doing the right thing.

I stick out my hand. "Hello," I say, "I'm Josie Saint-Martin, Diedre's granddaughter."

One brow lifts, but he accepts my handshake. "I'm well acquainted with your grandmother. A lot of your family, actually."

I laugh nervously. "Well, that's probably not good. But I would like to apologize formally for what happened to your store's window. That was wrong, and I'm sorry. I'd also like to say that it was not my intention to destroy your property. I was aiming for your sign."

Mr. Phillips coughs. The other man at the table laughs under his breath.

"Well, Miss Saint-Martin . . ." Mr. Summers starts.

"What I mean to say is that it was a moment of anger for what Adrian did to me and my cousin," I explain. "But no matter what he did, what I did was wrong. I feel terrible, because that's not who I am or more importantly, who I want to be in the future. And I know my grandmother talked to you about the window, and about Lucky Karras, and the whole mistake of him taking the blame for it, but that's all in the past."

"Oh?" he says, crossing his arms over a crisp white shirt.

"What I would like to do is to pay you back for the window," I tell him. "But I can't afford to do that. So instead, I was thinking . . . what if I took photographs of your window displays for your website? I'm a great photographer. You might even remember that I was up for consideration for an internship at *Coast Life*, but you thought I was too young."

"That's true," Mr. Phillips says, scratching his ear. "She's quite good, too. Has a professional portfolio. Her father—"

I shake my head. "I'd like to stand on my own merit, if you don't mind."

Mr. Phillips holds up both hands and smiles. "So be it."

Mr. Summers looks me over. "I admire both your apology and your offer, Miss Saint-Martin. I'm not sure if I'm in need of a photographer right now, but I'll think about it."

The restaurant's patio lights flip on and a buzz goes through the café tables. Uh-oh. That means the flotilla will be starting up soon. And now that I'm standing under mood lighting, a Juicy Clam waiter spots me and is coming to shoo me away from the patio ropes.

Time to flee.

"Um, okay, well . . . thank you for your time," I tell Levi Summers quickly. "I'll ask you again in the future. I'm tenacious. It runs in my family."

Mr. Summers smiles, but not unkindly. "You don't say . . ."

Ducking away, I wave goodbye to Mr. Phillips and head back down the pier to find Evie. She hasn't gone far, and Mom still hasn't found Aunt Franny and Grandma but is busy chatting at one of the food-truck windows.

"Hey," Evie calls, waving me over through the crowds. "What was that all about?"

"Just attempting to right a wrong," I say, and briefly tell her what I'm trying to do to pay for the window. When I look back up at Levi Summers and Mr. Phillips, I catch sight of the third man at the table. I should've introduced myself to him. Maybe it was rude not to have done so. "Hey, Evie? Do you know who that man with the ponytail is, sitting next to Levi Summers?"

She scrunches up her face to squint at the darkening pier. "Oh, him? That's Desmond Banks."

Desmond Banks . . . Bright red FOR RENT sign, darkened door. Next to the hand-dipped candle store that smells like Christmas. "The private investigator?"

"Former," Evie corrects. "Or more like disgraced. He used to run his own agency in South Harbor, a couple blocks from the Nook."

"I've seen his office."

"Well, a few years back, his files got hacked by some anonymous Golden and ten years of everyone's miscellaneous dirty laundry popped up in a Golden Academy forum. People's bank records, photos of affairs—all that kind of stuff. It was only up for an afternoon, and he recovered most of it when they busted the kid who did it, but who wants to hire a dumbass PI who was stupid enough to get hacked by a nerdy teen? The damage had been done to his reputation, and after trying in vain to keep it afloat, he finally shut down for good this past winter and is now 'retired.'"

All at once, several bells chime in my head, tiny thoughts all lighting up and connecting.

The private detective that my grandmother hired to investigate my father years ago.

My mother's nude photo.

"What's the matter, cuz?" Evie says.

"Did you ever ask Adrian where he got the photo of Mom?"

"Yeah," she says, "in his car, right before our wreck . . . He was coy about it. Said something smug about a trove of secret pictures that some of the Goldens keep on people around town. Decades worth of photos, or something. And when I told him that was super gross, he just said he was joking. I guess after the accident, I sort of forgot about it."

Oh my God.

I'm going to be sick.

Of course Lucky wasn't Adrian's source for the nude photo.

It was Grandma's bumbling private detective. If I had only taken one stinking minute out of my self-centered life to ask Evie about this. Communication breakdown number five-thousand-eighty-seven. Why didn't I ask her?

"Cousin?" Evie says, placing a steadying hand on my shoulder. "What's wrong?"

"Oh, nothing, nothing . . . I mean, so, hey? Question for you . . . What do you do when someone specifically asks you to trust them, and instead of doing that, you babble a bunch of emo nonsense at them and make wild accusations?" I say, feeling as if my knees might give out. "Basically, you've screwed up beyond repair."

"Well," she says, diplomatically, "most things that get screwed up can be fixed."

"But this isn't a thing. It's a person," I say in a panic.

Oblivious, Mom saunters back to us with a huge grin on her face and a red-and-white checked paper tray filled with hot food. "Ladies, welcome to the taste of summer. Chocolate chip cookie dough rolled up inside an egg roll skin, deep fried, swirled in icing. And it's on a stick—" Her smile fades. "What's wrong?"

"I'm sorry," I tell her and Evie, "but I can't wait for Grandma and Aunt Franny. I need to talk to Lucky right now. I need to get back to the boatyard."

"He's probably here, baby," Mom says. "They have a boat in the flotilla."

Oh God. Of course! "I've gotta go."

"But—"

"I love you, but I'll find you later, okay?"

Wide-eyed and confused, Mom stares at me, holding her chocolate-chip-cookie egg roll creation, as I swivel away and get my bearings. If the Karrases are in the flotilla, they'd be at the end of the line, not with the fancy boats. That means all the way around the Harborwalk, past Goodly Pier, the beach, and the Yacht Club.

I'll never make it before the flotilla starts.

But I have to try.

I focus on snaking through the Victory Day crowds. Got to get to Lucky. I can do this. I can make it. I have to. Because I was a complete moron, and I need to tell him before my chest explodes. Tonight. NOW.

It's getting darker outside as I jog through the boardwalk on the edge of Redemption Beach, heading around a clam shack, then a carousel, then a second clam shack. Head back up to the Harborwalk. Keep going.

Past a row of shops, the concrete dips down toward the water and intersects with a dock in front of the Beauty Yacht Club. Fewer tourists here, more locals. Lots of Goldens . . . a couple I recognize from the party that first night of summer. Maybe some of them saw the nude photo. I don't even care anymore. Like Lucky's dad says, it's only a body, and we all have them.

I just keep going.

My legs hurt. People stare at me, wondering why I'm running. Don't care. I take a shortcut through a grassy area of the yacht club—technically private grounds, but no one's paying attention—and as the sun falls behind the purpled horizon, an announcement blasts over the club's loudspeaker: "*Everyone aboard!*"

The flotilla is about to launch.

Crap!

I dart back onto the Harborwalk and jog faster, the soles of my sneakers smacking against the ridged concrete. It's easier to run now. The crowds thin to nothing, only the boaters and a few stray celebrants hurrying to catch a last-minute spot at the edge of the beach.

The flotilla lineup starts here with the big, fancy yachts—the ones I would have been on, had I gotten that magazine internship and been helping out during Regatta Week. Levi Summers's yacht is probably the first in line, and if I looked hard enough, I might even spot Adrian on crutches. But I don't look, because I don't care about him. He's a mosquito to me now.

The lamps along the Harborwalk dim. A cheer goes up. A loudspeaker announces something in a faraway voice. And like a game of dominos being played with lightning bugs, thousands of white lights suddenly ripple on across the darkness—a wave of fairy lights from stern to bow, deck to deck. It's shockingly pretty, and the delighted roar of the crowd behind me goes all the way through my spine.

The yachts get smaller. I slow down and begin looking at every boat in line, searching for the Karrases. What boat would they take out? The *Nimble Narwhal*, I assume. Problem is, all the fishing boats look pretty much the same when they're covered in white lights. I squint into the brightness, heart pounding, trying to catch my breath. And then—

A siren-like noise cuts through the twilight, and the crowd roars behind me again.

The torches have been lit. The flotilla begins moving.

Slowly, at first—just the big yachts up front.

But as I desperately look for the Karrases, I get more and more panicky. Maybe they aren't here. Maybe they're skipping it. It's only the biggest event of the summer—I should know where he is. And I *would* know it, *if I'd only trusted Lucky when he'd asked me to!*

Then—

Right there.

The *Narwhal*. I do see it.

I see it chugging away from the Harborwalk, three boats from the end of the line.

Already in the flotilla.

Already gone.

I'm too late.

END OF THE LINE: Red graffiti spray-painted over the private property sign posted at the southern end of the Harborwalk. *(Personal photo/Josephine Saint-Martin)*

25

And I know it's not rational, but it felt as if that was my last chance to fix things with Lucky, that watching the *Narwhal* getting smaller and smaller as it headed off with the other boats in the flotilla was like watching him sailing away to the other end of the world and not just to the other end of the harbor.

Like the universe was trying to tell me to quit.

To give up.

Accept defeat and move on.

And maybe that's not true, but it's enough to sober me up and make me step back to think about things. Because it's not as if having proof that Lucky didn't send Adrian the photo changed anything; I already knew in my heart he hadn't sent it anyway. I think it just felt like it gave me permission to go talk to him. Or a push. And then when that push didn't pan out, that felt like a sign.

"Do you want to talk about it?" Mom asks a few days later as she adds money to a parking meter where the Pink Panther is parked. It's almost lunchtime, and we're in the historic district while Evie watches the Nook. We're on a food mission. There's a colonial landmark tavern here called the Fife and Drum—the oldest tavern in Beauty. They have amazing lobster rolls on freshly baked bread with lobster that they bring in from up the coast. The lobster salad is on their menu all the time, but the lobster rolls are sort of a town secret: They only sell them one day a week between noon and one from June until October. They're dirt cheap, and they only sell one per customer. We're headed there now to stand in line.

"I hope this isn't bargain lobster that's going to make us sick," I tell Mom.

"Why would everyone in Beauty line up for food that makes them sick?"

"You have a point."

"Besides, it's the thrill of the unknown that makes it fun," she says, brows waggling behind her cat-eye glasses.

"Okay, *cookie egg roll*." The raw cookie dough inside made everyone violently sick. Even my grandma, which made it almost worth it, because my Aunt Franny said it was revenge for the bargain biscuits that Grandma made her eat in Nepal.

"It will be *fine*," she assures me as we pass a pair of cosplaying colonial men, bewigged and dressed in white breeches and red regimental coats, one of them toting a drum across his chest—we're getting close to the sandwich of our dreams. "Tell me what happened between you and Lucky on Victory Day at the flotilla."

"Nothing happened. I was wrong, that's all."

"About what? Come on, talk to me. What do you have to lose?" she asks, elbowing me playfully as she matches my hurried pace on the sidewalk.

"My self-worth and dignity?" I joke.

"Overrated," she says with a smile.

It's strange, having her poke around in my business. Not strange-bad. Just . . . strange. We're talking more often now, and I'm not quite used to it.

"It's not that I don't want to tell you," I say. "It's that it involves the photo, and I don't want to keep digging it back up again after we've buried it."

She groans. "That thing is worse than a B-movie monster that won't stay dead. Go on. Give it to me. Tell me what happened."

So I do. As we dart around the last of the summer tourists, I show her Adrian's texts and tell her about my fight with Lucky. I tell her everything, all the stupid things I said. The accusations I made, and how he asked me to trust him. How I couldn't, even after he trusted me that we weren't leaving town. I even tell her about seeing Desmond Banks before the flotilla, and how I could have avoided all this by just talking to Evie.

All of it.

When I'm done, she blows out a long breath, puffing out her cheeks. "Wow."

"Your daughter is kind of a dingbat."

"From a long line of dingbats," she says with a soft smile. "But hey. Let's not forget that he made a stool for the Nook with his own two hands. A beautiful stool. A work of art."

"He's a craftsperson, not an artist."

"Well, la-di-da," Mom says lightly.

I laugh. "But, okay. I see your point. Yeah, he did make the stool for us. That was something. Right?"

"Definitely. I think it's a clear sign that he's trying to talk to you."

"You do?"

"I can't read his mind or yours, but maybe, just based on what you've told me, maybe he realizes that you were going through some difficult things that day, and finding out about your father may have messed you up a little bit and made you act a little irrationally. Speaking from experience—when I found out the truth about your father, I packed up and took you away from Beauty for five years."

"Oh," I say as this clicks into place in my head.

"Yeah," she says, nodding. "So maybe *this* is how it affected you. And I can't be certain, but he seems like a smart guy, so maybe he worked that out for himself and is trying to establish a line of communication with you again, in his own way."

Was that possible?

"And," Mom continues, "if he's trying to communicate with you through his art—excuse me, through his *craft*—"

"He's a stickler about that."

"—then maybe you should do the same and communicate with him through *your* art."

I blink at her. "Through my photos?"

"Why not?" she says with a shrug. "That's what you're doing by taking pictures of your signs, right? Using photography to communicate? That's what it says in your portfolio."

"Well, yeah . . ."

"So use your photography to communicate with Lucky."

I think about this as we stroll past Lady Arabella's, an old-fashioned store that carries vintage toys, its window filled with jars of colorful marbles, hoops, tin soldiers, and cornhusk dolls. "So, you're saying I should send one of my photos to the boat-yard?" I ask Mom.

"Maybe?" she says, moving out of the way as a small child runs out of the toy store carrying a stuffed whale. "Send him a message. Strike up a conversation. See where it leads. Maybe even grovel a little, because that's something dingbats should probably do."

"Probably," I say with a groan.

"But shutterbug?"

"Yes?"

"If I'm wrong about this, and he's not ready to talk, then you need to respect that. You can't be an Adrian."

I nod, stomach dropping at that possibility forming in my head—that Lucky isn't ready to talk. Regardless, I think Mom may be onto something. I think this isn't the worst plan.

I think I want to try to strike up a conversation with Lucky again, and this may be a good way to try to do that. What do you know? Talking out my problems with real-life people actually results in real-life solutions.

"Hey, Mom? While we're talking about relationships, don't think I didn't notice that you still avoided driving down Lamplighter Lane on the way here. You can't avoid Drew Sideris forever, you know. This town is too small," I tell her, as Lucky once told me. "Maybe you should be striking up conversations of your own."

She gives me a sidelong glance. "Last time I checked, *I'm* the one who's supposed to be handing out advice."

"Saint-Martins have never been very good at following rules. Something about breaking them and doing it the right way . . . I can't remember."

Mom snorts a laugh. "Fine. I'll think about it, but that's all I'm promising. Now, come on, rebel."

As we round the corner of the block, heading toward the harbor, the Fife and Drum comes into view: gambrel roof, dusty blue clapboard walls, and white pediment-topped door. It's been standing here since the 1600s and will surely be standing here long after I'm gone. There's already a line queuing up for the lobster roll. People in Beauty are serious about their seafood. We should've come earlier, but if we hurry, we can still make it.

We both pick up the pace and jog toward the back of the line as the restaurant's server comes to do a head count. Another couple tries to beat us, but we're too competitive and have no shame whatsoever about racing for bargain lobster rolls.

"Victory," Mom says as we claim the last coveted spot in the queue.

I smile at her, and she smiles back, both breathless.

"Hey, look at us."

"A pair of old gal pals, scoring cheap seafood sandwiches," I agree.

"And *actually* talking."

"That, too," I say, feeling a little tender in my chest as a few knots that have been there for a long time begin to loosen. "Thanks for listening, Mom."

"It's not so scary, right?" she says, but what I think she's also saying is: *I'm glad you're not going to California.*

"It's almost as if we *like* each other, or something," I tease, but what I'm also saying is: *I'm not going anywhere. I just needed this.*

"Imagine that," she says with a gentle smile, slinging her arm around my shoulders. "Imagine that . . ."

I consider my Mom's suggestion to reach out to Lucky with a photograph during the remainder of my shift at the Nook that afternoon, and now I'm spending the night looking through prints of photographs. Nothing seems to fit. Or maybe I'm not sure what it is I want to say. I'm sorry I freaked out on you that day? Please forgive me for not trusting you, the one person in town who deserved my trust more than anyone? The one person who'd proved to me time and time again over the years that he was worth my trust?

How do you say that with a photograph? I'm not exactly sure I can.

But it's not until I'm shutting off the light in the stockroom and I catch sight of a box that an idea comes to mind. The box contains all of Grandma's postcards from Nepal—we took them down from the front counter after she returned. I thumb through them now, all the colorful photos that grace the fronts of each card, and I begin hatching a scheme.

A strategy. A plot. A plan.

I can make Lucky a postcard from one of my own photos.

And I know exactly which one.

In my darkroom, I find the right negative, and I develop the photo I took on Rapture Island of the dock house. Bordered by beach roses . . . before the storm.

It's a good photo. But it's the meaning behind it, what that building represents, that I'm hoping he understands.

I want to be sure I'm doing the right thing, myself. So I think about it. I sleep on it, even. And when I'm sure—as sure as someone who is teetering on the brink of uncertainty *can* be—the next morning before breakfast, I carefully mount the photo on a thick piece of paper using four archival corners. On the back of the paper, I write him a message:

> *Dear Lucky,*
> *Though I tried to catch you on the Narwhal*
> *before the flotilla in hopes that we could talk, I*
> *didn't make it in time. If you have a minute to*

listen, I'll be at our old meeting spot tonight after
work. Thanks for being patient with me.
Always your friend, no matter what,
Josephine

There. That's my message and my plan. And as the mid-August sun rises over the harbor, I'm somehow able to slip the note, unnoticed, into the slightly open crack of Lucky's helmet compartment on his Superhawk . . . before rushing away.

Okay. It's done. I did it.

It's sent. My postcard from paradise.

Nothing to do now but wait . . .

Hours.

And hours.

For the longest work shift in the entire history of the world to end.

And when it finally does, I wish I had a little longer, because I'm terrified to face him. And terrified that he won't show up. All the terrors, I have them. But I try my best to bottle them up, and with the sun warming my shoulders, I tell Mom and Evie where I'm going, cross the street toward the harbor, and head out to the southernmost point of Beauty.

The first few minutes of my walk, I toss looks behind me at the boatyard as the Karrases' big boat crane gets smaller and smaller, hoping I'll catch a glimpse of Lucky following me. But I don't. Seagulls soar over dark blue water as the sky becomes purple around the horizon, and to my right, the warehouse buildings get farther and farther apart with more parking lots between them.

Then I see it, right where the rocky shore curves inward.

The end of the Harborwalk. The concrete just stops, and there's a sign here that's been vandalized. It's so far away from the tourist area of town that no one's bothered to clean it up. I step through a flimsy gate, shoes crunching over gravel, and I search the wooded area that fans out from the rocks on the shore.

I see the old pier first, almost lost under the waves that lazily crash over it. And there's what I'm seeking. The old meeting place.

The North Star.

The abandoned cedar-plank building is easy to miss. Back in the 1940s or 1950s, it probably was a serviceable little boatshed, built to winter a fishing boat. Someone owned these woods—maybe they fished and hunted here, who knows. But the pier and the shed were lost to time long before Lucky and I found it.

And it looks like only two walls stand now, the two sides. The tree that was growing through the roof has fallen. Maybe taken by a storm. But the marker that provided the shed's name is still hanging on one of the standing walls, an old tin sign with a faded blue star and two hand-painted words: NORTH STAR.

The first sign I ever photographed.

Seeing it now brings back a rush of bright, sharp emotions and a flurry of memories. Lucky and I finding this place. Playing our poorly planned Harry Potter D&D campaigns and listening to music out here after school. Walking home together after dark.

I let these memories wash over me, breathing in the salt-tinged harbor air, until it all ebbs, and I'm settled again.

A tiny shape races toward me from the woods. I scoot back, unsure if I'm being attacked by a feral squirrel, but then there's a wagging pink tongue, and it's definitely of the canine variety.

"Bean the Magic Pup," I say, heart beating wildly as I crouch to scratch his ears and pick up his dragging leash. "Why are you loose and unsupervised?"

"He was chasing a rabbit," a gravelly voice says. "Until the rabbit started chasing him."

I stand up slowly.

Lucky appears out of the shadow of a tree.

Like a phantom.

He came. Thank goodness, he came.

Dressed in long shorts and a black T-shirt, he hovers for a moment, as if he's unsure whether he wants to come any closer. As if he might just keep walking right past me.

As if looking at me hurts too much.

It feels like a fist punching into my ribcage and squeezing painfully, wringing out anything left.

"You got my postcard. . . ." I gesture toward the boatshed. "Wasn't sure if you'd come."

"I did have to consider whether or not I should." In dappled sun reflecting off the water, I can see the white scars on the side of his forehead and the missing part of his eyebrow when he reaches out to take Bean's leash from me, careful not to touch my hand.

God. This is so hard.

He's so intimidating.

And I miss him so much.

I open my mouth and feel tears prick my eyes. I try to swallow them down, but it's no use. "Going to need you to press the button on the invisible wall now," I tell him in a small, cracking voice. "Because I was wrong, and I need to tell you I'm sorry."

He huffs out a breath through his nostrils and looks at the water as his small black dog sniffs around the gray rocks lining the edge of the shore. "No."

"No?"

"You do it. I don't own the wall."

"We both own the wall," I say, crying around my words. "Both of us. If we want to talk to each other, we can. But it's not just talking and being teeth-gratingly honest. It's listening, too—and that's partly where I screwed up."

"Is it?"

I nod, swiping away tears, but they're coming too fast. "If you don't want to listen to me, then you don't have to. And if I don't want to listen to you, then I can be a fool and talk over you when you're trying to tell me that you didn't give Adrian that photo."

"I tried to tell you," he says in a soft, emphatic voice.

"I'm so sorry. He told me it was you, and I made connections that weren't there. I jumped to conclusions. I stumbled over my own feet. Everything I knew was turned upside down in one day's time with my family, and it felt like nothing I knew was right, and . . . I just got scrambled."

He exhales a long breath, jaw working to one side. I can't tell if I've hurt him more or if he just can't forgive me. That thought makes me feel empty and hopeless.

"Josie?"

"Yes?"

"Can I be teeth-gratingly honest with you?"

"Yes," I say, bracing myself. "Please, Lucky. I wish you would."

For better or worse, I would rather him be honest than not talk to me.

Bean sits near a dilapidated dock post as Lucky's gaze shifts from the shoreline to my face. His eyes are glossy, and his brow lined and tense. "When I saw you in the car driving away from the bookshop that night with your family, I was already having a nervous breakdown that you might be leaving town—I didn't know what was going to happen. My parents were furious about us taking the boat out so far to the island, and everything was completely chaotic, and all I wanted was for you to tell me everything was going to be okay. That's all I wanted. But instead . . ."

"I raged out on you," I say, slumping.

"In the heat of the moment, I didn't fully grasp what you were going through with your father."

"I don't want to use him as an excuse. I don't want anything to do with him right now. Maybe one day I'll feel differently, but right now, I think he's wasted too much of me and my mom's energy. I wish I'd never bought into his lies, but I did. I bought into his, and I bought into Adrian's, too."

"Right, Adrian." Lucky scratches his clenched jaw. "After our fight, well . . . *I* knew I didn't give Adrian that photo. And it made me mad that you'd listen to him, but okay. I can understand it, I guess. Maybe? The thing that really hurt me in my bones was that you didn't trust me when I asked you to." He makes a fist and taps his chest with his free hand. "I'm talking deep."

"I am so sorry," I whisper. "I'm ashamed."

"Never," he says, taking a step closer to duck his head and catch my gaze with his. "None of this is anyone's fault. Okay, maybe your father can take some of the blame."

"And Adrian."

"And Adrian," he agrees. "And mistakes were definitely made by several parties, myself included. But what I'm trying to say is that there's room for a lot of things between us, but not shame."

My heart lifts and catches in my throat. "What about forgiveness? Is there room for that?"

"You told me to trust you. That was the last thing you told me when you were leaving in the car that night with your mom."

"I remember."

"No one hurts me like you do."

A knife-like pain stabs my heart. "I've never wanted to hurt anyone less."

"Josie?"

"Yes?"

"Can we just agree to smash the invisible wall for good? It's done nothing but keep us apart, and I don't want it up anymore. I'd rather be hurt than feel nothing at all. But right now, I'm just tired of missing you. Are you tired of missing me?"

"So very tired," I whisper.

"Then I need to tell you one more thing. Come here and listen."

Lucky reaches for my face, and I lean my cheek into his hand, solid and warm and familiar. Gravity tugs me into him, and his arm comes around my shoulders. He winds himself around me and pulls me closer, and we cling to each other. He's heavy against me, a brick wall, and nothing has ever felt so good.

He doesn't speak, but he says everything I need to know. That I'm forgiven. That it's okay. *We're* okay. That there's a bond between us that's changed into something different and stronger.

My best friend. My lover. My boy.

The one person in the world I can talk to without even saying a single word.

NOW LEAVING BEAUTY. HAVE A BEAUTIFUL DAY AND COME AGAIN SOON: Roadside sign on the highway north of Beauty, Rhode Island. *(Personal photo/Josephine Saint-Martin)*

26

October

There's a long-held belief in my family that all the Saint-Martin women are romantically cursed: unlucky in love, doomed to end up miserable and alone.

But as my grandmother would say, that's a load of bull.

The only thing we're cursed with is terrible communication skills, and that has nothing to do with any kind of witchy hex. Somewhere along the line, one of the Saint-Martins was a lousy communicator, and she taught the bad habit to her daughter, who then led by example and taught it to hers. And now here we are, three generations of women all facing the fact that we've been repeating the same mistakes that our stupid ancestors passed down to us.

All we can do is wake up. Be better. Admit when we're wrong, try to fix our mistakes, and smash all the invisible walls we can.

Who knew that would start with smashing a department store window?

Sometimes doing the wrong thing can point you in the right direction.

Sometimes being a little bad can turn out good.

And sometimes the places we think are portals to hell are actually just things we fear.

"Ugh. I'm not sure if this is the best idea. . . ." Mom frets near the old printing press in the Nook, brushing the front of her dress for the umpteenth time. "Maybe I should change. Or just leave town forever. Maybe I should just do that?"

"No," Evie says from behind her paperback, perched on our non-squeaky stool behind the bookshop register. "That color looks good on you. It's too brisk outside for the other dress. You're just nervous, which is understandable. But it's just a date."

"Not even a date," I assure her. "A double date isn't a date."

"Oh, it's *definitely* a date," Lucky says as he leans against the printing press, flipping the page of a book about ironwork in Victorian England. He looks up to see us all staring at him. "Hey. I'm just telling it like it is. It's a real date. Drew is ridiculously nervous too, if that helps. He's been pacing around the blacksmith studio chanting positive affirmations, driving me up the wall."

Mom clutches her stomach. "I'm going to be sick. I can't do this."

"Sure you can," he assures her. "My parents will be there to hold up the conversation."

The double date was Evie's idea, and the only way my mom would agree to go. Funny that a woman who's spent the last few years right-swiping anonymous strangers would be terrified. But she deleted her online dating apps, and right now, I've never seen her so nervous.

"It's going to be fine," I tell Mom. "All we're going to think about is what a fun, easy-breezy time you're going to have at the fall Renaissance Faire—"

"Revolutionary," Lucky corrects. "This is Beauty."

"At the Rev Faire," I say. "A fun, easy-breezy time, laughing at people dressed in Revolutionary War costumes mingling with people dressed in Renaissance costumes, eating giant turkey legs, and cheering on jousting contests. It's all perfectly weird and wacky, and you're just . . . reconnecting with an old friend."

"Who may or may not still be madly in love with you after all these years," Evie says.

"No pressure," Grandma teases, breezing past us as she makes her way to the children's section with a stack of books for story-time. "Tell him I said 'sorry, not sorry' about ending his stupid plan to marry you at Candy's Honeymoon Motel on Route 138 in the middle of the night before the ink was dry on your high school diplomas. If he still wants you, he'll have more class now."

"I'm seriously going to be sick," Mom mumbles.

"Don't listen to these bozos," Lucky tells her. "I know it's intense. He's just as nervous as you are, and maybe it'll be easier than you think. If you don't hit it off, no big deal."

Mom nods. "Maybe you're right. It's not a date. It's just walking around the woods, looking at things in tents. I can do that."

"All the food trucks will be there," I remind her. "Even the egg roll guys from Victory Day if you want to take your chances again. Eating things on sticks—your favorite."

"I do love food on sticks," she admits.

"And hey, my mom knows this is a high-pressure situation," Lucky says. "She's got your back. Both she and my dad will be there if you need an escape. Seriously, you'll be okay."

"You just need an emergency word if the date goes bad," Evie says. "Something to signal Kat and Nick that they need to get you out of there, stat. Like . . . 'huzzah!'"

"Do you know how many people will be saying 'huzzah' at a Ren Faire?" Lucky says. "I guarantee you that you'll be hearing a million versions of 'huzzah,' 'wench,' 'master,' 'ladies,' 'lords,' 'doth,' 'taketh' . . ."

"Pray, my lord, Phantom," Evie says to Lucky in a terrible accent, "what oil dost thou prefer for polishing thoust sword?"

"Not sure why I even come in here sometimes," Lucky says, burying his nose back in his book. "The customer service is atrocious."

I loop my arm around his waist, and he slings an arm over my shoulders. "Probably because we're the only bookshop in town."

"Oh, *r-i-i-ight*," he murmurs, smiling down before quickly kissing my forehead.

Evie bats dramatic, long eyelashes at us from the counter.

"You two make me sick in the best way possible. Madame Evie says the spirits are delighted—please don't stop."

I stick out my tongue at her playfully, and then I tell Mom, "Don't use 'huzzah' as your emergency word. Use 'cornucopia.' Like, 'Wow, there sure is a cornucopia of food trucks here today.' Inform Lucky's mom when she comes in, so she knows to help you if she hears it."

"I don't need an emergency word," Mom says. "Evie, I'll be back to close up the shop."

"If you aren't, you aren't. It's Saturday, and I'm perfectly capable of closing this shop on my own. Grandma's here for storytime, my mom's coming by any second, and Vanessa's meeting me here later, so I won't be alone."

Vanessa from Barcelona has been meeting Evie here almost every day since their fall semester started back at community college. It's kind of nice. Maybe even *more* than nice . . . Starting to suspect that Vanessa and Evie's friendship might be a little like mine and Lucky's.

Mom turns to me. "Are you guys set to go? This is a big day for you, too."

Maybe. Maybe not.

Lucky and I are taking a little afternoon trip on his Superhawk to a town outside Providence. Turns out one of my half-sisters lives there. She's two years younger than me, and Henry Zabka hasn't really been much of a father to her, either. Maybe we won't connect, but I thought . . . why not?

Gotta try, right?

Plus, I'm experimenting with some new pictures, and a road trip is a good opportunity for camera time. The leaves are beautiful, and the weather's good. I'm still photographing signs—I still love the poetry of billboards and forgotten flyers stapled to telephone poles. But I'm taking Lucky's advice and am trying to include people in the shots. It's not as hard as I once thought. The light's tricky on faces, but you know, as a wise woman once told me: If it was easy, any clown would do it.

"Don't worry about us," I tell Mom. "We'll be back by nine."

"Or ten," Lucky says. "We'll both have our phones on. Promise, cross our hearts, we will not be taking a boat out to Rapture Island or any other island."

My mom makes him swear that same thing every time we leave the town limits now. It's mostly a joke . . . *mostly*. "And you'll be careful on the drive to Providence?"

"Very careful," Lucky assures her. "Helmets on."

He points to the counter, where our helmets sit side by side. I'm no longer wearing his cousin Gabe's sparkly tri-corn. Lucky got me my own full-face helmet—safety first—and on the back, in a compact silver font, it says SHUTTERBUG.

Mom nods. "Just take it slow around that Dead Man's Curve on the highway where Evie wrecked." Evie. Not Adrian. Because we don't speak that jerk's name anymore. We haven't seen him around here lately, but word on the street is that he's already moved back into his apartment at Harvard, but he's not taking any classes. As long as he stays out of Beauty and away from Evie, I honestly don't care.

Evie says I should turn the poster-on-the-door incident into a plus and spread my own rumor around Golden Academy that my subscription service *is* nudes. Get people to fork over cash, then *kablam*! They subscribe and get photos of all my signs instead. Fleece the Goldens.

Tempting as that scam may be, I don't need that kind of energy in my life right now. Besides, I've picked up eight new online subscribers this month without resorting to trickery. I have a strong suspicion it may be members of the Karras family, but maybe one day Levi Summers himself will subscribe. I still haven't given up on convincing him to let me do photography to pay him back for the department store window. One of these days, he's going to say yes. . . .

The door to the bookshop swings open, and Kat Karras's dark head pops inside. "He's here, Winona. Ready to go?"

Mom looks as if she may faint. So I duck away from Lucky for a moment to walk over to her, and I squeeze her hand and smile, nodding. "You can do it," I whisper. "We Saint-Martins are not cursed."

"Not cursed," she whispers back. "Definitely not cursed."

Mostly not cursed.

But it's okay. We can break the curse ourselves. No magic spell needed. No special charm. All we have to do is decide that we're ready to smash down a few invisible walls.

And that's exactly what we do.

Acknowledgments

Oh, reader. This book nearly broke me. Not even kidding. It took *many* drafts, some blubbering, a lot of self-doubt, and the very fine skills of the Amazing Nicole Ellul, the best of all the caped superheroes—editor!—to bring this story to life. So first off, thank you, Nicole, for being so patient. I'm sure you wanted to slap me silly on more than one occasion.

Other people of note who have my gratitude: Laura Bradford, my agent. Taryn Fagerness sells my books to beautiful publishers across vast oceans. Laura Eckes created the beautiful cover for this book. I don't even know all the countless people behind the scenes at Simon & Schuster who champion my books, but some of them are Mara Anastas, Lauren Carr, Savannah Breckenridge, Emily Hutton, Emily Ritter, Liesa Abrams, Rebecca Vitkus, Elizabeth Mims, Clare McGlade, Lauren Forte, Jessi Smith, Tom Daly, Caitlin Sweeny, Alissa Nigro, and Anna Jarzab. There's even a team of Simon & Schuster folks in the

UK who do wonderful things for me, and they include Olivia Horrox and Laurie McShea.

Fist bumps to my personal support team: Brian, Luna, Iorek, Karen, Ron, Gregg, Heidi, Hank, Charlotte, Patsy, Don, Gina the Survivor, Shane, and Seph.

The rumors are true: Like the characters within these pages, I really was a bookseller for the better part of a decade. I did everything from cleaning toilets to managing stores to making buying decisions for a national chain. So for every bookseller that has recommended my books to customers, I realize that I owe you *everything*. Thank you.

And if you were one of the readers that took advice from a bookseller and purchased this book based on that advice . . . thank you for trusting them. Book people are good people.

About the Author

Jenn Bennett is an award-winning author of young adult books, including *Alex, Approximately*; *Serious Moonlight*; *Starry Eyes*; *The Lady Rogue*; and *Chasing Lucky*. Her books have earned multiple starred reviews, won the prestigious RITA Award, and been included on *Kirkus Reviews* and *Publishers Weekly* Best Books annual lists. She lives near Atlanta with one husband and two dogs.

If you liked CHASING LUCKY, you'll love all these other swoon-worthy stories by JENN BENNETT!

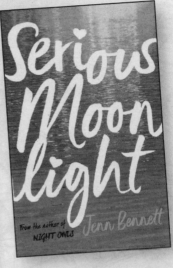

Praise for _Alex, Approximately_

★"A must for romance readers."

—_Booklist_, STARRED REVIEW

★"An irresistible tribute to classic screwball-comedy romances that captures the 'delicious whirling, twirling, buzzing' of falling in love."

—_Kirkus Reviews_, STARRED REVIEW

"A sexier, modern version of _You've Got Mail_ and _The Shop Around the Corner_, this will hit rom-com fans right in the sweet spot."
—_BCCB_

"A strong addition to romance collections."—_SLJ_

"Sympathetic characters and plenty of drama."—_Publishers Weekly_

Praise for _Starry Eyes_

★"A sweet and surprisingly substantial friends-to-more romance."

—_Kirkus Reviews_, STARRED REVIEW

"Vivid plots and endearing characters make this novel impossible to put down."

—_SLJ_

"A layered adventure–love story that's as much about the families we have and the families we make ourselves as it is about romance."

—_Booklist_

Praise for _Serious Moonlight_

A _Kirkus Reviews_ Best Book of 2019

★"An atmospheric, multilayered, sex-positive romance from the talented Bennett."
—_Kirkus Reviews_, STARRED REVIEW

"Compulsively readable and enormously fun, this is a first purchase for YA collections."
—_SLJ_

"Romance fans won't be disappointed." —_BCCB_